MY
SISTER'S
GRAVE

Also by Robert Dugoni

The David Sloane series
The Jury Master
Wrongful Death
Bodily Harm
Murder One
The Conviction

Stand-alone novel
Damage Control

Nonfiction with Joseph Hilldorfer
The Cyanide Canary

MY
SISTER'S
GRAVE

ROBERT DUGONI

THOMAS & MERCER

Published by Thomas & Mercer, Seattle

www.apub.com

Amazon, the Amazon logo, and Thomas & Mercer are trademarks of Amazon.com, Inc., or its affiliates.

ISBN-13: 9781477825570
ISBN-10: 1477825576

Cover design by Salamander Hill Design Inc.
Library of Congress Control Number: 2014939862
Printed in the United States of America

To my brother-in-law, Robert A. Kapela:
May you find in God's embrace the peace,
love, and comfort that eluded you in the
final years of your life.

PART I

Better that ten guilty persons escape
than that one innocent suffer.
— Sir William Blackstone,
Commentaries on the Laws of England

CHAPTER 1

Her tactical instructor at the police academy had liked taunting them during early morning drills. "Sleep is overrated," he'd say. "You will learn to do without."

He'd lied.

Sleep was like sex. The less you had, the more you craved it, and Tracy Crosswhite hadn't had much of either lately.

She stretched her shoulders and neck. With no time for a morning run, her body felt stiff and half-asleep, though she didn't remember sleeping much, if at all. Too much fast food and too much caffeine, her doctor said. Good advice, but eating well and exercising took time Tracy didn't have when investigating a homicide, and giving up caffeine would be like cutting off gasoline from a car engine. She'd die without it.

"Hey, the Professor's in early. Who died?"

Vic Fazzio leaned his considerable girth against Tracy's cubicle wall. It was an old Homicide joke, but never stale when punctuated by Faz's hoarse voice and New Jersey accent. With a salt-and-pepper pompadour and fleshy features, the Homicide section's self-proclaimed "Italian Goombah" could have served as one of those silent bodyguards in mafia movies. Faz held the *New York*

Times crossword puzzle and a library book, which meant the coffee had kicked in. God help anyone if they had to use the men's room while Faz was there. He was known to stew for half an hour over his answers or when reading a particularly compelling chapter.

Tracy handed him one of the crime scene photos she'd printed out that morning. "Dancer over on Aurora."

"Heard about it. Kinky shit, huh?"

"I saw worse working sex crimes," she said.

"I forgot. You gave up sex for death," he said.

"Death is easier," she said, stealing another of Faz's punch lines.

The dancer, Nicole Hansen, had been found hog-tied in a cheap motel room on Aurora Avenue in North Seattle. A noose was fastened around her neck and the rope threaded down her spine, binding her wrists and ankles—an elaborate setup. Tracy handed Faz the medical examiner's report. "Her muscles cramped and eventually seized. When they did, she straightened her legs to relieve the pain. She ended up strangling herself. Nice, huh?"

Faz considered the photograph. "Wouldn't you think they'd have used a slipknot or something to get out of it?"

"That would be logical, wouldn't it?"

"So, what's your theory? Some guy sat there getting his jollies watching her die?"

"Or they screwed up, and he panicked and fled. Either way, she didn't tie herself."

"Maybe she did. Maybe she's like Houdini."

"Houdini untied himself, Faz. That was the trick." Tracy took back the report and photograph and set them on her desk. "So here I sit at this ungodly hour, just you, me, and the crickets."

"Me and the crickets've been here since five, Professor. You know what they say. Early bird catches the worm."

"Yeah, well, this early bird's so tired she wouldn't know a worm if it crawled out of the ground and bit her on the butt."

"So where's Kins? How come you're having all the fun?"

She checked her watch. "He'd better be buying me a cup of coffee, but at this rate I could have brewed it myself." She nodded at the book. "*To Kill a Mockingbird*. I'm impressed."

"I'm trying to better myself."

"Your wife picked it out for you, didn't she?"

"You bet." Faz pushed away from the wall. "Okay, time for my smart time. The *Mockingbird*'s singing, and I'm percolating."

"TMI, Faz."

He started from the bull pen, then turned back, pencil in hand. "Hey, Professor, help me out. I need a nine-letter word for 'makes natural gas safe.'"

Tracy had been a high school chemistry teacher before making a career change and attending the academy. She received her nickname there. "Mercaptan," she said.

"Huh?"

"Mercaptan. They add it to natural gas so you can smell it if you have a leak in the house."

"No kidding. What's it smell like?"

"Sulfur. You know, rotten eggs." She spelled it.

Fazzio licked the tip of his pencil and wrote in the letters. "Thanks."

As Faz departed, Kinsington Rowe walked into the A Team's bull pen and handed Tracy one of two tall cups. "Sorry," he said.

"I was about to call search and rescue."

The A Team was one of the Violent Crime Section's four homicide teams, each consisting of four detectives. Tracy, Kins, Faz, and Delmo Castigliano, the other half of the Italian Dynamic Duo, made up the A Team. They sat with their desks in the four corners of one large cubicle, their backs to each other, which is how Tracy preferred it. Homicide was a fishbowl, and privacy was already at a premium. In the center of their square, they shelved Homicide binders below a work-space table. They each kept the felony assault files they were working at their respective desks.

Tracy cradled the cup. "Come to me you bittersweet nectar of the gods." She took a sip and licked foam from her upper lip. "So what took you?"

Kins grimaced as he sat. A running back for four years at the U and one year in the NFL, Kins retired when doctors misdiagnosed an injury that had left him with a degenerative hip. He'd eventually need it replaced but said he was holding out so he only had to have it done once. In the interim, he dealt with the pain by chewing on Advil.

"Your hip that bad?" she asked.

"Used to just be when it got cold."

"So get it fixed already. What are you waiting for? I hear it's routine now."

"Nothing's routine when the doctor has to slip that mask over your face and tell you nighty-night."

He looked off, still grimacing, an indication that something more than his hip was bothering him. After six years working side by side, Tracy knew Kins's tells. She knew his moods and his facial expressions. She knew first thing in the morning whether he'd had a bad night or gotten laid. Kins was her third Homicide partner. The first assigned to work with her, Floyd Hattie, had announced that he'd rather retire than work with a woman, then did so. Her second partner lasted six months, until *his* wife had met Tracy at a barbecue and couldn't deal with her husband sharing close quarters with a single then-thirty-six-year-old five-foot-ten blonde.

When Kins had volunteered to work with Tracy, she might have been just a tad sensitive.

Fine, but what about your wife? she'd asked. *Is she going to have a fucking problem?*

I hope not, Kins had said. *With three kids under the age of eight, that's about the last fun thing we do together.*

She knew immediately he was someone she could work with. They'd struck a deal—total honesty. No hard feelings. It'd worked for six years.

"Something else bothering you, Kins?"

Kins blew out a breath and met her gaze. "Billy stopped me in the lobby," he said, referring to the A Team's sergeant.

"I hope he had a good reason to keep me from my coffee. I've killed for less."

Kins didn't smile. The chatter of the morning news from the television hanging over the B Team's bull pen filtered through the room. A phone rang unanswered on someone's desk.

"Something to do with Hansen? The brass busting his chops over this one?"

He shook his head. "Billy got a call from the medical examiner's office, Tracy." He made eye contact. "Two hunters found the remains of a body in the hills above Cedar Grove."

CHAPTER 2

Tracy's fingers twitched with anticipation. The light breeze that had periodically kicked up throughout the day gusted, blowing open the back flap of her weathered duster. She waited for the wind to calm. After two days of competition, one shooting stage remained to determine the 1993 Washington State Single Action Shooting Champion. At twenty-two, Tracy was already a three-time winner, but she'd lost that title last year to Sarah, four years her junior. This year, the two sisters entered the final stage virtually tied.

The range master held the timer close to Tracy's ear. "Your call, Crossdraw," he whispered. Her cowboy name was a play on their last name, as well as the type of holster she and Sarah favored.

Tracy dipped the brim of her Stetson, took a deep breath, and gave deference to the best Western movie ever made. "Fill your hands, you son of a bitch!"

The timer beeped.

Her right hand drew the Colt from her left holster, cocked the hammer, and fired. Gun already drawn and cocked in her left hand, she took down the second target. Finding her rhythm and gaining speed, she shot so fast that she could barely hear the ting of lead over the discharge of the guns.

Right hand. Cock. Fire.

Left hand. Cock. Fire.

Right hand. Cock. Fire.

She took aim at the bottom row of targets.

Right, fire.

Left, fire.

Three final shots rang out in rapid succession. Bam. Bam. Bam. Tracy twirled her guns and slapped them down on the wood table.

"Time!"

A few spectators applauded, but their clapping quieted as more began to realize what Tracy already knew.

Ten shots. But only nine tings.

The fifth target in the bottom row remained upright.

Tracy had missed.

The three spotters standing nearby each holding up one finger to confirm it. The miss would be costly, a five-second penalty added to her time. Tracy eyed the target, disbelieving, but staring at it wasn't going to make it fall. Reluctantly, she collected her revolvers, slapped them in their holsters, and stepped aside.

All eyes turned to Sarah, "The Kid."

———

Their rugged carts, handmade by their father to hold their guns and ammunition, rattled and shook as Tracy and Sarah pulled them across the dirt-and-gravel parking lot. Overhead, the sky had rapidly blackened. The thunderstorm would arrive sooner than the weatherman had predicted.

Tracy unlocked her blue Ford truck's camper shell, lowered the tailgate, and wheeled on Sarah. "What the hell was that?" She did a poor job keeping her voice low.

Sarah tossed her hat into the truck bed, blonde hair falling past her shoulders. "What?"

Tracy held up the Championship silver belt buckle. "You haven't missed two plates in years. Do you think I'm stupid?"

"The wind kicked up."

"You're a terrible liar, you know that?"

"You're a terrible winner."

"Because I didn't win; you let me win." Tracy waited for two spectators to hurry past, the first drops of rain starting to fall. "You're lucky Dad wasn't here," she said. August 21 was their parents' twenty-fifth wedding anniversary, and James "Doc" Crosswhite hadn't been about to tell his wife she'd have to forsake Hawaii to celebrate at a dusty shooting range in the state's capital. Tracy softened, though she remained agitated. "We've talked about this. I've told you, we both have to try our best or people are going to think the whole thing is rigged."

Before Sarah could further respond, tires crunched gravel. Tracy diverted her attention as Ben swung his white pickup around her Ford, smiling down at them from inside the cab. Though he and Tracy had been dating for more than a year, Ben still smiled every time he saw her.

"We'll talk about this more when I get home tomorrow," Tracy said to Sarah and stepped away to greet Ben as he dropped from the cab and slipped on the leather car coat Tracy had bought him last Christmas. They kissed. "Sorry I'm late. Whoever outlawed drinking and driving never drove through Tacoma traffic. I could use a beer." When Tracy straightened the collar of his jacket, Ben glanced at the belt buckle in her hand. "Hey, you won."

"Yeah, I won." Her gaze shifted to Sarah.

"Hey, Sarah," Ben said, looking and sounding confused.

"Hey, Ben."

"You ready?" he asked Tracy.

"Give me a minute."

Tracy shed her duster and red bandanna, tossing both into the truck bed. Then she sat on the edge of the tailgate and held up a leg for Sarah to pull off her boot. The sky had turned completely black. "I don't like the idea of you driving alone in weather like this."

Sarah tossed the boot into the bed and Tracy raised her other leg. Sarah grabbed the heel. "I'm eighteen. I think I can drive myself home; it's not like it never rains here."

Tracy looked to Ben. "Maybe she should just come with us."

"She doesn't want to do that. Sarah, you don't want to do that."

"No, I definitely don't want to do that," Sarah said.

Tracy slipped on flats. "There's supposed to be thunderstorms."

"Tracy, come on. You act like I'm ten years old."

"Because you act like you're ten years old."

"Because you treat me like I'm still ten years old."

Ben checked his watch. "I hate to break up this intelligent discourse, ladies, but Tracy, we really have to go if we're going to keep that reservation."

Tracy handed her overnight bag to Ben and he took it to the cab as Tracy addressed Sarah. "Stay on the highway," she said. "Don't take the county road. It'll be dark and the rain will make it harder to see."

"The county road is faster."

"Don't argue with me. Stay on the highway and double back off the exit."

Sarah held out her hand for the truck keys.

"Promise me," Tracy said, not relinquishing them without Sarah's commitment.

"Fine, I promise." Sarah crossed her heart.

Tracy pressed the keys into Sarah's hand and curled her fingers over them. "Next time, just knock down the damn targets." She turned to leave.

"Your hat," Sarah said.

Tracy removed her black Stetson and popped it on Sarah's head. When she did Sarah stuck out her tongue. Tracy wanted to be angry, but Sarah was impossible to stay mad at. Tracy felt a grin inch across her own face. "You're such a brat."

Sarah gave her an exaggerated smile. "Yes, but that's why you love me."

"Yeah, that's why I love you all right."

"And I love you too," Ben said. He'd pushed open the passenger door and was leaning across the cab. "But I'll love you more if we make that reservation."

"I'm coming," Tracy said.

She hopped in and shut the door. Ben gave Sarah a wave and made a quick U-turn, heading for the line of cars forming at the exit, the falling rain now looking like flecks of molten gold in the truck's headlights. Tracy shifted to look out the cab window. Sarah remained standing in the rain, watching them leave, and Tracy felt a sudden urge to go back, as if she'd forgotten something.

"Everything okay?" Ben asked.

"Fine," she said, though the urge persisted. She watched as Sarah opened her hand, realized what Tracy had done, and looked quickly again at the cab.

Tracy had pressed the silver belt buckle into Sarah's palm along with the truck keys.

She would not see either again for twenty years.

CHAPTER 3

Cedar Grove Sheriff, Roy Calloway, still wore his fly-fishing vest and lucky cap, but he was already feeling far removed from the gentle rocking of the flat-bottomed boat. Calloway had driven straight to the station from the airport, his wife silent in the passenger seat, none too pleased to have their fly-fishing trip cut short, their first real vacation in four years. She hadn't made an effort to kiss him when she'd dropped him off, and he'd decided it best not to push the issue. He'd hear more about it at dinner for sure, and he'd say, "This one couldn't be helped," and she'd say, "I've been hearing that for thirty-four years."

Calloway entered the conference room and shut the door. His deputy, Finlay Armstrong, stood at the head of the rough-hewn wood table wearing his khaki uniform. Finlay looked pale beneath the fluorescent lights, but his complexion was robust compared to Vance Clark's pallid coloring. The Cascade County prosecutor sat at the far end of the room looking sickly, his checked sport coat draped over a chair, the knot of his tie lowered, the top button of his shirt undone. Clark didn't bother to get up. He gave Calloway a subtle nod.

"Sorry you had to come back for this, Chief." Armstrong stood in front of a paneled wall containing a photo gallery of Cedar Grove's sheriffs. Calloway's photograph had hung last on the right for thirty-four years. At six five, he still maintained the barrel chest of the man in that photograph, though he couldn't help but notice when he looked in the mirror each morning that the weathered lines on his face, which had once been hard edges to complement chiseled features, had become soft creases, and that his hair had thinned noticeably and turned gray.

"Don't sweat it, Finlay." Calloway tossed his cap onto the table, rolled out a chair, and sat. "Tell me what you got."

In his midthirties, tall and lean, Armstrong had been with Calloway for more than a decade, and was next in line to have his picture hung on the conference room wall. "Call came in this morning from Todd Yarrow. He and Billy Richmond were cutting through the old Cascadia property to their duck blind when Hercules took off on a scent. Yarrow said they had a hell of a time getting him to come back. When he did, Hercules had something hanging from his mouth. Yarrow grabs it thinking it's a stick and gets this white, slimy stuff on his hand. Billy says, 'That's a bone.' They didn't think much of it, figured Hercules dug up a deer carcass. Then Hercules takes off again, barking and making a hell of a racket. This time they chased after him and found him pawing at the ground. Yarrow couldn't call him off. Finally had to grab him by the collar and pull him away, and that's when he saw it."

"Saw it?" Calloway asked.

Armstrong played with the buttons of his iPhone as he stepped around the table. Calloway removed the half-lens reading glasses from the pocket of his fishing vest—he could no longer thread the flies onto the line without them—slipped them on and took the phone, extending his arm to focus. Armstrong leaned over his shoulder and used his fingers to enlarge the picture. "Those white lines there, those are bones. It's a foot."

The bones were encased in dirt, like a fossil being unearthed. Armstrong flipped through a series of photographs showing the foot and the grave site from various distances and angles. "I told them to mark the spot and meet me at their vehicle. They had the bone in the back of Todd's Jeep." Armstrong slid his finger across the screen until he came to an image of a single bone beside a flashlight. "The anthropologist in Seattle wanted it to scale. She said it looks like a femur."

Calloway glanced to the end of the room, but Vance Clark's gaze remained focused on the table top. Calloway directed his question to Armstrong. "You called the medical examiner?"

Armstrong took back his phone and straightened. "They had me talk to a forensic anthropologist." He checked his notes. "Kelly Rosa. She said they'd send a team, but they couldn't get here till tomorrow morning. I had Tony sit on the site so no other animals could get to it. Going to need to send someone to relieve him."

"She thinks it's human?"

"Doesn't know for certain, but she said it's the right length for a femur, a female. And you see the white stuff, the slimy stuff Yarrow got on his hands?" Armstrong rechecked his notes. "She called it adipocere, decomposed body fat. Stinks like rotting meat. Body's been there for a while."

Calloway folded his cheaters and slipped them back into his vest. "You up for walking them through it when they get here?"

"Sure, no problem," Armstrong said. "You going to be here too, Chief?"

Calloway stood. "I'll be here." He pulled open the door, in search of coffee. Armstrong's next question stopped him.

"You think it could be her, Chief? You think it could be that girl went missing back in the nineties?"

Calloway looked past Armstrong to where Clark remained seated. "I guess we're going to find out."

CHAPTER 4

Shafts of morning light filtered through the thick canopy of trees, casting shadows on the rock wall climbing straight up from the edge of the county road. A century before, tons of the mountain had been sheared away by dynamite, picks, and shovels to carve the road for mining trucks, revealing hidden springs that wept like tears down the stone face, streaking it with rust and silver mineral deposits. Tracy drove on autopilot, the radio off, her mind numb. The medical examiner's office had not had further information. Kelly Rosa had been out of the office and the minion Tracy had spoken with could only confirm what Kins had told her—a deputy from Cedar Grove had called with a photo of what appeared to be a human femur, unearthed by a dog belonging to two hunters on their way to their duck blind in the hills above the town of Cedar Grove.

Tracy took the familiar exit, made a left at the "Stop" sign, and a minute later turned onto Market Street. She stopped at downtown Cedar Grove's one and only traffic light and contemplated what had once been her hometown, but which now looked so tired and worn that it was foreign to her.

—

Tracy stuffed her change into the front pocket of her jeans, grabbed her popcorn and Coke from the counter, and looked about the theater lobby, but she didn't see Sarah.

Saturday mornings when Hutchins' Theater had a new movie, their mother gave Tracy six dollars, three dollars each for her and Sarah. The movie was $1.50, which left change for popcorn and a drink, or to buy an ice cream at the mercantile store after the show.

"Where's Sarah?" Tracy asked. At eleven, Tracy was responsible for Sarah, though she'd recently relented to Sarah's desire to carry her own movie money. Tracy had noticed that Sarah had not bought popcorn or a drink and had pocketed the extra $1.50. Now she was nowhere to be seen, which was not untypical.

Dan O'Leary pushed thick, black-framed glasses back onto the bridge of his nose, a persistent habit. "I don't know," he said, looking about the lobby. "She was just here."

"Who cares?" Sunnie Witherspoon had her popcorn and was waiting by the swinging doors to enter the darkened theater. "She always does this. Let's go. We're going to miss the previews."

Tracy liked to say Sunnie and Sarah had a love-hate relationship. Sarah loved to bug Sunnie and Sunnie hated it. "I can't just leave her, Sunnie." She asked Dan, "Did she go to the bathroom?"

"I can go look." Dan took two steps before the realization hit. "Wait. No, I can't."

Mr. Hutchins leaned his forearms on the counter. "I'll tell her you all went in and send her in, Tracy. You kids go on in so you don't miss the previews. I got the trailer for Ghostbusters.*"*

"Come on, Tracy," Sunnie whined.

Tracy took a final look about the lobby. It would be just like Sarah to miss the previews. Maybe she'd learn a lesson. "Okay, thanks, Mr. Hutchins."

"I can carry your soda," Dan said. His hands were empty. His parents only gave him enough money for the movie.

Tracy handed him the drink and used her free hand to cup the popcorn and keep it from spilling as she walked. Mr. Hutchins always filled her and Sarah's boxes until they overflowed. Tracy knew it had something to do with her father taking care of Mrs. Hutchins, who had lots of medical problems on account of her diabetes.

"It's about time," Sunnie said. "I'll bet all the good seats are taken."

Sunnie used her back to push open the swinging door and Tracy and Dan followed her in. The lights were out, and when the door shut, Tracy had to pause to let her eyes adjust to the dark. She heard kids already in their seats laughing and calling out names, eager for Mr. Hutchins to climb into the booth and start the projector. A couple of parents were trying unsuccessfully to shush them. Tracy loved everything about Saturdays at Hutchins' Theater, from the smell of the butter-flavored popcorn to its maroon carpet and velvet seats with the threadbare armrests.

Sunnie was halfway down the aisle when Tracy saw the shadow lurking behind a row of seats, too late to warn her before Sarah sprang her surprise.

"Boo!"

Sunnie let loose a bloodcurdling scream that silenced the theater. What followed was an equally recognizable laugh.

"Sarah!" Tracy yelled.

"What is wrong with you!" Sunnie shouted.

The lights in the theater burst on, bringing a chorus of booing. Mr. Hutchins hurried down the aisle, looking worried. Popcorn littered the worn carpet alongside Sunnie's discarded red-and-white-striped box.

"It was Sarah," Sunnie said. "She scared me on purpose."

"No, I didn't," Sarah said. "You just didn't see me."

"She was hiding, Mr. Hutchins. And she did it on purpose. She always does this."

"I do not," Sarah said.

Mr. Hutchins looked to Sarah, but rather than get mad, Tracy thought he looked like he was trying not to smile. "Sunnie, why don't you go back up and ask Mrs. Hutchins for another box of popcorn?" He raised his hands. "Sorry folks, just a bit of a delay while I get the sweeper. Only take a minute."

"No, Mr. Hutchins." Tracy looked to Sarah. "Sarah, you get the sweeper and clean it up."

"Why do I have to clean it up?"

"Because you made the mess."

"Uh-uh, Sunnie did."

"You clean it up."

"You're not the boss of me."

"Mom put me in charge. So you clean it up, or I'll tell Mom and Dad that you've been keeping the money Mom gives you for popcorn and ice cream."

Sarah scrunched her nose and shook her face. "Fine." She turned to go, stopped, and said, "Sorry, Mr. Hutchins. I'll clean it fast." Then she ran up the aisle and shoved open the door. "Hey, Mrs. Hutchins, I need the sweeper!"

"Sorry, Mr. Hutchins," Tracy said. "I'll tell my mom and dad what she did."

"No need to do that, Tracy," he said. "I think you handled it very maturely, and I think Sarah learned her lesson. That's just our Sarah, right? She does keep things interesting around here."

"Sometimes too interesting," Tracy said. "We're trying to get her to stop."

"Oh, I wouldn't do that," he said. "It's what makes Sarah, Sarah."

A horn honked. Tracy glanced in the rearview mirror and saw a man in the cab of a weathered truck pointing at the overhead signal. The light had turned green.

She drove past the movie theater, but the marquee was now pocked with rock holes and the windows that had advertised the feature attraction and upcoming movies boarded over with plywood. A breeze swirled newspaper and debris in the recessed area behind the ticket booth. The rest of the one- and two-story brick and stone buildings of downtown Cedar Grove were in similar distress. "For Lease" signs filled half the windows. In another, a Chinese buffet, which had replaced the Five 'n' Dime, advertised a $6.00 lunch special on a piece of cardboard. A thrift store had replaced Fred Digasparro's barbershop, though the red-and-white spiral pole remained fixed to the wall. A café advertised espresso drinks beneath faded letters whitewashed across the brick façade of what had been Kaufman's Mercantile Store.

Tracy turned right onto Second Avenue. Halfway up the block, she pulled into the parking lot. The black stenciled letters on the glass door to the Cedar Grove Sheriff's Office had not changed or faded, but she had no illusions about this homecoming.

CHAPTER 5

Tracy showed her badge to the deputy seated at the desk inside the glass doors and told him she was with the group from Seattle. He did not hesitate to direct her to the conference room down the hall.

"I know the way," she said.

When she opened the door to the windowless room, the conversation abruptly stopped. A uniformed deputy stood at the head of the wooden table, marker in hand, topographical map pinned to a cork board behind him. Roy Calloway sat closest to the door, eyebrows inched together and looking worried. On the opposite side of the table, Kelly Rosa, a forensic anthropologist from Seattle, sat along with Bert Stanley and Anna Coles, volunteers from the Washington State Patrol's Crime Scene Response Team. Tracy had worked multiple homicides with them.

Tracy didn't wait for an invitation to enter, knowing it wouldn't come. "Chief," she said, which was what everyone in Cedar Grove called Calloway, though technically he was the sheriff.

Calloway stood from the table as Tracy stepped past his chair and slipped off her corduroy jacket, revealing her shoulder holster and the badge clipped to her belt. "What do you think you're doing?"

She draped her jacket over the back of a chair. "Let's not do this dance, Roy."

He stepped toward her, straightening to his full height. Intimidation had always been his staple. To a young girl, Roy Calloway could be terrifying, but Tracy was no longer young or easily intimidated.

"I agree, let's *not* do this. So, if you're here on police business, you're out of your jurisdiction. If—"

"I'm not here as a police officer," she said. "But I'd appreciate a professional courtesy."

"Can't do it."

"Roy, you know I wouldn't do anything to jeopardize the integrity of a crime scene."

Calloway shook his head. "You're not going to get that chance."

The others looked on, uncertainty etched on their faces.

"Then I'm asking you for a favor . . . as a friend of my father's."

Calloway's blue eyes narrowed. His brow furrowed. Tracy knew she'd struck a deep wound, one that had never healed. Calloway and her father had hunted and fished together, and her father had cared for Calloway's aging parents before they died. The two men had also borne the guilt and the burden of being unable to find Sarah.

Calloway pointed a finger at her like he'd done when she was a kid riding her bike on the sidewalk. "You'll stay out of the way. If I tell you to leave, you will leave. Do we understand one another?"

Tracy was in no position to tell him she'd investigated more murders in a year than he'd investigated his entire career. "We do."

Calloway gave her a lingering glare before returning his attention to his deputy. "Go on, Finlay," he said, and retook his seat.

The deputy, whose badge read "Armstrong," took a moment to regain his train of thought before returning his attention to the topographical map. "This is where they found the body." He drew an X where the two hunters had apparently stumbled across the remains.

"That can't be," Tracy said.

Armstrong turned from the map, looking uncertain. He glanced at Calloway.

"I said, go on, Finlay."

"There's an access road here," Armstrong continued. "It was cut for a development."

Tracy said, "That's the old Cascadia property."

Calloway's jaw muscles tensed. "Continue, Finlay."

"The site is about half a mile from the access road," Finlay said, sounding less certain. "We've set a perimeter here." He drew another small X. "The grave itself is shallow, maybe a couple feet. Now—"

"Wait," Rosa said, lifting her head from taking notes. "Hold on. Did you say the grave was *shallow*?"

"Well, the foot wasn't very deep."

"And the grave looked to you otherwise undisturbed?" Rosa asked. "I mean other than where the dog had dug."

"Looked that way; I suppose it could just be a leg and foot."

"Why do you ask?" Calloway asked.

"The glacial till in the Pacific Northwest is rock hard," Rosa said. "It makes digging a grave very difficult, particularly in this type of terrain, which I'm assuming has an extensive root system. I'm not surprised the grave is shallow. What is surprising is that no other animals have disturbed it before now."

Tracy spoke to Rosa. "That area was just starting to be developed into a golf and tennis resort to be called Cascadia. They'd cleared some of the trees and brought in temporary trailers to use as a sales office to pre-sell the lots. You remember that body we found out in Maple Valley a few years back?"

Rosa nodded and directed her question to Armstrong. "Could the body have been buried in a hole created from a tree uprooted during the development?"

"I don't know," Armstrong said, shaking his head and looking confused.

"What difference does that make?" Calloway asked.

"For one, it could be indicative of a premeditated act," Tracy said. "If someone knew the area was being developed, they could have planned to use the hole."

"Why would a killer use a hole in a place that he knew was going to be developed?" Rosa asked.

"Because he also knew the development was never going to be built," Tracy said. "It was a big story around here. The resort was going to have a big impact on the local economy and make Cedar Grove a vacation destination. The developer submitted land use applications for a golf course and tennis resort, but shortly thereafter the Federal Energy Commission approved the construction of three hydroelectric dams across the Cascade River." Tracy stood, walked to the front of the room, and held out her hand for Finlay's marker. The deputy hesitated before handing it to her. She drew a line. "Cascade Falls was the last dam to go online. That was mid-October, 1993. When it did, the river backed up and the lake's perimeter expanded." She drew the lake's new perimeter. "It flooded that area."

"Which put the grave site under water and out of reach of animals," Rosa said.

"And out of our reach." Tracy turned to Calloway. "We searched that area, Roy."

Tracy knew. She'd not only been part of the search team, she'd kept the original topographical map after her father had died. In the intervening years, she'd gone over it so many times she knew it better than the lines on the palm of her hand. Her father had divided the map into sectors to ensure a thorough and systematic search. They'd gone over each sector twice.

When Calloway continued to ignore her, Tracy spoke to Rosa. "They took down Cascade Falls earlier this summer."

"And the lake receded back to its natural dimensions," Rosa said, understanding.

"They just reopened that area to hunters and hikers," Armstrong said, also catching on. "Yesterday was opening day of duck season."

Tracy looked to Calloway. "We went over that area before it flooded, Roy. There was no body there."

"It's a big area. You can't rule out the possibility we missed it," he said. "Or that it isn't her."

"How many other young women disappeared around here during that time, Roy?"

Calloway didn't answer.

Tracy said, "We searched that area twice and did not find *any* body. Whoever put the body there had to have done so after we'd searched and just before the flood."

CHAPTER 6

Tracy bolted upright, the bedsheet slipping to her waist. Disoriented, she thought the clatter that had startled her from sleep was the bell echoing through the halls of Cedar Grove High, signaling that she was late to teach her next chemistry class.

"Phone," Ben moaned. He lay on the mattress beside her, a pillow pulled over his head to block out the slats of sharp, morning light filtering through the blinds. The phone finally cut off midring.

Tracy fell back onto her pillow, but now her mind wanted to continue orienting itself. Ben had picked her up from the shooting competition to go to dinner. In her mind she watched him push back his chair and drop to one knee. The ring! Her mouth inched into a sleepy grin and she held up her left hand, tilting the diamond to reflect the prisms of light. Ben had been so nervous he could hardly get the words out.

Her thoughts shifted again, this time to Sarah. Tracy had meant to call Sarah with the news when she got to her rental but then one thing had led to another with Ben, though Sarah apparently already knew. Ben told Tracy that Sarah had helped plan the evening. It was why Sarah had missed the two targets. She had wanted Tracy to win so she wouldn't go off to get engaged in a bad mood.

Feeling guilty for having scolded Sarah, Tracy rolled over and checked the time on the digital alarm clock on the carpet beside the mattress. It glowed red numerals: 6:13 a.m. Sarah would never get out of bed this early to answer the extension in the hall of their parents' home. Tracy would have to wait to call her.

No longer interested in sleep, Tracy rolled close to Ben, spooning his body and feeling the heat radiate from him. When Ben didn't react, she pressed closer and ran her fingers over the ridges of his stomach muscles and took him in her hand, feeling him harden.

The phone rang.

Ben groaned, and not in a good way.

Tracy threw off the sheet, rolled out of the bed and stumbled over the clothes they had hastily discarded last night. She snatched the phone from its cradle on the wall in the kitchen. "Hello?"

"Tracy?"

"Dad?"

"I called earlier."

"Sorry, I must not have heard—"

"Is Sarah with you?"

"Sarah? No. She's at home."

"She isn't home."

"What? Wait, aren't you still in Hawaii? What time is it there?"

"Early. Roy Calloway said he couldn't get a hold of anyone at the house."

"Why was Roy calling the house?"

"They found your truck; did you have car trouble last night?"

Tracy was having difficulty tracking the conversation. Her head pounded from too much red wine and too little sleep. "What do you mean they found it? Found it where?"

"The county road. What happened to it?"

She felt a sense of dread wash over her. She'd told Sarah to stay on the highway. "Are you sure?"

"Yes, I'm sure! Roy recognized the sticker in the back window. Sarah's not with you?"

She felt sick to her stomach, lightheaded. "No, she drove home."

"What do you mean she drove home? Weren't you with her?"

"No, I was with Ben."

"You let her drive home from Olympia alone?" He was starting to shout.

"I didn't let her . . . Dad, I got . . ."

"Oh my God."

"She's probably at home, Dad."

"I just called there twice. No one answered."

"She never answers. I'm sure she's asleep."

"Roy knocked. He knocked on the front door—"

"I'm driving over there now, Dad. Dad. I said I'm going over there now. Yes, I'll call you when I get there. I said I'll call you when I get there."

She hung up the phone, trying to make sense of it.

Roy Calloway said he couldn't get a hold of anyone at the house.

They found your truck.

She took a deep breath, fighting against the spreading anxiety, telling herself not to panic, telling herself that everything was fine.

I just called there twice.

Sarah was probably asleep and either hadn't heard the phone ring or had ignored it. It would be just like her to ignore the phone.

Roy knocked. He knocked on the front door—

No one answered.

"Ben!"

CHAPTER 7

Tracy parked at the end of the caravan of cars lining the gravel road leading to the never-built entrance to the Cascadia Resort. She pulled her hair into a ponytail, then sat on her rear bumper and exchanged her flats for hiking boots. Though the sky was clear and the temperature October crisp, she tied a Gore-Tex jacket around her waist, knowing that rain could come quickly and the temperature dropped when the sun dipped below the treetops.

After they'd gathered, Finlay Armstrong led them down a dirt trail, Calloway behind him, followed by Rosa and her team. Rosa carried a dig bag, which was the size of an overnight bag with multiple pockets on the outside for things like scrapers, brushes, and small hand tools. Stanley and Coles carried sawhorses, a screen, and white buckets. The needles of the ponderosa pines had begun to turn a familiar soft shade of gold, and those that had fallen created a natural ground covering and familiar scent. The leaves of the maple and alders also hinted at the impending fall. Farther along the path, they passed the "No Trespassing" signs Tracy and Sarah and their friends had thrown rocks at as they rode their bikes along the mountain trails to reach Cascade Lake.

Half an hour into their hike, they stepped from the path into an area that had been partially cleared. The last time Tracy had been to this site, single-wide construction trailers had served as Cascadia's temporary sales offices.

"You wait here," Calloway said.

Tracy held back as the rest of the group walked closer to where a deputy stood beside wooden stakes driven into the ground. Yellow-and-black crime-scene tape strung between the stakes created a crude rectangle, perhaps eight feet wide and ten feet long. In the lower right quadrant, Tracy saw what looked like a stick protruding from disturbed soil. Her chest tightened.

"We'll set the second perimeter here," Calloway said to Armstrong, keeping his voice soft and reverent. "Use the tree trunks."

Armstrong grabbed the roll of crime-scene tape and began defining the second perimeter, which Tracy thought was overkill. No one else was coming. No one in Cedar Grove still cared, and the press would not find their way to this remote area of the North Cascades.

Armstrong approached where Tracy stood, looking almost apologetic. "I'm going to need you to step back, Detective," he said.

She stepped back as Armstrong finished wrapping the yellow-and-black tape between the trees.

Rosa quickly went to work. After restaking the grave to increase its dimensions, she used string to divide the plot into smaller sections, then dropped to her knees by the section with the protruding foot and methodically began brushing away the dirt. She used hand trowels to scoop soil into one of the five-gallon buckets. Each bucket was labeled with a capital letter corresponding to a particular section of the dig site, *A* through *D*. Stanley periodically dumped the dirt onto the screen set between the two sawhorses and sifted it. Anna Coles took photographs. Any bones or bone fragments found would be given a lowercase letter. Everything else—bits of clothing, metal, buttons—would be numbered. Rosa worked methodically, without breaks. She'd want to complete the task before the fall light fell below the treetops.

Shortly after one thirty, Tracy sensed the first break in Rosa's routine. The anthropologist stopped digging and sat back. She spoke to Stanley, who began handing her progressively smaller brushes from the dig bag as Rosa went back to whisking away dirt, though in a more and more concentrated area. After another half hour, Rosa stood. Whatever she'd unearthed, she now held in her gloved hand. She discussed the object with Roy Calloway, and then gave it to Stanley, who slipped the object inside a plastic evidence bag and labeled it with a black marker. After cataloguing it, Stanley handed the bag not to Rosa, but to Calloway, who seemed to be contemplating what Rosa had unearthed.

Then he turned and directed his gaze to Tracy.

She felt a surge of adrenaline. Sweat trickled from her armpits and rolled down her sides beneath her shirt.

As Calloway approached, her heart pounded. When he handed her the evidence bag she could not bring herself to look at it. She continued to study Calloway's face until the sheriff could no longer meet her gaze and looked away.

Tracy looked down at what Kelly Rosa had unearthed, and her breath caught in her chest.

CHAPTER 8

Tracy felt sick to her stomach. "You okay?" Ben reached across the cab and touched Tracy's shoulder, but she did not acknowledge him. She kept her gaze directed out the window, on the side of the mountain and the bits of shale littering the edge of the road. She had not found Sarah's boots on the front porch or in the entryway of their home. Sarah had not answered when Tracy had rushed up the grand staircase shouting her name. Sarah was not asleep in her bed or taking a shower. She was not in the kitchen eating or in the family room watching television. Sarah was not home. And there was no indication that she had been.

"There," Ben said as they came around another bend in the road.

Her blue truck looked abandoned, parked along the shoulder that sloped into the North Cascades wilderness.

Ben made a U-turn, parked behind Roy Calloway's Suburban and turned off the engine. "Tracy?"

She felt paralyzed. "I told her not to take the county road. I told her to stay on the freeway and double back. You heard me tell her."

Ben reached across the seat and squeezed her hand. "We're going to find her."

"Why is she so stubborn all the time?"

"It's going to be all right, Tracy."

But the sense of dread that had enveloped her as she had hurried from room to room in her parents' home grew more constricting. She opened her car door and stepped down onto the dirt shoulder.

The morning's temperature had continued to rise. The asphalt was already dry and showed no lingering hint of yesterday's heavy evening rains. Insects danced and buzzed about her as Tracy approached the truck. Weak and lightheaded, she stumbled. Ben steadied her. The shoulder of the road seemed narrower, the drop-off steeper than she recalled.

"Could she have slipped?" Tracy asked Roy Calloway, who stood waiting at the bumper of her truck.

Calloway held out his hand and took the spare key. "We'll take this one step at a time, Tracy."

"What's wrong with it?"

Tracy had been expecting one of the tires to be flat, or the body to be dented, or the hood to be raised to indicate a problem with the engine, though that was not likely. Their father was religious about bringing the cars to Harley Holt for servicing.

"We'll get that figured out," Calloway said. He slipped on a pair of blue latex gloves and opened the driver's door. A discarded Cheetos bag and empty Diet Coke bottle remained on the passenger-side floorboard—Sarah's breakfast the morning they drove to the competition. Tracy had given her a hard time for eating that crap. Her light-blue fleece remained rolled in a ball on the narrow bench seat where she'd put it. She looked at Calloway and shook her head. Everything looked as she remembered it. Calloway leaned across the steering wheel, inserted the key in the ignition, and turned it. The engine whimpered. Then it clicked. He leaned in farther and considered the dash.

"It's empty."

"What?" she asked.

Calloway stepped back so Tracy could lean in. "She ran out of gas."

"That can't be," Tracy said. "I filled up Friday night so we wouldn't have to do it that morning."

"Maybe it's just not registering because the engine is dead?" Ben suggested.

"I don't know," Calloway said, though he sounded skeptical.

Calloway removed the key and walked to the back of the truck. Tracy and Ben followed. Tinted glass prevented them from seeing inside the camper shell. At the back, Calloway said, "Why don't you turn around?"

Tracy shook her head. "No."

Ben wrapped an arm around her shoulders. Calloway unlocked the canopy door and bent to peek inside the bed before letting the door lift open. He lowered the tailgate. Again, everything remained seemingly as Tracy remembered. Their rugged carts were strapped to the bed walls. Tracy's duster lay strewn with her boots and red bandanna.

"Isn't that her hat?" Calloway pointed to the brown Stetson.

It was. Then Tracy remembered plopping her black Stetson on Sarah's head. "She was wearing mine."

Calloway started to raise the gate.

"Can I go in?" Tracy asked. Calloway stepped back. She climbed in, uncertain what she was looking for but feeling the same urgency she'd felt when she and Ben had driven off the night before, as if she'd forgotten something. She unlocked their rugged carts. The shotguns and rifles remained racked, barrel up, like pool cues in a rack. Sarah's pistols were stored in an interior drawer, the ammunition in the lock box. In a second drawer, where Sarah kept buttons and badges from other competitions, Tracy found the photograph of Wild Bill presenting her with the silver belt buckle: Sarah and the third place finisher stood on each side of her. She slid the photograph into her back pocket, lifted the duster, and checked the pockets.

"It isn't here," she said climbing out.

"What isn't here?" Calloway asked.

"The championship buckle," Tracy said. "I gave it to Sarah last night before we left."

"I'm not following," Calloway said.

"Why would she take the buckle and not take her guns?" Ben asked.

"I don't know. It's just . . ."

"It's just what?" Calloway asked.

"I mean, she wouldn't have had any reason to take the belt buckle unless she intended to give it back to me this morning, right?"

"She walked away," Calloway said. "Is that what you're saying? She had time to decide what to take and started walking."

Tracy looked down the deserted road. The white center line snaked with the hillside's contours, turning and disappearing around a bend. "So where is she?"

CHAPTER 9

The silver plating had lost its luster, but the cast image of a cowgirl firing two single-action revolvers and the lettering etched along the perimeter remained distinct: *1993 Washington State Champion.*

They'd found the belt buckle.

They'd found Sarah.

The emotion that welled inside Tracy surprised her. It wasn't bitterness or guilt. It wasn't even sorrow. It was anger, and it coursed through her like venom. She'd known. She'd always known Sarah's disappearance wasn't what everyone had wanted her to believe. She'd known there'd been more to it. And now she had a sense that she could finally prove it.

"Finlay." Calloway's voice sounded as if it were coming from the far end of a long tunnel. "Take her out of here."

Someone touched her arm. Tracy pulled away. "No."

"You don't need to be a part of this," Calloway said.

"I left her once," she said. "I'm not leaving her again. I'm staying. To the end."

Calloway nodded to Armstrong, who stepped back to where Rosa had resumed digging. "I'll need that back," Calloway said.

He held out his hand for the belt buckle but Tracy continued to trace the surface with her thumb, feeling the contour of each letter. "Tracy," Calloway said.

She held out the buckle, but when Calloway grasped it she did not release her grip, forcing him to look her in the eye. "I told you, Roy. We searched this area. We searched it twice."

—

She kept her distance the remainder of the afternoon, but she could see enough to know that Sarah had been buried in a fetal position, legs higher than her head. Whoever had used the hole created when the root ball was pulled free of the ground had misjudged the size of the hole, which was not uncommon. Spatial perception can become distorted when a person is under stress.

Only after Kelly Rosa had zipped closed the black body bag and padlocked the zipper did Tracy hike out of the woods back to her car.

She navigated the turns down the mountain without thought, her mind dulled. The sun had dipped below the tree line, causing shadows to creep across the road. She'd known, of course. It was why detectives were trained to work so hard to recover anyone abducted within the first forty-eight hours. After that, statistics showed that the odds of finding the person alive plummeted. After twenty years, the odds of finding Sarah alive had been infinitesimal. And yet there had remained that small part of her, the part that Tracy shared with other families whose loved ones had been abducted and never found. It was the part of every human being that clung to the hope, no matter how unlikely, that they could beat the odds. It had happened before. It had happened when a young woman in California, missing eighteen years, walked into a police station and said her name. Hope had been reignited that day for every family who had ever lost a loved one. It had flared for Tracy. Someday that would be Sarah. Someday that would be her sister. It could be so cruel, hope. But for twenty years it was all she'd had to hold on to, the only thing to push back the darkness that lingered on the periphery, searching for every opportunity to enshroud her.

Hope.

Tracy had clung to it, until that very last moment when Roy Calloway had handed her the belt buckle, and extinguished the final, cruel, flicker.

She drove past the spot on the county road where, twenty years earlier, they'd found her blue truck, and it felt as if just days had passed. Miles down the road, she took the familiar exit and drove through a town she no longer recognized or felt connected with. But rather than turn left for the freeway entrance, she turned right, driving out past the single-story houses she remembered as vibrant homes filled with families and friends, but which now looked tired and worn. Farther out of town, the size of the houses and the yards increased. She drove on autopilot, slowing to turn when she saw the river rock gateposts. She stopped at the bottom of a sloped driveway.

Bright perennials, regularly tended by her mother, had once filled the flowerbeds, but they had been replaced by the bare stalks of dormant rose bushes. At the top of a manicured lawn outlined by neatly trimmed English boxwood hedges was a severed stump, where the weeping willow had once stood like an open umbrella. Christian Mattioli had enlisted an architect from England to design a two-story, Queen Anne–style home when he had founded the Cedar Grove Mining Company and the town of Cedar Grove had sprung to life. As the story went, Mattioli later requested that the architect add a third story to ensure the home would be the tallest and grandest in Cedar Grove. A century later, long after the Cedar Grove mines had closed and most of the residents had moved on, the house and yard had fallen into disrepair. However, Tracy's mother had fallen in love at first sight with the fish-scale siding and the turrets rising above the low-pitched gabled roofs. Tracy's father, in search of a country medical practice, had bought her the property and together they had restored everything from the Brazilian-wood floors to the box-beam ceilings. They'd stripped the paneled wainscoting and cabinetry to the original mahogany and refurbished the marble entryway and crystal chandeliers, making the structure once again the grandest in Cedar Grove. But they'd done more than refurbish a structure. They'd created a place for two sisters to call home.

Tracy turned off the bathroom light and stepped into her bedroom wearing her red fleece pajamas. A towel turban entwined her hair. She sang along to Kenny Rogers and Sheena Easton's version of "We've Got Tonight," which played on her boom box as she leaned across the bench seat and considered the night sky out her bay window. A magnificent full moon cast the weeping willow in a pale blue light. Its long braids hung motionless, as if the tree had fallen into a deep sleep. Fall was slipping quietly into winter and the weatherman had predicted the nighttime temperature would dip below freezing. To Tracy's disappointment, however, the sky sparkled with stars. Cedar Grove Grammar School shut down for the first winter snow and Tracy had a test on fractions in the morning. She was less than fully prepared.

She hit the "Stop" button on the boom box, cutting off Sheena but continuing to sing. Then she clicked off her desk lamp. Moonbeams spilled across her down comforter and throw rug, disappearing again when she switched on the lamp clipped to the headboard. She picked up A Tale of Two Cities; they'd been slogging their way through the story the entire semester. She didn't much feel like reading, but if her grades slipped, her father wouldn't take her to the regional shooting tournament at the end of November.

She continued singing the lyrics to "We've Got Tonight" as she pulled back the comforter.

"Boo!"

Tracy screamed and stumbled backward, nearly falling over.

"Oh my God! Oh my God!" Sarah had popped out from beneath the covers like she'd been spring-loaded, and now lay on her back laughing so hard she could barely catch her breath to speak the words.

"You are such a brat!" Tracy yelled. "What is wrong with you?"

Sarah sat up, trying to talk in between her high-pitched giggles and gasps for air. "You should have seen your face!" She imitated Tracy's shocked look, then fell back onto the comforter holding her stomach, continuing to laugh.

"How long have you been under there?"

Sarah got to her knees and balled her fist as if singing into a microphone and mimicked Tracy singing the lyrics.

"Shut up." Tracy undid her turban, flipped her hair forward and rubbed vigorously with the towel.

"Are you in love with Jack Frates?" Sarah asked.

"That is none of your business. God, you are such a child."

"No duh. I'm eight. Did you really kiss him?"

Tracy stopped drying her hair and lifted her head. "Who told you that? Did Sunnie tell you that? Wait." She glanced at her bookshelf. "You read my diary!"

Sarah picked up the pillow and began making kissing noises. "Oh, Jack. Let's make it last. Let's find a way!"

"That is private, Sarah! Where is it?" Tracy leaped onto the bed, straddling Sarah, pinning her arms and legs. "Not cool. Totally not cool. Where is it?" Sarah started laughing again. "I mean it, Sarah! Give it back!"

The door opened. "What is going on?" Their mother entered in her pink robe and slippers, holding a brush. Her blonde hair, freed from its customary bun, fell to the middle of her back. "Tracy, get off of your sister."

Tracy slid off. "She hid under my covers and scared me. And she took my . . . she hid under the covers!"

Abby Crosswhite walked to the bed. "Sarah, what have I told you about scaring people?"

Sarah sat up. "Mom, it was so funny. You should have seen her face." She made a face that looked like an overexcited chimpanzee. Their mother covered her mouth, trying hard not to laugh.

"Mom!" Tracy said. "It's not funny."

"All right. Sarah, I want you to stop scaring your sister and her friends. What have I told you about the boy who cried wolf?"

"One of these times you're going to hide and no one will ever find you," Tracy said.

"Mom!"

"And I won't even look for you."

"Mom!"

"Enough," their mother said. "Sarah, go to your own room." Sarah slid off Tracy's bed and started for the door to the adjoining bathroom. "And give your sister back her diary."

Tracy and Sarah both froze. Their mother was like that, psychic or something.

"It's impolite to be reading about her kissing Jack Frates."

"Mom!" Tracy said.

"If you're embarrassed to have it read, then you probably shouldn't be doing whatever you're writing about in the first place. You're too young to be kissing boys." She turned to Sarah, who stood just inside the bathroom between their rooms making smooching noises. "Enough, Sarah, give it back."

Sarah walked back to the bed, savoring each step as Tracy glared at her. Sarah pulled the flowered book from beneath the covers and Tracy snatched it from her hand, taking a swipe at her. Sarah ducked and ran from the room.

"You're not supposed to be reading my diary, Mom. It's a total invasion of my privacy."

"Turn around. You'll get tangles." Abby Crosswhite ran the brush through Tracy's hair, and she relaxed at the feel of bristles tickling her scalp. "I didn't read your diary. That was a mother's intuition. Nice admission of guilt, however. The next time Jack Frates comes over, tell him your father would like a word."

"He won't come over. Not with that brat here."

"Don't call your sister a brat." She pulled the brush through a final time. "Okay, bed." Tracy slid under the covers, feeling the lingering warmth of Sarah's body. She adjusted a pillow behind her back, and her mother bent and kissed her forehead. "Good night." Her mother picked up the wet bath towel from the floor and closed the door halfway, then leaned back in. "And Tracy?"

"Yeah?"

Her mother belted out the song lyrics.

Tracy groaned. When the door shut, she climbed from bed, closed the door to the bathroom, and looked for a better hiding place for her diary. Finally, she slipped it beneath her sweaters on the top shelf of her closet, where Sarah couldn't easily reach. Back beneath the covers, she opened Dickens.

She'd been reading for nearly half an hour, and had just flipped forward to find the end of the chapter, when she heard the bathroom door creak open. "Go to bed," she said.

Sarah swung from the door handle into Tracy's peripheral vision. "Tracy?"

"I said, go to bed."

"I'm scared."

"Too bad."

Sarah stepped to the edge of the bed. She'd dressed in one of Tracy's flannel nightgowns. The hem dragged on the floor. "Can I sleep with you?"

"No."

"But it's scary in my room."

Tracy pretended to continue reading. "How can you be scared in your room and not scared hiding under covers?"

"I don't know. I just am."

Tracy shook her head.

"Please," Sarah pleaded.

Tracy sighed. "Fine."

Sarah leaped onto the bed and climbed over her, scurrying under the covers. Settled, she asked, "What was it like?"

Tracy looked down from her book. Sarah lay staring up at the ceiling. "What was what like?"

"Kissing Jack Frates."

"Go to sleep."

"I don't think I'll ever kiss a boy."

"How do you plan on getting married if you never kiss a boy?"

"I'm not going to get married. I'm going to live with you."

"What if I get married?"

Sarah's face scrunched in thought. "Could I live with you?"

"I'll have a husband."

Sarah bit at a fingernail. "Could we still see each other every day?"

Tracy lifted her arm. Sarah slid closer. "Of course we will. You're my favorite sister, even if you are a brat."

"I'm your only sister."

"Go to sleep."

"I can't."

Tracy put Dickens on the nightstand and slid beneath the covers. She reached overhead for the power switch to her lamp. "Okay, close your eyes."

Sarah did so.

"Now take a deep breath and let it out." When Sarah exhaled, Tracy said, "Ready?"

"Ready."

"*I am not . . .*"

"*I am not . . . ,*" Sarah repeated.

"*I am not afraid . . .*"

"*I am not afraid . . .*"

"*I am not afraid of the dark,*" they said in unison, and Tracy clicked off the light.

CHAPTER 10

As a younger man, Roy Calloway had liked telling people he was "tougher than a two-dollar steak." He could go for days on just a few hours of sleep and hadn't taken a sick day in thirty-plus years. At sixty-two, it was getting harder to keep those kinds of hours, or to convince himself that he wanted to. He'd been knocked down by the flu twice the last year, the first time for a week, the second for three days. Finlay had served as the acting sheriff, and Calloway's wife had been quick to point out that the town hadn't burned to the ground or suffered a crime wave without him.

Calloway hung his coat on the hook behind the door and took a moment to admire the rainbow trout he'd caught on the Yakima River the previous October. The fish was a beauty, twenty-three inches and just under four pounds, with a colorful underbelly. Nora had had it stuffed and hung it on his office wall when Calloway had been out. Lately, she'd been after him hard to retire; the fish was meant to serve as a daily reminder there were more to catch. Subtle his wife was not. Calloway had told her the town still needed him, that Finlay wasn't ready. What he hadn't said was that he still needed the town, and the job. A man could only fish and golf so much, and he'd never been much for travelling. He couldn't stand the thought of becoming one of "those guys" wearing the white, soft-soled orthotics, standing on the deck of a cruise ship pretending to have something in common with everyone besides being one step from the grave.

"Chief?" The voice came through the phone speaker.

"I'm here," he said.

"Thought I saw you sneak in. Vance Clark's here to see you."

Calloway looked up at the clock: 6:37 p.m. He wasn't the only one working late. He'd been expecting a visit from Cedar Grove's Prosecuting Attorney, but had thought it would not be until the morning.

"Chief?"

"Send him back."

Calloway sat at his desk beneath the sign his staff had given him the year he had become Sheriff.

> *Rule #1: The Chief is always right.*
> *Rule #2: See Rule #1.*

He wondered.

Clark's shadow passed the smoked-glass panes leading to Calloway's office door. He knocked once and entered with a limp. Years of running had taken their toll on Clark's knees.

Calloway rocked back in his chair and put his boots up on the corner of his desk. "Knee bothering you?"

"Aches when the weather starts to get cold." Clark shut the door. He had a hangdog look about him but that was not unusual. A monk's ring of hair displayed a full brow that seemed perpetually furrowed.

"Maybe it's time to give up the running," Calloway said, though he knew Clark wouldn't stop running for the same reason he wouldn't stop being Sheriff. What else would he do?

"Maybe." Clark sat. The fluorescent tubes hummed overhead. One had an annoying tick and occasionally flickered, as if about to go out. "I heard the news."

"Yeah, it's Sarah."

"So what do we do now?"

"We don't do anything."

Clark's brow creased. "And if they find something in the grave that contradicts the evidence?"

Calloway lowered his boots to the floor. "It's been twenty years, Vance. I'll convince her that, now that we've found Sarah, it's time to let the dead bury the dead."

"What if you can't?"

"I will."

"You couldn't before."

Calloway flicked the head of the Félix Hernández bobblehead doll his grandson had given him for Christmas and watched it bob and twitch. "Well, this time I'll just have to do a better job of it."

After a moment of seemingly deep thought, Clark said, "Are you driving down for the autopsy?"

"I sent Finlay. He found the body."

Clark exhaled and swore under his breath.

"We were all in agreement, Vance. What's done is done. Sitting here worrying about something that may never happen isn't going to change anything."

"Things have already changed, Roy."

CHAPTER 11

Tracy kept her head down as she stepped from the elevator and made her way to her cubicle. She'd meant to get in early, but traffic had turned the two-hour drive back to Seattle from Cedar Grove into three and a half, she'd drunk Scotch for dinner, and had forgotten to set her alarm. Or she'd slept through it. She didn't know.

She draped her Gore-Tex jacket over the back of her chair, dropped her purse inside her cubicle cabinet, and waited for her computer screen to come to life. Her head felt like someone was drumming inside her skull, and a handful of Tums had not extinguished the small brushfire in her stomach. Kins's chair creaked and rotated, but when she did not turn to acknowledge him, she heard him rotate back to his computer. Faz and Delmo were not yet at their desks.

Tracy started going through her e-mails. Rick Cerrabone had sent her several that morning. The King County prosecutor wanted copies of the witness statements and Tracy's affidavit to complete the search warrant Tracy was seeking for Nicole Hansen's apartment. He'd sent a second e-mail half an hour after the first.

Where are witness statements and affidavit? Can't go to judge without.

Tracy picked up the phone, about to call Cerrabone, when she saw an e-mail above his second message. Kins had copied her on his reply. She opened it. Kins had provided the witness statements and sworn out an affidavit. She swiveled her chair toward him, annoyed that he'd responded for her, even more annoyed that he'd done the affidavit when she was the lead detective. Kins glanced over his shoulder, caught her glare, and rotated to face her.

"He called me, Tracy. I figured you had enough on your plate and took care of it."

She swung back to her keyboard, hit "Reply All" and started to type a nasty response. After a minute she sat back, read what she'd written, and deleted it. She took a breath and pushed back from the keyboard. "Kins?"

He faced her.

"Thanks," she said. "What did Cerrabone say about the search warrant?"

Kins walked over, hands thrust in his pants pockets. "Should have it later this morning. You all right?"

"I don't know. I don't know what I'm feeling. My head hurts."

"Andy came by," he said, referring to their lieutenant, Andrew Laub. "He wants to see you."

She laughed, rubbed her eyes, and pinched the bridge of her nose. "Great."

"Why don't we go get some breakfast? We can take a drive and talk to that witness down in Kent in that felony assault case."

Tracy pushed back her chair. "Thanks, Kins, but the sooner I get this out of the way . . ." She gave him a resigned shrug. "I don't know." She made her way around the perimeter of the cubicles and down the hall.

Andrew Laub had been the A Team's sergeant for two years before his promotion to lieutenant. That had earned him a small interior office with no window and a removable nameplate in the slot beside his door. Laub sat sideways at his desk, eyes focused on the computer screen, fingers pecking at the keyboard. Tracy knocked on the door frame.

"Yeah?"

"This a bad time?"

The clicking stopped. Laub turned. "Tracy." He motioned her in. "Close the door."

She entered and shut the door. The photographs on the shelves behind Laub served as a biography. He was married to an attractive redhead. They had twin daughters, though not identical, and a son who looked a lot like his father, with the same red hair and freckles. The boy apparently played football. "Take a seat." The light from his desk lamp reflected in his glasses.

"I'm fine."

"Take one anyway."

She sat.

Laub removed his glasses and set them on his desk pad. Red impressions marked where the nose pads had pinched the bridge of his nose. "How you holding up?"

"I'm good."

He eyeballed her. "People care, Tracy. We all just want to make sure you're all right."

"I appreciate everyone's concern."

"The medical examiner has the remains?"

Tracy nodded. "Yeah. Brought her back last night."

"When will you get the report?"

"Maybe a day."

"I'm sorry."

She shrugged. "At least now I know. That's something."

"Yeah, that's something." He picked up a pencil, tapping the eraser on his desk pad. "When's the last time you slept?"

"Last night. Slept like a baby."

Laub leaned forward. "You want to tell everyone else you're fine, that's your prerogative, but you're my responsibility. I need to know you're okay; I don't need you to be a hero."

"I'm not trying to be anyone's hero, Lieutenant. I'm just trying to do my job."

"Why don't you take some time? Sparrow can handle the Hansen case," he said, referring to Kins by the nickname he'd picked up working undercover with narcotics. He'd grown his hair long and sported a wispy goatee, making him look like the Johnny Depp character, Captain Jack Sparrow.

"I can handle it."

"I know you can handle it. I'm saying, don't. I'm saying, go home, get some sleep. Take care of what you need to take care of. The job will still be here."

"Is that an order?"

"No, but it's a very strong suggestion."

She got up from her chair and made it as far as the door.

"Tracy—"

She faced him. "I go home and I have nothing but the walls to look at, Lieutenant. Nothing but time to think about things I don't want to think about." Tracy paused to get her emotions under control. "I don't have any pictures in my cubicle."

Laub set down the pencil. "Maybe you should talk to somebody?"

"It's been twenty years, Lieutenant. I've gone through it every day for twenty years. I'll get through these days the same way I got through those, one bad day at a time."

CHAPTER 12

The second morning after Sarah's disappearance, Tracy's father entered his den looking utterly exhausted, despite a shower. Her parents had flown the red-eye from Hawaii. Her mother had not come home. When the plane had landed, she had gone directly to the American Legion building on Market Street to mobilize the volunteers already gathering there. Her father had come home to meet with Roy Calloway and had asked Tracy to stay in the event that the Sheriff had additional questions, though she'd already answered so many she couldn't think of what else he could ask her.

Did you notice anyone at the competition acting peculiar, hanging around, seeming to take an unusual interest in Sarah?

Did anyone approach either of you, for any reason?

Did Sarah ever indicate that she felt threatened by anyone?

Calloway asked for a list of the boys Sarah had dated. Tracy could not think of a single person on it who would have any reason to harm Sarah. Most of them had been her friends since grammar school.

Her father's hair, a premature gray, hung in ringlets over the collar of his long-sleeved shirt. Ordinarily it contrasted with his youthful demeanor and inquisitive blue eyes. This morning he looked his fifty-eight years. His eyes were puffy and bloodshot behind his round, wire-rimmed glasses. Usually fastidious about his appearance, several days' growth competed with his thick mustache, the ends of which he kept long enough to wax into sharp points when he competed in shooting tournaments as "Doc" Crosswhite.

"Tell me about the truck," her father said to Calloway, and it was not lost on Tracy that it was her father, not Calloway, asking the questions. At parties in their home, her father was never boisterous or demonstrative, but a crowd always seemed to find him. Holding court, Tracy's mother called it. When James Crosswhite spoke, people listened, and when he asked questions, they gave him answers. At the same time, her father had a quiet and respectful manner about him that made you feel as if you were the only person in the room.

"We had it towed to the police impound," Calloway said. "Seattle is sending a forensic team to check for fingerprints." He looked to Tracy. "It appears she ran out of gas."

"No." Tracy stood near a red ottoman that matched two leather chairs. "I told you, I filled up before we left Cedar Grove. There should have been three-quarters of a tank."

"We'll take a closer look," Calloway said. "I've sent a bulletin to every police department in the state, as well as Oregon and California. Canadian Border Patrol has also been notified. We faxed Sarah's graduation photo."

James Crosswhite ran a hand over the stubble on his chin. "Somebody passing through?" he asked. "Is that what you're thinking?"

"Why would someone passing through take the county road?" Tracy said. "They would have stayed on the highway."

Her father's eyes narrowed but she caught his gaze too late. He stepped to her and took hold of her left hand. "What is that? Is that a diamond?"

"Yes."

Her father looked away, jaw clenched.

Calloway intervened. "You've reached out to her friends?"

Tracy shielded her hand behind her thigh. She'd spent hours calling everyone she could think of. "No one has seen her."

"Why didn't she take her guns?" her father asked, though seemingly to himself. "Why wouldn't she take one of the pistols?"

"She had no reason to feel threatened, James. I'm guessing she ran out of gas and started walking toward town."

"You've searched the woods?"

"Nothing to indicate she slipped or fell."

Tracy had never thought that likely. Sarah was too athletic to have tumbled off the side of the road, even in the dark and the rain.

"Sit tight," Calloway said.

"I'm not going to sit tight, Roy. You know I'm not built that way." He turned to Tracy. "Get that flier we talked about made up and get it down to your mother. Find a photograph that looks like Sarah, not her graduation picture. Bradley can make the copies for you at the pharmacy. Tell him to run off a thousand to start and put it on my store tab. I want them everywhere from here to the Canadian border." He turned to Calloway. "We're going to need a topographical map."

"I've called Vern. He knows these mountains better than anyone."

"What about dogs?"

"I'll look into it," Calloway said.

"Somebody coming home from somewhere? Someone who lives here?"

"Nobody here would do such a thing, James. Not to Sarah."

Her father looked about to say something else but stopped as if he'd lost his train of thought. For the first time in her life, Tracy saw fear pass over him, something gray and dark and ethereal. "That kid," he said. "The one they just paroled."

"Edmund House," Calloway whispered. He stood, as if paralyzed by the name. Then he said, "I'm on it." Calloway quickly slid apart the panel doors, hurrying across the marbled foyer to the front door.

"Jesus," her father said.

CHAPTER 13

The Spartan interior of the coffee shop beneath the building that housed the new offices of the King County Coroner on Jefferson Street reminded Tracy of the coffee shops in hospitals, before someone had decided that, just because a relative was sick, it didn't mean their family had to suffer too. Apparently intended to be some sort of modern decor, the floors were linoleum, the tables stainless steel, and the chairs plastic and uncomfortable. Kelly Rosa hadn't suggested the café for its ambiance. She'd chosen it for its location: close to, but not actually her office.

Tracy scanned the café tables but did not see Rosa. She ordered black tea and sat at a table near windows with a view of the sloped sidewalk, answering e-mails and text messages on her iPhone. Within a minute of sitting, she recognized Rosa making her way down the sidewalk, despite the hood of a green raincoat protecting her from a light sprinkle. Rosa lowered the hood as she entered the coffee shop and spotted Tracy. She did not look like a person who hiked through hillsides and swamps to find and examine the remains of persons long dead. She looked like a middle-aged soccer mom who drove a minivan, which Rosa did when not searching for human remains.

Rosa gave Tracy a hug before sliding off her coat.

"Can I get you anything?" Tracy asked.

"No, I'm good," Rosa said, sitting across from her.

"How are the kids?"

"My fourteen-year-old is taller than me. Not a big accomplishment, I know, but she takes great pleasure in hovering over me." If Rosa hit five feet, it was only by the width of one of her blonde hairs. "My eleven-year-old is starring in the school play. *The Wizard of Oz.*"

"She's Dorothy?"

"Toto. She thinks she's the star." Tracy smiled. Rosa sat forward and gripped Tracy's hand. "I'm very sorry, Tracy."

"Thanks. I appreciate you making the time."

"Of course."

"You've confirmed it's her?" It was a formality, but Tracy knew from experience that Rosa would have had to run an X-ray of Sarah's jaw and teeth through the Missing and Unidentified Person's Unit and the National Crime Information Center.

"Two positive hits."

"What else can you tell me?"

Rosa exhaled a sigh. "I can tell you that big sheriff doesn't want me telling you anything."

"He said that?"

"His intent was clear."

"Roy Calloway has never been subtle."

"Good thing I don't work for him." Rosa smiled, but it quickly waned. "But are you sure you want me to go through this? These are hard enough when they're anonymous."

"No, I'm not sure, but I need to know what you found."

"How much do you want me to tell you?"

"As much as I can stand; I'll tell you when I can't."

Rosa rubbed her hands together before forming a steeple at her chin, like a child preparing to pray. "As you suspected, the killer used a hole created by the root ball. Shovel marks indicate he tried to enlarge the hole but either misjudged the size, got lazy, or ran out of time. The body was positioned with the legs higher than the head and bent at the knees. That's why the dog uncovered the foot and leg first."

"I gathered as much."

"The position of the body in the hole, with bent knees and hunched back, also indicates rigor mortis prior to burial."

Tracy felt her pulse thicken. "Prior? You're sure?"

"I'm sure."

"How much prior to burial?"

"That I can't be certain. I can make an educated guess."

"But definitely *before* burial."

"That would be my strong opinion."

"Were you able to determine a cause of death?"

"The skull was fractured in the back, just above the spine. Whether that was the cause of death, I also can't be certain. It's just been too long. There were no other bone fractures, Tracy. Nothing to indicate she'd been beaten."

Rosa was being kind. The lack of fractures was not conclusive evidence a victim had not been beaten or tortured, especially when the remains were so decomposed. "What other personal effects did you find besides the belt buckle?" Tracy knew from experience that any organic materials, such as cotton and wool, would have long since deteriorated but inorganic material, like metals and synthetic fibers, would remain.

Rosa pulled out a small notebook from her jacket and flipped through it. "Metal rivets with 'LS&CO S.F.' on them."

Tracy smiled. "Levi Strauss & Company," she said. "Sarah was a rebel."

"I'm sorry?"

"Levi Strauss supports the anti-gun lobbyists. We wore Wrangler or Lee, but Sarah thought they made her butt look big so she wore Levi's. You had to know her to appreciate her."

"Let's see. Seven metal snaps." Rosa looked up from her notes. "I'm assuming from a long-sleeved shirt. Two were smaller in diameter, I'm thinking for the cuffs."

Tracy reached into her briefcase at the side of her chair and pulled out a framed photograph, the championship photo of Tracy and Sarah and the third place finisher. "Like this?"

Rosa considered the photograph. "Yeah. Though the buttons are no longer black."

Sarah had worn long-sleeved shirts made by Scully. She'd worn her white-and-black-embroidered shirt at the competition that day. Tracy took back the picture.

Rosa reconsidered her notes. "Bits and pieces of plastic."

Tracy's stomach cramped, but she fought to remain focused. Sarah's killer had had to bend her body to fit her into the hole. He'd also apparently stuffed her into a common garbage bag.

Rosa hesitated. "You okay?"

Tracy took a deep breath and forced herself to say the words. "A garbage bag?" she asked. The bag could be significant. Calloway claimed Edmund House had confessed to immediately killing Sarah and burying her body. The theory was that House had stumbled upon Sarah walking on the road and attacked her. If so, it would have been more than fortuitous if he'd had a garbage bag in the truck to use.

"I think so."

"What else?"

"Trace amounts of synthetic fibers."

"How big?"

"The fibers? Fifty microns."

"Carpet fibers?"

"Likely."

"You think her body could have been rolled up in a carpet?"

"No. If that had been the case, I would have expected to find remnants of the carpet, or at least a lot more fibers than we did. These were likely fibers that she came into contact with, maybe inside a vehicle?"

Edmund House had been living with his uncle, Parker House, and driving one of the many vehicles Parker restored on his property and resold, a red Chevy truck. He'd gutted the cab down to the metal. Carpet fibers in the grave also did not fit with Calloway's testimony that Edmund House had confessed to raping, strangling, and immediately burying Sarah's body. "Anything else?"

"Some jewelry."

Tracy leaned forward. "What specifically?"

"Earrings. And a necklace."

Her pulse raced. "Describe the earrings?"

"They were jade. Oval-shaped."

"Teardrops?"

"Yes."

"And the necklace, sterling silver?"

"Yes."

Tracy slid the photograph back across the table. "Like this?"

"Exactly like that."

"Where are they now?"

"The sheriff's deputy took possession of everything."

"But you photographed and catalogued everything?"

"Always. Regular routine." Rosa gave her a quizzical look. "Tracy?"

Tracy pushed back her chair and slipped the photograph into her briefcase. "Thanks, Kelly. I appreciate this." She started from the table.

"Tracy?"

She turned back. Rosa continued, "What about her remains?"

Tracy paused and closed her eyes, pressing the heel of her palm against her forehead, feeling the onset of a crushing headache. She retook her seat.

After another moment, Rosa asked, "What's going on?"

Tracy considered what to say, how much to reveal. "It's better if you don't know too much, Kelly. You may end up being a witness, and it's best if your opinions remain untainted by anything I might tell you."

"A witness?"

Tracy nodded.

Rosa's eyes narrowed in question, but she apparently decided to let it go. "Okay. But if I could offer a suggestion . . ."

"Please."

"Let me send her remains directly to a funeral home. It's easier. You don't want to have to transport them."

Twenty years ago, some in Cedar Grove had suggested a service. They'd been seeking closure, but James Crosswhite wouldn't hear any talk of funerals or funeral homes. He would not hear any discussion that his baby girl was dead. Tracy no longer had any such hope, but now she had something she'd been waiting twenty years for. Hard evidence.

"I think that would be best," Tracy said.

CHAPTER 14

Early on the morning of the third day after Sarah's disappearance, Tracy opened the front door to find Roy Calloway standing on the porch, kneading the brim of his hat. From his expression, Tracy knew Calloway had not come bearing good news.

"Morning, Tracy. I need to speak to your father."

Tracy had dragged her parents home when darkness had made searching the hills above Cedar Grove no longer practical. She had worked beside her father, who had been using his den as their command center. He had called police stations, congressmen, everyone he knew in positions of power. Tracy had called radio stations and newspapers. Sometime after eleven, as her father studied a topographical map, Tracy had curled up in one of the red leather chairs to take a fifteen-minute nap. She had awoken beneath a blanket, the morning sun streaming through the leaded glass. Her father remained seated at his desk, the sandwich she'd made him the night before untouched. He was using a ruler and compass to divide the topographical map into quadrants. She got up to make coffee but found a pot already brewing in the kitchen. Her mother had evidently left earlier that morning without awakening her. About to pour a cup for her father, she'd heard the knock on the front door.

"He's in his den," she said.

The sliding doors behind her were already pulling apart, and her father stepped out, fitting his glasses behind each ear. "I'm here," he said. "Tracy, make some coffee."

"Mom has a pot brewing." She followed them into the den.

"Did you speak to him?" her father asked.

"He says he was at home."

Tracy knew they were talking about Edmund House.

"Can anyone verify that?"

Calloway shook his head. "Parker worked the night shift at the mill and got home late. He says he found Edmund asleep in his bedroom."

When Calloway didn't immediately continue, her father said, "But?"

Calloway handed her father Polaroid photographs. "He has scratch marks on the side of his face and the back of his hands."

Her father held one up to the light. "How did he explain these?"

"He said a piece of wood exploded on him while he was working in the metal shed where Parker makes his furniture. He said it splintered and cut him."

Her father lowered the picture. "I've never heard of such a thing."

"Neither have I."

"These look like someone raked fingernails across his face and arms."

"I thought so too."

"Can you get a search warrant?"

"Vance already tried," Calloway said, frustration seeping into his voice. "He called Judge Sullivan at home. Sullivan turned him down. He said there wasn't enough evidence to invade the sanctity of Parker's home."

Her father massaged a kink in the back of his neck. "What if I call Sullivan?"

"I wouldn't. Sullivan goes by the book."

"He's been in my damn house, Roy. He comes to my Christmas party."

"I know."

"What if he has Sarah there? What if he has her somewhere on that property?"

"He doesn't."

"How do you know?"

"It's Parker's property. I asked if I could take a look around, and he gave his consent. I searched every room and every building. She isn't there and I didn't see any sign to indicate she had been."

"There could be other evidence—blood in his car or in the house."

"There could be, but to bring in a forensic team—"

"He's a Goddamn felon, Roy. A convicted rapist who has scratch marks on his face and arms and no one to account for his where-abouts. How the hell is that not enough?"

"I said the same thing to Vance, and he made the same argu-ment to Judge Sullivan. House did his time for that crime."

"I called King County, Roy. House got off on a damn plea because the police screwed up. They say he raped and beat that poor girl for more than a day."

"And he did his time, James."

"Then you tell me, Roy, where's my daughter? Where's my Sarah?"

Calloway looked upset. "I don't know. I wish I did."

"So this is what, just one big coincidence? They let him out, he comes to live here, and now Sarah's missing?"

"It's not enough."

"He has no alibi."

"It's not enough, James."

"Who then? A drifter? Someone passing through? What are the odds of that?"

"The bulletin is out to every law enforcement agency in the state."

James Crosswhite rolled up the topographical map and handed it to Tracy. "Take this to your mother down at the American Legion building. Tell her to give it to Vern and get the teams together. We're going back out. This time I want the search done in a systematic manner so there is no margin for error." He looked to Calloway. "What about dogs?"

"The closest team is in California. Flying them is a problem."

"I don't care if they're in Siberia. I'll pay whatever it takes to get them here."

"It's not the cost, James."

Her father turned to Tracy as if surprised she hadn't left. "Did you hear me? I said get going."

"Aren't you coming?"

"Do as I say, damn it!"

Tracy flinched and stepped back. Her father had never raised his voice to her or to Sarah. "Okay, Daddy," she said, walking past him.

"Tracy." He gently touched her arm, taking a moment to regain his composure. "You go on, now. Tell your mother I'll be down shortly. The sheriff and I have a few more matters to discuss."

CHAPTER 15

A week after they'd located Sarah's remains, Tracy drove back to Cedar Grove. Though the drive from Seattle had been mostly in sunshine, as she approached, a dark cloud had gathered and now hung over the town, as if to mark the somber reason for her return. She was coming home to bury her sister.

Traffic was lighter than she'd expected and she arrived half an hour early for her meeting at the funeral home. She looked around the dilapidated storefronts and shops, before spotting the neon sign in the shape of a cup of coffee on what had been Kaufman's Mercantile Store. The air was heavy with the earthy scent of impending rain. Tracy fed a quarter into the meter, though she doubted there was a meter maid within a hundred miles, and entered The Daily Perk. Long and narrow, the space had once been the mercantile store's soda and ice cream counter. Someone had built a false wall to divide the space into a coffee shop and a Chinese restaurant. The decor was a mishmash of furniture that resembled a college apartment. The couch was threadbare and covered with newspapers. The lath and plaster walls displayed long cracks that were poorly disguised by a fresco painting of a window looking out on a city sidewalk of people walking past brownstones. It seemed an odd choice for a rural coffee shop. The young woman behind the counter had a nose ring, a stud piercing her lower lip, and the service skills of a government employee one week from retirement.

When the girl didn't bother to greet her, Tracy said, "Coffee. Black."

She took the cup to a table by the real window and sat looking out on a deserted Market Street, remembering how she and Sarah and their friends used to get in trouble for riding their bikes on the crowded sidewalk. They'd lean them against the wall, never bothering to lock them, and go inside the stores to buy supplies for whatever Saturday adventure they'd planned for that week.

—

Dan O'Leary stood forlornly over his bike. "Damn it."

"What's the matter?" Tracy had just exited Kaufman's after stuffing a length of thick rope, a loaf of bread, and jars of peanut butter and jelly into her backpack. With the leftover quarter, she'd bought ten pieces of black licorice and five pieces of red. Her father had given her the money that morning, when she'd asked permission for her and Sarah to ride their bikes to Cascade Lake. Sarah had found the perfect tree for a summer rope swing. Tracy was surprised her father had given her the money so readily. This was ordinarily the type of extravagance that she and Sarah were expected to pay for with their allowance money. Now a high school sophomore, Tracy also earned money working part-time in the ticket booth at Hutchins' Theater. Her father not only gave her the money, he told her to spend it all, and said that Mr. Kaufman "was having trouble making ends meet." Tracy suspected that was because Mr. Kaufman's son, Peter, who was in Sarah's sixth-grade class at Cedar Grove Grammar School, had been sick and in and out of the hospital for most of the year.

"Flat tire," Dan said, sounding as deflated as his bike's front wheel.

"Maybe it's just low on air," Tracy said.

"No. It was flat this morning so I pumped it up before we left. It must have a hole. Great. Now I can't go." Dan slid his backpack off his shoulder and sank onto the sidewalk.

"What's the matter?" Sarah asked, exiting the store with Sunnie.

"Dan's got a flat tire."

"I can't go," he said.

"Let's ask Mr. Kaufman to use the phone to call your mom," Tracy said. "Maybe she'll come down and buy you a new tube."

"I can't," Dan said. "My dad's been on my ass about being irre-sponsible. He says money doesn't grow on trees."

"So you're not going?" Sunnie said. "We had it all planned out."

Dan lowered his head to his forearms crossed over his knees. He didn't bother to fix his glasses when they slipped down the bridge of his nose. "You guys just go without me."

"Okay," Sunnie said, getting her bike.

Tracy glared at her. "We're not going without him, Sunnie."

"We're not going? It's not our fault he's got a lousy bike."

"Quit it, Sunnie," Sarah said.

"You quit it. Who invited you anyway?"

"Who invited you?" Sarah spat back. "I found the tree, not you."

"Stop it, both of you," Tracy said. "If Dan can't go, then none of us is going." Tracy grabbed Dan's arm. "Come on, Dan, get up. We'll push your bike to my house. We can tie the rope on one of the branches of the weeping willow and make a swing there."

"Are you kidding? What are we, six years old?" Sunnie said. "We were going to jump in the lake. What are we going to do, jump in the lawn?"

"Let's go." Tracy looked about but did not see her sister. She sighed. "Where's Sarah?"

"Great," Sunnie said. "Now she's disappeared again. This day is getting worse by the minute."

Sarah's bike remained against the building, but she was nowhere to be seen. "Wait here." Tracy went back into the store and found Sarah at the counter talking to Mr. Kaufman. "Sarah, what are you doing?"

Sarah reached into her pocket and pulled out a wad of dollar bills and quarters, dropping it on the counter. "Buying Dan a new tire," Sarah said. She swung her head to get strands of hair out of her face. It drove their mother crazy, but Sarah refused to wear a clip or pull her hair back in a rubber band.

"Is that your movie money you've been saving?"

Sarah shrugged. "Dan needs it more than me."

"Here you go, Sarah." Mr. Kaufman handed Sarah the box with the new tire tube. "This should be the right size."

"Do I have enough, Mr. Kaufman?"

Mr. Kaufman scooped the money from the counter without counting it. "I think it's plenty. You sure you can fix it? It's a pretty big job." He looked at Tracy and winked.

"I've seen my Dad do it. It's only the front tire so I don't have to take the chain off."

"Maybe your big sister can help you," he said.

"No, I can do it."

He reached beneath the counter and handed Sarah a wrench and a flat-head screwdriver. "Well, you'll need these. You let me know if you need any help."

"I will. Thanks, Mr. Kaufman." Sarah took the box and the tools and ran out of the store shouting, "Dan, I got a new tire, so now you can go!"

Tracy watched out the window. Dan looked confused, then surprised, and finally popped to his feet grinning.

"You let me know if you need any help, okay, Tracy?" said Mr. Kaufman.

"I will," Tracy said.

He handed her a bike pump. "Just bring it back with the tools when you're done." He looked out the window. Sarah and Dan had dropped to their knees, and Sarah was fitting the wrench onto the front nut. "She's a pistol, that sister of yours."

"Yeah, she's something. Thanks, Mr. Kaufman." Tracy started from the store but turned back when Mr. Kaufman called her name. He held out one of the extra-big Hershey's bars, the kind her mother bought to make s'mores when they went camping. "Oh no, Mr. Kaufman. I don't have any more money."

"It's a gift."

"I can't take that," she said, remembering her father saying that Mr. Kaufman was having trouble making ends meet. She already suspected that the tire cost more than Sarah had put on the counter.

Mr. Kaufman looked as if he was about to cry. "Do you know she rides her bike all the way to the hospital to visit Peter?"

"She does?" The hospital was one town over in Silver Spurs. Sarah would have been in big trouble if their parents found out.

"She brings him coloring books," he said, eyes moist. "She said she'd been saving her popcorn money."

CHAPTER 16

Tracy shook the rain from her jacket as she entered the front door of Thorenson's Funeral Home. Old Man Thorenson, which is what they'd called Arthur Thorenson when they were kids, had once embalmed everyone who died in Cedar Grove, including both her mother and her father. But when Tracy had called earlier in the week, she'd spoken to Darren, his son. Darren had been a few years ahead of her at Cedar Grove High and had apparently gone into the family business.

She introduced herself to the woman seated at a desk in the lobby and declined a seat or a cup of coffee. The lighting inside the building seemed brighter than she remembered, and the walls and carpeting a lighter color too. The smell, however, had not changed. It smelled like incense, an odor Tracy had come to associate with death.

"Tracy?" Darren Thorenson approached in a dark suit and tie, arm outstretched. He took her hand. "It's good to see you, though I'm sorry about the circumstances."

"Thanks for taking care of all the arrangements, Darren." In addition to cremating Sarah's remains, Thorenson had notified the cemetery workers and obtained a minister for the service. Tracy hadn't wanted a service, but she also wasn't about to dig a hole in the middle of the night and unceremoniously dump her sister in the ground.

"Not a problem." He led her into what had been his father's office when Tracy and her mother made the arrangements for her father's funeral and when Tracy had returned after her mother had died of cancer. Darren took the seat behind the desk. A portrait of his father, younger-looking than Tracy recalled, hung on the wall beside a family photograph. Darren had married Abby Becker, his high school sweetheart. They apparently had three kids. He looked like his father. Heavyset, Darren combed his hair back off his forehead, which accentuated his bulbous nose and thick, black-framed glasses, like the kind Dan O'Leary had worn as a kid.

"You've redecorated," Tracy said.

"Slowly," he said. "It took some time to convince Dad that *reverent* didn't have to mean *bleak*."

"How is your father?"

"He still threatens to come out of retirement from time to time. When he does, we stick a golf club in his hand. Abby said to pass along her condolences."

"Did you have any problems with the plot?"

Cedar Grove Cemetery had existed longer than the town, though no one knew the date of the first burial since its earliest graves were unmarked. Volunteers tended to the upkeep, pulling weeds and mowing the grass. If someone died, they dug the grave. They worked for free, the unspoken understanding being that someday someone would repay the favor. Because of limited space, the City Council had to approve every burial. Cedar Grove residency was mandatory. Sarah had died a Cedar Grove resident, so that wasn't the issue. Tracy had requested that her sister be buried with their parents, though technically her parents were in a two-person plot.

"Not a bit." Darren said. "It's all taken care of."

"I guess we better get your paperwork taken care of."

"That's all done too."

"Then I'll just write you a check."

"It's all good, Tracy."

"Darren, please, I can't ask that of you."

"You didn't ask it of me." He smiled, but it had a sad quality to it. "I'm not going to take your money, Tracy. You and your family, you've been through enough."

"I don't know what to say. I appreciate this. I really do."

"I know you do. We all lost Sarah that day. Things were never the same around here. It was like she belonged to the whole town. I guess we all did back then."

Tracy had heard others say similar things—that Cedar Grove hadn't died when Christian Mattioli had closed the mine and much of the population had moved away. Cedar Grove had died the day Sarah disappeared. After Sarah, people no longer left their front doors unlocked or let their kids roam freely on foot and bicycle. After Sarah, they did not let their children walk to school or wait for the bus unaccompanied by an adult. After Sarah, people weren't so friendly or welcoming to strangers.

"He's still in jail?" Thorenson asked.

"Yeah, he's still in jail."

"I hope he rots there."

Tracy considered her watch.

Darren stood. "You ready?"

She wasn't, but she nodded anyway. He led her into the adjoining chapel, the rows of chairs empty. The room had been unable to accommodate the crowd for her father's wake. A crucifix hung on the front wall. Below it, on a marble pedestal, was a gold-plated container the size of a jewelry box. Tracy stepped closer and read the engraving on the plate.

Sarah Lynne Crosswhite
The Kid

"I hope it's okay," Darren said. "That's how we all remember her, the kid following you all over town." Tracy wiped a tear away with a tissue. "I'm glad you're going to be able to put Sarah to rest and put this behind you," Darren continued. "I'm glad for all of us."

—

The cars parked bumper to bumper on the one-way road leading into the cemetery were more than Tracy had anticipated, and she suspected she knew who was responsible for getting the word out, and why. Finlay Armstrong stood in the road directing traffic, rain sheeting off the clear poncho that protected his uniform and dripping from the brim of his hat. Tracy lowered her window as she pulled to a stop.

"Don't worry about parking. You can leave it in the road," Finlay said.

Darren Thorenson, who'd followed Tracy in his own car, opened a large golf umbrella to shield her from the rain as she stepped from the car, and they walked up the hill toward a white awning covering her mother and father's plot at the top of a knoll overlooking Cedar Grove. Thirty to forty people sat in white folding chairs beneath the canopy. Another twenty stood outside its perimeter beneath umbrellas. Those people seated stood when Tracy stepped beneath the cover. She took a moment to acknowledge the familiar faces. They'd aged, but she recognized friends of her parents, adults who had once been kids that she and Sarah had gone to school with, and teachers who'd become Tracy's colleagues when she'd returned briefly to teach chemistry at Cedar Grove High. Sunnie Witherspoon was there, as was Marybeth Ferguson, one of Sarah's best friends. Vance Clark and Roy Calloway stood outside the tent. So did Kins, Andrew Laub, and Vic Fazzio, who had all driven up from Seattle and brought Tracy some semblance of reality. Being back in Cedar Grove was still surreal. It felt as if

she'd become stuck in a twenty-year time warp, things both familiar and foreign. She couldn't equate what she was seeing with what
she remembered. This was not 1993. Far from it.

The crowd had left the first row of chairs vacant, but now the
empty seats beside Tracy only served to amplify her isolation.
After a moment, she sensed someone step beneath the canopy to
the seat beside her.

"Is this seat taken?" She had to take a moment to peel away
the years. He'd ditched the black frames for contacts, revealing the
blue eyes that had always held a mischievous glint. The crew cut
had been replaced with gentle waves that fell to the collar of his
suit jacket. Dan O'Leary bent and gently kissed Tracy's cheek. "I'm
so sorry, Tracy."

"Dan. I almost didn't recognize you," she said.

He smiled, keeping his voice low. "I'm a bit grayer, not much
wiser."

"And a little taller," she said, bending back her head to look up
at him.

"I was a late bloomer. I grew a foot the summer of my junior
year." The O'Learys had moved from Cedar Grove after Dan's sophomore year in high school. His father had taken a job at a cannery
in California. It had been a sad day for Tracy and the other members of their posse. Dan and Tracy had stayed in touch for a while,
but those were the days before e-mail and texting and they had
soon fallen out of touch. Tracy seemed to recall that Dan had graduated and gone to college on the East Coast and remained there
after graduating, but had also heard that his mother and father had
returned to Cedar Grove when his father had retired.

Thorenson approached and introduced the minister, Peter
Lyon. Lyon, tall with a full head of red hair and fair skin, wore a
white, ankle-length alb with a green rope tied around his waist.
A matching green stole was draped over his shoulders. Tracy and
Sarah had been raised Presbyterian. After Sarah disappeared,

Tracy's faith had ranged from agnostic to atheist. She hadn't set foot in a church since her mother's funeral.

Lyon offered his condolences, then stepped to the head of the grave and began with the sign of the cross. He thanked those who had come, raising his voice to be heard over a burst of rain pattering on the canopy. "We have come today to inter the remains of our sister, Sarah Lynne Crosswhite, in the earth. Our loss is great and our hearts are heavy. In times of trouble and pain we turn to the Bible, the Word of God, for our comfort and our salvation." The minister opened his Bible and read from it. Finishing, he said, "I am the resurrection and the life, sayeth the Lord. He who believes in me will live, even though he dies; and whoever lives and believes in me will never die." He closed his missal. "Sarah's sister, Tracy, will now come forward."

Tracy stepped to the edge of the grave and inhaled a deep breath. Darren Thorenson handed her the gold-plated box and gave her a hand as she knelt on a cloth spread over the ground, though she still felt moisture seep through her nylons. She placed Sarah's remains in the grave and then scooped up a handful of moist soil. Tracy closed her eyes, imagining Sarah lying in bed beside her as she had frequently done when they were children and when they had shared a hotel bed while traveling to shooting competitions with their father.

Tracy, I'm scared.

Don't be afraid. Close your eyes. Now take a deep breath and let it out.

Tracy's chest heaved. Her eyes watered. "I am not . . . ," she whispered, fighting to keep her voice even as she spread her fingers and let the clumps of dirt fall onto the box.

I am not . . .

"I am not afraid . . ."

I am not afraid . . .

"I am not afraid of the dark."

A sudden gust of wind rippled the canopy and blew strands of hair in Tracy's face. She smiled at the recollection and folded the strands behind her ear.

"Go to sleep," Tracy whispered, and wiped away the tear rolling down her cheek.

—

Those in attendance came forward to drop handfuls of dirt and flowers into the grave and to offer their condolences. Fred Digasparro, who had owned the barber shop, needed the assistance of a walker, a young woman at his side. Hands that had shaved men with a straight razor now trembled as he reached to take Tracy's hand. "I had to come," he said, with his Italian accent. "For your father. For your family."

Sunnie quickly embraced Tracy, sobbing. They had been inseparable throughout grammar school and high school, but Tracy had not stayed in touch, and now the contact felt uncomfortable and the tears forced. Sunnie and Sarah had never been close; Sunnie had been jealous of Tracy and Sarah's relationship.

"I'm so sorry," Sunnie said, drying her eyes and introducing her husband, Gary. "Are you staying for a few days?"

"I can't," Tracy said.

"Maybe a cup of coffee before you go? A few minutes to catch up?"

"Maybe."

Sunnie handed her a slip of paper. "This is my cell phone. If you need anything, anything at all . . ." She touched Tracy's hand. "I've missed you, Tracy."

Tracy recognized most of the faces that came forward, though not all. As with Dan, for some she had to peel away the years to find the person that she'd known. Toward the end of the procession, however, a man in a three-piece suit stepped forward, a pregnant woman at his side. Tracy recognized him but could not put a name with his face.

"Hey, Tracy. It's Peter Kaufman."

"Peter," she said, now seeing the boy who had left Cedar Grove Grammar School for a year while suffering from leukemia. "How are you?"

"I'm great." Kaufman introduced his wife. "We live over in Yakima," he said, "but Tony Swanson called and told me about the service. We drove over this morning."

"Thanks for coming all that way," Tracy said. Yakima was a four-hour drive.

"Are you kidding? How could I not come? You know she used to ride out to the hospital every week and bring me candy and a coloring book or a book to read?"

"I remember. How are you?"

"Cancer free for thirty years. I've never forgotten what she did. I used to look forward to seeing her each week. She raised my spirits. She was like that. She was a special person." Tears welled in his eyes. "I'm glad they found her, Tracy, and I'm glad you gave us all this chance to say good-bye."

They spoke for another minute; Tracy was in need of another Kleenex by the time Peter Kaufman departed. Dan, who had stood back a respectful distance while she had greeted those who'd come, stepped forward and handed her a handkerchief.

Tracy gathered her emotions and blotted her eyes. When she'd regained some semblance of composure, she said, "So I don't understand; I thought you lived back east. How'd you find out?"

"I did live back east, just outside of Boston. But I've moved back. I live here now—again."

"In Cedar Grove?"

"It's a bit of a story, and you look like you could use a break from the past." Dan slipped her a business card and gave her a hug.

"I'd like to catch up when you feel up to it. Just know how sorry I am, Tracy. I loved Sarah. I truly did."

"Your handkerchief," she said, holding it out.

"You can hang on to that," Dan said.

She noticed that the handkerchief was embroidered with his initials, DMO, which made her consider the cut of his tailored suit and the quality of his tie. Having spent time with attorneys, she knew both were high-end, which didn't exactly fit the image of the boy she'd known, who'd worn hand-me-downs. She looked at his business card. "You're a lawyer," she said.

He gave her a wink. "Recovering."

The card included a business address for the First National Bank building on Market Street in Cedar Grove. "I'd like to hear that story, Dan."

"Just give me a call." He gave her a gentle smile before opening a golf umbrella and stepping out from beneath the canopy into the rain.

Kins approached with Laub and Faz. "You want some company on the drive back?"

"I know a great place to eat on the way," Faz said.

"Thanks," she said. "But I'm going to stay another night."

Kins said, "I thought you wanted to come straight back to Seattle?"

She watched as Dan reached an SUV, pulled open the door, lowered his umbrella, and slid inside. "My plans just changed."

CHAPTER 17

First National Bank's fortune had been literally tied to Christian Mattioli's fortune. Established to protect the considerable wealth of the founders of the Cedar Grove Mining Company, including Mattioli, the bank had nearly died when the mine had closed and he and his cohorts had left town. The Cedar Grove residents had rallied together, transferring savings and checking accounts and making a commitment to the bank for their mortgages and small-business loans. Tracy wasn't certain when the bank had folded for good and vacated the building. Judging from the register inside the vacant lobby, the opulent, two-story brick building had since been carved into office spaces, though many of those offices were currently vacant.

As she climbed the interior staircase, she looked down on the intricate mosaic floor that depicted an American eagle with an olive branch in its right foot and thirteen arrows in its left. Dust had settled over it, along with sporadic cardboard boxes and debris. She recalled teller cages, bank officer desks, and sprawling potted ferns. Her father had brought her and Sarah to the bank to open their first savings and checking accounts. First National's president, John Waters, had initialed and stamped their books.

Tracy found Dan's office on the second floor and stepped into a tiny reception area with a vacant desk. A sign told her to ring the bell. She slapped it with the palm of her hand, resulting in an obnoxious clang. Dan came around the corner in khakis, leather boat shoes, and a blue-and-white-striped button-down shirt. She was still having trouble accepting that the man before her was the same kid she'd known in Cedar Grove.

He smiled. "Have any trouble finding parking?"

"There's quite the selection out there, isn't there?"

"The City Council wanted to put in those automated parking meters. Someone did the math and determined it would take ten years before the revenue generated would pay for them. Come on in."

Dan led her into an octagon-shaped office with rich, dark molding and wainscoting. "It was the bank president's office," he said. "I pay fifteen dollars a month more in rent to say that."

Law books filled bookshelves, but she knew they were mostly for show. Everything was now accessed online. Dan's ornate desk faced the arched bay window still bearing the maroon-and-gold lettering that had advertised the building as the First National Bank. From it, Tracy looked down on Market Street. "How many times do you think we rode our bikes down that street?" she asked.

"Too many to count. Every day of the summer."

"I remember the day you got the flat tire."

"We were going to the mountains to put up that rope swing," he said. "Sarah bought me the tube and helped me fix the tire."

"I remember, she used her own money," Tracy said. She turned from the window. "I'm surprised you came back here to live."

"So was I."

"You said it was a long story."

"Long. Not interesting. Coffee?"

"No thanks. I'm trying to cut back."

"I thought coffee was a prerequisite for being a cop."

"That's donuts. What do lawyers eat?"

"Each other."

They sat at the round table beneath the window. A law book wedged in the sash held up the lower pane, allowing fresh air into the office.

"It's good to see you, Tracy. You look great, by the way."

"I think you better get some new contacts. I look like hell, but thanks for being kind." His comment made her even more self-conscious about her appearance. Not having intended to stay another night, she hadn't brought much to wear. Before leaving Seattle, she'd thrown jeans, boots, a blouse, and her corduroy jacket into her car to change into after Sarah's service. She'd slipped the same clothes on in the morning. Before leaving her motel room, she had stood at the mirror contemplating pulling her hair into a ponytail but decided it only accentuated her crow's-feet. She had left her hair down. "So, why did you come back?" she asked.

"Oh, it was a combination of things. I'd burned out practicing at a big law firm in Boston. Every day just became a grind, you know? And I'd made enough money and thought I wanted to try something different. Seemed my wife had the same idea; she was trying a different man."

Tracy grimaced. "I'm sorry."

"Yeah, so was I." Dan shrugged. "When I suggested I was going to quit law, she suggested we quit each other. She'd been sleeping with one of my partners for more than a year. She'd grown accustomed to the country club lifestyle and was afraid of losing it."

Dan was either over the pain or hid it well. Tracy knew that some pain never fully resolved. You just suppressed it beneath a façade of normalcy. "How long were you married?"

"Twelve years."

"Do you have kids?"

"No."

She sat back. "So why Cedar Grove? Why not someplace . . . I don't know."

He gave her a resigned smile. "I thought about moving to San Francisco and looked into Seattle. Then Dad died and Mom got sick, and someone needed to take care of her. So I came home figuring it a temporary situation. After a month, I decided I'd die of boredom if I didn't do something so I hung out a shingle. I do mostly wills, estate planning, a few DUIs, anything that walks in the door that is boring and can pay a $1500 retainer."

"And your mom?"

"She died a little over six months ago."

"I'm sorry."

"I miss her, but we had time to get to know one another in a way we never had before. I'm grateful for that."

"I envy you."

His brow furrowed. "Why would you say that?"

"My mom and I never really had much of a relationship after Sarah disappeared, and then after my father . . ." She let it drift and Dan didn't press her, which made her wonder how much he knew.

"That must have been a terrible time for you."

"Yeah, it was," she said. "It was awful."

"I hope yesterday brought some closure."

"Some," she said.

Dan stood. "You sure I can't get you any coffee?"

She suppressed a smile, seeing him again as the young boy who didn't like heavy conversations and would quickly change the subject. "Really, I'm fine. So tell me what type of law did you practice?"

Dan sat again and folded his hands in his lap. "I started out doing antitrust work and realized it *is* truly possible to die of boredom. Then a partner brought me in on a white-collar criminal-defense case, and I found that I really liked it. And, if I say so myself, I was pretty good in court." He still had a boyish grin.

"I'll bet juries loved you."

"Love's a strong word," he said. "Worshipped, maybe." He laughed and she heard the boy in that too. "I defended the CEO of a big corporation, and when I got a defense verdict, every attorney in my firm who had a client who'd gotten his hand caught in the cookie jar or a relative who'd drunk too much at the company Christmas party came to me. That evolved into larger white-collar criminal-defense cases, and before I knew it, I'd developed a good practice." He tilted his head, as if studying her. "Okay, your turn. Homicide detective? Wow. What happened to teaching?"

She waved him off. "You don't want to hear about that."

"Hey, come on, now. What about that good for the goose thing? Wasn't your dream to become a teacher at Cedar Grove High and raise your kids here?"

"Don't make fun."

He scoffed. "Hey, *I* live here now. And that's what you always said, you were going to teach, and you and Sarah were going to live next door to each other."

"I did teach, for a year."

"Cedar Grove High?"

"The Fighting Wolverines," she said and made claws with her hands.

"Let me guess, chemistry?"

Tracy nodded. "Very good."

"God, you were such a nerd," he said.

She displayed mocked indignity. "I was a nerd? What about you?"

"I was a dork. Nerds are smart. There's a subtle distinction. And are *you* married, with kids?"

"Divorced," she said, "No kids."

"I hope it ended better than mine."

"I doubt it, but at least mine was short. He felt like I was cheating on him."

"*Felt* like?"

"With Sarah."

Dan gave her a quizzical look.

Sensing the timing to be right, Tracy said, "I left teaching and joined the police academy, Dan. I investigated Sarah's murder for more than ten years."

"Oh," he said.

She reached into her briefcase and pulled out the file she'd brought with her, setting it on the table. "I have Bekins boxes filled with witness statements, trial transcripts, police reports, evidence reports, everything. What I didn't have was forensics from a grave site. Now I do."

"I don't understand. They convicted someone, didn't they?"

"Edmund House," she said, "a paroled rapist living with an uncle in the mountains outside of town. House was the low-hanging fruit, Dan. He'd spent six years at Walla Walla after pleading guilty to having sex with a sixteen-year-old high school student when he was eighteen. He was initially charged with first-degree rape, kidnapping, and assault, but a legal question arose over the admissibility of certain evidence found in a shed on the property where he'd kept her against her will."

"No warrant?"

"The court held that the shed was an extension of the home and the police needed a search warrant. The evidence was tainted and a judge ruled it inadmissible. The prosecutor said he had no choice but to offer the plea. After Sarah disappeared, Calloway targeted House from the start, but he didn't have any hard evidence to dispute House's alibi he was at home sleeping the night Sarah disappeared. His uncle was working a graveyard at the mill."

"So what changed?" Dan asked.

Seven weeks had passed since Sarah's disappearance when Tracy answered the door to find Roy Calloway outside, looking anxious.

"I need to speak to your father," he said, stepping past Tracy and knocking on the panel doors to James Crosswhite's office. When he got no answer, Calloway slid the doors apart. Her father lifted his head from his desk, eyes bloodshot and bleary. Tracy stepped in and removed the open bottle of Scotch and a glass from his desk.

"Roy's here, Dad."

Her father took a moment to put on his glasses, squinting at the sharp light filtering in the leaded-glass window. He had not shaved in days. His hair was disheveled and had grown well past the collar of his button-down shirt, which was wrinkled and stained. "What time is it?"

"We have a possible development," Calloway said. "A witness."

Her father stood, stumbled, and braced a hand on the desk to regain his balance. "Who?"

"A salesman driving back to Seattle the night Sarah disappeared."

"He saw her?" James Crosswhite asked.

"He recalls a red truck on the county road. A Chevy stepside. He also recalls a blue truck parked along the shoulder."

"Why didn't he come forward earlier?" Tracy asked. The tip line had long been disbanded.

"He didn't know. He travels twenty-five days out of the month. The trips blur together. He said he recently saw a newscast about the investigation, and it triggered his memory. He called the police station to make a report."

Tracy shook her head. She'd followed every newscast for seven weeks and had not seen anything recently. "What newscast?"

Calloway gave her a quick glance. "Just a story on the news."

"What channel?"

"Tracy, please." Her father raised his hand, cutting her off. "It should be enough, shouldn't it? It puts his alibi in question."

"Vance is renewing his request for warrants to search the property and the truck. The Washington State Patrol Crime Lab has a team on standby in Seattle."

"How soon will we know?" her father asked.

"Within the hour."

"How could he have not known before?" Tracy asked. "It's been all over the local news. We posted fliers. Didn't he see the billboards offering the ten-thousand-dollar reward?"

"He travels," Calloway said. "He hasn't been home."

"For seven weeks?" She turned to her father. "This doesn't make sense. He's probably just after the money." Her father and some others in the town had offered a $10,000 reward for information leading to the arrest and conviction of whoever had taken Sarah.

"Tracy, go home and wait there." Her father had never referred to the house she'd rented when she took the job teaching at Cedar Grove High as her home. "I'll call you when we know more."

"No, Dad, I don't want to go. I want to stay."

He steered her to the panel doors. She could tell by the firmness of his grip that his decision was not debatable. "I'll call as soon as I know anything," he said, and then slid the doors closed behind her. She heard the lock click shut.

CHAPTER 18

Tracy handed Dan a copy of Ryan Hagen's witness statement. "It busted House's alibi."

Dan put on a pair of cheaters to read the statement. "You sound skeptical."

"The cross-examination by House's attorney was less than stellar. No one ever asked Hagen for details about the newscast or to produce any receipts. Salesmen don't spend their own money. If Hagen had stopped to eat and to fill the tank, as he testified, he would have had a receipt. I didn't find one."

Dan looked up from the report, eyeing her over the cheaters. "But this guy's recollection was enough to get the ball rolling."

"Enough for the county prosecutor to get Judge Sullivan to issue search warrants for the uncle's home and truck."

"And they found something?"

"Hair and blood. And Calloway testified that when he confronted House with the evidence, House changed his story and said he'd picked up Sarah walking along the side of the road, drove her into the mountains, raped and strangled her, and then immediately buried her body."

"Then why didn't they find it?"

"Calloway said House refused to tell them where he'd buried Sarah without a deal, and that they'd never be able to convict him without a body."

Dan lowered the statement. "Wait, I'm confused. If he confessed, what kind of deal could he hope to get?"

"Good question. House denied confessing at the trial."

Dan shook his head as if having trouble following her. "Didn't Calloway record it? Didn't he get a signed statement?"

"No. He said House just blurted out the information to taunt him and then refused to repeat it."

"And House denied saying it at trial?"

"That's right."

"So you're telling me that his attorney put him on the stand when the prosecution's case was circumstantial and they had no forensics from a crime scene?"

"That's what I'm telling you."

"How did House explain the hair and blood?"

"He said it was planted by someone trying to frame him."

Dan scoffed. "Sure they did—the last defense of the guilty."

Tracy shrugged.

"You believe him?"

"House went away for life and Cedar Grove was supposed to get a chance to heal. It never did. Not me. Not my family. No one."

"You have doubts."

"Twenty years' worth." She slid another file across the table. "Will you take a look?"

Dan ran a finger along his upper lip. "What are you hoping to find?"

"Just an objective opinion."

Dan did not immediately answer. He also didn't take the file. Then he said, "Okay. I'll take a look."

She removed her checkbook and a pen from her handbag. "You said you have a fifteen-hundred-dollar retainer?"

He reached across the table and gently touched her hand. It surprised her, as did the fact that his hand was rough, though his fingers were long and sinewy. "I don't charge my friends, Tracy."

"I can't ask you to work for free, Dan."

"And I can't take your money. So if you want my opinion, you need to put your checkbook away. Wow, I'll bet no attorney has ever uttered those words before."

She laughed. "Can I pay you with something else?"

"Dinner," he said. "I know a good place."

"In Cedar Grove?"

"Cedar Grove still holds a few surprises. Trust me."

"Isn't that what every lawyer says?"

—

Tracy left First National Bank and looked up at the bay window cantilevered over the sidewalk. She'd never shared the contents of her investigation with anyone before. There'd been no need, not without forensics from the grave. Until then, all she'd had was an unsupported hypothesis. Kelly Rosa's revelations had changed that.

"Tracy?" Sunnie Witherspoon stood beside a parked van, keys in one hand, a plastic bag from a hardware store in the other.

"Sunnie."

Sunnie stepped onto the sidewalk. She wore slacks, a blouse, and sweater. Her hair was styled and her makeup heavy. "I thought you'd left."

"I had a few loose ends to take care of. I was actually just heading out."

"Do you have time for coffee?" Sunnie asked.

Tracy wasn't looking for a long trip down memory lane. "It looks like you're dressed up to go someplace."

"No," Sunnie said. "I just needed to run an errand at the hardware store for Gary." An awkward pause followed.

With no easy retreat, Tracy relented. "Is there a place?"

They walked across the street to The Daily Perk, ordered coffee, and sat at a table outside that wobbled when Tracy set her mug down. So much for her doctor's orders that Tracy cut down on her caffeine intake.

Sunnie sat across the table, smiling. "It's so strange seeing you here. I mean, I'm sorry that you are, the reason, but it's so good. It was a nice service."

"Thanks for being there."

"Everything changed, didn't it?"

Sunnie had caught Tracy in midsip of her coffee. She swallowed and set down her cup. "I'm sorry?"

"After Sarah died, everything kind of changed."

"I guess so."

"Though I'm still here." Sunnie's smile had a sad quality to it. "I'll never leave." She looked indecisive. Then she said, "You haven't made it to any of the reunions."

"Not really my thing."

"It's just that people ask about you, and they still talk about what happened."

"I didn't want to talk about it anymore, Sunnie."

"I'm sorry. I didn't mean to upset you. We don't have to talk about it. Let's talk about something else."

But Tracy knew talking about what had happened to Sarah and its aftermath was exactly why Sunnie wanted to have coffee. It wasn't to allow two old friends to catch up. It was for the same reason so many had come to a service for a family that had, for all intents and purposes, departed Cedar Grove twenty years earlier. And it wasn't just because Roy Calloway had gotten the word out. The search for Sarah and the trial had given them all something to focus their attention on, but it had not brought back Sarah. It had not brought closure to Sunnie or anyone else still living in Cedar Grove, any more than it had brought closure to Tracy or her parents. Now, sitting across from a person who at one time had been someone Tracy had entrusted with her deepest teenage thoughts and secrets, Tracy couldn't bring herself to tell Sunnie that they might be about to relive that nightmare all over again.

CHAPTER 19

Tracy killed the engine and let her truck roll to a silent stop. She scanned the darkened street before exiting to the ambient light from a full moon. A year after the trial and she still searched for shadows lurking behind trees and seeping out from behind bushes. As children, Tracy and Sarah had called these unseen horrors bogeymen. Back then, they had been made-up monsters conjured by the vivid imaginations of two sisters. Now they were frighteningly real.

She climbed the porch steps and fit her key into the deadbolt. It turned with a snap that made her pause and listen for sounds inside the house. Not hearing anything, she pressed her shoulder to the door and applied pressure. The wood expanded in the winter and that had caused the door to stick in the jamb. When Tracy felt the door slide free of the threshold, she pushed the door open and stepped quietly inside.

The light came on, startling her. She dropped her keys.

"Jesus. You scared me," she said.

Ben sat in the recliner dressed in jeans and a flannel shirt. "I scared you? You're coming home at this hour, no phone call, no note, and I scared you?"

"I meant I didn't see you sitting there. Why were you sitting in the dark? Why do you have all your clothes on?"

"You didn't see me because you weren't home. Where were you, Tracy?"

"I was working."

"At one in the morning?"

"You know what I meant; I was working on Sarah's case."

"What a surprise."

"I'm tired," she said, not wanting to get into the debate again.

"You didn't answer my question."

She spoke over her shoulder as she walked from the room. "Yes, I did."

"No. You told me what you were doing. I asked where you were."

"It's late, Ben. Let's talk in the morning."

"I'll be gone in the morning." She stepped back into the room. Ben had stood and she noticed that he was also wearing his work boots. "I'm leaving. I can't live like this."

She stepped toward him. "It's not going to always be like this, Ben. I just need more time."

"How long is it going to take, Tracy?"

"I don't know."

"And there lies the problem."

"Ben—"

"I know where you were."

"What would you have me do?"

"Move on, Tracy. That's what people do."

"My sister was murdered."

"I was here, remember? I've been here, every single day. I sat by your side every day of the trial and I sat through the sentencing. You just haven't noticed."

She took a few more steps toward him. "Is that what this is about? You want my attention?"

"I'm your husband, Tracy."

"And you should support me."

He started for the door. "I was going to leave in the morning. My truck is packed. I think it's better that I leave now, before either of us says something we'll regret."

"Ben, it's late. Wait until the morning. We can talk this through."

He gripped the doorknob. "What did he tell you?"

"What?"

"What did Edmund House tell you?"

He'd followed her to the prison. "I asked him about the case. I asked him about what Chief Calloway said about him confessing that he'd killed Sarah. I asked him about the jewelry."

"Did you ask him if he killed her?"

"He didn't kill her, Ben. The evidence—"

"A jury convicted him, Tracy. A jury considered the evidence and convicted him. Why isn't that enough?"

"Because the evidence is wrong. I know it."

"And is that going to change by morning? Is there anything more I can say that will get you to stop this?"

She touched the sleeve of his shirt. "Don't make me choose, Ben. Please don't make me choose between you and my sister."

"I never would have done that to you. You did that on your own." He pulled open the door and stepped out.

Tracy followed him onto the porch, suddenly afraid. "I love you, Ben. I don't have anyone else but you."

He stopped. After a moment, he turned to face her. "Yeah, you do. And until you put them both to rest, there's no room for me. There's no room for anyone."

She hurried toward him, holding him. "Ben, please. We can work this out."

He placed his hands on her shoulders. "Then come with me."

"What?"

"We can pack your things in an hour. Come with me."

"Where?"

"Away from here."

"But my mother and father—"

"They want nothing to do with me, Tracy. I'm the reason you left Sarah alone that night. I'm the reason she's dead. They won't even talk to me. They hardly talk to you anymore. There's nothing here."

She stepped back. "I can't, Ben."

"Can't or won't?" Tears pooled in his eyes. "A part of me will always love you, Tracy. That's the pain I'm going to have to get over. I can't do it living here. You have your own pain to get through, and I don't think you can do it here either, but you're going to have to figure that out on your own."

He climbed into the truck cab and shut the door. For a moment, she thought he might reconsider, that he might open the door and get out, come back to her. Then he started the engine, gave her one final glance, and backed out of the driveway, leaving her alone.

CHAPTER 20

Tracy sensed a car slowing as it approached and instinctively reached for the Glock in her purse. The car pulled up beside her and came to a stop. Roy Calloway sat with his elbow bent out the window. "Tracy."

She took her hand off the gun. "Are you following me, Sheriff?"

"I understood you were leaving town."

Tracy looked about the motel parking lot. "I did leave town. I'm in Silver Spurs. What are you doing here?"

Calloway threw the car into park and slid out, leaving the engine running and the door open. Chatter spilled from the radio mounted to his dash. "A little bird tells me you've been talking to people around town."

"Seems like the polite thing to do after being away so long. What business is it of yours?"

"I'd like to know what you've been talking to them about."

Part of her wanted to stand up to Calloway and let him know she wasn't the little girl buying his line of bullshit anymore. But that would likely cause a prolonged confrontation and she was mentally and physically drained. She just wanted to get inside her room for the night. "I don't think that's any of your business, unless you're going to tell me it's a crime in Cedar Grove to talk to people." She started up the staircase. "I'm tired and I'd like to take a hot shower."

"What did you and Dan O'Leary have to talk about?"

"Old times. It was a regular stroll down memory lane."

"Is that it?"

"It's all you're going to get."

"Goddamn it, Tracy. Don't be so damned stubborn."

The adamancy with which he spoke caused her to stop and face him. Calloway had grown red in the face, which was unlike the man she remembered, but maybe that was because the man she remembered had always gotten his way. Seemingly regaining his composure, Calloway said, "Do you think you're the only one who's suffered? Look at all the people who came out to the service to pay their respects yesterday."

She stepped down. "Did you have something to do with that, Roy?"

"People are looking for closure. They need this to be over."

"They need it, or you need it?"

He pointed a finger at her. "I did my job. You of all people should understand that. I followed the evidence, Tracy."

"Not to the grave."

"We didn't have a grave."

"Now we do."

"Exactly. We found Sarah. So let the dead bury the dead."

"You said that to me once before. Do you remember? But here's the thing I've learned, Roy. The dead don't bury the dead. Only the living can do that."

"And now you've buried Sarah and put her to rest. She's at peace. She's with your parents. Let it go, Tracy. Just let it go."

"Are you giving me an order, Chief?"

"Let me make this clear to you. You may be a big-time homicide detective in Seattle, but here you have no jurisdiction. Here, you're just a citizen. I'm the law. I suggest you remember that and don't go running around chasing ghosts."

Tracy tempered her anger with the knowledge that there was nothing Calloway could do to her. It was bluster. Calloway was fishing for information, trying to make her angry enough to slip and say something about what she'd been doing and why.

"I have no intention of chasing ghosts," she said.

He seemed to study her. "So I can assume you'll be going back to Seattle?"

"Yeah, I'll be going back to Seattle."

"Good." He gave her a nod, slid back into the Suburban, and shut the door. "Then you have a safe drive home."

She watched the SUV drive off, the taillights illuminate as Calloway slowed to make the turn, and the car disappear around the corner. "Not ghosts, Roy. Not chasing ghosts. I'm chasing a killer," she said.

—

As she made her way up the outdoor stairs another thought struck her, and she fumbled in her purse, retrieving her cell phone and Dan's business card. She hurried into her room and called his number. Dan answered on the third ring.

"Dan? It's Tracy."

"You're not going to be one of those clients who calls all the time, are you? Because if you are, it's okay. I was just about to call you."

"Do you still have my file?"

"Right here on my kitchen table. We spent the afternoon together. Why, what's wrong?"

She breathed a sigh of relief. "Roy Calloway's been following me. He knows I came to talk to you and wanted to know what about."

"What do you mean he's been following you?"

"I mean he just accosted me outside my hotel room in Silver Spurs and wanted to know why I went to see you. Has he tried to talk to you?"

"No, but I left the office early. He hasn't been here. Why are you staying in Silver Spurs?"

"I just didn't want to stay in Cedar Grove. After the service, it was just too much."

"No, I mean, why didn't you go back to Seattle?" When she didn't immediately answer, Dan said. "You knew I'd call, didn't you. You knew I'd call about the file."

"I suspected you might."

"Where are you staying in Silver Spurs?"

She checked her key ring, the old-fashioned kind that was actually a key and not an activation card. "The Evergreen Inn."

"Check out. You can stay here. I have an extra room."

"It's fine, Dan."

"It probably is, but I've been through the materials you gave me, Tracy. Not in detail, but enough to have a lot of questions."

She felt a familiar rush of adrenaline. "What kind of questions?"

"I'm going to need to review whatever else you have."

"I can get it to you."

"That's for another time. For tonight, check out of wherever you're staying and come here. There's no reason for you to stay in a motel."

She wasn't quite sure what to make of his invitation. Was he worried about her because of Calloway, or because of something he'd discovered in her file? Was it just a childhood friend being hospitable, or was there something else motivating him, like the attraction Tracy had felt when Dan had first stepped to her side during Sarah's service and kissed her cheek? She pulled back the drapes and peeked out the window at the dirt-and-gravel parking lot and to the grove of trees on its far side. The shadows had begun to creep around the trunks.

"Besides, you owe me a dinner," Dan said.

"Where should I meet you?"

"Do you remember how to get to my parents' house?"

"Like the back of my hand."

"Meet me here. I have the best alarm system in town."

CHAPTER 21

Tracy heard that alarm system going off as she drove up the driveway of what had been Dan O'Leary's childhood home. She did not recognize the Cape Cod house on the large lot, recalling a one-story yellow clapboard rambler. Set back on a manicured lawn, the house was now two stories tall, with dormer windows, a large front porch, and white Adirondack sitting chairs. The clapboard had been replaced with pale blue shingles and gray trim that had a definite East Coast feel to them.

Dan opened the front door and stepped out into the light of a full moon. Two *very big* dogs flanked him. They looked like bulldogs on steroids, with stunted black muzzles and short hair that exposed muscular, broad chests. With them sitting at his sides, Dan looked like an Egyptian pharaoh.

Tracy stepped away from the car, shouldering her overnight bag. "Is it safe?"

"It will be, once you're properly introduced." Dan looked comfortable in faded jeans with a hole in one knee, a black V-neck sweater over a white T-shirt, and bare feet.

"I don't like the sound of that," she said, approaching on a stone path in a rich-green lawn that looked and smelled like it had been freshly mowed.

"Just hold out the back of your hand and let them smell you."

"I really don't like the sound of that."

"Don't be a ninny."

Tracy held out her hand. The smaller of the two dogs stretched his neck and brushed his cold nose across the back of her hand. As he did, Dan said, "This is Sherlock."

"You're kidding?" *No shit, Sherlock* had been one of Dan's favorite expressions.

Dan turned his attention to the other dog. "And this—"

"Let me guess. Ex-Lax," she said. Dan's other favorite boyhood expression had been *smooth move, Ex-Lax.*

"Now that would just be gross. No, this big boy is Rex, as in T. rex." T. rex didn't bother to sniff her hand. "He's a bit more reserved than Sherlock."

"What breed are they?"

"Rhodesian and Mastiff mix. They weigh in at a combined two hundred eighty-six pounds and their food bill is twice the size of mine. Go ahead and take them inside. I'll put your car in the garage in case anyone is nosy." She'd noticed a freestanding garage at the back of the property.

Tracy stepped into a den with an L-shaped couch facing a brick fireplace, over which hung a large flat-screen television. The den flowed into a kitchen with a table and chairs, granite counters, barstools, and incandescent lighting. Tile samples rested against the kitchen splash behind the sink. Dan closed the door behind her and handed her back her keys.

"You're remodeling," she said.

"That's an understatement. After forty years, it needed a makeover."

He walked into the kitchen, but the dogs kept their attention on Tracy. She dropped her bag on one of the barstools. "You're planning on staying?"

"After all the work I just put in, I better get some enjoyment out of it."

"*You* did this?"

"You don't have to sound that surprised." He opened the refrigerator.

"I just don't remember you being that handy."

Dan spoke from behind the door. "You'd be amazed what you can learn when you're bored, motivated, and have access to the Internet. Are you hungry?"

"Don't go to any bother, Dan."

"No bother. I did tell you I know a great restaurant." He returned with a plate containing four large hamburger patties. "I was just about to make my famous bacon cheeseburgers."

She laughed. "I can feel my arteries hardening already."

"Please don't tell me you've become one of those grain-eating vegan types."

"With my schedule? I'm lucky to see a vegetable unless it's a tomato on a Whopper bun."

"Technically, a tomato is a fruit."

"Whatever. What, are you also a horticulturist now?"

"If you're nice, after dinner I'll show you my vegetable garden."

"You must have been *really* bored." She stepped to his side of the counter. "What can I do to help?" Side by side, Dan was a good four inches taller. The sweater accentuated his broad shoulders and a trim chest. She elbowed him playfully and hit a solid torso. "I seem to recall a guy with a lot more baby fat. I know it isn't the diet."

"Yeah, well some of us weren't blessed with the Crosswhite long legs and muscle-tone gene."

"I'll have you know I work out four days a week," she said.

"I'll have you know it shows."

"Oh God, I sounded like one of those middle-age women fishing for a compliment, didn't I?"

"If you were, I was hooked. Come on, why don't I show you to your room? You can take a hot shower and relax while I get dinner started."

"I think that sounds even better." She grabbed her bag and followed him to the stairs.

"Should I have a glass of red wine waiting, or are you going to tell me you've given up alcohol?"

"Only the kind that's good for you."

She followed him into a room at the top of the stairs and was again surprised by the furnishings, a wrought-iron bed and early American antiques, with a bushy broom in one corner and a bed warmer in another. Over the bed hung a painting of a woman lighting a fire in a darkened pioneer home. Tracy dropped her bag on the bed. "Okay, I'll buy the remodel, but no way you decorated on your own." She guessed a girlfriend.

"*Sunset Magazine.*" Dan shrugged. "Like I said, I was bored." He closed the door and left her to settle in.

Tracy sat on the edge of the bed, considering their banter, which in some respects felt like old times, though Dan was definitely now more adept at his comebacks than she remembered. She found herself smiling. Was Dan flirting with her, or were his comments just an adult version of the ribbing they used to give one another when they were kids? It had been a long time since anyone had flirted with her.

"I'll have you know it shows?" she said, groaning at the sound of it. "Way to look needy."

When Tracy stepped out of the shower, her limited choice of clothing became even more frustrating. She left her blouse out instead of tucking it into her jeans to create a different look and pulled her hair back into a ponytail, her crow's-feet be damned. She applied mascara and eye shadow, added a touch of perfume to her wrists and neck, and headed downstairs to the smell of bacon and hamburgers wafting from the grill, announcers providing the play-by-play of a college football game on the flat-screen.

Dan stood at the counter beating the contents of a glass bowl with a whisk. A pie crust with lemon filling sat on the counter.

"Are you making a lemon meringue pie?"

He muted the volume on the TV. "Don't make fun. It was my mother's recipe and it happens to be my favorite. And if I can ever get the damn egg whites to fluff, you'll know why."

"You're using the wrong bowl."

Dan gave her a skeptical look. "How could there be a *wrong* bowl?"

She stepped to his side of the counter. "Where do you keep your bowls?"

He pointed to a lower cabinet. Tracy found a copper bowl, transferred the egg whites into it, and took the whisk. In no time at all, she whisked the egg whites into foam. "Mrs. Allen would be appalled. Don't you remember anything from chemistry class?"

"Isn't that the class I cheated off of you in?"

"You cheated off me in every class."

"And look how well it's done for me. I can't even beat egg whites."

"It has to do with one of the proteins in the egg whites reacting with the copper of the bowl's surface. A silver-plated bowl will do the same thing." She poured in the sugar Dan had in a measuring cup to finish the meringue, spooned it on top of the filling, and slid the pie into the oven, setting the timer. "Didn't you promise me a glass of wine?"

He poured two glasses, handed her one, and raised his. "To old friends."

"Speak for yourself."

"We're the same age," he said.

"Haven't you heard? Forty is the new twenty."

"The memo hasn't reached my back and knees. Fine." He raised his glass again. "To good friends."

"That's more like it."

She moved to the other side of the counter and sat beneath an incandescent light, watching as he turned the onions he'd added to the grill. She smelled their sweet scent. "Can I ask you something?"

"I'm an open book."

"It's just you here."

"Just me and the boys," he said. The two dogs sat at the edge of the tile between the rooms, watching as Dan walked to the fridge.

"So why did you go to the trouble?"

He opened the fridge. "You mean the remodel?"

"Everything. The remodel, the furnishings, two dogs. It must have been a lot of effort."

He grabbed a jar of pickles and a tomato and set them on a plastic cutting board. "It was. That's why I did it. I went through the 'woe is me' period, Tracy. Finding out your wife is cheating on you isn't exactly confidence building. I felt sorry for myself for a while. Then I got angry with the world, with her, with my ex-partner for sleeping with her." He fished out a pickle and sliced it as he continued talking. "When Mom died that put me into an even deeper funk. One morning I woke up and decided I was tired of looking at the same damn walls. I went into the toolshed, got Dad's sledgehammer, and started knocking them down. The more I knocked down, the better I felt. Once the walls were down, the only thing I could do was rebuild."

"So this was your diversion."

He washed the tomato at the sink and began to cut it with precise strokes. "All I know is, the more I rebuilt, the more I realized that just because things hadn't worked out as I'd planned didn't mean things couldn't work out at all. I wanted a home. I wanted a family. Getting another wife was not on the horizon, and frankly, I wasn't looking. So I went and got Rex and Sherlock and we created a home." The two dogs whined at the mention of their names.

"How'd you start?"

"One swing of the hammer at a time."

"Do you ever talk to your ex?"

"Every once in a while she'll call. Things with my partner didn't work out."

"She wants you back."

He used a spatula to transfer the burgers to a plate. "I think she was fishing about the possibility at first. What she probably really misses is the country-club lifestyle. She figured out pretty quick that the guy she married didn't exist anymore."

Tracy smiled. "I think the finished product looks pretty good, Dan."

He stopped transferring the sliced tomatoes and pickles from the cutting board to a plate. "Oh no."

"What?"

"Did that sound like a middle-aged man fishing for a compliment?"

She threw a crumpled napkin at him.

Dan had set the table while she was in the shower. He placed the plate of hamburgers on it beside a tossed green salad. "This okay?" he asked.

"Fishing for another compliment?"

"You know it."

"It's perfect."

As Tracy made up her burger with condiments, Dan said, "Okay, my turn. Do you still compete in those shooting tournaments?"

"I don't really have a lot of free time."

"But you were so good."

"Too many painful memories. The last time I saw Sarah was the 1993 Championship in Olympia."

"Is that why you also never come back to Cedar Grove? Because the memories are too painful?"

"Some," she said.

"And yet you're about to dig up those memories all over again."

"Not dig them up, Dan. Hopefully bury them for good."

CHAPTER 22

After dinner, Tracy walked into the den and picked up a golf club leaning against the wall. At the other end of a narrow strip of Astroturf was what looked like a tin ashtray.

"Do you play?" Dan stood in the kitchen drying the last of the dishes and stacking them into the cupboards.

She lined up a golf ball, tapped it, and watched it roll down the Astroturf. It hit the ashtray, rolled over the top, and kept going, rattling along the hardwood to the baseboard, drawing Rex and Sherlock's attention from where they'd been lounging on the rug. "Like I said, not a lot of time for hobbies."

"You'd pick it up quick; you were always a good athlete."

"That was a long time ago."

"Nonsense. You just need the right instructor."

"Yeah? Can you recommend anyone?"

He set down the bowl he'd been drying, walked into the room, and set another golf ball at her feet. "Stand over the ball."

"You're going to give me a lesson?"

"I paid a lot of money to be a member of a country club. I was determined to get something out of it. Come on, stand over the ball."

"I don't think so."

"Feet shoulder-width apart."

"You're serious?"

"I'm a serious guy."

"Not the guy I remember."

"Yes, but I told you I've changed. I'm a hardened lawyer."

"And I've had hand-to-hand combat training."

"I'll remember that if I ever need a bodyguard. Now turn around. Feet shoulder-width apart."

She smiled and did as he said. Dan stepped close behind her and wrapped his arms around her shoulders. He touched her hands, trying to adjust her grip. "Loosen up. Relax. You're strangling it."

"I thought you were supposed to keep your arms stiff," she said, feeling suddenly warm.

"Your arms, not your hands. Soft hands. Light touch."

He placed his hands over hers on the shaft of the club, his breath warm against her neck, his voice soft in her ear. "Bend your knees." He touched the back of her knees with his own to make hers flex.

She laughed. "Okay. Okay."

"Now, it's a nice easy stroke back and forth, like a pendulum."

"That I can relate to," she said.

"I thought you might."

He guided her arms back and gently forward. The putter struck the ball and sent it rolling slowly down the green carpet. This time when it hit the tin cup the sides folded and the ball rolled up and came to rest in the center.

"Hey," she said. "I made it."

"You see," Dan said, his arms still around her, "I may not be any good in chemistry but I could teach you a thing or two."

She'd closed her eyes, imagining what she might do if Dan were to suddenly kiss her neck. Her knees felt weak at the thought.

"Tracy?"

"Huh?"

He let go of her arms. "Maybe we should talk about your file?"

She let out the breath she had been holding. "Yeah, I think that would be good. But first, bathroom?"

"Beneath the stairs."

Tracy found the bathroom, shut the door, and held on to the edge of the sink. In the mirror, her reflection stared back with flushed cheeks. She took a moment to regroup, turned on the faucet, and splashed cold water on her face. After drying her hands on a Boston Red Sox hand towel, she returned to the kitchen.

Dan stood near the table flipping through the pages of a yellow legal pad, each one filled with notes. He'd placed Tracy's file in the center of the table and he'd also refilled their wine glasses. "Do you mind if I stand? I think better on my feet."

"Be my guest." She sat at the table and took a much-needed sip of wine.

Dan said, "I have to tell you, I was skeptical when you came in this morning. I really thought I was just humoring you."

"I know."

"Am I that transparent?"

"I'm a detective, Dan." She set down her glass. "I'd be skeptical too. Ask me what you want."

"Let's start with the traveling salesman, Ryan Hagen."

—

Vance Clark stood at the counsel's table. "The State calls Ryan P. Hagen."

Edmund House, seated beside his court-appointed defense attorney, long-time Cedar Grove resident DeAngelo Finn, turned for the first time since he'd entered the courtroom in handcuffs. Clean-shaven with his hair cut short, House looked like an East Coast prep student.

He was dressed in gray slacks, the collar of a white button-down shirt protruding above a black V-neck sweater. His gaze locked on Hagen as he entered the courtroom, looking like he attended the same imaginary prep school in khakis, a blue sport coat, and a paisley tie, but then House's eyes shifted across the packed gallery and came to rest on Tracy. It made her skin crawl and she reached for Ben's hand, squeezing it tight.

"Are you all right?" Ben whispered.

Hagen pushed through the gate in the railing and took the witness stand. With thinning hair parted down the middle, Tracy thought Hagen had elfin features. Vance Clark walked the traveling auto-parts salesman through his job and how it required him to be on the road as many as twenty-five days each month, traveling throughout Washington, Oregon, Idaho, and Montana.

"Is it unusual for you to not keep abreast of the local news?"

"Not unless it's my Mariners or my Sonics." Hagen had the easy smile of someone in sales and looked to be enjoying the spotlight. "I'm not much for picking up an out-of-town newspaper or watching the evening news when I get to my hotel. I usually look for a game."

"So you were unaware of Sarah Crosswhite's abduction?"

"I hadn't heard about it, no."

"Can you tell the jury how you did come to hear about it?"

"Sure." Hagen turned to face the jurors, five women and seven men, all white. Two alternates sat in chairs just outside the railing. "I got home one night from an account at a reasonable hour, for a change. I was having a beer on the couch and watching my Mariners when a story came on during a break about a missing woman from Cedar Grove. I have a number of clients up that way, so I paid attention. They showed a picture of her."

"Did you recognize the woman?"

"I'd never seen her."

"What happened next?"

"They said she'd been missing a while, and they showed a photograph of her truck, a blue Ford, abandoned along the shoulder of the county road. That jarred my memory."

"Jarred it how, Mr. Hagen?"

"I'd seen the truck before. I was certain it was the truck I saw one night when I was driving back home from visiting accounts up north. I remembered because not many people use the county road anymore, with the interstate, and it was raining hard that night and I thought, 'Bummer of a night to have your truck break down.'"

"Why did you drive the county road that evening?"

"It's a shortcut. You learn them all when you drive as much as I do."

"Did you remember the particular night?"

"Not initially, no. But I remembered it was in the summer because the storm surprised me. I'd even debated not taking the county road because of it. It's dark. There aren't any street lights."

"Were you subsequently able to determine the night?"

"I keep a calendar of my appointments and went and checked. It was August 21."

"Of what year?"

"1993."

Hagen had his calendar in his lap. After introducing it into evidence, Clark asked that it be shown to the jury. Then Clark asked Hagen, *"And do you recall anything else about that evening?"*

"I remembered that I'd seen a red truck. It was driving toward me."

"And why would you remember that?"

"Like I said, there were no other cars on the county road that night."

"Did you get a look inside the cab?"

"Not really, no. But I got a good look at the truck. It was a Chevy stepside. Cherry red. You don't see too many of those. It's a classic."

"What did you do then?"

"*The news program put up a phone number for the Sheriff's Office, so I called and told the person what I'd seen. I got a call back from the sheriff saying he was following up. So I told him what I just told you.*"

"*Did you recall anything else while talking to Sheriff Calloway?*"

"*I recall thinking that I had stopped to get gas and something to eat that night, and thinking that maybe if I hadn't, I could have reached that girl first.*"

DeAngelo Finn objected and asked that the statement be stricken. Judge Sean Lawrence, a big man with a full head of red hair, sustained it.

Clark left that final thought with the jury and sat.

Finn stepped forward, notepad in hand. Tracy knew DeAngelo and his wife, Millie. Her father cared for Millie, who had debilitating arthritis. Balding, Finn parted his hair low on his head and combed it over the top. No more than five foot six, the hem of his suit pants dragged on the marble floor as he made his way to the podium, and the cuffs of his jacket reached the palms of his hands, as if he'd bought the suit off a department store rack that morning and hadn't had time to have it tailored.

"*You say you saw this truck along the shoulder. Did you see anyone standing beside the truck or walking along the road?*" *Finn had a high-pitched voice that the expansive courtroom swallowed.*

Hagen said he had not.

"*And this red truck you claim to have seen, you didn't get a look in the cab, is that right?*"

"*That's right.*"

"*So you didn't see a blonde woman in that cab, did you?*"

"*I did not.*"

Finn pointed at House. "*And you didn't see the defendant in that cab, did you?*"

"*I didn't.*"

"*Didn't catch the license plate number?*"

"No."

"Yet you claim to recall this truck that you admit you saw for just a fraction of a second on a dark and rainy evening?"

"It's my favorite truck," Hagen countered, the salesman's smile returning. "I mean, cars and trucks are what I do for a living. It's my job to know them."

Finn's mouth opened and closed like a fish out of water. His eyes shifted between his notepad and Hagen several times. After several uncomfortable seconds, Finn said, "So your focus was on the truck and you didn't see anyone in the cab. No further questions."

CHAPTER 23

Dan flipped through his notes. "I'm having a hard time believing that, seven weeks after the fact, Hagen made note of a red truck he passed briefly on a dark road in heavy rain. Finn never really explored it in cross-examination?"

Tracy shook her head. "He also never questioned Hagen about the news station Hagen claimed to be watching, or sent subpoenas to get copies of any of the newscasts during that period."

"What would he have found if he had?"

"I have every tape of every newscast. I didn't find any newscast even remotely like the one Hagen described during the time period he claims to have seen it. Sarah's disappearance was old news by then. You know how it is. The press, police, everyone in town was absorbed with it initially, but as the weeks passed, so did their interest. I don't blame them. After seven weeks, Sarah's disappearance was a footnote unless something significant happened to draw attention back to it. Nothing had."

"What about the reward?"

"That also never came up at trial."

Dan squinted as if fighting a headache. "Given that Hagen's testimony provided Calloway and Clark what they needed to convince Judge Sullivan to issue the search warrants, Finn should have jumped all over Hagen about every detail, especially because Hagen also laid the groundwork for Calloway's testimony the next day."

Roy Calloway sat in the witness chair as if he was seated in his living room and everyone else in the courtroom was an invited guest. The rain ticked off the second-story wood-sash windows, sounding like birds pecking against the glass. Tracy looked out at the trees in the courthouse square, their soaked limbs sagging. Smoke curled from the chimneys of houses in the near distance, but the bucolic image only seemed to magnify the illusion that Edmund House had exposed. Small towns were not immune to violent crimes.

Far from it.

Clark stepped to the railing of the jury box. "When did you next return to Parker House's property, Sheriff Calloway?"

"About two months later."

"Can you explain the circumstances?"

"We got a witness tip."

"And can you tell the jury where that tip led?"

"To Ryan Hagen."

"You interviewed Mr. Hagen?"

"I did," Calloway said, and over the next five minutes he confirmed what Hagen had testified the prior day.

"And what was the significance of the red Chevy pickup?"

"I knew Parker owned a red Chevy and I remembered seeing it in his yard the morning Sarah was reported missing."

"Did you confront the defendant with this new evidence?"

"I told him we had a witness. I asked if he had anything to add."

"And what did the defendant say?"

"At first he didn't say much, except that I was harassing him. Then he said, 'Okay, yeah, I was driving that night.'"

"Did he say anything else?"

"He said he'd been drinking at a bar in Silver Spurs and was driving home on the county road because he was afraid of being pulled over on the interstate. He said he passed a blue Ford truck on the shoulder and a little farther down saw a woman walking in the rain. He said he gave her a ride to an address in Cedar Grove, dropped her off there, and that was the end of it. He said he never saw her again."

"Did he identify the woman?"

"I showed him a photograph and he positively identified Sarah Crosswhite."

"Did he provide the address where he claimed to have driven her?"

"Not the address, but he described Sarah's home."

"Did Mr. House say why he didn't tell you this when you first questioned him?"

"He said he'd heard in town that a woman was missing, saw one of the fliers, and recognized the photograph on the flier as the woman he gave a ride to. He said he was afraid nobody would believe him."

"Did he say why?"

Finn objected and Lawrence sustained it.

"What did you do next, Sheriff Calloway?"

"I brought the information to your attention and asked that you secure search warrants for Parker House's property and truck."

"Did you take part in those search warrants?"

"I executed them, but we brought down crime scene investigators from the Washington State Patrol Crime Lab to do the forensic work. Based on the evidence located that day, we arrested Edmund House."

"Did you talk with him again?"

"In custody."

"And what did Mr. House tell you?"

Calloway turned his focus from Clark to Edmund House, who sat with his hands in his lap, face impassive. "He smiled. Then he said we would never convict him, not without a body. He said if the prosecutor cut him a deal, he'd tell me where to find Sarah's body. Otherwise, he said, I could go to hell."

CHAPTER 24

Dan paced near the flat-screen television. They'd moved to the family room. Tracy sat on the couch listening as Dan alternately asked questions and thought out loud.

"The obvious question is, if Calloway was telling the truth, why would Edmund House change his story? He'd already spent six years in prison, which means he'd likely received a pretty good legal education. One has to assume he would have known that changing his alibi would be enough for Calloway to get the search warrants. And if he was going to change his alibi, why would he tell Calloway he'd been drinking at a bar in Silver Spurs, something Calloway could so easily refute, though he apparently never did?"

Tracy said, "I spoke to every bartender in Silver Spurs. No one remembered Edmund House, and no one remembered Calloway coming in and asking any questions."

"Another reason to suspect Calloway lied about the confession," Dan said.

"Something else. Finn never cross-examined Calloway about it at trial," Tracy said.

"A mistake, for sure," Dan agreed, "but that's not what got House convicted. What got him convicted was what they found at the property."

—

Late in the afternoon, the storm intensified, causing the lights hanging from the courthouse's ornate box-beam ceiling to flicker. The wind had also kicked up, the trees outside the courtroom windows now swaying violently, their limbs shimmering.

"Detective Giesa," Vance Clark continued, "with respect to the truck, would you tell the ladies and gentlemen of the jury what you found?"

Detective Margaret Giesa looked more like a runway model than a detective, with long, light-brown hair and blonde highlights. Perhaps five foot four, she looked considerably taller in four-inch heels and wore well a gray, pinstriped pants suit. "We located multiple strands of blonde hair varying in lengths from eighteen to thirty-two inches."

"Would you show the jurors exactly where your team found these strands of hair?"

Giesa left her chair and used a pointer to direct the jury's attention to a blown-up photograph of the interior of the red Chevy stepside that Clark had set on an easel. "On the passenger side, between the seat and the door."

"Did the Washington State Patrol Crime Lab run tests on those strands of hair?"

Giesa considered her report. "We examined each strand under a microscope and determined that some had been pulled out by the root. Others had broken off."

Finn stood. "Objection. The officer is speculating that the hairs had been pulled out by the roots."

Lawrence sustained it.

Clark looked glad to have the phrase repeated. "Do we humans shed hair, Detective?"

"Shedding hair is a natural process. We shed hair every day."

He patted his bald spot. "Some of us more than others?"

The jurors smiled.

Clark continued. "But you also mentioned that your team found some hair that had been broken off. What did you mean by that?"

"I mean that we did not find a root ball. Under a microscope, one expects to find a white bulb at the base. Breakage is usually the result of damage to the hair follicle by external factors."

"Such as?"

"Chemical treatments, heat from styling tools, or rough handling come to mind."

"Can someone tear out another person's hair by the root, say, during a struggle?"

"They can."

Clark acted as if he was reviewing his notes. "Did your team locate anything else of interest in the truck cab?"

"Trace amounts of blood," she said.

Tracy noticed several jurors turn their attention from Giesa to Edmund House.

Again using the photograph, Giesa explained where her team had located the blood inside the truck cab. Clark then placed a blown-up aerial photograph of Parker House's property in the mountains on the easel. It showed the metal roofs of several structures and the shells of cars and farm equipment amid a grove of trees. Giesa pointed to a narrow building at the end of a footpath leading from Parker House's one-story home.

"We found woodworking tools and several pieces of furniture in various stages of completion."

"A table saw?"

"Yes, there was a table saw."

"Did you find any blood inside that shed?"

"We did not," Giesa said.

"Did you find any blonde strands of hair?"

"No."

"Did you find anything of interest?"

"We found jewelry inside a sock in a coffee can."

Clark handed Giesa a plastic evidence bag and asked her to unseal it.

The courtroom grew silent as Giesa reached inside the bag and held up two silver pistol-shaped earrings.

—

Dan stopped pacing. "That's when you really began to suspect something was wrong."

"She wasn't wearing the pistol earrings, Dan. I know she wasn't, and I tried to tell my father that afternoon," Tracy said. "But he said he was tired and wanted to get my mother home. She wasn't doing well. She was an emotional wreck, physically weak, and becoming more and more reclusive. After that, every time I tried to bring up the subject, my father would tell me to let it alone. Calloway and Clark told me the same thing."

"They never heard you out?"

She shook her head. "No. So I decided to keep the information I had to myself until I could prove them wrong."

"But you couldn't leave it alone."

"Could you have, if it had been your sister, and you'd been the one who left her?"

Dan sat on the coffee table facing her. Their knees nearly touched. "What happened wasn't your fault, Tracy."

"I had to know. When no one else was going to do anything about it, I decided to do it myself."

"So that's why you quit teaching and became a cop."

She nodded. "After ten years of using all my free time to read transcripts and hunt for witnesses and documents, I sat down one evening, opened up the boxes, and realized that I'd gone over *all* the records and interviewed *all* the witnesses. I'd reached a dead end. Unless they found Sarah's body, I had nowhere to go. It was a horrible feeling. I felt like I'd failed her all over again, but it's like you said, the world doesn't stop so you can grieve. One day you wake up and realize you have to move on because . . . well, what are you going to do? So I put the boxes in a closet and tried to move on."

He touched her leg. "Sarah would have wanted you to be happy, Tracy."

"I was fooling myself," she said. "There wasn't a day that went by that I didn't think of her. There wasn't a day I wasn't tempted to pull out the boxes, that I didn't think I had missed something, that there had to be one more piece of evidence. And then I was sitting at my desk and my partner said they'd found her grave." She exhaled. "Do you know how long I've waited for someone to tell me I'm not just some obsessed crazy person?"

"You're not a crazy person, Tracy. Obsessed, maybe."

She smiled. "You always could make me laugh."

"Yes, but unfortunately that usually wasn't my intention." Dan sat back and exhaled. "I don't know what happened back then, Tracy, not for certain, not yet, but what I do know is, if you're right about this, if House was framed, it wasn't orchestrated by one person. This was a conspiracy and Hagen, Calloway, Clark—even Finn, potentially—would have had to have been a part of it."

"And someone with access to Sarah's jewelry and our home," Tracy said. "I know."

Roy Calloway's Suburban was parked in the driveway of her parents' home behind another sheriff's vehicle and alongside a Cascade
County fire truck and ambulance. The sirens were silent and no
strobes pierced the early morning darkness. It gave Tracy a strange
sense of relief. Whatever the emergency was, it couldn't be too bad if
the lights were off. Could it?

Calloway's call had awakened her at just after four in the morning. Though Ben had been gone three months, Tracy had kept the
rental house. Home no longer held the fond memories it once had for
her. Her mother and father remained reclusive and quiet. Her father
had quit working at the hospital and was rarely seen around town.
They had not held their annual Christmas Eve party since Sarah's
disappearance. Her father had also started to drink at night. She
heard the slur in his voice when she called to check up on them and
smelled it on his breath when she visited. She also did not feel fully
welcome there anymore. There was an elephant in the room nobody
wanted to acknowledge. The memory foremost on their minds was
the one they wanted to forget. They were each wracked with their
own guilt—Tracy, for having left Sarah to drive home alone, and
her parents, for having gone to Hawaii instead of being at home that
fateful weekend. Tracy rationalized it all by telling herself she was
too old to be running home to her parents anyway, and that home
was no longer home.

In his call, Calloway had told her to get dressed and get to her
parents' house. "Just get here," he'd said, when she'd attempted to
question him further.

She hustled up the front steps to the sound of chatter from the
emergency vehicle radios. Medical and police personnel milled about
the porch and grand foyer. Nobody seemed to be in a particular
hurry, and she took that as another good sign. One of Calloway's
deputies saw her come in and knocked on the doors to her father's
den. Moments later, it was Roy Calloway, not her father, who slid
them apart. She saw others in the room behind him, though not her

father or her mother. The deputy said something to Calloway, who slid the doors closed. He looked pale and sickly. Stricken.

"Roy?" she asked, stepping toward him. "What is it? What happened?"

Calloway wiped at his nose with a handkerchief. "He's gone, Tracy."

"What?"

"Your father's gone."

"My father?" She hadn't even considered her father. She'd been certain something had happened to her mother. "What are you talking about?" When she tried to step past him, Calloway blocked her path, holding her by the shoulders. "Where is my father? Dad? Dad!"

"Tracy, don't."

She fought to free herself. "I want to see my father."

Calloway took her out onto the porch and pressed her shoulders to the side of the house, restraining her. "Listen to me. Tracy, stop and listen to me." She continued to struggle. "He used the shotgun, Tracy."

Tracy froze.

Calloway lowered his hands and took a step back. He glanced away, exhaling before regrouping and reconsidering her. "He used the shotgun," he said.

CHAPTER 25

A week after she'd buried Sarah's remains, Tracy slid onto a bench seat attached to a table in the visitor's area of Walla Walla State Penitentiary. "Let me do the talking," she said.

"I will," Dan said, taking a seat beside her.

"Don't promise him anything."

"I won't."

"He'll try to cut a deal."

Dan reached over and gripped her hand. "You told me that too. Calm down. I've been in prisons before, though admittedly the ones I've been in looked more like country clubs. This looks like an austere high school cafeteria."

Tracy looked to the door but did not see Edmund House. He was imprisoned in the D Unit of the penitentiary's West Complex, the prison's second-highest security unit. His placement reflected the severity of his crime, murder in the first degree, not his behavior during his time served. Tracy's phone calls over the years had revealed House to be a model inmate who kept mostly to himself, reading in his cell or working in the library on one of the many appeals he had filed during his years of incarceration.

Having forensic evidence from the grave to support her ten-year theory that House had been framed and Sarah's killer remained at large would do her no good unless she could get the evidence before a judge and get the witnesses back on the witness stand, under oath, and subject to thorough cross-examination. The only way to do all of that was to get Edmund House a post-conviction relief hearing, the precursor to a new trial. They could not do that without House's cooperation. She hated the thought that she needed House or that her fate was tied to him in any way. During her previous two trips to visit him, House had toyed with her and her fragile emotions. She hadn't realized it at the time, but she realized it now in hindsight. House had seemingly held all the cards. That was no longer the case. If House wanted a new trial and a chance to get out of prison, he had to cooperate.

The voices of the inmates and visitors seated at the surrounding tables echoed loudly. Tracy checked her watch and looked again to the door. She noticed an inmate lingering at the entrance, eyes scanning the tables. His gray braid hung well past muscled shoulders. She started to dismiss him. He looked nothing like Edmund House, but his gaze found hers and his mouth inched into a "look what the cat dragged in" grin.

"That can't be him, can it?" Dan said, also looking to the door.

At his trial, the newspapers had likened Edmund House's thick hair and burning good looks to James Dean. The face of the man walking toward them had broadened with age and weight, but the changes in House's facial features and the length of his hair was not the most striking change in his appearance. Not by a long shot. The muscles of his neck and chest pressed taut the fabric of his prison-issued T-shirt and pants, as if the seams might burst. Filing appeals was not the only thing House had done to pass his time in prison.

House stopped at the edge of the table and took a moment to appraise them. "Tracy Crosswhite," he said, as if savoring the name. "I thought you'd given up. What's it been, fifteen years?"

"I haven't kept track."

"I have. Little else to do in here."

"You could file another appeal." The prison information network, like the drug and illegal steroid network, was intricate and extensive. She needed to know if House already knew they'd found Sarah's grave.

"I plan on it."

"Yeah? What are the grounds this time?"

"Ineffective assistance of counsel."

"Sounds like you're reaching."

"Am I?"

She estimated House to be two hundred fifty pounds of thick muscle. Prison had washed dull the once-sparkling blue eyes, but not the piercing quality of his gaze.

A correctional officer approached. "Take a seat, please."

He sat. They were separated by just the width of the table. The closeness made her skin crawl, as it had whenever House had looked her up and down in the courtroom. "You've changed," she said.

"Yeah, I got my GED and I'm working toward my AA. How about that? Maybe I'll become a teacher when I get out of here." House looked to Dan.

"This is Dan," Tracy said.

"Hello, Dan." House extended his hand. Dark-blue letters, prison tats made with the ink of ballpoint pens, ran vertically along the inside of his forearm as thick as a mooring line.

"Isaiah," House said, catching Dan's focus on the tattoo. He kept his grip on Dan's hand and rotated his forearm so the words could be read.

To open the blind eyes,

to bring out the prisoners from the prison,
and them that sit in darkness
out of the prison house.

"Proper English would have been 'those that sit in darkness,' but I don't question the writer," House said. "Dan have a last name?"

The correctional officer stepped forward again. "No prolonged contact."

House released Dan's hand.

"O'Leary," Tracy said.

"Dan have a tongue?"

"O'Leary," Dan said.

"So what brings you here, Tracy and friend Dan, after all these years?"

"They found Sarah," she said.

House arched his eyebrows. "Alive?"

"No."

"That doesn't help me. Though I am curious, where did they find her?"

"Not relevant at this moment," Tracy said.

House tilted his head, eyes narrowing. "When did you become a cop?"

"What makes you think I'm a cop?"

"Oh, I don't know, your whole demeanor, your posture, the tone of your voice, your reluctance to introduce friend Dan or provide information. I've had a few years to make some observations. You've changed too, haven't you, Tracy?"

"I'm a detective," she said.

House grinned. "Still hunting for your sister's killer; any new leads you'd like to share?" He turned to Dan. "What do you think about my chances on my latest appeal, Counselor?"

At Tracy's instruction, Dan had dressed down in blue jeans and a Boston College sweatshirt. "I'd have to review your file," he said.

"Two for two," House said. "Watch me go three for three. You already have, and you agree. That's why you're sitting here with Detective Tracy." He looked at her. "They found your sister's remains and something about the crime scene confirms what you and I discussed all those years ago. Someone planted evidence to frame me."

Tracy regretted those previous visits. With the experience and training she'd received at the academy and as a patrol officer before becoming a detective, she knew she'd told House too much.

House shifted his gaze between her and Dan. "Am I getting warm?"

"Dan would like to ask you a few questions."

"I'll tell you what, when you're ready to stop playing games and start talking like a normal human being instead of talking in cop speak, come back and see me." House slid from the table.

Tracy said, "We leave and we don't come back."

"I leave and I don't come back. You're wasting my time. I have studying to do. I have finals coming up."

Tracy stood. "Let's go, Dan. You heard the man. He has studying to do." She started from the table. "Maybe you can teach in here. By the time you're done, you'd have tenure." She got half a dozen steps before House spoke.

"Fine."

She turned back. "Fine what?"

House bit at his lower lip. "Fine, I'll answer attorney Dan's questions." He shrugged and smiled, but it looked forced. "Why not, right? Like I said, not a lot to do in here." House sat and Tracy and Dan rejoined him at the table. "At least give me the courtesy of telling me why you came."

"Dan has reviewed your file. Incompetence of legal counsel might be a basis for a new trial. I'm not interested in that."

"You want to know who killed your sister," House said. "So do I."

"You told me once that you thought Calloway, or someone executing the search warrant, planted the earrings at your uncle's property. Tell Dan."

House shrugged. "How else did they get there?"

"The jury concluded you put them there," Dan said.

"Do I look that stupid? I'd been in prison six years; why would I keep evidence that would put me back in here?"

"Why would Calloway or anyone else frame you?" Dan asked.

"Because they couldn't find her killer, and I was the monster living in the mountains above the quaint little village, and I made people uncomfortable. They wanted to get rid of me."

"You have any evidence to support that?"

Tracy relaxed a bit. Now that he was in his element, Dan seemed more assured, confident, and less intimidated by House or their surroundings.

"I don't know," House said, looking between them. "Do I?"

"They ran a DNA test on the strands of blonde hair they found in your truck," Tracy lied. "They confirmed they belonged to Sarah. A billion-to-one odds."

"The odds are irrelevant if someone else put them there."

"You told Calloway you'd been out drinking and picked Sarah up and gave her a ride," Dan said.

"I didn't tell him anything of the sort. I wasn't even out that night. I was asleep. I would have been pretty stupid to make up a story so easy to refute."

"The witness says he saw your truck on the county road," Dan said.

"Ryan Hagen," House said with sarcasm. "The traveling auto-parts salesman. Convenient he would come forward after so much time had passed."

"You think he lied too. Why?" Dan asked.

"Calloway needed to put my alibi into question so he could obtain the search warrants. Before Hagen, Calloway's investigation was going nowhere."

"But why would Hagen lie and risk criminal prosecution?"

"I don't know, maybe to collect the ten-thousand-dollar reward being offered."

"No evidence of that," Dan said. Tracy had never found any proof of payment from her father to Ryan Hagen, and Hagen had denied receiving the reward at trial.

"Who was going to call him on it?" House let his question linger as he considered them both. "Who was a jury going to believe, a convicted rapist or Joe Q. Citizen? Putting me on the stand to refute it was the stupidest thing Finn could have done. It allowed them to ask me questions about my prior rape conviction."

"What about the blood they found in your truck?" Tracy asked.

House shifted his attention to Dan. "Mine. I didn't lie about it. I told Calloway I cut myself in the shop. I went to the truck for my smokes before I went inside." He looked to Tracy. "And don't insult me anymore about DNA. If they'd run a DNA test on the blood and proven it was your sister's, you wouldn't be sitting here. Why are you here?"

"*If* we were to get involved," Tracy said, "you'd need to cooperate fully. If at any time I think you're not telling the truth, we walk."

"I'm the *only* one who told the truth about that night." House sat back from the table. "Get involved how?"

Tracy nodded to Dan. He said, "I believe there could be new evidence, unavailable at your trial, which now raises a reasonable doubt about your guilt."

"Such as?"

"Before I discuss specifics, I need to first know if you want my assistance."

House studied him. "Do I want to retain you as my attorney, which would protect our conversations as privileged, and in which case Detective Tracy here would need to leave the table?"

"That's right," Dan said.

"First, you tell me what your intent is."

"I'd file a motion for post-conviction relief based on the new evidence and ask for a hearing in order to present it."

"Old Judge Lawrence still on the bench?"

"Retired," Tracy said.

Dan said, "The papers are filed with the Court of Appeals. If they grant a hearing, I'd ask that it be presided over by a judge brought in from outside Cascade County. It would pretty much force their hand."

"It wasn't the judge who convicted me; a Cascade County jury did that."

"There wouldn't be a jury this time. We'd present the evidence directly to the judge."

House considered the tabletop before lifting his gaze. "Would you get to put on witnesses?"

"I'd cross-examine the witnesses who testified at your first trial."

"Yeah? Would that include that big shot Calloway? Or is he retired too?"

"He testified the first time," Dan said.

"What's it going to be?" Tracy said.

House closed his eyes and took a deep breath. Dan looked like he wanted to say more to convince House, but Tracy shook her head to indicate he shouldn't oversell it. When House opened his eyes, he looked at her and grinned. "Looks like it's you and me again, Detective Tracy."

"It was never you and me, and it never will be."

"No? I've been filing appeals for nearly twenty years." He pointed to her left hand. "No wedding ring. No tan line from a ring you removed before coming here. Narrow hips. Flat stomach. Never married. No kids. What've you been doing with *your* time, Detective Tracy?"

"You've got ten seconds to make up your mind before we walk."

House again gave her that sick, beguiling grin. "Oh, I've made up my mind. In fact, I can already see it."

"See what?"

"The looks on the faces of all those people when they see me walking the streets of Cedar Grove again."

CHAPTER 26

Vance Clark was wearing a baseball cap and had his head down, but Roy Calloway still recognized him, reading at a table near the back of the bar. Clark looked up when Calloway slid back the chair opposite him. "I hope they have a killer happy hour," Calloway said. Clark had picked a bar in Pine Flat, two exits down the freeway from Cedar Grove. Calloway removed his jacket and hooked it over the back of the chair as he addressed an approaching waitress. "Johnnie Walker Black with a splash. Don't baptize it." He had to speak over the clatter of billiard balls and country music playing on an old-fashioned juke box.

"Wild Turkey," Clark said, though his glass on the table was still half-full.

Calloway sat and rolled up the sleeves of his flannel shirt. Clark flipped back to the first page of what he'd been reading and slid it across the table toward him. "Shit, Vance, you going to make me put on my glasses?"

"It's a pleading," Clark said.

"I can see that."

"Filed in the Court of Appeals. In re: Edmund House."

Calloway picked the papers up. "Well, it isn't his first appeal, and I'm sure it won't be his last. Did you drag me all the way out here just to show me this?"

Clark adjusted the bill of his cap and sat back, drink in hand. "House didn't file it. It was filed on his behalf."

"He's got an attorney?"

Clark drained his glass. The ice clinked. "I think you should put on your glasses."

Calloway pulled them from his pocket and slipped them on, eyeballing Clark before considering the pleading.

"The law firm is along the bottom of the page, right-hand side," Clark said.

"The Law Offices of Daniel O'Leary." Calloway flipped through the pages. "What are the grounds?"

"New evidence not available at the time of trial and incompetence of legal counsel. But it isn't an appeal. It's a motion for post-conviction relief."

"What's the difference?"

The waitress returned and set Calloway's drink on the table and replaced Clark's empty glass with a full one.

Clark waited for her to depart before he explained. "If the Court of Appeals agrees, they can remand it for a hearing. House would get to introduce evidence to prove his initial trial wasn't conducted fairly."

"You mean a new trial?"

"It's more of an evidentiary hearing, but if you're asking whether he'd get to put on witnesses, the answer is yes."

"DeAngelo seen this yet?"

"I doubt it," Clark said. "Technically he hasn't been House's legal counsel for years. The proof of service doesn't list him."

"You talk to him about it?"

Clark shook his head. "I didn't think it wise, with his heart condition and all. But he's listed as a witness, *if* the Court of Appeals grants the motion. So are you."

Calloway flipped the pages and found his name just above "Ryan P. Hagen," second from the bottom of the list. "Does it hold water?"

"Like the Hoover Dam." Clark slumped in his chair. "I thought you said you'd convinced her to let this go."

"I thought I did."

Clark's brow furrowed. "She's never let this go, Roy. Not from the very start."

CHAPTER 27

Ryan Hagen opened his front door and greeted Tracy with a sheepish smile. Then he acted as if he didn't recognize her. Four years since the trial, it was possible he didn't, but Tracy saw that moment of hesitation in his expression that indicated he remembered exactly who she was.

"Can I help you?" Hagen asked.

"Mr. Hagen, I'm Tracy Crosswhite. Sarah was my sister."

"Yes, of course," Hagen said, quickly resorting to his salesman's demeanor. He shook her hand. "I'm sorry. I see so many faces in my line of work they tend to blend together. What are you doing here?"

"I was hoping I could ask you a few questions," she said.

Hagen glanced over his shoulder into the small house. It was Saturday morning, and Tracy heard what sounded like cartoons coming from a television. Hagen had testified that he was married with two young children. He stepped out onto the tiny porch, closing the door behind him. His hair, currently not held in place by hair product, fell across his forehead, and his round shape was more pronounced in a T-shirt, plaid shorts, and flip-flops. "How did you find me?"

"You gave your address at trial."

"You remembered it?"

"I ordered the transcripts."

Hagen's eyes narrowed. "You ordered the transcripts? Why would you order the transcripts?"

"Mr. Hagen, I was wondering if you could tell me the television station you were watching when they ran the report on Edmund House that triggered your memory."

Hagen crossed his arms and rested them on his stomach. The smile faded. He looked bewildered. "I didn't say it was a report on Edmund House."

"Sorry, I meant the report on my sister being missing. Do you remember the station? Or maybe the broadcaster?"

His brow furrowed. "Why are you asking me these questions?"

"I know it's an inconvenience. It's just that . . . well, I have the newscasts for that time period and—"

Hagen unfolded his arms. "You have the newscasts? Why would you have the newscasts?"

"I was just hoping you could tell me—"

"I testified to everything at trial. If you have the transcripts, you know what I said. Now, I'm sorry, but I have things to do." He turned and reached for the door handle.

"Why did you say you saw the red Chevy stepside on the road, Mr. Hagen?"

Hagen turned back. "How dare you. I helped put that animal away. If it wasn't for me . . ." Hagen flushed.

"If it wasn't for you what?" Tracy asked.

"I'd like you to leave now." Hagen pushed on the door but it wouldn't open. He shook the handle.

"If it wasn't for you saying you saw the Chevy truck, we wouldn't have gotten the search warrant. Is that what you were going to say?"

Hagen banged on the door. "I told you I'd like you to leave."

"Is that what someone told you?" Hagen banged harder. "Is that why you said it? Did someone say it would help get the search warrants? Mr. Hagen, please."

The door pulled open. Hagen ushered a small boy away from the door and stepped across the threshold, turning to face her, already closing the door. "Don't come back," he said. "I'll call the police."

"Was it Chief Calloway?" Tracy said, but Hagen had shut the door.

CHAPTER 28

Dan had figured he'd hear from Roy Calloway, though not this quickly. Cedar Grove's sheriff sat in the lobby of Dan's office, casually flipping through a months-old magazine from a collection on the coffee table and biting into an apple. He was dressed in full uniform, his hat resting on the chair beside him.

"Sheriff. This is a surprise."

Calloway put down his magazine and stood. "You're not surprised to see me, Dan."

"I'm not?"

He chewed another bite of apple. "You did list me as a witness on that pleading you filed."

"Word always did travel fast here in Cedar Grove." With no court appearances, Dan had dressed casually in jeans and a button-down. He liked to wear slippers in the office. Now he wished he'd worn shoes, though the discrepancy in their heights wasn't nearly as significant as it had been back when Calloway used to stop Dan on his bike to ask what he was up to.

"What can I do for you, Sheriff?"

"How is it going to impact your business when word spreads you're representing Edmund House, the convicted murderer of one of Cedar Grove's own?"

"I suppose my criminal practice could pick up."

Calloway smirked. "Always the smart-ass, weren't you, O'Leary? I wouldn't count on that."

"Well, unless you have some stock tips to go along with your prediction for my legal career, I have work to do." Dan turned to leave.

"You have questions for me, Dan, here I am. I haven't hid a single day my thirty-five years on the job. Somebody has questions for me, I'm happy to answer them."

"I'm sure you would," Dan said. "But I have to do it in a court of law, after you're sworn to tell the truth, the whole truth, and nothing but the truth."

Calloway took another bite of his apple, taking a moment to chew before saying, "I did that once, Dan. Are you saying I lied?"

"That isn't for me to decide; that's for a judge."

"Judge already did that too. You're rehashing old business."

"Maybe. We'll see what the Court of Appeals has to say."

"What did she tell you, Dan?" Calloway paused and gave him a sardonic grin. "She tell you that no one asked Hagen the news show he was watching or that Sarah had different earrings?"

"I'm not going to discuss this with you, Sheriff."

"Hey, I know she's a friend, Dan, but she's been on this crusade for twenty years. She tried to use me and now she's using you. She's obsessed, Dan. It killed her father and drove her mother crazy and now she's sucking you into her fantasy. Don't you think it's time to put it to bed?"

Dan paused. When Tracy had first come to him, that had been exactly what he'd thought, that she was a sister unable to get past her guilt and grief, obsessed with trying to find answers to questions that had already been answered. But then he'd looked at the file and her reasoning had seemed just like the Tracy he'd always known, the leader of their little band of friends—practical, dogged, and logical. "You'd have to ask her that. I represent Edmund House."

Calloway held out the apple core. "Then maybe you could throw this out for me, since you're apparently adept at handling garbage."

Unruffled, Dan took the core. So far he'd found Calloway's attempts to intimidate him to be more pathetic than threatening. He tossed the core into a pail behind the desk on the first attempt. "I think what you're going to learn, Sheriff, is I'm adept at my job. You might want to remember that."

Calloway fit his hat onto his head. "I got a call from one of your neighbors. He says your dogs have been barking something fierce during the day, sometimes late at night. We do have an ordinance in town about dogs disturbing the peace. First offense is a fine. Second offense, we take the dogs."

Dan felt his anger build and fought to control it. Threaten him? Fine. Don't threaten innocent animals. "Really? You can't do any better than that?"

"Don't try me, Dan."

"I'm not going to try you, Sheriff, but if the Court of Appeals grants my petition, I am going to seriously cross-examine you."

CHAPTER 29

Tracy typed up the details of a recent witness interview regarding the Nicole Hansen case file. A month had passed since they'd discovered the young woman's body in the motel on Aurora Avenue, and pressure was building to find the young stripper's killer. The SPD had not had an unsolved homicide since Johnny Nolasco had become Chief of Investigations, something Nolasco was proud of and quick to point out. And Nolasco didn't need any additional reason to bust Tracy's chops. They had a turbulent history dating back to Tracy's time at the police academy, where Nolasco, one of her instructors, had demonstrated a simulated pat-down by grabbing her breast. Tracy had responded by breaking his nose and kneeing him in the nuts. She'd then further bruised his ego by breaking his long-standing shooting-range record.

Any thought that Nolasco had mellowed with age had vanished when Tracy had become Seattle's first female homicide detective. Nolasco, who'd risen to Chief of Investigations, had assigned her to work with his former partner, a racist chauvinist named Floyd Hattie. Hattie had made a stink about it and promptly dubbed her "Dickless Tracy." Tracy later learned that Hattie had already put in for retirement, meaning Nolasco had made the assignment just to embarrass her.

If nothing else, the Hansen investigation was keeping her busy and distracted. Dan said the State had sixty days to respond to Edmund House's Petition for Post-Conviction Relief, and he expected Vance Clark to take every one of those days. Tracy told herself she'd already waited twenty years, she could wait two more months, but now each day seemed like an eternity.

She answered her desk phone, noting it was an outside line.

"Detective Crosswhite, this is Maria Vanpelt from KRIX Channel 8."

Tracy immediately regretted answering. The Homicide Unit maintained a civil relationship with police beat reporters, but Vanpelt—whom they referred to as "Manpelt" for her proclivity to be seen draped on the arms of some of Seattle's more prominent men—was the exception.

Early in Tracy's career, Vanpelt had sought an interview for a story about discrimination against female officers in the Seattle Police Department. Tracy had declined. When Tracy had made Homicide, Vanpelt had requested another interview, ostensibly to profile Tracy as Seattle's first female homicide detective. Not wanting to draw any additional attention to herself, and now educated by others that hatchet jobs, not human-interest pieces, were Vanpelt's specialty, Tracy had again declined.

Their dicey professional relationship did not improve. Vanpelt had somehow obtained confidential information about a gang murder investigation on which Tracy was the lead detective. Two of Tracy's witnesses had been gunned down within hours of Vanpelt airing the information on her show, *KRIX Undercover*. Caught off guard by a competing news crew at the scene of the murders, an angry and frustrated Tracy had not minced her words about Vanpelt having blood on her hands. And the Homicide Unit had frozen Vanpelt out, refusing to talk to her, until Nolasco had issued an edict directing them to cooperate with all media.

"How'd you get my direct line?" Tracy asked. The media was supposed to go through the Public Information Office, but many reporters found ways to get through to direct desk numbers.

"Various channels," Vanpelt said.

"What can I do for you, Ms. Vanpelt?"

She said the name loud enough to get Kins's attention across the bull pen. Kins picked up his phone without even bothering to acknowledge her. They had a system in place.

"I'm hoping to get a comment for a story I'm working on."

"What's your story about?" Tracy mentally flipped through her case files. Only the Nicole Hansen investigation came to mind, and she had nothing new to discuss.

"Actually, it's about you."

Tracy leaned back in her chair. "And what makes me suddenly so interesting?" she asked.

"I understand your sister was murdered twenty years ago and that her remains were recently found. I was hoping you would be willing to discuss it?"

The question gave Tracy pause. She sensed more at play. "Who did you hear this from?"

"I have an assistant who goes through the court files," Vanpelt said, dismissing the question with a bullshit answer—but one intended to let Tracy know that Vanpelt knew about Dan's motion for post-conviction relief. "Would now be a good time to talk?"

"I don't think that story has much public appeal." Her second line began to buzz. She looked over at Kins, who held the receiver in his hand, but now she was curious as to what Vanpelt knew. "What's the premise?"

"I think that's pretty self-evident, don't you?"

"Enlighten me."

"A Seattle homicide detective who spends her days putting murderers behind bars seeks to free the man convicted of murdering her sister."

Kins gave her a "what's up?" shrug.

Tracy raised a finger. "Is that part of the court files?"

"I'm an investigative reporter, detective."

"Who's your source?"

"My sources are confidential," Vanpelt said.

"You like to keep certain information private."

"That's right."

"So you know how I feel. It's a private matter. I intend to keep it private."

"I'm going to report the story, detective. It would be better to have your side of the story when I do."

"Better for me or better for you?"

"Is that a 'no comment'?"

"I said it's a private matter, and I intend to keep it private."

"Can I quote you?"

"It's what I said."

"I understand the attorney, Dan O'Leary, was a childhood friend of yours. Care to comment on that?"

Calloway. Except the Sheriff would not have called Vanpelt. He would have called Nolasco, Tracy's superior. Rumors swirled that Nolasco was one of the men doing the hokey-pokey with Vanpelt and providing her with information. "Cedar Grove is a small town. I knew a lot of people growing up there."

"Did you know Daniel O'Leary?"

"There's only one middle school and one high school."

"That doesn't answer my question."

"You're an investigative reporter; I'm sure you'll figure it out."

"Did you recently accompany Mr. O'Leary to meet with Edmund House at the Walla Walla State Penitentiary? I've obtained a copy of Mr. House's visitor list for the month. Your name appears just above Mr. O'Leary's name."

"Then print that."

"So you won't comment?"

"As I said, this is a private matter unrelated to my job. Speaking of which, my other line is ringing." Tracy hung up the phone and swore under her breath.

"What did she want?" Kins asked.

Tracy looked across the bull pen. "To stick her nose up my ass."

"Vanpelt?" Faz slid his chair back from his desk. "That's her specialty."

"She says she's doing a story about Sarah, but she's more focused—" She decided not to finish her thought.

Kins said, "Don't sweat it too much. You know Vanpelt, the facts don't interest her."

"She'll get bored and go make up another story," Faz said.

Tracy wished it was that easy. She knew Vanpelt hadn't found the story on her own. It had to have come from Calloway, and that meant Calloway was talking to Nolasco, who didn't need much to make Tracy's life miserable.

It also wasn't the first time Calloway had threatened to get Tracy fired from her job.

—

The students in the front of the classroom flinched and leaned back when the spark shot a crackling white bolt across the gap between the two spheres. Tracy cranked the handle of the electrostatic generator, increasing the speed of the two rotating metal discs that caused the bolt to continue firing. "Lightning, ladies and gentlemen, is one of nature's most dramatic illustrations of the energy form scientists like *James Wimshurst* and *Benjamin Franklin sought to harness,"* she said.

"Wasn't he the dude who flew the kite in a storm?"

Tracy smiled. "Yes, Steven, he is the dude who flew the kite in a storm. What he and those other 'dudes' were trying to determine was whether energy could be converted into electricity. Can someone point to hard evidence that they succeeded?"

"The lightbulb," Nicole said.

Tracy released the handle. The spark died. Her freshmen sat in pairs at tables equipped with a sink, Bunsen burner, and microscope each. Tracy turned on a water faucet at a front table. "It helps if you think of electricity as a fluid capable of flowing through objects. When an electric current flows we call that what, Enrique?"

"A current," he said, generating laughs.

"I meant, when an electric current can flow through a substance we call that substance . . . ?"

"A conductor."

"Can you provide me with an example of a conductor, Enrique?"

"People."

The students again laughed.

"No joke," Enrique said. "My uncle was working a construction job in the rain, and he cut through an electrical line and nearly killed himself, except another guy yanked him off the saw."

Tracy paced the front of the room. "All right, let's discuss that scenario. When Enrique's uncle cut through the electrical line, what happened to the flow of electricity?"

"It flowed into his body," Enrique said.

"Which would be evidence the human body is, in fact, a conductor. But if that is the case, why didn't the coworker get shocked when he touched Enrique's uncle?"

When no student responded, Tracy reached below her desk and retrieved a nine-volt battery and a lightbulb in a bulb holder. Two lengths of copper wire extended from the battery, and a third wire extended from the bulb holder. The opposite ends were alligator clips. Tracy attached the alligator clips to a piece of rubber tubing. "Why didn't the bulb light?"

No one answered.

"What if the worker who touched Enrique's uncle was wearing rubber gloves? What could we conclude?"

"Rubber isn't a conductor," Enrique said.

"That's right, rubber is not a conductor. So the power from the battery will not flow through the rubber tubing." Tracy attached the clips to a large nail. The bulb lit. "Nails," Tracy said, "are made up mostly of iron. So what can we conclude about iron?"

"Conductor," the class said in unison.

The bell rang. Tracy raised her voice over the obnoxious clang and the scraping of barstool legs on linoleum. "Your homework is on the board. We will continue our discussion of electricity on Wednesday."

Back at her desk, Tracy began to put away the demonstration, preparing for her next period. The volume of noise from the hallways increased, which meant someone had opened the door to her classroom. "If you have questions, please see me during my regular office hours; you'll find them posted on my door along with a sign-up sheet."

"This won't take long."

Tracy turned toward the voice. "I'm preparing for a class."

Roy Calloway let the door shut behind him. "You want to tell me what it is you think you're doing?"

"I just did."

Calloway approached her table. "Questioning the integrity of a witness who had the courage to come forward and do his civic duty?"

Hagen had called Calloway, which Tracy had thought likely when he'd shut the door in her face that Saturday. "I didn't question his integrity. Did he tell you I questioned his integrity?"

"*You did everything but call him a liar.*" Calloway leaned his palms flat on her table. "*You want to tell me what you think you're trying to accomplish?*"

"*I just asked him the news program he was watching.*"

"*That is not your place, Tracy. The trial is over. The time for asking questions is done.*"

"*Not all the questions got asked.*"

"*Not all the questions needed to be asked.*"

"*Or answered?*"

Calloway pointed a finger at her, the way he used to when she was young. "*Leave it alone. Okay? Let it be. I know you also drove to Silver Springs and have been talking to bartenders.*"

"*Why didn't you, Roy? Why didn't you check to make sure House wasn't telling the truth?*"

"*I didn't need to check to know he was lying.*"

"*How, Roy? How did you know?*"

"*Fifteen years of police work, that's how. So we're clear, I don't want to hear about you ordering any more transcripts or harassing witnesses. I do, and I'll have a talk with Jerry and tell him how one of his teachers isn't committed to teaching, that she'd rather play junior detective. Do you understand?*"

Jerry Butterman was Cedar Grove High's principal. Tracy fumed at the fact that Calloway would threaten her this way. At the same time, she wanted to laugh. He had no idea the threat was hollow, no idea that Tracy did not intend to play "junior detective." She'd decided to jump in with both feet. At the end of the school year, she'd leave Cedar Grove and move to Seattle to join the police academy. "*Do you know why I became a chemistry teacher, Roy?*"

"*Why?*"

"*It's because I could never just accept the way things were. I needed to know why they were that way. It used to drive my parents crazy, me always asking 'why.'*"

"*House is in prison. That's all you need to know.*"

"I tell my students it's not the result that's important. It's the evidence. If the evidence is suspect, so is the result."

"And if you want to continue teaching your students, I'd suggest you take my advice and focus on being a teacher."

"That's the thing, Roy. I've already made that decision too." The bell rang and the door to the classroom was pulled open. Tracy's fourth-period students hesitated at the sight of Cedar Grove's sheriff standing in their classroom. "Come on in," Tracy said, stepping out from behind her table. "Take your seats. Chief Calloway was just leaving."

CHAPTER 30

Late in the afternoon, Tracy and Kins returned from Kent. They'd interviewed an accountant whose fingerprint had matched a latent print that CSI had recently pulled from the motel room where Nicole Hansen had suffocated. "Did he confess?" Faz asked.

"Praise the Lord and hallelujah," Kins said. "He's a regular Bible-toting, psalm-spewing churchgoer who just happens to also have a proclivity for young prostitutes. He also has a rock-solid alibi for the night Hansen strangled herself."

"So why the print?" Faz asked.

"He'd been in that room the week before with a different young lady."

Tracy dumped her purse inside her cabinet. "You should have seen the look on his face when I said we'd need to talk to his wife to confirm he was really asleep beside her the night Hansen died."

"Looked like he'd seen the Lord himself," Kins said.

"That's our job," Faz said. "Solving murders and helping people find religion."

"Praise the Lord." Kins waved his hands over his head.

"You thinking of a career change?" Billy Williams stood just outside their bull pen. Williams had been promoted to Detective

Sergeant of the A Team when Andrew Laub had made Lieutenant. "Because if you are, let me tell you as someone raised Baptist in the south, you're going to need to be a lot more convincing than that to get people to open up their wallets."

"We were just talking about another witness in the Hansen case," Kins said.

"Anything we can work with?"

"Wasn't there that night. Doesn't know Hansen. Feels awful and will go forth and sin no more."

"Praise the Lord," Faz said.

Williams looked to Tracy. "Got a minute?"

"Yeah, what's up?"

He turned and nodded over his shoulder for her to follow him.

"Ooh, the Professor is in trouble," Faz said.

Tracy gave them a shrug, made a face, and followed Williams to the soft interrogation room around the corner and down the hall. Williams closed the door behind her.

"What's up?" she asked.

"Your phone's going to ring. The brass have been meeting."

"What about?"

"Are you helping some lawyer get the guy who killed your sister a new trial?"

She and Williams had a good relationship. As a black man, Williams could relate to the subtle and not-so-subtle discrimination Tracy had encountered as a woman in a predominantly male occupation. "It's complicated, Billy."

"No shit. So it's true?"

"It's also personal."

"The brass are concerned about how it reflects on the department."

"By 'brass,' do you mean Nolasco?"

"He's in on it."

"What a surprise. Vanpelt called me this morning to advise that she's doing a story on the same subject and asking me to comment. She seemed to have a lot of details for someone who ordinarily doesn't concern herself with facts."

"Look, I'm not going there."

"I'm not asking you to. I'm just telling you that Nolasco's not concerned about how it reflects on the department; he sees it as another opportunity to bust my ass. So if I tell him 'fuck how it reflects on the department,' I'd appreciate a little support. Unless he's got a problem with how I'm doing my job, this isn't his problem or his business."

"Don't shoot the messenger, Tracy."

She took a moment to check her temper. "Sorry, Billy. I just don't need this right now."

"Where's the information coming from?"

"I got a hunch it's a sheriff in Cedar Grove who's had a twenty-year hard-on for me and doesn't want me anywhere near this."

"Well, whoever he is, he seems intent on making this difficult for you. Manpelt loves the personal shit."

"I appreciate the heads-up, Billy. Sorry I snapped."

"What's the word on the Hansen case?"

"We're coming up empty."

"That's a problem."

"I know."

Williams pulled open the door. "Promise me you'll play nice."

"You know me."

"Yeah, that's what I'm afraid of."

—

The phone on her desk did indeed ring, and later that afternoon Tracy was last to enter the conference room she'd been summoned to. The very fact that she'd been invited to the gathering was unusual. Normally Williams would simply inform her of any decisions made by upper management. She figured Nolasco wanted her there to call her out in front of Williams and Laub and otherwise run around the room pissing on chairs.

Nolasco stood on one side of the table with Bennett Lee from the Public Information Office. Lee wouldn't be present unless Nolasco was expecting Tracy to approve a statement for the media. She was going to disappoint him. It certainly wasn't the first time she had over the years and likely would not be the last. She stepped to the side of the table with Williams and Laub.

"Detective Crosswhite, thanks for joining us," Nolasco said. "Do you know why you're here?"

"Can't say I do." She played the game because she did not want to reveal that Williams had tipped her off. They all took their seats. Lee had a notepad on the table, pen in hand.

"We got a call from a reporter requesting a comment for a story she's working on," Nolasco said.

"Did you give Vanpelt my direct line?"

"Excuse me?"

"Vanpelt called my direct line. Is she the reporter requesting a comment?"

Nolasco's jaw stiffened. "Ms. Vanpelt is under the impression you are assisting an attorney trying to obtain a new trial for a convicted killer."

"Yeah, that's what she said."

"Can you enlighten us?" Now in his late fifties, Nolasco remained lean and in good physical condition. He parted his hair down the middle. A few years back he'd started dyeing it an odd shade of brown, almost like rust, which stood out even more because it was a different color from the natural shade of his wedge-shaped mustache. Tracy thought he looked like an aging porn star.

"It isn't complicated. Even a hack like Vanpelt has the basic facts correct."

"What facts are those?" Nolasco asked.

"You already know them," she said. Nolasco had been one of the initial screeners of Tracy's application for admittance into the Academy. He'd also been present at her oral board exams when the board had asked about her sister's disappearance. Tracy had been forthright in her application and that interview.

"Not everyone here does."

She fought not to let him get under her skin and turned to face Laub and Williams. "Twenty years ago my sister was murdered. They never found her body. Edmund House was convicted on circumstantial evidence. Last month they found my sister's remains. The forensics at the grave site conflict with evidence offered at House's trial." She avoided specifics, not wanting Nolasco to share any information with Calloway or Vanpelt. "His attorney has used that conflict to file a motion for post-conviction relief." She returned her focus to Nolasco. "So, are we finished here?"

"Do you know the lawyer?" Nolasco asked.

Tracy felt herself getting angrier. "It's a small town, Captain. I knew everyone growing up in Cedar Grove."

"There's an indication you've been conducting your own investigation," Nolasco said.

"What indication would that be?"

"Have you been conducting your own investigation?"

"I've had doubts about House's guilt since they first arrested him."

"That doesn't answer my question."

"Twenty years ago I questioned the evidence that led to House's conviction. It made some people in Cedar Grove less than happy with me, including the Sheriff."

"So you *have* been conducting an investigation," Nolasco said.

Tracy knew what he was driving at. Using her official position on a personal investigation would be grounds for a reprimand and perhaps suspension.

"Define 'investigation.'"

"I think you're familiar with the term."

"I've never used my official position as a homicide detective, if that's what you're asking. Anything I've done has been on my own time."

"So it's an investigation?"

"More like a hobby."

Nolasco lowered his head and rubbed his brow, as if fighting a headache. "Did you facilitate an attorney's access into Walla Walla to meet with House?"

"What did Vanpelt tell you?"

"I'm asking you."

"Maybe *you* should just tell *me* the facts and save everybody a lot of time."

Williams and Laub cringed. Laub said, "Tracy, this isn't an inquisition."

"Sounds like one, Lieutenant. Do I need a union rep here?"

Nolasco's lips pinched. He was growing red in the face. "It's a simple question. Did you facilitate an attorney's access to speak with House?"

"Define 'facilitate.'"

"Did you assist in any manner?"

"I drove with the attorney to the facility in his car, on a day I was off duty. Didn't even pay for the gas. We entered through the public access on a day scheduled for inmate visitations just like everyone else."

"Did you use your badge number?"

"Not to get in."

"Tracy," Laub said. "We're getting inquiries from the press. It's important we're all on the same page, saying the same thing."

"I'm not saying anything, Lieutenant. I told Vanpelt it's a private matter and nobody's damn business."

"That's not reasonable given the public nature of the proceedings," Nolasco said. "Whether you like it or not, it's in the public domain, and our job is to make sure it does not reflect badly on this department. Vanpelt is asking for an official comment."

"Who gives a shit what Vanpelt is asking for?"

"She's the police beat reporter for the number one news station in town."

"She's an ambulance chaser. She's a hack. And she's unethical. Everyone knows that. No matter what I say, she'll twist it to create a seeming conflict. I'm not playing her game. It's personal. We don't comment on personal matters. Why is this being treated differently?"

Laub said, "I think what the Captain is asking is, Tracy, do you have a suggestion for how we should respond?"

"More than one," she said.

"Something printable?" Laub asked.

"Say it's a personal matter and neither I nor the department will comment on ongoing legal proceedings. That's how we handle open files. Why should this be any different?"

"Because it is not one of our files," Nolasco said.

"Bingo," Tracy said.

Laub turned to Nolasco. "I don't disagree with Detective Crosswhite. We gain nothing by making a statement."

Williams backed her too. "Vanpelt will report what she wants regardless of what we say. We've been down this road before."

"She's going to run a story that one of our homicide detectives is assisting an attorney in getting a convicted killer a new trial," Nolasco said. "We say 'no comment,' it's a tacit admission we condone it."

"If you feel compelled to make a comment, tell her I'm interested in a thorough resolution of my sister's murder," Tracy said. "How does that reflect on the department?"

"That sounds good to me," Laub said.

"There are some people in Cedar Grove who think there already was a thorough resolution twenty years ago," Nolasco said.

"And they didn't like me asking questions then either."

Nolasco pointed his pen at her. She wanted to reach out and snap his finger. "If there is something to cast doubt on this man's guilt, it should be brought to the attention of the Sheriff's Office in Cascade County. That's their jurisdiction."

"Didn't you just tell me you didn't want me involved? Now you want me to provide the sheriff with information?"

Nolasco's nostrils flared. "I'm saying, as a law-enforcement officer, you have a professional obligation to share information with them."

"I tried that once; it didn't get me very far."

Nolasco set his pen down. "You realize that your assisting a convicted murderer reflects on the entire Violent Crimes Section."

"Maybe it will show we're impartial."

Williams and Laub did a poor job suppressing smiles. Nolasco was not amused. "This is a serious matter, Detective Crosswhite."

"Murder always is."

"Perhaps I should ask if this is going to impact your ability to perform your job?"

"With all due respect, I thought finding murderers *was* my job."

"And you should be devoting your time to finding out who killed Nicole Hansen."

Laub intervened again. "Can we all take a deep breath? Are we at least in agreement that the department will issue a statement that neither Detective Crosswhite nor anyone else will comment on ongoing legal proceedings and refer all questions to the Sheriff's Office in Cascade County?"

Lee started scribbling.

"You are not to use your official position or any of this department's resources to investigate the matter. Do I make myself clear?" Nolasco was no longer trying to mask his annoyance.

Tracy said, "Are we equally clear that the department is not to put words in my mouth?"

"Nobody's going to put words in your mouth, Tracy," Laub said. "Bennett can put together a statement and we will review it together. Does that work for everyone?"

Nolasco did not answer. Tracy wasn't about to capitulate without some show of good faith from him.

"I can't protect you on this," Nolasco finally said. "This is outside the department's business. Something goes sideways, you're on your own."

Tracy wanted to laugh at the suggestion that Nolasco had ever had her back. She also wanted to scream. "I wouldn't have it any other way," she said.

—

Kins spun his chair toward her when Tracy returned to the bull pen, her adrenaline still pumping from the confrontation with Nolasco. "What's going on?"

Tracy sat and rubbed her hands over her face, massaging her temples. She opened her desk drawer, shook out two ibuprofen, tilted back her head, and swallowed them without water. "Vanpelt wasn't asking about the ME's office finding Sarah's remains," she said. "She wanted to know if I was helping an attorney get Edmund House a new hearing. The brass got wind of it and aren't happy."

"So just tell them you're not." When she didn't immediately respond, Kins said, "You're not, are you?"

"You know that cold case we have, the elderly woman on Queen Anne a year ago?"

"Nora Stevens?"

"Does it bother you, Kins, not knowing?"

"Of course it bothers me."

"Imagine how much it would bother you after twenty years, and it had been someone you loved. How far would you go to get answers?"

CHAPTER 31

Tracy knocked on the door and stepped back, letting the screen door slap shut. When no one answered, she cupped her hands to the window and tried to look through white lace curtains. Seeing no one, she walked along the covered porch to the side of the house and leaned over the railing. A late-model Honda Civic sat parked in the driveway in front of a freestanding garage.

She called out, got no answer, and walked back toward the porch steps, about to descend when she saw a figure through the window crossing the living room. The front door pulled open.

"Tracy."

"Hello, Mrs. Holt."

"I thought I heard someone knock. I was in the back doing some needlepoint. Well, this is certainly a surprise, hearing from you. What are you doing back in Cedar Grove?"

"I needed to take care of a few matters involving my parents' estate."

"I thought you'd already sold the house?"

"A few loose ends," she said.

"That must have been heart wrenching. Harley and I had such wonderful memories of our times there, especially the Christmas parties. Well, come in, come in. Don't stand out in the cold."

Tracy wiped her feet on a welcome mat and stepped inside. The furnishings were simple but neat. Framed photographs lined the mantel and rested on doilies on the dining room credenza. A china cabinet was filled with porcelain figurines, a collection of some kind. Carol Holt closed the door behind her. Tracy estimated her to be in her midsixties, heavyset with short silver hair and matching glasses. She still apparently favored stretch pants, long sweaters, and colorful beaded necklaces. When Sarah had disappeared, Carol Holt had made sandwiches at the American Legion building for the volunteers searching the hillsides.

"What are you doing now?" Mrs. Holt asked. "I heard you live in Seattle."

"I'm a police officer."

"A police officer," she said. "Wow. I'll bet that's exciting."

"It has its moments."

"Sit down and visit for a bit. Can I get you anything? A glass of water or coffee?"

"No, Mrs. Holt, thank you. I'm fine."

"Please, dear, I think you're old enough to call me Carol now."

They sat in the living room, Tracy on a maroon couch with crocheted throw pillows. One said "Home Sweet Home" with a picture of the front of the house. Carol Holt sat in a nearby chair.

"So what brought you by to visit?" she asked.

"I was on my way back to Seattle, and I drove by the service station to talk to Harley, but it looks like it's closed." That wasn't exactly true. Tracy had planned the visit to Cedar Grove, but not to settle her parents' estate. She'd hunted down Ryan Hagen's former employer a month earlier and had found some interesting documents. She'd hoped Harley Holt had additional documents that would further enlighten her.

"I'm sorry, Tracy. I lost Harley a little over six months ago."

Tracy felt suddenly deflated. "I didn't know, Carol. I'm so sorry. How did he die?"

"Pancreatic cancer. It got in his lymph nodes and they just couldn't stop it. At least he didn't suffer long."

Tracy couldn't recall a time when she'd dropped a car off at Harley's station for servicing and Harley hadn't been there to greet her with a cigarette in his mouth. "I apologize."

"Nothing to apologize for." Carol Holt smiled, close-lipped, but her eyes had filled with tears.

"Are you doing okay?" Tracy asked.

Carol gave a resigned shrug and twisted her necklace. "Well, it's hard, but I'm trying to stay active and make the best of it. What else are you going to do, right? Oh Lord, why am I telling you something like that. You've certainly had more than your fair share of tragedy."

"It's okay."

"My kids visit with the grandkids and that helps." She slapped her thighs with both hands. "So tell me, what is it you wanted to discuss with Harley after all these years?"

"Actually, I was hoping to talk a little shop with him. Harley worked on just about everyone's car in Cedar Grove, didn't he?"

"He sure did. Your father was a regular customer. Harley appreciated that about him. Such a shame what happened. Your father was such a good man."

"Do you know who Harley bought his car parts from, Carol?"

Carol Holt made a face like she'd been asked a question on quantum physics. "No. I didn't get too involved in any of that, dear. I imagine he bought them from any number of places."

"I remember he had all those cabinets in his office," Tracy said, getting to the reason for her visit.

Carol Holt threw up her hands. "That office was an abomination, but Harley didn't have a problem with it. He had his own way of doing things."

"How long ago did he close the station?"

"It was when he retired. He was hoping our son Greg might take it over, but Greg had different plans. Three, four years ago, I suppose."

"Would you happen to still have a key to the building?"

Her eyebrows arched. "I wouldn't know. I suppose it's somewhere around here. What is it you're looking for?"

"I'm curious about something, Carol. I know it sounds crazy, but I was hoping I could just take a look through Harley's records to satisfy my curiosity."

"I'd be happy to help, honey, but I'm afraid you won't find anything at the service station. Harley cleared it out when he closed it."

"I was afraid of that when I went by earlier and looked through the windows, but I thought, nothing ventured, nothing gained. Well, I better let you get back to your needlepoint, and I better get started back to Seattle."

"What about the records?"

"I'm sorry?"

"You said you wanted to go through his records."

"I thought you said he threw them out?"

"Harley? You saw his office. That man never threw out a scrap of paper in his life. You'll have to dig a bit to reach them, though."

"You have the records here?"

"Why do you think I park in the driveway? Harley brought everything from the station here and put it in the garage. He kept telling me he was going to go through them, but then he got sick and, to be honest, I haven't given them a second thought until you brought them up."

CHAPTER 32

Tracy gave up and got out of bed at just after two in the morning. During her years investigating Sarah's disappearance and murder, she'd rarely slept through the night. It had gotten better when she'd finally put the boxes in the closet, but now her insomnia had returned. Roger, her black tabby, followed her into the living room, meowing loudly.

"Yeah, well, I'm not happy to be awake either," she said. She grabbed her laptop and a down comforter, along with the remote control, and sat on the sofa in her seven-hundred-square-foot apartment in Seattle's Capitol Hill district. She hadn't rented the apartment for its amenities or its view—which was of another brick apartment building directly across the street. She'd rented it because it was the right price and in the right location for when your profession didn't include the initials "Dr." before your name but required you to live close and be frequently on call.

Roger leaped into her lap and, after a moment kneading the blanket to get comfortable, curled into a ball. Tracy reconsidered her conversation with Dan earlier that evening. After she'd told him about Maria Vanpelt and the meeting with Nolasco, Dan had broached the subject of him driving down to Seattle the upcoming

Friday, taking her to the Chihuly glass exhibit, and then getting dinner.

Since her initial visit to Cedar Grove to bury Sarah's remains, Tracy had, in the intervening weeks, made several additional trips to provide Dan with the rest of her files and go over what her investigation had revealed. She'd spent the night twice. Nothing romantic had happened between them since her impromptu golf lesson. Tracy was wondering if she had misinterpreted Dan's intentions, though *she* had certainly felt the sexual tension and didn't think she had been imagining it. A part of her wanted to act on it, but she worried that a relationship with Dan would not be wise under the circumstances. Not to mention the fact that she did not see herself ever moving back to Cedar Grove, where Dan had clearly reestablished a home. It was a complication she had decided to put aside. The Chihuly invitation, however, forced her to reconsider his possible intentions. She could not rationalize the invitation as work related, not to mention the fact that it put their sleeping arrangements at the center of a target. She only had one bedroom. Caught off guard, she'd accepted, and had spent the rest of the evening wondering if she'd made the right decision.

She fired up her laptop, pulled up the Washington State Attorney General's website, and typed her username and password to log into the Homicide Investigation Tracking System, or HITS. The searchable database contained information on more than 22,000 homicides and sexual assaults across Washington, Idaho, and Oregon that had occurred since 1981. Assuming Hansen had been murdered and hadn't died from a sex act gone horribly wrong, studies had revealed that persons who killed in such a unique manner often practiced their craft in order to perfect it. So, after the long days at the office working on the case, Tracy would drag herself home and sit at the computer running searches and reviewing cases similar to Nicole Hansen's murder.

Her initial search using the key words "motel room" had reduced the 22,000 cases to 1511. She'd added the word "rope," but not "strangulation," because she wanted to keep the search broad enough to capture cases in which the victim had been bound, though maybe not strangled. That further reduced the field of cases to 224. Of those 224, 43 of the victims had not been sexually assaulted—Nicole Hansen's autopsy had revealed no semen in her body cavities. That anomaly could be explained by the fact that it would have been a near physical impossibility to have intercourse with Hansen with her body hideously contorted and bound. Hansen had also not been robbed. Her wallet, flush with cash, had been left untouched on the motel dresser. That ruled out the second most logical motive, again assuming Hansen had been murdered.

Tracy had been focused on those forty-three cases, reviewing the HITS forms on file. After an hour, she'd considered three more of the cases. None seemed promising. She closed the laptop and leaned back against the pillows. "Like searching for a needle in a haystack, Roger." The cat was already purring.

Tracy envied him.

CHAPTER 33

Friday afternoon, Tracy's phone vibrated as she and Kins drove west across Lake Washington on the 520 floating bridge. Traffic was heavy with people trying to get downtown. Tall cranes jutted high above the darkened water on floating platforms, helping construct a badly needed second bridge parallel to the first one, but screwups in the concrete pontoons that would keep the second bridge afloat had delayed completion until sometime in 2015.

Tracy checked her most recent calls and saw that she'd missed two previous calls from Dan. She called him back.

"Hey," she said. "Sorry I missed your calls. We've been running around today tracking down witnesses and talking with experts about the rope in that murder in North Seattle."

"I got a surprise this afternoon."

"A good surprise or a bad surprise?"

"I'm not sure. I was in court most of the day, and when I got back to the office I found a copy of Vance Clark's Opposition to the Petition for Post-Conviction Relief in my fax machine."

"They filed early?"

"Apparently."

"What do you make of it?"

"Haven't read it yet. Thought I'd call you first and let you know."

"Why would he file early?"

"It could be he decided to keep it simple, make the Court of Appeals think the petition lacks merit. I won't know until I read it. Anyway, it sounds like you've got your hands full."

"Email it to me and we can talk more about it tonight at dinner."

"Yeah, about that," Dan said. "I'm sorry, but I'm going to have to cancel."

"Everything okay?"

"Yeah, just some things to take care of. Okay if I call you later?"

"Sure," Tracy said. "We'll talk tonight." She hung up, uncertain what to make of Dan breaking their date. Though initially concerned about it, she'd begun to look forward to it and where it might lead. She'd planned to buy a couple of Dick's hamburgers—the $1.39 variety—and serve them at her apartment just to tweak him.

"New development?" Kins asked.

"I'm sorry, what?"

"I said, new development?"

"They filed the opposition to the petition. We weren't expecting it for another two weeks."

"What's it mean?"

"Don't know yet," she said, still hearing the uncertainty in Dan's voice.

CHAPTER 34

Dan O'Leary tilted back his head to apply eyedrops. His contact lenses felt glued to his corneas. Outside his bay window, rain fell in the shafts of yellow light from the street lamp. He had the window open so he could listen to the storm as it rolled in from the north, bringing the sodden, earthy smell of rain. As a boy, he used to sit at his bedroom window watching for lightning strikes over the North Cascades, counting the seconds between the strike and the clap of thunder exploding across the mountain peaks. He'd wanted to be a weatherman. Sunnie had said that she thought that would be the most boring job on the planet, but Tracy had said Dan would be good on television. Tracy had always been that way, even when other kids had treated him as the dork he'd sometimes been. She'd always stood up for him.

When he'd seen her at Sarah's memorial service, alone, his heart had bled for her. He'd always envied her family, so close and loving and caring. His house had not always been that way. Then, in a relatively short period of time, Tracy had lost everything she'd loved. When he'd stepped to her side at the service, it had been as her childhood friend, but he also could not deny he had been physically attracted to her. He had given her his card in hope that she might call him, and come to see him not as the boy she'd known, but as the man he'd become. That hope had faded when she had come to his office and asked him to review her file. Strictly a business meeting.

Later, he'd invited her to his home out of concern for her safety, but seeing her again, he hadn't been able to help hoping that something might spark between them. When he'd wrapped his arms around her to putt the golf ball, something had stirred inside that he had not felt in a very long time. He'd spent the past month tempering those feelings with the realization that Tracy remained deeply wounded and was not only vulnerable, but distrustful— about Cedar Grove and everything and everyone she associated with it. Dan had suggested the Chihuly glass exhibit and dinner to remove her from that environment, then realized that he'd placed her in an awkward dilemma. Did she invite him to spend the night or did he get a hotel? He'd sensed that he was rushing her, that she wasn't ready for a relationship, and that she had enough on her plate with the recent discovery of Sarah's remains and now the potential for another emotionally draining hearing.

He'd also had professional concerns. Tracy was not his client. Edmund House was his client. But Tracy had all the information Dan needed to prepare properly for the post-conviction relief hearing, should a court of appeals grant House that right. Under the circumstances, Dan thought it best to remove any undue pressure on Tracy and bow out of their date until they were both in a better place and time.

Sherlock grunted and twitched, asleep beside Rex on the throw rug in front of Dan's desk. Dan had begun bringing the dogs to work after Calloway's threat to impound them. He didn't mind. They were good company, except for the fact that every noise caused them to bolt upright and race into the reception area barking. For the moment, at least, they were quiet.

He refocused on Vance Clark's Opposition to the Petition for Post-Conviction Relief. His intuition that Clark had filed his opposition early in order to insinuate to the Court of Appeals that the petition had no merit had been correct. Clark had kept his arguments simple. He'd stated that the petition failed to show any impropriety in the prior proceedings that would warrant a hearing to determine if Edmund House should get a new trial. He reminded the Court that House had been the first individual in the state of Washington to be convicted of first-degree murder based solely on circumstantial evidence because House had refused to tell authorities where he'd buried Sarah Crosswhite's body, though he'd confessed to killing her. Clark had written that House had instead tried to use the information as leverage to force a plea, and that he should not now benefit from that strategy. Had House advised authorities of the location of Sarah Crosswhite's body twenty years ago, Clark concluded, any exculpatory evidence could have been introduced during his trial. Of course House had not done so because it would have been conclusive evidence that he'd committed the crime. Either way, House was guilty. He'd received a fair trial. Nothing that Dan had introduced in his petition for post-conviction relief changed that.

Not a bad argument, except it was completely circular, premised upon a court accepting that House had confessed to the murder and used the location of the body as leverage for a lesser sentence. DeAngelo Finn had done a poor job cross-examining Calloway on the lack of a signed or taped confession, which would have been any defense attorney's first plan of attack. Finn had compounded his mistake by putting House on the witness stand to deny confessing, which had put his credibility at stake and allowed the prosecution to successfully argue that House's prior rape conviction was now fair game, allowing them to question him about it at his trial. That had been the death knell. Once a rapist, always a rapist. Finn should have moved to exclude the introduction of

House's alleged confession as suspect due to the lack of any sup-porting evidence and highly prejudicial to House's case, avoiding the entire fiasco. Even if the motion had been denied, House would have established strong grounds for an appeal. Finn's failure to do so, regardless of the exculpatory evidence found at the grave, was itself a basis for a new trial.

Sherlock rolled and lifted his head. A second later, someone rang the reception bell.

Sherlock's nails clicked on the hardwood, Rex close behind, followed by a chorus of barks and baying. Dan checked his watch, started for the door, then paused to pick up the autographed Ken Griffey, Jr., baseball bat that he'd also started bringing to the office.

CHAPTER 35

Sherlock and Rex had pinned an African-American man with his back against the door. The man looked and sounded seriously intimidated. "The sign said to ring the bell."

"Off," Dan said, and both dogs obediently stopped barking and sat. "How'd you get in?"

"The door was unlocked."

Dan had taken Sherlock and Rex out earlier in the evening to conduct their nightly business. "Who are you?"

The man eyed the dogs. "My name is George Bovine, Mr. O'Leary." Dan recognized the name from Tracy's files even before Bovine continued, "Edmund House raped my daughter, Annabelle."

Dan leaned the baseball bat against the side of the reception desk. Thirty years earlier, Edmund House had been convicted on a charge of sex with a minor and served a six-year sentence. George Bovine had testified during the sentencing phase of House's trial, after his conviction for the murder of Sarah Crosswhite. "What are you doing here at this time of night?"

"I drove from Eureka."

"California?"

Bovine nodded. Soft-spoken, he looked to be in his late sixties, with a gray, close-cropped beard and studious tortoiseshell glasses. He wore a maroon golf cap and a V-neck sweater beneath a jacket.

"Why?"

"Because this is a matter to be handled in person. I intended to try to see you tomorrow morning. I only stopped by to make sure I had the correct address, and saw the lights in the window. The door to the building was unlocked, and when I came upstairs, I noticed the lights that I'd seen from the street were coming from your suite."

"Fair enough, but it doesn't answer my question. Why did you drive all this way, Mr. Bovine?"

"Sheriff Calloway called me. He says you're attempting to secure a new trial for Edmund House."

Dan began to understand where this was headed, though he was surprised Bovine had been so forthright. "How do you know the Sheriff?"

"I testified at Edmund House's sentencing."

"I know. I've read the transcript. Did Sheriff Calloway ask you to convince me not to represent Mr. House?"

"No. He simply told me you were seeking a new trial. I've come on my own."

"You understand why I have trouble believing that."

"All I ask is for a chance to speak with you. I'll say my piece. I won't say it twice. Then I'll leave you be."

Dan considered the request. He was skeptical, but Bovine sounded sincere. He'd also just driven eight hours and not tried to hide the purpose for his visit. "You understand I have a confidential relationship with my client."

"I understand, Mr. O'Leary. I'm not interested in what Edmund House has to say."

O'Leary nodded. "My office is in the back." He snapped his fingers and the two dogs turned and sped down the hall. Inside

Dan's office, they retook their spots on the throw rug but remained upright and alert, ears perked.

Bovine removed his jacket, still glistening with drops of rain, and hung it on the rarely used coatrack near the door. "They're awfully large, aren't they?"

"You should see my food bill," Dan said. "Can I offer you a cup of stale coffee?"

"Yes, please. It's been a long drive."

"How do you take it?"

"Black," Bovine said.

Dan poured a cup and handed him a mug and the two men settled into chairs at the table beneath the window overlooking Market Street. When Bovine raised his mug to take a sip of coffee, Dan noticed a tremor in his hand. Outside the window, the rain sheeted across the sky and beat hard on the flat roof, pinging as it funneled through the gutters and downspouts. Bovine lowered his mug and reached into his back pocket to remove his wallet. His hands shook even more as he struggled to pull photographs from their plastic slips, and Dan wondered if perhaps he had Parkinson's disease. Bovine set one of the photographs on the table. "This is Annabelle."

His daughter looked to be in her early twenties, with straight dark hair and skin lighter than her father's. Her blue eyes also indicated a mixed-race heritage. But it was not the color of Annabelle Bovine's skin or her eyes that caught Dan's attention. It was her utterly flat expression. She looked like a cardboard cutout.

"You'll notice the scar descending from her eyebrow."

A thin line, barely detectable, curved from Annabelle's eyebrow to her jaw in the shape of a sickle.

"Edmund House told the police he and my daughter had consensual sex." Bovine placed a second photograph beside the first. The young girl in it was almost unrecognizable, her left eye swollen shut, the cut on her face caked in blood. Dan knew from Tracy's file that House had raped Bovine when she was sixteen. Bovine started to lift his mug but his shakes had become more pronounced and he lowered it back to the table. Then he closed his eyes and took several measured breaths.

Dan gave the man a moment before he said, "I don't know what to say, Mr. Bovine."

"He hit her with a shovel, Mr. O'Leary." He paused again and took another breath, but this time it was sharp and rattled in his chest. "You see, Edmund House was not content to just rape my daughter. He wanted to hurt her, and he would have continued to hurt her had she not found the will to escape."

Bovine's face inched into a resigned grimace. He removed his glasses, wiping the lenses with a red handkerchief. "Six years. Six years for ruining a young woman's life because someone made a mistake gathering the evidence. Annabelle was a bright, outgoing young woman. We had to move; the memories were too horrific. Annabelle never returned to school. She cannot work. We live on a quiet street not far from the water in a quiet town with little crime. It's peaceful there. And every night we deadbolt our doors and check every window. It's our routine. Then we climb in bed and we wait. My wife and I wait for her screams. They call it Rape Trauma Syndrome. Edmund House served six years. We've served nearly thirty."

Dan recalled similar testimony from the sentencing transcript, but hearing a father's anguish brought the impact home. "I'm sorry. No one should have to live that way."

Bovine's mouth pinched. "But someone will, Mr. O'Leary, if you do what they say you're attempting to do."

"Sheriff Calloway shouldn't have called you, Mr. Bovine. It isn't fair to either of us. I don't mean to in any way diminish what happened to your daughter or your family—"

Bovine raised a hand but did so in the same understated manner that he spoke. "You're going to tell me that Edmund House was a young man when he raped my daughter, that it occurred nearly thirty years ago, that people can change." The thin-lipped, ironic smile returned. "Let me save you the trouble." Bovine looked to Sherlock and Rex. "Edmund House is not like your dogs. He cannot be trained. And he cannot be called off."

"But he does deserve a fair trial, just like everyone else."

"But he's not like everyone else, Mr. O'Leary. Prison is the only place for violent men like Edmund House. And make no mistake. Edmund House is a very violent man." Bovine quietly picked up the photographs and slipped them back in his wallet. "I said my piece. I won't take up any more of your time." He stood and retrieved his jacket. "Thank you for the coffee."

"You have a place to stay?" Dan asked.

"I've made arrangements."

Dan walked George Bovine back to the reception area. Bovine pulled open the door but looked back again at Rex and Sherlock. "Tell me, would they have bitten me if you hadn't called them off?"

Dan petted them about their heads. "Their size is intimidating, but their bark is worse than their bite."

"But still very much capable of causing damage, I'd imagine," Bovine said, stepping into the hall, the door swinging shut behind him.

CHAPTER 36

Tracy was running on fumes, unable to recall the last time she'd slept through the night. She felt the fatigue in her limbs and heard it in her voice as she and Kins sat in the conference room with Faz and Del, updating Billy Williams and Andrew Laub on the A Team's active files.

During the weeks since Dan had filed his reply brief to Vance Clark's Opposition to the Petition for Post-Conviction Relief, Tracy and Kins had retraced many of their steps in the Nicole Hansen investigation without success. They'd re-interviewed the motel owner and motel guests. They'd run latent fingerprints lifted from the motel room through King County's Automated Fingerprint Identification System and run down hits, crossing off persons with lock-tight alibis as potential suspects. They'd spoken again to the dancers at the Dancing Bare, to Nicole Hansen's family, to her friends, to a couple of ex-boyfriends. Tracy had created a timeline of the last few days of Hansen's life and had identified any person with whom she'd come into contact. They'd also executed search warrants that had been spectacularly unproductive.

"What about the employee files?" Laub asked.

"They came in late yesterday afternoon," Tracy said, referring to the files they'd subpoenaed of current and past Dancing Bare employees. "I got Ron getting a head start on them," she said, meaning the A Team's fifth wheel, Ron Mayweather. Each of the four Homicide teams had a fifth detective assigned to them for carrying out some of the more mundane tasks of investigative work.

Laub turned to Faz. "Where are we on the cars in the parking lots?"

Faz shook his head. "We got bubkes," he said. "We're still running down an out-of-state plate in California and one up in British Columbia. We're making nice to our buddies across the border."

"Anything on HITS?" Laub asked.

Tracy shook her head. "No."

When the meeting broke up, Tracy was craving caffeine, but Williams met her at the door. "Hang out a minute," he said, and she suspected she knew why.

When they were alone, Williams said, "Vanpelt's show last night created a shit storm. You can expect another phone call."

Vanpelt's early Christmas present had been an hour-long report profiling Edmund House, Cedar Grove, and Tracy on her show, KRIX Undercover. Vanpelt had spliced historical photographs of the town with photographs of Tracy, Sarah, their parents, and Edmund House. She'd used interviews of Cedar Grove residents discussing how Sarah's disappearance had shattered the town's bucolic existence, the emotional impact the trial had had on the town, and how they felt about the possibility of going through it all over again. No one was happy about having their lives dragged back through the media mud.

Tracy leaned against the conference room table. "I thought it might," she said to Williams. "How bad is it?"

"Media fielded two dozen requests for interviews from the local and national media, and that was before the Seattle Times ran the story on the front page this morning. They want an interview. So do CNN, MSNBC, and half a dozen others."

"I'm not doing it, Billy. It won't end the inquiries. It will only heighten the attention."

"Laub and I agree," Williams said. "And we've told Nolasco as much."

"Yeah? What did he say?"

"He said, 'what do we do if House gets a new hearing?'"

—

Nolasco rarely looked happy, but that afternoon when Tracy entered the conference room he was scowling like he'd received Botox injections while constipated. Lee again sat beside him, his chin resting on the palm of his hand and his eyes locked on a single sheet of paper on the table, no doubt another statement they'd ask Tracy to sign. She just couldn't seem to keep from disappointing them.

"What's the status of the Hansen investigation?" Nolasco asked, before Tracy had the chance to sit. Tracy didn't think for a minute Nolasco had called the meeting to discuss the Hansen case.

"Not much different from when we spoke last night," she said, pulling out a chair.

"And what are you doing to change that?"

"At the moment I'm sitting in here, so not much."

"Maybe it's time we brought in the FBI."

"I'd rather work with a Boy Scout troop." In Homicide, FBI stood for "Famous But Idiots."

"Then I suggest you get me something to take upstairs."

Tracy bit her tongue as Nolasco gave a nod to Lee, who reached below the table and retrieved a half-inch-thick stack of paper.

"We started getting these just after Ms. Vanpelt signed off last night," Nolasco said, sliding the stack to her. Tracy flipped through copies of e-mails and transcribed phone messages. They weren't pretty. Some called her unfit to wear the uniform. Others asked for her head on a platter.

"They want to know why a Seattle homicide detective sworn to serve and protect the public is working to free a piece of shit like Edmund House," Nolasco said.

"These are the haters," Tracy said. "They live for this. Are we going to start making decisions to appease the fringe now?"

"The *Seattle Times*, NBC, CBS, are they also the fringe?"

"We've been through this. They're interested in sound bites and ratings."

"Maybe," Nolasco said, "but in light of recent events, we believe it prudent the department issue a statement on your behalf."

"We've prepared something for your consideration," Lee said.

"Consideration," Nolasco said. "Not approval."

Tracy motioned for Lee to slide the single sheet of paper across the table, though she had no intention of signing anything. They could issue what they wanted. They couldn't make her attach her name to it.

> Detective Crosswhite has had no official role in
> the investigation or in the proceedings to obtain
> Post-Conviction Relief for Edmund House. Should
> Detective Crosswhite be called upon to participate
> in these proceedings, it will be as a member of the
> victim's family. She has not, and will not, officially
> or unofficially use her position as a Seattle homi-
> cide detective to influence the proceedings in any
> manner. She will have no comment on the pro-
> ceedings or the results of those proceedings now or
> in the future.

She slid it back. "First you want me to comment. Now you're forbidding it? I don't even know what this means."

"It means you will testify if subpoenaed," Nolasco said. "That will be your only involvement. You are not to serve in any manner as a consultant for the defense."

"Involvement in what?" She glanced to Laub and Williams, but they looked as confused as Tracy felt.

"We thought you knew," Nolasco said, looking suddenly uneasy.

"Knew what?"

"The Court of Appeals granted Edmund House's Petition for Post-Conviction Relief."

—

Kins stood as Tracy hurried back to her cubicle to gather her things. "What happened?"

Tracy slipped on her coat, still not fully comprehending what she'd just heard. She'd waited twenty years, but now it seemed as if everything was moving too fast. She was having trouble processing it.

"Tracy?"

"The Court of Appeals granted the petition," she said. "Nolasco just told me."

"How the hell did he know?"

"I don't know. I need to call Dan." She grabbed her phone from her desk and started from the bull pen.

"When's the hearing?"

"I don't know that either." She rushed to catch the elevator, seeking a private place to call Dan and take a moment alone to absorb everything. She felt like she'd taken a punch to the head and was still clearing cobwebs. The post-conviction relief hearing was the platform Tracy needed to demonstrate that the inconsistencies in the testimony and the evidence introduced at Edmund House's first trial raised serious questions about his guilt. If Dan could get a judge to agree, the court would be forced to order a new trial, bringing Tracy one giant step closer to getting the investigation into Sarah's death re-opened.

As the elevator descended, she squeezed her eyes shut. After twenty years, Sarah might finally get justice, and Tracy might finally get answers.

PART II

. . . there is nothing so dangerous as a maxim.
—C. J. May, "Some Rules of Evidence: Reasonable
Doubt in Civil and Criminal Cases" (1876)

CHAPTER 37

Judge Burleigh Meyers chose to hold the preliminary hearing in the temporary chambers assigned to him rather than open court because of what he called "the significant media interest in the matter." Dan had asked for, and Meyers had agreed to, Tracy's presence at the hearing, though Meyers noted it was an unusual request for defense counsel. He was clearly familiar with the nuances of the case. Dan's background check of Meyers indicated that that was no accident.

Meyers had served more than thirty years on the bench in Spokane County, mostly to critical acclaim, before retiring. The Spokane County Bar Association gave him high marks for the manner in which he had conducted himself and his courtroom. Dan had also learned that both Meyers's clerk and bailiff had retired rather than be assigned to work for another judge, which he took as a good sign. He'd found home numbers for each and called to pick their brains. They had both described Meyers as a man who worked long hours, conducted much of his own research, and who could agonize for days over his decisions, though he was not afraid to pull the trigger. He was what Dan and Tracy had hoped for, an intelligent judge willing to make a tough call. They also said

Meyers ran a tight ship and would not be influenced by the media attention, which was likely why the Court of Appeals had asked him to preside over the hearing.

Tracy sat off to the side watching as Meyers wheeled the leather chair from behind the desk, its wheel squeaking. He positioned it so he faced O'Leary and Clark, who sat side by side on a cloth sofa. To Tracy the office had the feel of an austere stage production, the walls devoid of any paintings or photographs and not a scrap of paper to be found anywhere in the room. Dan had told her that Meyers's clerk had also said the judge's willingness to come out of retirement was definitely not because he was bored. Apparently Meyers owned a sixty-acre cattle ranch and did much of the heavy lifting himself.

Tracy guessed Meyers to be six four and ruggedly handsome, with the robust, weathered skin of someone who kept in shape mending fences, making barn repairs, and lugging hay bales. With silver hair and crystal-blue eyes, Tracy thought he looked a bit like Paul Newman.

"I accepted this assignment on one condition," Meyers said. He wore slippers, and when he crossed his legs, his blue jeans inched up to reveal argyle socks. "My wife loves the sun and she loves to ride. So I tow a two-horse trailer all over the western states in search of both. She plans to be on a trail ride in Phoenix at the end of the month, gentlemen. And let me tell you, my wife does not like to be disappointed, and I really don't like to disappoint her. In other words, I may be semi-retired, but that does not mean I have time to waste. I intend to move this matter forward expeditiously."

"The defense is prepared to do just that, Your Honor," Dan said.

Clark looked troubled. "Your Honor, I have several other matters on my calendar, including an upcoming trial—"

Meyers cut him off quickly. "While I am sympathetic to your schedule, Mr. Clark, the statute requires the prosecuting attorney to obtain a *prompt* evidentiary hearing. I'd suggest you clear your calendar and give this matter top priority. As for your scheduled trial, I have already spoken to Judge Wilber and he has agreed to kick it over a month."

Clark sighed. "Thank you, Your Honor."

"Will the defense seek to conduct any pre-trial discovery?" Meyers asked.

Tracy's file had more information than Dan ever could have gathered on his own, including the trial transcripts and Kelly Rosa's forensic report. He'd told her that further depositions would only serve to delay the proceedings and give subpoenaed witnesses the chance to become conveniently unavailable, or think through their prior testimony and come up with something new. He also did not want to further educate Clark on how he intended to attack the State's witnesses' previous trial testimony.

"The defense is prepared to move forward," he said.

"The prosecution would like to conduct depositions," Clark said. "We are compiling a list."

"Your Honor," Dan said, "the prosecution cannot put on new evidence in this hearing and the defense intends to call just the State's witnesses from Mr. House's initial trial. The only new witnesses will be the medical examiner, to testify concerning the forensics from the grave, and a DNA expert. I see no reason why the prosecutor cannot speak to their witnesses on their own time. We're also happy to make our expert available after hours."

"Mr. Clark?"

Vance Clark sat up. "We will endeavor to speak to the witnesses," he said.

"Any pre-hearing motions?" Meyers asked.

"The prosecution moves to exclude Detective Crosswhite from the courtroom," Clark said.

Tracy glanced at Dan. "On what grounds?" Dan asked.

"Detective Crosswhite will be a witness for the defense," Clark said to Meyers. "As such, she should not be allowed in the courtroom until such time as she has testified, just as any other witness."

"Detective Crosswhite is not a witness for the defense," Dan said. "She is the decedent's sister. We expect her testimony will be factual and pertain to the events of the day her sister disappeared. The State can talk to her whenever they want. Moreover, Detective Crosswhite is not like any other witness. I would have assumed the State would want Detective Crosswhite—"

Meyers cut him off. "Mr. O'Leary, you will try your case and allow the State to make its own decisions." He waved off a response by Clark. "I'm going to deny the motion, Mr. Clark. Detective Crosswhite has a right to be present as a member of the deceased's family, and I fail to see how it will prejudice the State's prosecution of this matter. Now, one other subject: We all know the significant media attention that has been given to this matter. I will not allow this to become a spectacle or a zoo. The reporters have a right to be present, and I have agreed to a single camera feed. While I am not going to impose a gag order on either of you or your witnesses, I am going to appeal to your oath as officers of this court that you will adjudicate this matter before me, not the media. Am I making myself clear?"

Clark and Dan verbally acknowledged Meyers's admonition. Meyers seemed pleased. He clasped his hands as if to lead them in solemn prayer. "Well, then, since we are all present and accounted for, and I've been given that behemoth of a courtroom out there at the taxpayers' expense, I'm going to suggest we begin bright and early Monday morning. Do I hear any objections?"

Having been forewarned of the potential wrath of a woman forced to forego her horseback ride, neither Dan nor Clark voiced any.

CHAPTER 38

DeAngelo Finn knelt in the soil with his back to the sidewalk, unaware that he was being watched. The cloud layer had lifted, and the respite from the persistent rain had provided an opportunity for Finn to put his vegetable garden to bed for the winter. Tracy watched him as she finished talking to Kins, who'd called to tell her that Nolasco had officially transferred the Nicole Hansen case to the Cold File Division.

"He pulled it from us?" Tracy asked.

"It's a power play. He doesn't want it on the section's books. He said we can't devote the manpower to a file going nowhere. Between you being gone and my workload, there just aren't enough bodies to go around."

"Shit, I'm sorry, Kins."

"Don't sweat it. I'll still work the edges, but Nolasco's right. We've exhausted our leads. Unless something comes up there's no place else to go."

Tracy felt a twinge of remorse. She knew from experience that, until the killer was found and convicted, Hansen's family would have no closure.

"You do what you need to do," Kins said. "The work will be here when you get back, unfortunately. Death and taxes, my father used to say. Those are the two things you can count on. Death and taxes. Keep me posted on what happens."

"Likewise." Tracy disconnected and took a moment before stepping from the car. The sun was bright enough that she donned sunglasses, though the temperature remained cool enough that each breath marked the air as she approached the gate in the picket fence. She had not detected any reaction from DeAngelo when she'd parked or when she closed the car door and detected none now.

"Mr. Finn?"

The gloves bunched around Finn's fingertips as he struggled to grip another weed.

She raised her voice. "Mr. Finn?"

He turned his head and she saw the hearing aid attached to the arm of his glasses. Finn hesitated before removing his gloves and setting them on the ground. He adjusted his glasses and reached for a cane at his side, unsteady as he got to his feet and approached the fence. He was bundled in a knit Mariners ski cap and a matching team jacket that hung from his shoulders like a hand-me-down from an older brother. Twenty years ago, Finn had been on the heavy side. Now he looked rail thin. Thick lenses magnified his eyes and made them appear watery.

"It's Tracy Crosswhite," she said, removing her sunglasses.

Finn gave no initial indication that he recognized her or her name. Then, slowly, he smiled and pushed open the gate. "Tracy," he said. "Of course. I'm sorry. I don't see too well anymore. I have cataracts, you know."

"Getting the garden ready for winter?" she said, stepping into the yard. "I remember my father doing the same thing every fall—pulling the weeds, adding fertilizer to the soil, and covering the beds with black plastic."

"If you don't get the weeds in the winter they go to seed," he said. "Surest way to ruin a spring garden."

"I remember my father saying something similar."

Finn gave her an envious smile and reached out to touch her arm, leaning in to speak conspiratorially. "No one could compete with your father's tomatoes. He had that greenhouse, you know."

"I remember."

"I told him it was cheating, but he said I was welcome to bring my plants over anytime. He was a prince of a man, your father."

She looked about the tiny plot of soil. "What do you grow?"

"A little of this and a little of that. I give most of it to the neighbors. It's just me now. Millie died, you know."

She didn't know, but she assumed that had been the case. Finn's wife had already had health issues twenty years ago, when Tracy's father had cared for her. "I'm sorry," she said. "How are you doing?"

"Come on inside and visit," he said. Finn had trouble lifting his legs to climb the three concrete steps to the back door, a task that left him winded and flushed. Tracy also noticed a tremor in his hands when he unzipped his jacket and hung it on a hook inside the mudroom. Vance Clark's motion to quash Dan's subpoena to have Finn testify at the hearing had been accompanied by a doctor's report. According to the report, Finn had a heart condition, emphysema, and a host of other physical ailments that made the stress of testifying injurious to his already precarious health.

Finn led her into a kitchen that time had not touched. Dark wood cabinets made a contrast to the bright floral wallpaper and pumpkin-colored Formica. Finn moved a stack of newspapers and a bundle of mail from a chair to make a place for Tracy to sit at the table, then filled a kettle at the faucet and set it on a Wedgewood stove. She noticed a portable oxygen machine in the corner and felt heat blasting from the floor vents. The room held the odor of fried meat. A greasy cast-iron skillet sat on the front burner.

"Can I help with something?" she said.

He waved her off, pulled two mugs from a cabinet and dropped in tea bags, making small talk. When he opened the refrigerator door, she saw mostly empty shelves inside. "I don't keep much in the house. I don't get many visitors."

"I should have called," she said.

"But you were afraid I might not wish to speak to you." He peered at her over the top of his mottled lenses. "I'm old, Tracy. I don't see or hear too well anymore, but I still read the newspaper every morning. I don't imagine you came by to ask about my garden."

"No," she said. "I came by to talk to you about the hearing."

"You came by to see if I really was too sick to testify."

"You look like you're getting around all right."

"You have good days and bad days when you get to be my age," Finn said. "And you never can predict which it's going to be."

"How old are you, Mr. Finn?"

"Please, Tracy, I feel like I've known you since you were born. Call me DeAngelo. And to answer your question, I'll be eighty-eight in the spring." He rapped knuckles on the counter. "God willing." He fixed his eyes on her. "And if not, I'll get to see my Millie, and that's not a bad thing, you know."

"Edmund House was your last trial, wasn't it?"

"I haven't seen the inside of a courtroom in twenty years, and I don't intend to ever see one again."

Steam whistled from the spout of the kettle, and Finn shuffled about to fill both mugs. Tracy declined cream or sugar. Finn set the mugs on the table and sat across from her dunking his tea bag. The mug shook when he raised it to take a sip. "Millie's health had already been in decline. I hadn't intended to take any more trials."

"Why did you?"

"Judge Lawrence asked me to defend Edmund House as a favor. No one else would. When the trial ended, I came home. Millie and

I thought we'd share a few years together, do those things we'd put off because I was always in court. Travel a bit. Life doesn't work out the way we plan, does it?"

"Do you remember the trial?"

"You want to know if I did my best for that young man."

"You were a good lawyer, DeAngelo. My father always said that about you."

Finn gave her a wry smile. Tracy could not help but think it held a secret—and the knowledge that no one was going to force an eighty-eight-year-old man with a bad heart and emphysema to testify. "I have no guilt or misgivings about how I handled that matter."

"That doesn't answer the question."

"We're not always entitled to the answers."

"Why not in this instance?"

"Because the answers can be hurtful."

"My family's gone too, DeAngelo. It's just me."

His gaze lost focus. "Your father always treated me with respect. Not everyone did. I didn't come from one of those prestigious law schools and I'm not exactly cut from the textbook image of a trial attorney, but your father always respected me and he was so very kind to my Millie. I appreciated that, more than you will ever know."

"Enough to throw your final case if he asked?"

It had always been her theory that her father, not Calloway or Clark, had orchestrated Edmund House's conviction. Finn didn't flinch. He placed his hand atop hers and gave it a gentle squeeze. Finn's hand was small and spotted with age. "I'm not going to try to dissuade you from what you've come back to do. I understand there is a part of you that clings to your sister and to a different time. We all cling to that time, Tracy, but it doesn't mean we're going to get it back. Things change. As do we. And many things changed the day your sister disappeared, for all of us. But I'm so very glad you stopped by this afternoon to visit."

Tracy had her answer. If Finn had been part of a conspiracy to frame Edmund House, he would take it to his grave. They made small talk about Cedar Grove and the people who'd lived there for another twenty minutes. Then Tracy pushed back her chair. "I appreciate the cup of tea, DeAngelo."

Finn walked her through the mudroom to the back door, and she stepped out onto the small porch, feeling the discrepancy between the warm house and the cool air and smelling the rich odor of the fertilizer DeAngelo had been adding to the soil. She thanked him again, but as she turned to leave, he reached out and rested his hand on her arm.

"Tracy," he said. "Be careful. Sometimes our questions *are* better left unanswered."

"There's no one left to hurt, DeAngelo."

"But there is," he said, and he gave her that gentle smile again as he stepped back and shut the door.

—

Tracy picked at a carton of chicken in black bean sauce with chopsticks. Reams of paper, yellow legal pads and trial transcripts, lay strewn across Dan's kitchen table. They'd taken a break to eat and to watch the evening news. Dan had muted the sound while they talked.

"He didn't even disagree with me," Tracy said, recounting her conversation with DeAngelo Finn again. "He just said he had no guilt or misgivings."

"But he didn't say he defended him to the best of his abilities."

"No, he definitely didn't say that."

"We don't really need him to prove he did not defend House to an acceptable standard," Dan said, reading an article on the front page of the *Seattle Times* on the impending hearing. The *Times* had run a comprehensive story, along with Sarah's senior year class picture, a twenty-year-old photo of Edmund House, and a more recent photograph of Tracy. The Associated Press had picked up the story and run it in dozens of newspapers across the country, including *USA Today* and the *Wall Street Journal.*

"There was something more there, Dan." She spiked her chopsticks in the carton and sat back. Rex padded over and stuck his head in her lap, a rare sign of affection. "You need some attention?" she asked, rubbing his head.

"Careful. He's a master manipulator. What he wants is some chicken."

She scratched Rex behind the ears. Sherlock, not to be left out, attempted to nuzzle Rex out of the way. "Are you still thinking about opening with Calloway?"

Dan folded the newspaper and set it on the table. "Right out of the chute."

"My guess is he'll feign a lack of memory and refer you to his testimony at trial."

"I'm counting on it. I intend to pick apart his testimony." Dan snapped his fingers and pointed, and the two dogs dutifully went into the family room and lay on the rug. "The more he evades answering my questions the better. I just need to pin him down and let the testimony of the other witnesses discredit him. And if I can get under his skin, he might just say more than he otherwise would."

"He does have a temper." She glanced at the television. "Hang on. That's Vanpelt."

Maria Vanpelt stood on the sidewalk outside the Cascade County Courthouse, the bronze letters on the sandstone visible over her right shoulder. Dan followed Tracy to the couch, picked up the remote, and hit the "Mute" button as Vanpelt strolled toward the courthouse steps while noting how she had been the one who "broke" the story of Tracy Crosswhite's involvement in securing Edmund House a hearing.

"She makes it sound like Watergate, doesn't she?" Dan said.

At the base of the courthouse steps, Vanpelt pivoted and faced the camera. In the background, Tracy detected multiple news vans parked along the street nearest the courthouse entrance, staking out territory.

"It seems it is not just Edmund House on trial here, but the entire town of Cedar Grove. The question remains—what really happened all those years ago? The disappearance of a prominent doctor's daughter. A massive search. The dramatic arrest of a paroled rapist. And a sensational murder trial that may have put an innocent man behind bars. Neither side is talking tonight, but we'll all know soon enough. The hearing of Edmund House begins tomorrow morning, and I'll be there, inside the courtroom, bringing you up-to-the-moment reports on the day's events."

Vanpelt looked one last time over her shoulder to the courthouse before signing off.

Dan muted the television again. "It looks like you've managed to do what no one else could."

"What's that?"

"Make Cedar Grove relevant again. It's been mentioned on every news show and in every major newspaper in the country. And, I'm told, every hotel between Cedar Grove and the courthouse is full. People are renting out rooms in their homes."

"I think she's got more to do with that than I do," Tracy said, referring to Vanpelt. "She's wrong about the trial having been sensational, though. I remember it as almost boring. Vance Clark was methodical and plodding, and I recall DeAngelo as competent but subdued, like he was resigned to the outcome."

"Maybe he was."

"In fact, I remember a strange detachment by the whole town, as if no one wanted to be there but felt an obligation to attend. I've often wondered if my father had something to do with that also, whether he made some calls so the judge and jury would see the support for Sarah and the impact the crime had on the town."

"Like he wanted to ensure the jury didn't hesitate when it came time to sentence House."

She nodded. "He didn't believe in the death penalty, but he wanted House to get life without parole. I remember that. But he seemed more detached than anyone."

"How so?"

"My father was a note taker. I remember he'd take notes of even casual phone conversations. During the trial he kept a note-pad on his lap, but he never wrote a single word." Dan glanced at her. "Not one," she said.

Dan ran a hand over a day's growth of stubble on his chin. "How are you holding up?"

"Me? I'm fine."

He seemed to give her answer consideration. "You never let your guard down, do you?"

"I don't have a guard up." She stepped to the kitchen, clearing cartons from the table to make room so they could get back to work.

Dan leaned against the counter, watching her. "Tracy, you're talking to a guy that had his guard up for two years so no one would see how much my ex-wife had hurt me."

"I think we should concentrate on the case and psychoanalyze Tracy some other time."

He pushed away from the counter. "Okay."

She set down a carton. "What do you want me to say, Dan? Do you want me to go to pieces and break down and cry? What good is that going to do?"

He raised both hands in mock surrender, pulled out his chair at the kitchen table, and sat. "I just thought it might help to talk."

She stepped toward him. "Talk about what? Talk about Sarah's disappearance? Talk about my father putting a shotgun in his mouth? I don't need to talk about it, Dan. I lived it."

"All I asked was how you're doing."

"And I said I was fine. Do you want to be my psychiatrist, too?"

His eyes narrowed. "No, I don't. I don't want to be your psychiatrist. But I would like to be your friend again."

Dan's answer caught her off guard. She approached where he was sitting. "Why would you say that?"

"Because what I feel like is your lawyer and that's causing me enough ethical turmoil. Be honest. Would you have given me the time of day if I hadn't told you I was a lawyer that day at Sarah's funeral?"

"That's not fair."

"Why not?"

"Because it isn't personal."

"I know. You've made that clear also." He opened his laptop.

She moved her chair closer to his and sat. She'd known this moment would come, when they would try to clarify their relationship. She just hadn't thought it would be the night before the hearing. But now that it was before them, she saw no reason not to get it said and done. "I didn't want to give anyone in Cedar Grove the time of day, Dan. It wasn't just you. I didn't want to be back here."

He typed, not looking at her. "I get it. I understand."

Tracy reached out and put her hand over the keyboard. Dan sat back. "I just want this to be over," she said. "You can understand that, can't you? Once it's over, then I can move on with my life, all of my life."

"Of course I can understand it. But Tracy, I can't guarantee you that's going to happen."

His words had an uncharacteristic edge and she realized the stress Dan was also enduring. He'd borne it so well Tracy had forgotten that tomorrow morning, he was not just stepping into a courtroom, but one that would likely be filled with a hostile audience and media throng, and doing so on behalf of a childhood friend who had been on a twenty-year quest for that moment.

"I'm sorry, Dan. I didn't mean to put any undue pressure on you. I know this has been stressful, especially living here again. And I know there are no guarantees."

He kept his voice soft. "Judge Meyers could deny House a new trial. He could grant it. Either way, you could be no closer to knowing what happened than you are right now."

"That's not true. The hearing will expose the inconsistencies. It will make public what I've known privately all these years, that things at the first trial were not as they seemed."

"I'm worried about you, Tracy. What are you going to do then? What if you still can't convince anyone to reopen the investigation?"

She'd asked herself the same question many times, but she still didn't have a ready answer. Outside, a gust of wind rattled the window, causing Rex and Sherlock to raise their heads, ears perked and faces curious.

"I don't know." She shrugged and gave him a wistful smile. "There, I said it. Okay? I don't know what I'll do. I'm trying to take this one day at a time, one step at a time."

"Can I give you a suggestion, from experience?"

She shrugged. "Sure."

"The first thing you need to do is stop blaming yourself for what happened."

Tracy closed her eyes and felt a lump in her throat. "I should have driven her home that night, Dan. I never should have left her alone."

"And I kept telling myself, if I'd been home more, my wife wouldn't have been sleeping with my partner."

"It's not the same thing, Dan."

"No, it isn't. But you're blaming yourself for something you didn't do. My wife broke our marriage vows, and whoever killed Sarah is responsible for her death. Not you."

"She was my responsibility."

"Nobody took better care of a sister than you, Tracy. No one."

"Not that night. I didn't take care of her that night. I was mad at her for letting me win and I didn't insist that she come with us." Her voice cracked. She fought back tears. "I live with that every day. This hearing, this is my way of taking care of her, my way of making up for leaving her alone that night. I don't know what's going to happen, Dan, but I need to know what *did* happen. That's all I'm asking. After that, I'll take it from there."

Rex got up and padded to the front window, placing his paws on the sash and peering out into the yard. Dan pushed away from the table and out of his chair. "I better let them out." He started into the family room. "What is it, boy? You need to go out and take care of business?"

Tracy looked out the window facing the yard. Soft landscape lights lit the flowerbeds and lawn, reflecting in the glass and making it difficult to see the shadow that stepped out from behind the trunk of the tree at the edge of the property.

"Dan!"

The front window exploded.

Tracy knocked back her chair and managed to half tackle, half drag Dan to the floor. She held him down, waiting for additional gunfire. None came. Outside, a truck engine revved. Tires squealed. Tracy rolled off Dan, grabbed the Glock from her purse, flung open the front door, and raced across the lawn. The vehicle had sped to the end of the block, too far for her to catch, too far for her to see a license plate. When it slowed to take the turn, however, she noticed that only the right brake light lit up.

When she rushed back into the house, Dan was on his knees with towels, frantically trying to stanch Rex's bleeding as the big dog's fur matted with blood.

CHAPTER 39

Tracy lowered the tailgate on Dan's Tahoe while speaking into her cell phone. "This is Detective Tracy Crosswhite, Seattle Homicide," she said out of habit. Dan slid Rex into the back and handed Tracy the keys. He climbed in with the dog. "I'm reporting a shooting in the six hundred block of Elmwood Avenue in Cedar Grove. Requesting all available units in the area to respond."

Tracy slammed shut the tailgate and slid into the cab. "Suspect vehicle is likely a truck headed east on Cedar Hollow toward the county road." She backed quickly down the driveway, bouncing into the street, tires squealing. "Vehicle's left rear taillight is out." She removed the phone from her ear and shouted to Dan. "Where am I going?"

"Pine Flat."

She tossed her phone on the passenger seat and punched the accelerator. Sherlock whined and whimpered. In the rearview mirror Tracy could see him peering over the back seat at his fallen buddy. Dan continued applying pressure to Rex's wounds, his cell phone wedged between his shoulder and jaw as he carried on his own conversation with the veterinary clinic.

"He's bleeding from multiple wounds. We're about seven to eight minutes away."

"How's he doing?" Tracy yelled.

"Vet's going to meet us. I can't stop the bleeding." Dan sounded panicked. "Come on, Rex. Hang in there, buddy. Hang in there with me."

She turned onto the county road and came up quickly behind a slow-moving van. When it didn't accelerate, she swerved to pass but had to retreat when she saw headlights. An eighteen-wheel truck blew past, creating a rush of wind sufficient to shake the Tahoe. After it had passed, Tracy swerved into the outside lane, saw no headlights, and stepped on the accelerator again. No sooner had she done so when more headlights appeared around the next turn. She had the pedal to the floor and not much distance between her and the oncoming vehicle. When she'd cleared the van's hood, Tracy swerved back into her lane, eliciting prolonged honks from both vehicles.

She passed two additional cars before reaching the exit for Pine Flat. Dan provided final directions to an A-frame split-log building. She braked, the Tahoe skidding to a stop in a dirt-and-gravel parking lot. Jumping out, she left the engine running. A man and a woman burst out the front door of the clinic as Tracy opened the tailgate. Dan slid out carrying a bloodied Rex, rushing him up the steps into the building.

When Dan went inside Tracy shut off the engine. Though the weather had turned bitterly cold and she was underdressed in a long-sleeved shirt and jeans, she remained too amped to sit, too angry to do nothing. She used one of the towels Dan had been using to stanch Rex's wounds and wiped up the blood in the back of the Tahoe before closing the tailgate. She paced the dirt and gravel and made another call. The dispatcher at the Sheriff's Office said that Roy Calloway was not in, but a unit had responded to the shooting at Dan's home. Tracy told the woman she was at the Pine Flat Veterinary Hospital and asked to be kept advised.

She tried to temper her anger so it wouldn't cloud her thinking. It had been buckshot. She knew from the way the window had shattered and the multiple wounds that Rex had sustained. Tracy had hunted enough deer with her father to know the most important thing now was whether or not one of those pellets had hit a vital organ. She crossed her arms against the cold. The night sky had clouded over, blotting out the stars and calming the wind. A chime hung motionless from the roof eaves.

Tracy paced until the cold began to make her joints ache and her fingers and toes became numb. She climbed the wooden steps to the porch. A yellowed light fixture above the front door emitted a tepid glow. About to go inside, Tracy noticed headlights on the asphalt road and, a moment later, recognized the Suburban that slowed into the parking lot and parked beside Dan's Tahoe. Roy Calloway stepped out wearing a flannel shirt, blue jeans, and a Carhartt jacket. His boots thumped on the wood stairs.

"You come to tell me 'I told you so'?" she said.

"I came to see if you were all right."

"I'm all right."

"How's the dog?"

She nodded to the clinic. "Don't know yet."

"You get a look?"

"Yeah, I got a look. It was a truck," she said.

"You get a license plate?"

"Too far. They had the lights off."

"How do you know it was a truck?"

"From the sound of the engine and the height of the brake light off the ground."

He gave it some thought. "Won't limit it much, not around here."

"I know. The left brake light was out, though."

"That will help."

"It was a shotgun," she said. "Buckshot. Some idiot trying to scare us."

"Dan's dog may disagree."

"There were no curtains, Roy. I was sitting in front of the kitchen window. If they'd wanted to kill me they had a clean shot to do it. It was just a shot across the bow. The media has everyone in town stirred up. You know anything about that?"

Calloway scratched at the back of his neck. "I'll have my deputies make some inquiries, try to find out if anyone was out drinking and spouting off."

"That might not limit the pool much either."

"I sent Finlay over to the house. Told him to call Mack at the lumberyard to get some plywood and board up the window."

"Thanks. I'll let Dan know." She reached for the door to enter the hospital.

"Tracy?"

She really didn't want to hear what he had to say or get into an argument. At the moment, she just wanted to get in out of the cold and find out how Rex was doing. But she turned and faced him. Calloway looked to be struggling to find words, which was unlike him. After a moment, he said, "Your father was one of my best friends. I'm not saying it's the same thing, but there's not a day goes by that I don't think about him and Sarah."

"Then you should have found the person who killed them."

"I did."

"The evidence suggests otherwise."

"You can't always trust the evidence," he said.

"I don't."

He looked like he was going to get angry, which was his way. Then he just looked tired, and for the first time, Roy Calloway looked old. His voice grew soft. "Some of us couldn't run off, Tracy. Some of us had to stay here. We had jobs to do. We had a town to think of, a place that people still called home. And it was a good place to live until then. Folks just wanted to put it behind them and move on."

"Doesn't look like any of us got very far," she said.

He showed her his palms. "What do you want from me?"

They were well beyond this. The conversation was going nowhere and she was starting to get a chill. "Nothing," she said and started again for the door.

"Your father . . ."

She took her hand off the knob. DeAngelo Finn had also invoked her father's name that afternoon. "What, Roy? My father what?"

Calloway bit at his lower lip. "Tell Dan I'm real sorry about the dog," he said, and started down the steps.

—

From the look on Dan's face, Tracy was convinced Rex had died. He sat in the reception area with his elbows propped on his knees, his hands beneath his chin. Sherlock lay on the floor in front of him, head resting on his paws, eyes looking up from beneath a worried brow.

"Have you heard anything?" she asked.

Dan shook his head.

"Calloway just came by," she said. "He's going to ask around, see if anyone was mouthing off. And he's going to get someone to board up the window."

Dan didn't respond.

"You want a cup of coffee?" Tracy asked.

"No," he said.

She sat in the chair beside him, the silence uncomfortable. After a minute, she reached out and touched his arm. "Dan, I don't know what to say. I shouldn't have brought you into this. It wasn't fair to you. I'm sorry."

Dan stared at the floor, seemingly giving her words consideration.

"Look if you want to bow out . . ."

Dan turned his head and looked at her. "I got involved because a childhood friend asked me to take a look. I took the case though because what I found didn't make sense, and it appears that an innocent man may have been railroaded. If that's true it means someone got away with murder, someone who lived or still lives in this town. I've chosen to live here again. This is my home now, Tracy, for better or for worse, and it was better once, wasn't it?"

"Yes, it was," she said, recalling that Calloway and DeAngelo Finn had said very much the same thing.

"I'm not trying to get back what we had growing up. I know that was a long time ago, but maybe . . ." He blew out a breath. "I don't know."

Tracy didn't push him. They sat in silence.

Forty-five minutes after they'd brought Rex in, an interior door to the left of the reception counter opened and the veterinarian entered. Tall and rangy, he looked like he was seventeen. He made Tracy feel old. She and Dan stood. Sherlock lurched to his feet.

"You got some dog there, Mr. O'Leary."

"Is he going to be all right?"

"It looked worse than it is. The buckshot did some damage, but it was mostly superficial, in part because he's so darn muscular."

Dan heaved a sigh of relief, removed his glasses, and pinched the bridge of his nose. His voice shook. "Thank you. Thank you for everything."

"We're going to keep him sedated to keep him quiet. We can do that better here. I'd say maybe day after tomorrow you can take him home, if you think you can keep him down."

"I have a hearing starting. I'm afraid I'm not going to be home much the next few days."

"We can keep him here. Just let us know what you decide." The veterinarian took Sherlock's head in his hands. "You want to see your buddy now?"

Sherlock's tail began to whip the air. He shook free his head, ears flopping and chain collar rattling. He and Dan followed the veterinarian, but Tracy held back, feeling this was not her place. Sherlock stopped and looked back at her in question, but Dan continued through the door without stopping.

CHAPTER 40

The morning came quickly. It had been after midnight by the time Tracy had gotten to her motel in Silver Spurs. She'd lain down on the bed but sleep had not come easily. She remembered seeing the glow of the clock on her nightstand at 2:38 a.m., and had gotten up from the bed for good at 4:54 a.m.

When she pulled back the drapes, she saw a white curtain of snow falling from a low gray sky outside the window. The snow already blanketed the ground and clung to tree limbs and power lines. It tempered the sounds of the small town, giving everything a false sense of calm.

Tracy had reserved the motel room while in Seattle, wanting to avoid the potential of a reporter snapping a photo of her and Dan leaving Dan's home together in the morning. After the shooting, Dan had pressed her to stay at the house, debating the wisdom of her being alone at the motel. She'd dismissed his concern as she'd dismissed the threat when Roy Calloway had brought it up. "It's just some crazy who had too many beers," she'd said. "If the person had wanted to kill me, he had a clean shot to do it, and he wouldn't have used buckshot. I have my Glock. That's all the protection I need." In truth, she hadn't wanted to put Dan or Sherlock in any further danger.

—

She drove into the Cascade County Courthouse parking lot an hour before the hearing, hoping to avoid much of the press. The parking lot was already three-quarters full, and cameramen and reporters buzzed about the news vans parked along the street. When they spotted Tracy, they wasted little time filming her as she crossed the parking lot toward the courthouse. The reporters shouted out questions.

"Detective, will you talk about the shooting last night?"

"Do you fear for your life, detective?"

Tracy headed for the expansive courthouse steps leading to the building's peaked pediment, ignoring the questions.

"Why were you at Dan O'Leary's house?"

"Do the police have any suspects?"

As she neared the steps, the pack of reporters and cameramen grew thicker, making her progress more difficult. A line of hopeful spectators bundled in winter clothes flecked with snow also blocked the front entrance, snaking down the steps and spilling along the sidewalk, adding to the congestion.

"Will you be testifying, Detective?"

"That will be up to the attorneys," she said, remembering that she and her family had never waited in line to enter the courthouse during Edmund House's trial.

"Have you spoken to Edmund House?"

She pressed on through the crowd to the south side of the building and the glass-door entrance that had been reserved for family members, witnesses, and counsel during House's trial. The correctional officer just inside the door didn't hesitate to open it when Tracy rapped on the glass. He also didn't ask her for any ID before ushering her inside.

"I was Judge Lawrence's bailiff the first go-round," he said. "I guess this is like déjà vu all over again. They're even using the same courtroom."

—

To accommodate the anticipated crowd, Judge Meyers had indeed been assigned the ceremonial courtroom on the second floor where Edmund House had been tried twenty years earlier. When the correctional officer allowed Tracy to enter the courtroom early, she stepped back in time to those awful days. Almost everything about the courtroom remained the same, from the rich marble floor to the mahogany woodwork and the vaulted box-beam ceiling, from which hung the bronze-and-stained-glass light fixtures.

Tracy had always likened courtrooms to churches. The ornate judge's bench, like the hanging cross, was the focal point, elevated at the front of the room looking down on the proceedings. Counsel sat at two tables facing the bench. A railing with a swinging gate separated them from the gallery, which at present was a dozen empty pews on each side of an aisle. Witnesses would enter the courtroom at the back of the gallery and walk down the aisle, pushing through the gate and proceeding between counsel tables to the slatted wooden chair on the elevated witness stand. The jury box was to the right of the witness stand. To the left were the wood-sash windows that at present displayed the still-heavy snowfall.

Only the technology had changed. A flat-screen television occupied the corner of the room where an easel had formerly been used to display photographs to the jury, and computer screens adorned each counsel table, the bench, and the witness stand.

Dan had set up at the table on the left, closest to the windows. He looked back over his shoulder and gave Tracy a brief glance when she entered, then went back to reviewing his notes. Despite the prior evening's events, Tracy thought he looked sharp in a navy-blue suit, white shirt, and solid silver tie. By contrast, Vance Clark, who stood at the table beside Dan's and closest to the empty chairs in the jury box, already looked spent. He had his blue sport coat off and the sleeves of his shirt rolled up his forearms. Hands pressed flat on the table, Clark was hunched over a topographical map, head bowed and eyes closed. Tracy wondered if he'd ever pondered the possibility that he might someday be back in this courtroom, sitting opposite the same defendant he'd convicted twenty years earlier. She doubted he had.

When the courtroom door swung open behind her, more of Tracy's past entered. Parker House, Edmund's uncle, hesitated when he saw her, as if trying to decide whether to enter or to leave. He'd aged. Tracy estimated him to be in his midsixties now. His hair had thinned and turned gray, but it still hung in strands over the collar of his Carhartt jacket. His face, tanned and weathered from years working outdoors, had sagged from the effects of a lifetime of hard living and hard drinking. Parker thrust his hands in the pockets of worn blue jeans, lowered his eyes, and made his way along the back wall to the opposite side of the courtroom, the sound of his scuffed, steel-toed work boots echoing. He took his seat in the first row behind Dan, the same seat where he'd sat throughout the first trial, usually alone. Tracy's father had made it a point to greet Parker each morning of the trial. When Tracy had asked him why, her father had said, "Parker is suffering too."

Tracy approached Parker's seat. He had his head turned away from her, looking at the snow continuing to fall outside the windows. "Parker?"

Parker looked surprised to hear his name, and after a seeming moment of indecision, he stood. "Hey, Tracy." His voice was barely above a whisper.

"I'm sorry to put you through this again, Parker."

His eyebrows inched together. "Yeah," he said.

Not knowing what else to say, she let him be. Instinctively, she also went to the first pew, behind the prosecutor's table. It had been the pew in which she had sat with her mother and father and Ben, but the familiarity of her surroundings suddenly overwhelmed her, and she realized her emotions were more raw, and the edge between composure and tears more thin, than she was willing to admit.

She stepped to the second row and sat.

As she waited, Tracy alternately checked e-mails on her phone and looked out the wood-sash windows. The trees in the court-house square looked as if they had been flocked, and the rest of the landscape had become a brilliant, pristine white.

Ten minutes before nine, the bailiff unlocked the courtroom doors and pushed them open. The crowd steadily streamed in, fill-ing the pews as if at a movie theater, taking the best seats and dis-carding coats, hats, and gloves to save seats for others.

"No saving seats, folks," the bailiff said. "It's first come, first served, around here. Please put your coats and gloves under the pew so we can make room for the people still standing in the cold."

If the gallery filled, as anticipated, it would hold more than 250 people. Based on the length of the line that had snaked down the courthouse steps and along the sidewalk, Tracy suspected some of them would be turned away at the door or forced to sit in the courtroom next door and watch the news feed instead.

Vanpelt entered with a press credential dangling from a string around her neck and sat near the front, behind Parker House. Tracy counted a dozen other men and women wearing press credentials. She recognized many of the people, the same faces who had attended Sarah's interment, but this time none of them approached Tracy, though a few acknowledged her with a nod or a wistful smile that quickly faded.

With the gallery full, the doors to the courtroom again opened. Edmund House entered flanked by two correctional officers. The gallery fell silent. Those who had attended the first trial alternately looked on disbelievingly at the dramatic change in House's physical appearance or whispered their disbelief to those around them. Unlike his trial, no one had attempted to clean House up to make a favorable impression on a jury. There would be no jury this time. He shuffled forward in his prison uniform—khaki pants and a short-sleeved shirt that revealed his tattooed arms. His long, braided ponytail reached the center of his broad back, and the chains connecting the manacles around his ankles and leading up his legs to the belly belt rattled and clinked as the guards led him to counsel table.

At his trial, House had seemed indifferent to the stares of the spectators, but now he looked bemused by their attention. It made her think of his comment when she and Dan had first visited him in prison, about what it would be like to see the faces of Cedar Grove's citizens when he walked the streets as a free man again. Hopefully, that would not be for a while. She surveyed the courtroom, noting two additional officers had entered and were standing near the courtroom exit, and that a fifth had taken up a position beside the elevated bench.

House turned, facing the gallery as the correctional officers removed the restraints from his wrists and ankles. Dan placed a hand on House's shoulder and whispered in his ear, but House kept his gaze on his uncle, though Parker did not look up. Parker kept his head down, looking like a penitent praying in church.

Judge Meyers's clerk, who had left when House had entered, returned through the door to the left of the bench and called the proceedings to order. Meyers followed quickly on his clerk's heels, took the stairs to his bench, and in rapid succession dispensed with preliminary matters, including expected courtroom decorum. Then, without fanfare or preface, Meyers turned to Dan.

"Mr. O'Leary, as the burden rests with the defendant at this hearing, you may proceed."

Twenty years later, they were underway.

CHAPTER 41

Edmund House's spine stiffened when Dan stood and said, "The defense calls Sheriff Roy Calloway."

House watched Calloway intently from the moment the Cedar Grove Sheriff entered the courtroom. Calloway stepped through the swinging gate and paused to return House's glare, long enough that one of the guards moved toward the table, but Calloway gave House a final, smug smile and crossed the well to the witness chair.

Cedar Grove's sheriff looked even more imposing when he stepped up onto the elevated platform to take his oath to tell the truth, the whole truth, and nothing but the truth.

Calloway dwarfed the witness chair when he sat. Dan led him through the preliminaries. Meyers quickly facilitated this. "I'm familiar with the witness's background and it is noted in the record. Let's move to the substance of the matter." His wife's trail ride was calling.

O'Leary complied. "On August 22, 1993, do you recall receiving a call from one of your deputies about a blue Ford truck seemingly abandoned along the side of the county road?"

"Not *seemingly* abandoned. Abandoned."

"Will you tell the court what you did as a result of that call?"

"My deputy at the time had already run the plates and said they came back registered to James Crosswhite. I knew Tracy Crosswhite, his daughter, drove that vehicle."

"You were friends with James Crosswhite?"

"Everyone was friends with James Crosswhite."

The low murmur and subtle nods caused Meyers to raise his head, though not his gavel.

"What happened next?"

"I drove out to the vehicle."

"Did the car appear in any way disabled?"

"No."

"Did you attempt to get inside?"

"The doors were locked. There was no one inside the truck cab. The camper shell windows were tinted but I banged on the side and got no response." Calloway's tone fluctuated between disdain and boredom.

"What did you do next?"

"I drove to the Crosswhite home and knocked on the door but again got no answer. So I thought I better call James."

"Was Dr. Crosswhite home?"

"No. He and Abby had gone to Maui to celebrate their twenty-fifth wedding anniversary."

"You knew how to reach him?"

"James had provided me the hotel number in case I needed to get a hold of him. It was something he did whenever he left town."

"What was James Crosswhite's response to the news that you'd located his daughter's truck?"

"He told me the girls had been at the Washington State shooting championships that weekend and that Tracy had recently moved into a rental house. He said if the girls had car trouble, they could have spent the night there. He said he'd call Tracy and suggested I hang tight until he called me back."

"Did he call you back?"

"He said he'd reached Tracy but she'd told him Sarah had driven the truck home alone. He said Tracy was heading home and would meet me at the house with a key."

"Was Sarah home?"

"We wouldn't be here if she was."

"Just answer the question," Meyers said.

Dan considered his notes on his iPad before taking Calloway through his and Tracy's inspection of the car and the house. "What did you do next?"

"I had Tracy begin to call Sarah's friends to see if she'd spent the night someplace."

"Did you think that likely?"

Calloway shrugged his big shoulders. "It had rained hard the previous night. I thought if Sarah had some kind of car trouble and started to walk it was more likely she would have just walked home."

"So you were already suspecting foul play?"

"I was doing my job, Dan."

"Answer the questions you're asked and refer to the attorneys in this courtroom as 'Counselor,'" Meyers said.

"Who was the last person to see Sarah?" Dan said, and Tracy saw him flinch at his mistake.

Calloway pounced on it. "Edmund House."

This time Meyers silenced the murmur with a single rap of his gavel.

"Other than your belief concerning the defendant—"

"It isn't a belief, *Counselor*. House told me he was the last person to see Sarah, just before he raped and strangled her."

"Your Honor, I would request that you instruct the witness to allow me to finish asking my question before he answers."

Meyers leaned closer to the witness chair and looked down at Calloway. "Sheriff Calloway, I'm not going to tell you again to treat these proceedings and those participating in them with respect. Wait until the question is finished before you answer."

Calloway looked like he'd bitten into something tart.

Dan moved a few feet to his left, the blanket of snow falling out the windows now a backdrop. "Sheriff Calloway, who do you personally know to have been the last person to have seen Sarah Crosswhite alive?"

Calloway took a moment. "Tracy and her boyfriend spoke to Sarah in a parking lot in Olympia."

"You met with Tracy and her father James Crosswhite in the family home the following morning, is that correct?"

"James and Abby took a red-eye home."

"Why did you meet with James Crosswhite?"

Calloway looked to Meyers as if to ask, *How long do I have to answer these stupid questions?* "Why did I meet with the father of a missing woman? To set up a plan to try to find Sarah."

"You believed Sarah had met with foul play?"

"I considered it a distinct possibility."

"Did you and James Crosswhite discuss potential suspects?"

"Yeah. One. Edmund House."

"Why did you suspect Mr. House?"

"House had been paroled for rape. The facts of that case were similar. He'd abducted a young woman."

"Did you speak with Mr. House?"

"I drove out to the property. His uncle, Parker House, and I woke him."

"He was asleep in bed?"

"That's why we woke him."

"And did you take note of anything about Mr. House's appearance?"

"I noted scratches on his face and forearms."

"Did you ask Mr. House how he'd sustained his injuries?"

"He said he'd been working in the woodshop and a piece of wood splintered. He said he quit after that, watched television, and went to bed."

"Did you believe Edmund House?"

"Not for a second."

"You'd already decided he had something to do with Sarah's disappearance, hadn't you?"

"I'd decided that I'd never heard of a piece of wood splintering and causing the kind of injuries I noted on his face and arms. That is the question you asked me."

"What did you think caused his injuries?"

Again Calloway paused, perhaps anticipating where Dan was headed with his questions. "I thought it looked like someone had raked fingernails across his face and scratched his forearms."

"Fingernails?"

"That's what I said."

"Did you do anything further as a result of that suspicion?"

"I took some Polaroids, and I asked Parker if I could take a look around his property and he gave his consent."

"What did you find?"

Calloway shifted as if uncomfortable. "It was only a visual inspection."

"You didn't find any evidence Sarah had been there, did you?"

"Again, it was only a visual."

"So would the answer to my question be 'no'?"

"The answer would be I did not find Sarah."

O'Leary let it go. "Was a search conducted in the foothills above Cedar Grove?"

"Yes."

"A thorough search?"

"It's a big area."

"Did you consider the search thorough?"

Calloway shrugged. "We did the best we could, given the terrain."

"And was Sarah's body found?"

"Jesus," Calloway uttered under his breath, though the court-room microphone picked it up. He sat forward. "We never found Sarah and we never found her body. How many times do I have to answer that question?"

"That's for me to decide, Sheriff Calloway, not you," Meyers said. He looked to Dan. "Counselor, I think we've established the decedent was never found."

"I'll move on." Dan took Calloway through the seven weeks of tips leading up to the phone call from Ryan P. Hagen. Then he handed Calloway a multipage document. "Chief Calloway, this is the log of tips received in the Sarah Crosswhite investiga-tion. Would you please identify for me the tip received from Mr. Hagen?"

Calloway quickly flipped through the document. "I don't see one," he said. Dan retrieved the document, about to return it to the evidence table when Calloway said, "The call could have come in directly to the police station. The tip line was no longer being advertised."

Dan frowned but maintained his composure. "Do you have a record of those telephone calls?"

"Not anymore. We're a small police department, Counselor."

Dan took Calloway through his conversation with Ryan Hagen. "Did you ask him about the news program he was watching?"

"I might have."

"Did you ask him the name of the client he was visiting?"

"I could have."

"But you didn't note either in your report, did you?"

"I didn't always write everything down."

"Did you speak to the client Mr. Hagen said he had visited that day?"

"I saw no reason not to take the man at his word."

"Chief Calloway, isn't it true that your police agency had received a number of false reports from people claiming to have seen Sarah?"

"I seem to recall a few."

"Didn't one man claim Sarah visited him in a dream and was living in Canada?"

"I don't recall that one," Calloway said.

"And wasn't James Crosswhite offering a ten-thousand-dollar reward for information leading to an arrest and conviction?"

"He was."

"It was on a billboard outside of town, was it not?"

"It was."

"But you didn't think it wise to confirm if this witness was telling you the truth?"

Calloway leaned forward. "We'd never released any information that Edmund House was a person of interest in the investigation or that we believed him to be driving a red Chevy truck. In fact, the truck wasn't registered to Edmund. It was registered to Parker. So there was no way Hagen would have known the significance of having seen a red truck."

"But you knew Edmund House drove a red Chevy stepside, didn't you, Sheriff Calloway?"

Calloway glared at him.

"The witness will answer the question," Meyers said.

"I knew it," Calloway said.

"Did Mr. Hagen say why he'd recalled this one particular vehicle?"

"You'd have to ask him."

"But I'm asking you, as a law enforcement officer in charge of an investigation into the abduction of your good friend's daughter. Did you think to ask him why he remembered this one particular truck that flashed by for a brief second during a storm on a dark road?"

"I don't recall," Calloway said.

"I don't see that in your report either. Can I assume you also didn't ask him that question?"

"I didn't say I didn't ask. I said not everything went into the report."

"Did you confirm he even had an appointment?"

"He had it written in his calendar."

"But you didn't confirm it."

Calloway slapped the table beside the witness chair and rose from his seat. "I thought it important to find Sarah. That's what I thought important. And I busted my ass to do just that." Meyers rapped his gavel, the sharp snap of wood against wood competing with Calloway's escalating volume. The guard at the front of the courtroom moved quickly to the base of the platform. Undeterred, Calloway pointed at Dan. "You weren't here. You were back at your East Coast college. Now you come back here twenty years later and question me about how I did *my* job? You second-guess and speculate and insinuate about something you know nothing about."

"Sit down!" Meyers had stood too, his face flushed with anger.

A second correctional officer positioned himself at the base of the witness stand, and the two who had escorted House into the courtroom moved swiftly back to House's side.

Calloway's glare remained on Dan, who remained firmly fixed in the middle of the courtroom. At counsel table, Edmund House sat watching the spectacle with a bemused smile.

"Sheriff, if I have to have you escorted from this courtroom in handcuffs, it will not be with any joy or pleasure, but I will not hesitate to do so if you so much as raise your voice again," Meyers said in a steely tone. "At present, this is my courtroom, and when you disrespect it, you disrespect me. And I will not be disrespected. Do I make myself perfectly clear?"

Calloway turned his glare from Dan to Meyers, and for a moment, Tracy thought the sheriff might just dare Meyers to have him handcuffed. Instead, Calloway looked out at the gallery and the many Cedar Grove residents and media. Then he sat.

Meyers retook his seat and took a moment to rearrange papers, as if to give everyone in the courtroom a chance to catch their collective breath. Calloway took a sip of the water he'd been provided and set the glass back on the table. Meyers looked to Dan. "You may continue, Counselor."

Dan asked, "Sheriff Calloway, did you ever consider that Mr. Hagen could have written the appointment in his calendar after the fact?"

Calloway cleared his throat, his gaze now fixed on a corner of the ceiling. "I told you, I saw no reason not to take the man at his word."

O'Leary took Calloway through his further questioning of Edmund House.

"I told him I had a witness who could put a red Chevy stepside on the county road that night," Calloway said.

"And what was his response?"

"He smirked. He said I'd have to do better than that."

"Did you do better than that?"

Calloway's lips pinched. This time, when he looked past Dan, his gaze settled on Tracy.

"Do you need me to repeat the question?" Dan said.

Calloway looked at Dan. "No. I told House that the witness would also testify he saw a man driving the truck with a blonde woman in the cab."

DeAngelo Finn had never brought this up at House's initial trial, and it wasn't in any report Tracy had ever found. She knew Calloway had perpetrated the ruse because he had divulged the information to her father during one of their many conversations in her father's den.

"Did Mr. Hagen tell you that?"

"No."

"Then why did you say he had?"

"It was a ruse, Counselor, to see if House would take the bait. It's not an uncommon interrogation technique."

"You don't deny it was untrue."

"As you so aptly put it, I was trying to find the killer of a good friend's daughter."

"And you would have said anything to accomplish that, wouldn't you?"

"Argumentative," Clark said, and Meyers sustained the objection.

"What did Mr. House say in response to this ruse?"

"He changed his story. He said he'd gone out that night, that he'd been drinking, and when he was driving back he saw the truck on the side of the road and a little ways farther he saw Sarah. He said he stopped and offered her a ride and drove her home."

"Did you note the name of the bar at which Mr. House said he'd been drinking in your report?"

"I don't believe I did."

"Did you ask Mr. House the name of the bar?"

"I don't recall."

"Did you talk to anyone to try to confirm whether Mr. House had, in fact, been drinking in their establishment?"

"He told me he had."

"But you didn't note the name of the tavern and you never tried to confirm Mr. House had been at a bar that night, did you?"

"No."

"As with Mr. Hagen, you chose to take Mr. House at his word?"

"I didn't see why House would make up a lie—" Calloway caught himself.

"Did you want to finish your answer?"

"No. I'm done."

Dan stepped closer. "You didn't see why Mr. House would implicate himself by saying he was with the victim. Is that what you intended to say?"

"Sometimes people who lie forget their own lies."

"I have no doubt," Dan said, which brought Clark to his feet, but Dan quickly continued. "Did you tape this conversation?"

"I didn't get the chance."

"Didn't you consider this important information, Sheriff Calloway?"

"I thought it important that House had changed his alibi. I thought it important to get that information in front of Judge Sullivan so we could get search warrants for the property and House's truck. My priority remained finding Sarah."

"And you could not get those search warrants without Mr. Hagen's statement that he saw the red Chevy stepside on the county road, could you?"

"I wasn't privy to Judge Sullivan's decision-making process."

Dan took Calloway through the execution of the search warrants. "And what did James Crosswhite tell you when you showed him the earrings?"

"He positively identified them as belonging to Sarah."

"Did he tell you how he could be so certain?"

"He said he'd given Sarah the earrings as a gift when she won the Washington State Shooting Championship the prior year."

"Did you confront Edmund House with this new evidence?"

"He called it 'bullshit.'" Calloway looked past Dan to where House sat. "He leaned across the table and smiled at me. Then he said he hadn't driven Sarah home. He said he'd driven her into the foothills, raped her, strangled her, and buried her body. He laughed. He said without a body we'd never convict him. He laughed about it like it was one big game."

The crowd stirred.

"And you have this confession on tape?"

Calloway bit his lower lip. "No."

"After the first confession, weren't you better prepared?"

"I guess not."

"Just one more question, Sheriff." Dan used a remote control to display a blowup of the topographical map of the area above Cedar Grove on the flat-screen television. "I wonder if you'd note on this map where it was that Sarah's remains were recently found."

CHAPTER 42

Later in the afternoon, after Clark's attempt to rehabilitate Calloway, and with a black *X* on the topographical map to mark the spot where the hunter's dog had found Sarah's remains drawing the attention of the gallery, Calloway stepped down from the witness stand. Dan had told Tracy his intent was to follow Calloway with a series of witnesses whose testimony he anticipated to be brief. He wanted to avoid having the inconsistencies between Calloway's current testimony and his trial testimony become lost in too many details. Dan wanted Meyers thinking about them overnight.

Dan called Parker House. Parker looked as uncomfortable now as Tracy recalled from the trial. He left his jacket in the pew and took the oath to tell the truth in a wrinkled, short-sleeved white shirt. When he sat, he absentmindedly picked at the hair on his arm, and the heel of his right boot shook to a silent beat.

"You were working the graveyard?" Dan asked.

"That's right."

"What time did you get home?"

"Wasn't till late. I'd say ten that morning."

"That's what you testified to during the trial."

"Then that's probably right."

"What time did your shift at the mill end?"

"That would have been right around eight."

"What did you do between the time your shift ended and the time you arrived home?"

Parker shifted in his chair and glanced at the faces in the gallery, though not at his nephew. "Went out for a few drinks."

"How many is a few?"

Parker shrugged. "I don't recall."

"You testified at trial that you had three beers and a shot of whiskey."

"Then that's probably right."

"Do you recall the name of the bar?"

Parker was starting to look like a man with a bad back trying to get comfortable in the chair. Clark took the opportunity to stand and object. "Your Honor, none of this is relevant, and it is clearly making the witness uncomfortable. If the counsel's intent is only to embarrass . . ."

"Not at all, Your Honor," Dan said. "Just trying to establish if the witness was competent to assess what he claims to have seen when he arrived home that morning."

"I'll allow it," Meyers said. "But make it quick."

"I don't recall the bar," Parker said, which was plausible after twenty years. But he had also claimed to not recall the name of the bar during the trial, which, given that there weren't many in the small towns, seemed less plausible. But Vance Clark had not pressed him on it. Nor had DeAngelo Finn.

"And when you got home, where was Edmund?"

"Sleeping in his room."

"Did you wake him?"

"Not right then, no."

"When did you wake him?"

"When the sheriff arrived. I'd say eleven."

"And did you notice anything different about Edmund's appearance from when you'd last seen him?"

"You mean the scratches on his face and arms?"

"Did you notice scratches on his face and arms?"

"Had to. They was right there to see."

"He hadn't tried to cover them with makeup or anything?"

"Don't think we had anything like that. It was just him and me. There wasn't no women." When the gallery smiled, Parker gave a sheepish grin and, for the first time, considered his nephew. His smile quickly faded.

"Did he tell you and Sheriff Calloway how he got the scratches?"

"He said he was working in the furniture shed and a piece of wood he was stripping got all bound up in the table saw and it splintered and cut him."

"What did Sheriff Calloway say or do?"

"He took some Polaroids of Edmund's face and arms and then he asked if he could look around."

"Did you grant him permission?"

"I said he could."

"Did you accompany him?"

"Nope."

"Did you see the sheriff go into the furniture shed?"

"Yeah, I saw him do that."

"And did you see him go inside the cab of the red Chevy?"

"Yep, he done that too."

"Were you restoring that truck, Parker?"

"I was."

"But you let Edmund drive it."

Parker nodded. "Yeah. He didn't have no car and he took a liking to it."

"Was there carpet in that truck at that time?"

"No. I'd stripped it down to the metal."

"Leather or cloth seats?"

"Leather."

"One more question, Parker. Did you keep any black plastic in that truck, you know, for garbage bags, or maybe to lay over a garden in the winter?"

"Didn't have no garden, so no need for that."

"So you didn't keep any in the truck?"

"Not that I was aware of."

"Did you keep any at the house?"

"You still mean the garbage bags?"

"Yes."

"No. I composted most of the garbage. The rest I just piled up and when the pile got big enough I drove it myself to the dump in Cascadia. We don't have no garbage service on the mountain."

Clark declined to ask Parker any questions, and Dan finished the day by calling Margaret Giesa. She was the CSI detective who had executed the search warrants on Parker House's property and truck and discovered the Colt-pistol earrings in the coffee can. Giesa had retired and moved to a small town in Oregon with her husband, Erik, but otherwise she hadn't changed much from the woman Tracy remembered from the first trial, still stylishly dressed and wearing the four-inch pumps.

Dan put Giesa through her search of the property to reestablish what her team had found that day, and spent most of his time discussing the earrings she had found in the coffee can in the furniture shed and the strands of blonde hair recovered from the cab of the Chevy. He methodically walked her through the chain of custody. It was tedious and time-consuming but necessary to prevent any argument that someone had tampered with the evidence or switched it in the twenty years since Giesa and her team had found it and relinquished custody to the Washington State Patrol Crime Lab, where it had been stored.

After Giesa had stepped down from the witness chair, Judge Meyers wrapped up the day's proceedings. Concerned about the weather reports, Meyers provided his clerk's desk number and said that, in the event that he had to postpone the proceedings, the court would establish a recorded message for the press and the public. When he banged his gavel, Maria Vanpelt and the other reporters made a beeline for Tracy, who moved just as quickly for the courtroom doors. There, she unexpectedly met Finlay Armstrong, who guided her into the hall past the blinding lights atop the cameras and escorted her down the interior staircase as the reporters hurled questions after her.

"Will you comment on the proceedings, Detective?" Vanpelt asked.

Tracy ignored the questions. Finlay guided her across the parking lot to her car, through snow that was nearly a foot deep in some places.

"I'll meet you here in the morning," Finlay said.

"Did the Sheriff ask you to do this?" Tracy asked.

Finlay nodded and handed her a business card. "If you need anything just give a call."

No sooner had Tracy pulled from the parking lot when her cell phone rang. Though Dan had cautioned that trials were like marathons, and this had been only the first mile, she could hear from the tone in his voice that he was pleased with the way the day had gone.

"I'm heading over to Pine Flat to visit Rex. Meet me there. We can discuss tomorrow."

———

Dan was with the veterinarian when Tracy arrived in the hospital, so she put up the hood of her jacket and stepped back outside, pacing the porch while checking e-mails and returning phone messages. The light had faded to dusk, the sky hidden beneath a low-lying fog that continued to spew snow and did not appear ready to let up anytime soon. The thermometer next to the frozen wind chimes indicated the temperature had fallen to twenty-four degrees.

Tracy checked in with Kins. As she filled him in on the day, she noticed a car parked at the edge of a pristine, snow-covered field. The hood and roof of the car were covered in two inches of snow, but the wiper blades had recently cleared the windshield. It was too far for Tracy to see clearly, especially with the fading light and persistent snowfall, but she had a sense that someone was sitting behind the steering wheel, maybe a reporter. She was contemplating driving over to find out when Dan opened the door and stuck his head out. He was smiling, a good sign.

"Are you trying to catch pneumonia?" Dan asked.

"How's he doing?"

"Come in and see for yourself."

Inside, Tracy was surprised to see Rex up and about in the reception area, though moving gingerly. He looked like something out of the circus, with a plastic cone about his head to keep him from licking his bandages. She put out her hand and Rex didn't hesitate to come to her, his nose cold and wet in her palm.

Dan stood beside the vet and his wife, explaining to Tracy, "We're trying to decide what to do. I hate to leave him here, but I think it's for the best, especially if I'm gone during the day."

"Not to worry," the vet said. "We'll take good care of him for as long as you need."

Dan dropped to a knee and took Rex's big head in his hands. "I'm sorry, buddy. One more night, then we'll get you home. I promise."

Tracy was moved by Rex's troubled brow and Dan's compassion. It was tough to keep her emotions in check as she watched the vet lead the big dog away. As they approached the door, Rex looked back, worried and forlorn, before reluctantly continuing. It was heartrending.

Dan stepped quickly out onto the porch and Tracy followed him. The car that had been parked across the snow-covered field was gone. She looked for it, but the streets were empty. Dan's Tahoe and her Subaru were the only cars in the parking lot. Across the field, smoke curled from chimneys atop the A-frame homes, and children bundled in hats, scarves, and gloves played in the snow. Otherwise, no one was braving the cold or willing to risk getting too far from home with the anticipated heavier snowfall.

"I hate to leave him here," Dan said, clearly emotional.

"I know, but you made the right decision."

"It doesn't make it any easier."

"That's how you know it was the right decision." She took his hand, which seemed to surprise him. "I think Rex and Sherlock are lucky you found them, Dan. And I think Roy Calloway now knows you're not the pudgy little kid with the glasses that he used to bully."

"Pudgy? Is that what you thought of me? I'll have you know that was undeveloped muscle."

She smiled, seeing in his face not only the boy who had been her friend but also the man he'd become—adept and strong enough to vanquish Roy Calloway, but sensitive enough to be brought to tears by one of his dogs. A good man, a man who'd been hurt and used humor to hide his pain, the type of man she'd hoped would someday come into her life. She'd been using the hearing to stall acknowledging her feelings for Dan because it had been so long since she'd allowed herself to become emotionally close to another human being, afraid that she could lose another person dear to her and not wanting to relive that pain.

Snow stuck to Dan's hair. "You were good today. Better than good."

"We've got a long way to go. Today was just about locking down Calloway's testimony. Tomorrow is about landing the real blows."

"Well, I was still impressed."

He gave her an inquisitive look. "You mean surprised."

"Not at all." She held up her free hand, thumb and index finger a fraction of an inch apart. "Okay, maybe just a little bit."

He laughed and squeezed her hand. "I'll let you in on a little secret. I surprised myself."

"Yeah? How so?"

"It's been a while since I was in a courtroom cross-examining a witness in a case that mattered. I guess it's like riding a bike."

"Except that didn't always go too well for you, as I remember."

His eyes widened with mock indignity. "Hey, it was one flat tire!"

She laughed while continuing to consider how their intertwined fingers seemed like a natural fit, and imagining what his fingers would feel like caressing her skin.

"Are you going to be all right in that motel?" Dan asked.

"I won't be eating anyone's famous bacon cheeseburgers, but I'll probably live longer for it."

"You know, not having you stay at the house had nothing to do with what happened to Rex," he said. "I'm sorry. I was upset and said some things . . ."

"I know." She closed the gap between them, looking for a cue. When he bent down she rose onto her toes and met him halfway. Despite the cold, his lips were warm and moist, and she didn't feel the least bit odd kissing him. In fact, it felt as natural as their hands felt twined together. When they parted lips, a snowflake landed on her nose. Dan smiled and brushed it aside.

"We're both going to catch pneumonia out here," he said.

"They gave me two keys to the room," she said.

She lay beside him in the sallow glow cast by the lamp mounted over the headboard of her motel bed. The snow had dampened all sound outside the room, and it was eerily silent but for the occasional hiss and tick of the radiator beneath the window.

"You okay? You're kind of quiet."

"I'm doing great. How about you?"

He squeezed her close and kissed the top of her head. "Any regrets?" he asked.

"Only that you can't stay."

"I'd like to," he said, "but Sherlock's a big baby without his brother, and I do have to prepare for a fairly important hearing tomorrow."

She smiled. "I think you would have been a good father, Dan."

"Yeah, well, some things aren't meant to be."

She propped herself onto an elbow. "Why didn't you have kids?"

"She didn't want kids. She told me before we got married, but I thought she'd change her mind. I was wrong."

"Well, now you have your boys."

"And I'm sure one of them is getting anxious."

He kissed her and rolled onto his side to get out of the bed, but she reached for his shoulder and pulled him back down. "Tell Sherlock I'm sorry you were late," she said, rolling on top of him and feeling him harden beneath her.

—

After, she lay beneath the covers watching him dress.

"Are you going to walk me to the door or just kick me to the curb?" he asked. She slipped out of bed to grab a nightshirt, surprised that she did not feel self-conscious standing naked before him. "I was only kidding," Dan said, "though I am enjoying the view."

Tracy slipped the shirt over her head and walked him to the door. Before opening it, he pulled back the curtain and looked out the window next to it.

"A media throng with cameras?" she said.

"Doubtful in this weather." He pulled open the door and she felt the chilled air on her still bed-warm skin. "It's stopped snowing. That's a good sign."

She looked past him. The snow had stopped, but recently, judging by the three-inch layer on the deck railing, and likely not permanently, given the cloud-darkened sky. "Remember snow days?" she asked.

"How could I forget? Those were the best days of school."

"We didn't have school."

"Exactly."

He bent and kissed her again, and goose bumps danced across her skin, causing her to fold her arms across her body.

"Is that from me or the cold air?" Dan said, smiling.

She winked. "I'm a scientist. Not enough empirical data yet."

"Well, we'll have to change that."

She hid behind the half-open door. "I'll see you in the morning."

His boots crunched fresh snow. When he reached the staircase, he turned back before descending. "Close the door before you freeze to death. And lock it."

But she waited until he'd reached the Tahoe and slid inside. About to shut the motel door, she noticed a car parked down the street—not the car so much as its windshield. It had been cleared. Once was odd. Twice was purposeful. If it was a reporter or a photographer, he was about to get the lesson of a lifetime about the perils of stalking a cop. She shut the door, quickly slipped on her pants, parka, and boots, grabbed her Glock, and pulled open the door.

The car was gone.

The hairs on the back of her neck tingled. She shut the door, bolted it, and called Dan.

"You miss me already?"

She pulled back the curtain, looking at the space where the car had been parked. The tires had left shallow impressions in the snow, which meant the car had parked after the snow had fallen but hadn't remained parked there long.

"Tracy?"

"Just wanted to hear your voice," she said, deciding that Dan had enough to worry about.

"Something up?"

"No. I'm just a worrier. A hazard of the job."

"Well, I'm fine. And I still have half of my security system at home."

"Not being followed?" she asked.

"If I were, I'd have to be an idiot not to know it. The roads are deserted. You okay?"

"Yeah, I'm fine," she said. "Good night, Dan."

"Next time I want to wake up beside you."

"I'd like that."

She disconnected and exchanged her clothes for pajama pants and her nightshirt. Before climbing back into bed, she pulled back the curtain and considered the empty space where the car had been. Then she slid the chain lock across the door, set her Glock on the nightstand, and turned off the light.

Dan's smell lingered on the pillow. He'd been a gentle and patient lover, his hands firm but his touch soft, just as she'd imagined. He'd given her time to relax, to free her mind until she was no longer thinking, just reacting to the motion of his body and the touch of his hands. When she'd climaxed, she'd clung to him, not wanting the feeling, or him, to leave her.

CHAPTER 43

She slept through the night, the first time in months, and the following morning awoke feeling refreshed, though anxious about the upcoming day. She didn't recall ever feeling nervous as a cop. The days when the shit hit the fan were the good days for her, the exciting days, the days when her shift flew by as if the hours were minutes. But the simple act of sitting through another day of the hearing provoked anxiety as the trial had all those years earlier.

She retrieved a copy of the *Cascade County Courier* in the motel lobby. The front page included an article on the hearing, with an accompanying photograph of Tracy entering the courthouse, but thankfully no picture of her and Dan kissing outside the veterinary clinic or entering her motel room together.

Finlay met her in the courthouse parking lot as planned and facilitated her access through the media and into the courtroom, and Tracy could not help but sense that Finlay took some pride in his role as her guardian.

As the 9:00 a.m. hour approached, Tracy expected fewer spectators, figuring the novelty of the first day would have worn off for some, and the worsening weather would deter all but the hardiest, but when the courtroom doors opened the pews again quickly filled. If anything, there were more people in attendance, perhaps intrigued by the article on the first day of the proceedings. Tracy counted four additional media badges.

House again entered the courtroom escorted by multiple correctional officers, but this time when he reached counsel table and faced the gallery to allow the officers to remove his handcuffs, House did not look to his uncle. He looked directly at Tracy. His gaze made her skin crawl, as it had twenty years earlier, but unlike that day, Tracy had no intention of looking away, not even when House's mouth inched into that familiar grin. She knew enough now to know that the stare and grin were his façade, meant to make her feel uncomfortable, but that House—while physically hardened in prison—very much remained emotionally stunted, the insecure kid who had abducted Annabelle Bovine because he couldn't bear the thought of her leaving him.

House broke his gaze when the clerk entered and commanded the room to rise. Judge Meyers resumed his seat, and day two was underway.

"Mr. O'Leary, you may continue," Meyers said.

Dan called Bob Fitzsimmons to the stand. Twenty years earlier, Fitzsimmons had been the managing partner of the company that entered into contracts with the State of Washington to construct three hydroelectric dams across the Cascade River, including Cascade Falls. Though now retired and in his seventies, Fitzsimmons looked as if he'd just stepped from the board meeting of a Fortune 500 company. He had a healthy head of silver hair and wore a pin-striped suit and lavender tie.

In short order, O'Leary had Fitzsimmons explain the process of obtaining the necessary federal and state paperwork to build the dams, a public process covered in the local newspapers.

"Naturally the dam backed up the river," Fitzsimmons said, legs crossed. "You need to create a ready source of water in the event of a drought."

"And what was the ready source of water for Cascade Falls?" O'Leary asked.

"Cascade Lake," Fitzsimmons said.

O'Leary used two diagrams to compare the size of Cascade Lake before the dam went online and after the area had flooded. The increased area included the location where Calloway had put an X to signify where Sarah's body had eventually been discovered.

"And when did that area flood?" O'Leary asked.

"October 12, 1993," Fitzsimmons said.

"And was that date public knowledge?" O'Leary asked.

Fitzsimmons nodded. "We made sure it was in all the newspapers and the local broadcasts. It was a state mandate and we did more than the state required."

"Why was that?"

"Because people hunted and hiked in that area. You didn't want anyone trapped out there when the water came."

O'Leary sat. Clark approached. "Mr. Fitzsimmons, did your company do anything else to ensure no one was 'trapped out there when the water came,' as you put it?"

"I don't understand the question."

"Didn't you also hire security personnel and put up roadblocks to keep people out of that area?"

"We did that several days before the plant went online."

"So it would have been extremely difficult for anyone to have entered that area, wouldn't it?"

"That was the intent."

"Did any of your security people report seeing anyone trying to enter the area?"

"Not that I recall."

"No reports of someone carrying a body down a trail?"

Dan objected. "The prosecutor is testifying, Your Honor."

Clark shot back, "Your Honor, that is exactly the insinuation being made here."

Meyers raised a hand. "I'll rule on the objections, Mr. Clark. The objection is overruled."

"Did you receive any reports of anyone carrying a body down a trail?" Clark asked.

"No," Fitzsimmons said.

Clark sat.

O'Leary stood. "How big an area is this?" He used the diagram to note the flooded area.

Fitzsimmons frowned. "My recollection is the lake was about two thousand five hundred acres and closer to four thousand five hundred after we went online."

"And how many trails cut across that area?"

Fitzsimmons smiled and shook his head. "Far too many for me to know."

"You put up roadblocks and posted security on the main roads, but you couldn't possibly have covered every point of ingress and egress, could you?"

"No way to do that," Fitzsimmons said.

O'Leary followed Fitzsimmons with Vern Downie, the man James Crosswhite had specifically enlisted to lead the search for Sarah in the hills above Cedar Grove because Vern knew those hills better than anyone. Tracy and her friends used to joke that Vern, with his thinning hair and five o'clock shadow on a craggy face, would have been a hit in horror movies, especially with a voice that rarely rose above a whisper.

In the intervening twenty years, Vern looked to have forsaken shaving altogether. His gray-and-silver beard started just a few inches below his eyes, obscured his neck, and extended nearly to his chest. He wore fresh blue jeans, a belt with a silver, oval-shaped buckle, boots, and a flannel shirt. For Vern, this was church attire.

His wife sat in the first row for moral support, as she had at the trial. Tracy recalled that Vern wasn't much for public anything, particularly public speaking.

"Mr. Downie, you're going to have to speak up to be heard," Meyers cautioned, after Vern whispered his name and address. Perhaps sensing Vern's anxiety, Dan eased him into his testimony with some background questions before getting to the substance of his examination.

"How many days did you search?" O'Leary asked.

Vern stuck out his lips and pinched them. His face scrunched with thought. "We were out there every day for the week," he said. "After that we went out couple times a week, usually after work. That was maybe a few more weeks. Until the area flooded."

"How many people were involved in the search initially?"

Vern looked to the gallery. "How many people in this room?"

Dan let the answer stand. It was the first light moment in two days.

Clark stood and approached the lectern. Again, he was brief. "Vern, how many acres are those foothills?"

"Hell, Vance, I wouldn't know that."

"It's a big area isn't it?"

"Yeah, it's big."

"Is it rugged?"

"Depends on your perspective, I guess. It can get steep and there's a lot of trees and shrub. Dense in places, that's for sure."

"A lot of places for someone to bury a body and not have it found?"

"I suppose," he said, and he glanced at Edmund House.

"Did you use dogs?"

"I recall they had dogs in Southern California but we couldn't get them up here. They wouldn't fly them."

"As systematic as your search was, Vern, do you believe you covered every square foot of those foothills?"

"We did our best."

"Did you cover every square foot?"

"Every square foot? No way to know that for sure. It's just too big. I guess we didn't."

—

Dan followed Downie with Ryan Hagen, the auto-parts salesman. Hagen took the stand looking like he'd put on thirty pounds since the Saturday morning when Tracy had surprised him at his home. Hagen's jowls fell over the collar of his shirt. His hairline had further thinned, and he had the ruddy complexion and bulbous nose of a man who liked his daily cocktails.

Hagen chuckled when Dan asked if he had a purchase order or other document to confirm his trip on August 21, 1993.

"Whatever the company, I'm sure it's long since gone out of business. Most of this is done over the Internet now. The traveling salesman has gone the way of the dinosaur." As she watched him, Tracy thought that the salesman might have left, but Hagen still had the salesman's smile and mannered charm.

Hagen also couldn't say which news broadcast he'd been watching.

"You testified twenty years ago you were watching your Mariners."

"Still a fan," Hagen said.

"So you know the Mariners have never been to the World Series."

"I'm an optimist." Others in the audience smiled along with Hagen.

"But it didn't happen in 1993, did it?"

Hagen paused. "Nope."

"In fact, they finished in fourth place and didn't make the play-offs that year."

"I'll have to take your word on that. My memory isn't *that* good."

"Which means their last regular season game was Sunday, October 3, a seven-to-two loss to the Minnesota Twins."

Hagen's smile waned. "I'll take your word for that also."

"The Mariners weren't playing in late October, 1993, when you claimed to have seen this broadcast, were they?"

Hagen kept smiling, but now it looked strained. "It might have been a different team," he said.

Dan let that answer linger before shifting gears. "Mr. Hagen, did you make service calls on any establishments in Cedar Grove?"

"I don't recall," Hagen said. "I had a big territory."

"Natural salesman," Dan said.

"I guess I am," he said, though he no longer looked the part.

"Let me see if I can help." Dan picked up a Bekins box and set it on the table. He made a production of pulling out the files and documents. Hagen looked perplexed by this turn of events and Tracy noticed his gaze shift to where Roy Calloway sat in the gallery. Dan pulled out a file Tracy had recovered from the file cabinets in Harley Holt's garage and moved to a position beside the lectern, blocking Hagen from making eye contact with Calloway. The records in that file documented regular orders of parts by Harley Holt from Hagen's company.

Dan asked, "Did you not call upon Harley Holt, the owner of Cedar Grove Service and Repair?"

"That was a long time ago."

Dan made a production of flipping through the documents. "In fact, you called on Mr. Holt fairly regularly, once every couple months or so."

Hagen smiled again, but he'd flushed and his brow glistened with perspiration. "If that's what the records show, I won't quibble with you."

"So you did spend some time in Cedar Grove, including during the summer and fall of 1993, didn't you?"

"I'd have to check my calendar," Hagen said.

"I did that for you," Dan said. "And I have copies here of purchase orders that contain both your and Harley's signatures on them, dated the same day that your calendar indicates you called upon the Cedar Grove Service and Repair."

"Well, then I guess I did," Hagen said, sounding less and less sure.

"So I'm wondering, Mr. Hagen, during those visits with Harley Holt, did the subject of Sarah Crosswhite's disappearance come up?"

Hagen reached for a glass of water next to the chair, took a sip, and returned the glass to the stand. "Could you repeat the question?"

"During your visits with Harley Holt, did the subject of Sarah Crosswhite's disappearance come up?"

"You know, I'm not really sure."

"It was big news in Cedar Grove, wasn't it?"

"I, I don't know. I suppose it was."

"They had a billboard right there on the highway offering a ten-thousand-dollar reward, didn't they?"

"I didn't receive any reward."

"I didn't say you did." Dan pulled out another document and acted as though he was reading it as he asked his question. "What I asked was, even though Sarah Crosswhite's disappearance was big news all over Cascade County, one of your geographic sales areas, are you saying you can't recall you and Mr. Holt *ever* discussing it?"

Hagen cleared his throat. "I believe we probably did, you know, in general. Not in any detail. That's the best I can recall anyway."

"So you knew about Sarah's disappearance before you ever saw a news program, didn't you?"

"The news program may have jogged my memory. Or I could have spoken to Harley about it after the fact. That's probably what it was. I'm not too sure anymore."

Dan held up more sheets of paper as he spoke. "It didn't come up in August or September or October."

"I don't recall specifically, is what I'm saying. I suppose it could have. Like I said, twenty years is a long time."

"During your visits to Cedar Grove, did you ever discuss Edmund House with anyone?"

"Edmund House? No, I'm pretty sure his name did not come up."

"Pretty sure?"

"I don't recall his name coming up."

Dan took another document from the file and held it up. "Did Harley ever tell you his service and repair shop had ordered parts for Parker House's vehicles and had done the maintenance on a red, Chevy stepside truck?"

Clark rose. "Your Honor, if Mr. O'Leary is going to ask questions from documents, I would ask that they be entered into evidence rather than continuing with this exercise to test Mr. Hagen's memory about discreet meetings that may or may not have occurred twenty years ago."

"Overruled," Meyers said.

Tracy knew Dan was acting. She had tried unsuccessfully to find a record that confirmed Harley had ordered a car part from Hagen for the Chevy Parker House had been restoring. Hagen, however, did not dare call Dan's bluff at this point. The salesman had turned a beet red and looked as though someone had put a hot plate beneath his seat.

"I believe we did discuss that," Hagen said, shifting to cross his legs and then parting them again. "It's kind of coming back now. I remember saying to Harley that I saw a red Chevy on the road that night, or something like that. That must have been how I remembered it."

"I thought you remembered it because you heard about it on a news program as you were watching a Mariners game and the Chevy stepside was your favorite truck?"

"Well, it was probably a little bit of both. It was my favorite truck, so when Harley mentioned that, you know, Edmund House drove one, then it clicked."

Dan paused. Judge Meyers looked down at Hagen with a furrowed brow.

Then Dan stepped directly beside the witness chair. "So you and Harley Holt did discuss Edmund House by name," he said.

Hagen's eyes widened. This time he could not muster a smile, not even a pained one. "Did I say Edmund? I meant Parker. Right. Parker House. It was his truck, wasn't it?"

Dan turned to Clark without providing an answer. "Your witness."

CHAPTER 44

When Judge Meyers returned to the bench for the afternoon session, he looked troubled, and considered the daunting blanket of snow continuing to fall outside his courtroom windows. "While I believe it is important to proceed expeditiously, I also do not want to be foolhardy," he said. "The weathermen indicate the snow is supposed to let up this afternoon. Having lived in the Pacific Northwest much of my life, I prefer my own method of meteorology; I stick my head out the front door." The audience chuckled. "That is precisely what I did during the break, and I didn't see any blue sky on the horizon. This will be our last witness of the day so as to avoid many of you driving home in the dark."

Dan displayed a series of charts and photographs on the flat-screen television as he walked Kelly Rosa, the King County forensic anthropologist, through her testimony. He started with Finlay Armstrong's phone call and the photograph of the bone.

"And how long does it take before body fat deteriorates and turns to adipocere?"

"It depends on a number of different factors: the location of the body, the depth of burial, soil and climate conditions. Generally, though, it happens over years, not days or months."

"So you concluded the remains had been buried for years. Why then were you puzzled?"

Rosa sat forward. "Normally a body buried in a shallow grave in the wilderness does not remain buried long. Coyotes and other animals will get to it."

"Were you able to resolve this mystery?"

"I was advised that the grave site, up until recently, had been covered by a body of water, making it inaccessible to animals."

"Did you conclude from the fact that animals had not desecrated the site—that is, scattered the bones—that the body had to have been buried shortly before the area was flooded?"

Clark stood. "Calls for speculation, Your Honor."

Meyers considered the objection. "As Dr. Rosa is an expert, she can answer as to her opinions and conclusions."

Rosa said, "I can only say that normally it would not have taken long for animals to get to a body buried in that shallow of a grave."

O'Leary paced. "I also noted in your report a wholly separate reason for your opinion that these remains were not buried immediately upon death. Can you explain why?"

"It has to do with the position of the body in the grave." Dan displayed a photograph of Sarah's remains on the flat-screen. The dirt had been whisked away to reveal a skeleton curled in what looked very much like a fetal position. The gallery fidgeted and emitted soft rumblings. Tracy lowered her gaze and covered her mouth, nauseated and light-headed. Her mouth watered. She closed her eyes and took short, quick breaths.

"It was clear the person tried unsuccessfully to bend the body to fit in the hole," Rosa continued.

"How long before burial did rigor mortis set in?" Dan asked.

"I can't say with any reasonable certainty."

"Were you able to determine the cause of death?"

"No."

"Did you note any injuries, broken bones?"

"I noted skull fractures at the back of the cranium." She used a diagram to show the location of the fractures.

"Could you determine what caused the skull fractures?"

"A blunt-force trauma, but from what . . ." She shrugged. "It's not possible to tell."

Rosa then explained how her team accounted for everything, from bone fragments to the rivets from Sarah's Levi's and the silver-and-black snaps of her Scully shirt. She also said she had unearthed pieces of black plastic of the same material as common lawn and leaf bags, as well as carpet fibers.

"And could you draw any conclusions from that?"

"What I can conclude is that the plastic was either placed underneath the body prior to the body being placed in the hole, or—"

"Why would someone do that?"

Rosa shook her head. "I don't have any idea."

"What is the other possibility?"

"The body was buried in a plastic bag."

Tracy struggled to control her breathing. She felt flushed. Perspiration trickled down her sides.

"Did you find anything else?"

"Jewelry."

"What in particular?"

"A pair of earrings and a necklace."

The crowd stirred. Meyers reached for his gavel but resisted rapping it.

"Can you describe the earrings?"

"They were jade, teardrop shaped."

Dan presented Rosa with the jewelry in question. "Would you show us on your diagram where you located each earring?"

Rosa used a pointer to note the two locations. "Near the skull. The necklace we found near the top of the spinal column."

"Did you reach any conclusions from the location of the jewelry?"

"I concluded the deceased was wearing the jewelry when placed in the grave."

—

Vance Clark left his tortoiseshell glasses on the table and moved purposefully toward the witness chair. He held no notes, arms crossed across his chest. "Let's discuss for a moment, Dr. Rosa, what you don't know. You don't know how the deceased died."

"I do not."

"You don't know how the deceased received the blunt-force trauma to the back of her skull."

"I do not."

"The killer could have banged her head against the ground while strangling her."

Rosa shrugged. "It could have happened that way."

"You have no evidence to determine whether the deceased was raped."

"I don't."

"You have no DNA evidence with which the killer could be identified."

"I don't."

"You believe the victim was killed sometime before burial but you don't know how long before."

"Not with any certainty."

"So you don't know if the killer buried the body immediately after death, then went back some time later and moved the body to where it was ultimately found."

"I don't know that," Rosa agreed.

"That could be a potential reason that rigor mortis had set in before the body was placed in this particular location, correct?

Edmund House could have killed her, buried the body, then later went back to move it, and found that rigor mortis had set in, correct?"

Dan stood. "Your Honor, now the State is clearly asking Dr. Rosa to speculate."

Meyers looked to be pondering the scenario. "I'll allow it."

"Dr. Rosa, do you need me to repeat my question?" Clark asked.

Rosa said, "No. The scenario is possible with one clarification. Rigor mortis dissipates after approximately thirty-six hours. So under the scenario you've posed, Mr. House would have had to have moved the body relatively quickly."

"But it is a possibility," Clark said.

"It is a possibility," she said.

"So there's quite a bit of speculation on your part, in addition to the science."

Rosa smiled. "I'm just answering the questions asked."

"I understand. But the only thing you can state definitively is that the deceased is, in fact, Sarah Lynne Crosswhite."

"Yes."

"Do you know what clothes the victim was wearing when she was abducted?"

"No."

"Do you know what jewelry the victim was wearing when abducted?"

"Again, I can only offer an opinion based upon what I located in the grave."

"I see you're wearing earrings today."

"I am."

"Have you ever put on a pair of earrings and then, perhaps undecided, brought a second pair?"

Rosa shrugged. "I don't know that I have."

"Have you known women who do that sort of thing?"

"I have," she said.

"It is a woman's prerogative to change her mind, is it not?" Clark smiled. "God knows my wife does."

The question brought a few snickers. It was a light moment in the darkest testimony so far and those in the gallery responded with nervous laughter. Even Judge Meyers smiled.

"That's what I tell my husband," Rosa said.

"And you have no idea whether the deceased had more than one pair of earrings or more than one necklace when she was abducted?"

"I do not."

Clark smiled for the first time in two days as he returned to his seat.

Dan stood. "No further questions," he said.

Meyers considered the clock on the wall. "We will end for the day. Mr. O'Leary, who do you intend to call tomorrow morning?"

Dan stood. "Weather permitting," he said, "Tracy Crosswhite."

CHAPTER 45

The media for the most part left Tracy alone, perhaps heeding Judge Meyers's warning that everyone get to where they were staying before nightfall. The inside of her car was cold as an icebox. Tracy started the engine and stepped out to clear the windshield while the defroster blasted hot air from the inside.

Dan called her cell phone. "I'm going to get Rex," he said. "The weather is supposed to get worse. No one is going to be out tonight. Stay at the house."

She flexed her fingers against the cold and looked at the cars departing the parking lot and lining the adjacent streets. "Are you sure?" she asked, but she was already contemplating making love to Dan and sleeping soundly beside him.

"I won't be able to sleep and Sherlock misses you."

"Only Sherlock?"

"He whimpers. It isn't pretty."

⎯

Rex greeted her at the door, his tail whipping the air.

"Well, I can see myself quickly becoming second fiddle around here," Dan said. "But at least they have good taste in women."

Tracy put down her suitcase and knelt to gently caress the dog's head beneath the plastic cone. "How are you, boy?"

When she stood, Dan said, "You doing okay?"

She stepped to him and let him wrap his arms around her, holding her. She'd felt the impact of Kelly Rosa's testimony more than she'd thought she would. Trained to disassociate herself from a victim, over her years as a homicide detective Tracy had investigated horrific crime scenes with a practiced detachment. She'd become desensitized in order to deal with very visual depictions of evil manifested in man's inhumanity to man. For years, she'd investigated Sarah's disappearance with the same learned detachment, not allowing herself to consider what despicable things her killer could have done to her. That detachment had had holes poked in it when she'd hiked into the mountains and seen Sarah's remains in the shallow grave. It had collapsed when she'd seen her baby sister's skeletal remains on the courtroom television and had to come to grips with hard evidence of the horrors Sarah had endured, and the indecency of her being stuffed in a garbage bag and dumped into a shallow hole like a bag of trash. Now, out of the public eye, away from the intrusion of the cameras into her personal life, Tracy wept, and it felt good to do so while being held by someone who had also known and loved Sarah.

After several minutes, Tracy stepped back and wiped her tears from her cheek. "I must look like a mess."

"No," Dan said. "You could never look like a mess."

"Thanks, Dan."

"What else can I do for you?"

"Take me away."

"Where?"

She tilted back her head and met his lips, kissing him. "Make love to me, Dan," she whispered.

—

Their clothes were spilled across the bedroom carpet, along with the decorative pillows. Dan lay beneath the sheet catching his breath. They'd kicked off the covers and the down comforter. "Maybe it's a good thing you stopped being a teacher. You would have broken a lot of high school boys' hearts."

She rolled over and kissed him. "And if I was your teacher, I would definitely have given you an A for effort."

"Only for effort?"

"And the results."

He put an arm behind his head and looked up at the ceiling, chest still rapidly rising and falling. "My first A, how do you like that? If only I had known back then that all I had to do was sleep with the teacher."

She punched him lightly and laid her chin on his shoulder. After a comfortable silence, she said, "Life has a way of throwing us curves, doesn't it? When you lived here, did you ever think you'd marry someone from the East Coast and live in Boston?"

"No," he said. "And when I lived in Boston, I never thought I'd be back in Cedar Grove sleeping with Tracy Crosswhite in my parents' bedroom."

"Kind of creepy when you put it like that, Dan." She ran her fingers over his chest. "Sarah used to say she was going to live with me. When I asked what she would do when I got married, she'd say we would live next door to each other, teach our kids to shoot, and take them to competitions just like we did with my dad."

"Would you ever consider coming back?" Her fingers stopped. He moaned and visibly cringed. "Sorry. I shouldn't have asked that."

After a moment, she said, "It's hard separating the good memories from the bad."

"What was I?"

She tilted her head to look into his eyes. "You were definitely one of the good memories, Dan, and getting better and better."

"You hungry?"

"Famous bacon cheeseburgers?"

"Carbonara. Another of my specialties."

"Are all your specialties fattening?"

"Those are the best kind."

"Then I'll jump in the shower," she said.

He kissed her and slid out of bed. "I'll have it on the table awaiting your arrival."

"You're going to spoil me, Dan."

"I'm trying."

He bent and kissed her again, and she was tempted to pull him back down to the bed, but he slipped away to descend the stairs. Tracy fell back, hugging a pillow to her chest, listening to Dan rummaging about the kitchen, drawers opening and closing, and pots and pans clanging. She'd been happy once in Cedar Grove. Could she be happy here again? Maybe all she needed was someone like Dan, someone to make Cedar Grove feel like home again. But even as she thought it, she knew the answer to her question. There was a reason for adages like "you can never go home again," just as there was a reason for stereotypes—because they were usually true. She groaned and threw the pillow aside, getting up. Now was not the time to consider the future. She had enough to worry about in the present.

She would be on the stand first thing in the morning.

CHAPTER 46

The storm did not hit Cedar Grove. For once, the weathermen had got it right. That was not to say the weather had improved. The morning temperature had plunged to eight degrees, one of the colder days on record in Cascade County. Still, it did not deter the spectators from filing into the courtroom for day three of the hearing. Tracy wore her black skirt and jacket, what she referred to as her trial suit. She'd brought heels in her briefcase, and once inside the courtroom, she removed her snow boots and slipped them on.

With reports that the predicted storm still continued to bear down on the region, Judge Meyers seemed more determined than ever to get the proceedings moving. His seat had barely hit his chair when he said, "Mr. O'Leary, call your next witness."

"The defense calls Tracy Crosswhite," Dan said.

Tracy felt Edmund House's gaze fix on her as she stepped through the gate and walked to the witness stand to take the oath to tell the truth. It made her sick, knowing she was House's best chance at freedom. She thought of what Dan had told her about his conversation with George Bovine, shortly after Annabelle's father had visited Dan's office to warn him about Edmund House. Bovine had said that prison was the only place for someone like Edmund House. Tracy didn't doubt it, but they were beyond that point.

Dan eased her into her testimony and Judge Meyers, perhaps sensitive to the emotional subject matter, did not rush him. After preliminary background matters had been dispensed with, Dan asked, "She was called your shadow, was she not?"

"Seemed she was always by my side."

O'Leary strolled close to the windows. Dark tendrils of clouds reached down from an ominous sky, from which a light snow had started to fall again. "Would you describe the physical location of your bedrooms growing up?"

Clark rose. He was objecting more to Dan's direct examination of Tracy than he'd objected during any other witness, clearly trying to disrupt the flow of Tracy's testimony and seemingly more concerned that Dan was going to try to slip in something inadmissible. "Objection, Your Honor. It's irrelevant."

"It's for foundational purposes," Dan said.

"I'll allow it, but let's move this forward, Counselor."

"Sarah's bedroom was just down the hall from mine, but it really didn't matter. She spent most nights in my bed. She was afraid of the dark."

"Did you share a bathroom?"

"Yes, between our bedrooms."

"And as sisters, did you borrow each other's things?"

"Sometimes more than I would have liked," Tracy said, trying to muster a smile. "Sarah and I were about the same size. We had similar tastes."

"Did that include the same taste in jewelry?"

"Yes."

"Detective Crosswhite, would you describe the events that took place August 21, 1993, for the court?"

Tracy felt her emotions welling and paused to gather herself. "Sarah and I were competing in the Washington State Cowboy

Action Shooting Championship," she said. "We were actually tied for the lead going into the final shooting stage, which was to shoot ten targets alternating using both hands. I missed a target, which is an automatic five-second penalty. In essence, I'd lost."

"So Sarah won?"

"No. Sarah missed two targets." Tracy smiled at the recollection. "Sarah hadn't missed two targets in two years, let alone in one stage."

"She did it on purpose."

"Sarah knew that my boyfriend, Ben, was coming to pick me up that evening, that he planned to propose at our favorite restaurant." Tracy paused and sipped her water, returning the glass to the table beside the chair. "I was upset because I knew Sarah had let me win. It colored my judgment."

"In what way?"

"The weather forecast was bad. Heavy rains and thunderstorms. Ben picked me up at the competition in order to make our reservation." Tracy felt the words sticking in her throat.

Dan helped her out. "So Sarah had to drive your truck home alone."

"I should have insisted that she come with us. I never saw her again."

Dan paused, as if out of respect. Quietly he asked, "Was there a prize associated with winning?"

Tracy nodded. "A silver-plated belt buckle."

O'Leary retrieved the pewter-colored buckle from the evidence table and handed it to her, identifying it by its designated evidence number. "The medical examiner testified that she uncovered this buckle in the grave with Sarah's remains. Can you explain how it could have got there if you'd won the buckle that day?"

"Because I gave Sarah the buckle."

"Why did you do that?"

"Like I said, I knew that Sarah let me win. So before I left I gave the buckle to her."

"And that's the last time you saw it?"

She nodded. She'd never contemplated that the brief moment she'd looked back through the window of the truck cab and seen Sarah standing in the rain, wearing Tracy's black Stetson, would be the last time she would ever see her sister. Tracy had thought about that moment often over the years, the fleeting nature of life and the unpredictability of the future even from one moment to the next. She regretted that she had been angry with Sarah that afternoon for letting her win. She'd allowed her personal pride to get the better of her, not knowing that Sarah's intentions had been altruistic, not wanting Tracy to depart on one of the biggest nights of her life feeling bad for coming in second.

Tracy fought against it, but a tear escaped the corner of her eye. She pulled a tissue from the box on a side table and dabbed at it. Some seated in the gallery had also begun to wipe away tears and blow their noses.

Dan gave Tracy a moment to regain her composure, acting as if he was searching his notes. Back at the podium, he asked, "Detective Crosswhite, would you tell the court what your sister was wearing the last time you saw her on August 21, 1993?"

Clark rose unexpectedly and came out from behind counsel table. "Your Honor, the State objects that the question by its very nature calls for the witness to speculate and therefore would be unreliable."

Dan met Clark before the bench. "The objection is premature, Your Honor. The State can certainly object to any particular question asked and cross-examine Detective Crosswhite concerning her recollection. That is not a valid reason to bar her testimony altogether."

Clark sounded almost exasperated. "With all due respect to Your Honor's ability to weed out such evidence, the State is concerned about an appellate record that includes speculation and supposition."

"And the State is free to voice those objections to preserve the appellate record," Dan said.

"I agree, Mr. O'Leary," Judge Meyers said, "but we all know this case has already been played out in the media far more than I would prefer, and I appreciate the State's concern about the record."

Clark jumped in. "Your Honor, the State would request an opportunity to voir dire the witness to see if there is any basis, independent of what evidence has been offered during this hearing, that this witness can recall after more than twenty years the specifics of what her sister was wearing on a particular day in August, 1993."

Meyers rocked in his chair, eyes narrowed with intrigue. Tracy was not surprised when he said, "I'll allow the State to voir dire the witness."

In her experience, when a judge knew it was likely that the outcome of a hearing would be headed to the Court of Appeals, he erred on being conservative in his rulings in order to limit the grounds for the appeal. By allowing Clark to examine Tracy's recollection, he was eliminating Clark's objection as a possible basis for the State to argue to the Court of Appeals that Meyers's ruling had been wrong. He thus minimized the possibility of having the matter remanded back into his lap.

Dan returned to his seat beside House, who leaned over and whispered something. Whatever House said, Dan did not respond.

Clark smoothed his tie, this one adorned with trout, as he approached the podium. "Ms. Crosswhite, do you recall what you were wearing August 21, 1993?"

"I can make an educated guess."

"A guess?" Clark glanced at Meyers.

"I was superstitious. I always wore a red bandanna, turquoise bolo tie, and my black Stetson during competitions. I also wore a long suede coat."

"I see. Was your sister superstitious?"

"Sarah was too good to be superstitious."

"So we can make no such *guesses* about what she might have worn that day, can we?"

"Only that she preferred to look better than everyone else."

Smiles creased several of the faces in the gallery.

"But she didn't have a particular shirt she wore to each competition?"

Tracy said, "She wore Scully. It's a particular brand. She liked the embroidering."

"How many Scully shirts did she own?"

"I'd guess ten or so."

"Ten," Clark said. "And no particular boots or hat?"

"She had several pairs of boots and I recall half a dozen hats."

Clark turned toward the jury box. Realizing it was empty and that he was without a jury to play to, he positioned himself near the railing separating the gallery. "So you have no basis to testify with any certainty as to what your sister wore on August 21, 1993, other than a *guess* after twenty years, or what you may have heard during this hearing, correct?"

"No. That's not correct."

Clark looked taken aback. Meyers's chair squeaked as he rocked, looking on intently. The gallery had gone silent. Clark stepped toward the witness chair, no doubt debating what was every lawyer's dilemma on cross-examination—whether or not to ask the next question and possibly open a Pandora's box without any idea of what was inside, or to move on to a different subject. The problem for Clark, Tracy knew from her experience as a trial witness in homicide cases, was that he had opened the subject matter, and that meant that, if *he* didn't ask the question, Dan would.

Clark's banter slowed, cautious. "You certainly don't remember what she was wearing."

"No. Not with certainty, I don't."

"And we've established she didn't have any superstitious articles of clothing she wore."

"She did not."

"So what other possible means . . ." Clark suddenly stopped.

Tracy did not wait for Clark to decide if he was going to finish his question. "A photograph," she said.

Clark flinched. "But surely not of that day."

"Yes, of that day," Tracy said evenly. "They took a Polaroid of the three top finishers. Sarah finished second."

Clark cleared his throat. "And you just happen to have kept this photograph for twenty years?"

"Of course I kept it. It's the last photograph ever taken of Sarah."

Because Tracy had removed the photograph from her rugged cart the morning she had met with Calloway to look inside her blue Ford, the photograph had never been inventoried and had never become a part of the police file.

Clark looked to Meyers. "Your Honor, the State would request a meeting of counsel in chambers."

"Denied. Are you finished with your voir dire?"

"Your Honor, the State objects. No such photograph was ever produced in this case. This is the first we have heard anything of it."

"Mr. O'Leary?" Meyers asked.

Dan stood. "As far as I know, Your Honor, the State is correct. The photograph certainly did not belong to the defense, and the defense had no means to produce it even if such a request had been made. However, the State clearly had access to it through Detective Crosswhite."

"The objection is overruled," Meyers said. "Mr. O'Leary, you may continue your examination."

Dan re-approached the lectern. "Detective Crosswhite, do you have that photograph with you today?"

Tracy reached into her briefcase and pulled out the framed photograph. The commotion from the gallery was enough for Judge Meyers to rap his gavel. After having the photograph marked and introduced into evidence, Dan asked Tracy to describe what Sarah was wearing in it and Tracy complied. Then Dan asked, "Can you describe the earrings and necklace your sister is wearing in that photograph?"

"The earrings are jade, teardrop shaped. The necklace is a silver strand."

"Do you recognize these?" O'Leary handed her the jade earrings Rosa had recovered from Sarah's grave.

"Yes. They're the same earrings Sarah is wearing in the photograph."

Dan retrieved the miniature, Colt-shaped pistol earrings introduced at House's original trial. The gallery stirred. "And these," he said, identifying them by their exhibit number. "Do you recognize these earrings?"

"Yes, those were also Sarah's."

"Was she wearing them the day she was abducted?"

Clark bolted from his seat. "Objection, Your Honor. The witness has testified she does not recall with certainty what her sister wore that day. The only thing this witness can testify to is whether they match the earrings in the photograph."

"I'll withdraw the question," Dan said. "Detective Crosswhite, are these earrings the earrings your sister is wearing in the photograph?"

"No," Tracy said. "They're not."

Dan replaced the earrings on the evidence table and sat. The murmuring had reached a sufficient volume for Meyers to rap his gavel. "I'll remind those seated in the gallery to maintain the decorum I discussed at the opening of these proceedings."

Clark stood and approached the witness stand with a seeming sense of urgency, his voice defiant. "You testified that your sister was fashion conscious, isn't that correct?"

"Yes, she was."

"You said she wore any number of different ensembles to these competitions, multiple shirts and pants and hats, correct?"

"Yes."

"Did she take additional clothes with her to these competitions and change her mind about what she was going to wear?"

"Sometimes more than once," Tracy said. "It was an annoying habit."

"Including changing her mind about what jewelry to wear," Clark said.

"I can think of occasions she did that, especially if the tournament was more than one day long."

"Thank you." Looking partially relieved, Clark quickly sat.

Dan stood. "Briefly, Your Honor." He crossed to the lectern. "Detective Crosswhite, the times you recall your sister changing her jewelry, do you recall a single instance in which she ever changed to the jewelry presented at Edmund House's initial trial? The pistol-shaped earrings identified as State exhibits Thirty-Four A and Thirty-Four B?"

"I never saw her do that, no."

Dan gestured toward Clark. "The State's question intimates that could have been a possibility; could it have been a possibility?"

Clark objected. "Again, the question asks this witness to speculate. She can testify as to what is in the photograph."

"The question does call for speculation, Mr. O'Leary," Meyers said.

"If the court will indulge me, Your Honor, I believe Detective Crosswhite will explain why it does not."

"I'll give you some leeway but make it quick."

"Could it have been a possibility that your sister wore these pistol-shaped earrings?" Dan asked.

"No."

"How can you be so emphatic given your testimony that your sister had a propensity to change her mind?"

"My father gave Sarah the pistol earrings and the necklace after she won the Washington State Cowboy Action Shooting Championship when she was seventeen. The year, 1992, is engraved on the back of each earring. Sarah wore them once. They gave her horrible ear infections. She couldn't wear anything but twenty-four-carat-gold or sterling-silver posts. My father thought they were sterling silver, but they clearly weren't. Sarah didn't want to upset him, so she never told him. She also never wore them again to my knowledge."

"Where did she keep them?"

"In a jewelry box on her dresser in her bedroom."

Meyers had stopped rocking. The gallery too had stilled. Out the windows the ethereal dark fingers reached further down from the sky and the snowfall had grown heavier.

"Thank you," Dan said and quietly returned to his seat.

Clark sat with his index finger pressed to his lips as Tracy left the stand. Her heels clicked the marble floor as she made her way across the well to the gallery. As she did, a sudden gust of wind rattled the windows, spooking those in the gallery who were sitting nearby them. One woman gasped and flinched. Otherwise, no one moved. Even Maria Vanpelt, resplendent in a royal-blue St. John pantsuit, sat still, looking pensive.

Only one person looked as if he'd enjoyed the morning's events. Edmund House rocked onto the back legs of his chair, smiling like a man who had just had his fill at a fine restaurant and had savored every last bite.

CHAPTER 47

At the start of the afternoon session, Judge Meyers retook the bench looking resigned. "It appears the weathermen got it partially correct," he said. "The third storm is approaching, though they expect it to hit sooner than anticipated, as early as late this afternoon. I am going to push counsel to finish the hearing today, if at all possible."

Dan immediately stood and announced that Harrison Scott would be the defense's last witness.

"Let's get to it, then," Meyers said.

Tall and lean, Scott took the witness chair in a steel-gray suit. In quick order Dan went through Scott's educational background as well as his credentials. Scott had been head of the Washington State Crime Labs in Seattle and Vancouver, Washington, before he had gone into private practice to start Independent Forensics Laboratories.

"What type of work does IFL specialize in?" O'Leary asked.

Scott pushed sandy-blond hair off his forehead. Except for the patches of gray at his temples, he looked too young for his impressive resume. He looked like he should be riding waves off the beaches of Southern California. "We do all disciplines of forensic work, from DNA analysis to processing latent fingerprints, firearm and tool-mark analysis, crime scene analysis, and micro-analysis of things such as hairs and fibers, glass, paint."

"Would you explain to the court what I asked your laboratory to do in this particular case?"

"You sought a DNA analysis on three blood samples and thirteen hair samples."

"Did I tell you where those samples were obtained?"

"The DNA samples you provided had been kept by the Washington State Patrol Crime Lab as part of a police investigation into the disappearance of a young woman named Sarah Crosswhite."

"Would you provide the court with a brief overview of DNA testing?"

"The court is familiar with DNA analysis and testing," Meyers said, scribbling notes and not raising his head. "Move along."

"Did you perform DNA testing on the blood and hair samples I provided to you?"

"We did," Scott said, and he provided an overview of the tests performed.

"Were those tests available back in 1993?"

"No, they were not."

"Starting with the blood, were you able to obtain a DNA profile from the samples provided?"

"Because of the age of the samples and the manner in which they had been stored, as well as possible cross-contamination, it was not possible to obtain a full DNA profile."

"Were you able to obtain a partial DNA profile on any blood sample?"

"Just one."

"And could you make any definitive conclusions about that sample based on that partial profile?"

"Only that it belonged to a male."

"You could not identify a specific individual?"

"No."

Dan nodded and checked his notes. Scott's findings confirmed House's assertion that the blood was his and lent some credibility to his contention that he'd cut himself working in the furniture shop and had gone to his truck to get his cigarettes before going inside to clean his scratches and scrapes. Dan continued. "Would you describe the testing performed on the hair samples?"

"We examined each sample microscopically. Of the thirteen strands of hair we examined, seven strands had roots which allowed us to run DNA profiles."

"And did you obtain a DNA profile on any of those seven strands?"

"We obtained DNA profiles from five strands."

"Did you run those profiles through the state and national databases that store DNA profiles?"

"Yes we did."

"And did those DNA profiles from the hairs match any DNA profiles stored in the state and national databases?"

"Yes, we obtained what we call 'positive hits' on three of the five samples."

"What does a positive hit mean?"

"It means that the DNA profile we obtained from three of the hair samples matched a DNA profile that is on file in the state and national databases."

"Thank you, Mr. Scott. Now, let's go back a moment. Did I provide you with any other item to test for DNA?"

"Yes, you provided me with a strand of blond hair and asked that it be independently analyzed."

"Did I tell you where I obtained that independent strand of blond hair?"

"No, you did not."

"Did you obtain a DNA profile from the independent strand of blond hair?"

"We did, and we ran that DNA profile through the state and national DNA databases and obtained a positive hit."

"Dr. Scott, would you identify the person in the state database whose DNA matched the DNA you obtained from the independent strand of blonde hair that I gave to you?"

"The DNA profile matched the DNA profile in the state database for a law enforcement officer, Detective Tracy Crosswhite."

Tracy felt the gaze of the gallery shift to her.

"Okay. You testified you also matched the DNA profile on three strands of hair in the police file to an individual's DNA profile in the state database. Would you identify *that* individual?"

"The DNA obtained from the three strands of hair also matched the DNA in the state database for Tracy Crosswhite."

The gallery stirred.

"Oh my God," someone muttered.

Meyers rapped his gavel once, restoring silence.

"Just to be clear, the DNA obtained from the three strands of hair in the police investigative file, which were obtained from the interior of the red Chevy stepside truck, belonged to Tracy Crosswhite?"

"That is correct."

"What are the odds that you're wrong?" Dan asked.

Scott smiled. "Billions to one."

"Dr. Scott, you said you also obtained a DNA profile for the two other strands of hair." Dan turned and pointed to Tracy. "Those two strands did not belong to detective Crosswhite?"

"They did not."

"Were you able to determine anything definitive about those samples?"

"Actually, yes. The two strands belonged to a person genetically related to Detective Crosswhite."

"Related how?" Dan asked.

"A sibling," Scott said.

"A sister?" Dan asked.

"Most definitely a sister."

CHAPTER 48

As Harrison Scott stepped down from the witness stand following Vance Clark's brief cross-examination, Judge Meyers turned his attention to Vance Clark. "Mr. Clark, does the State wish to call any witnesses?"

Meyers's tone intimated he didn't think it wise, and for all practical purposes, who could the State call? The witnesses from 1993 had all been on the stand, and this time they had been less than stellar in their performances.

Clark rose. "The State does not, Your Honor."

Meyers nodded. "Then we'll be in recess." Without further explanation why he had recessed instead of summarily ending the day's proceedings, Meyers quickly left the bench. The moment the door leading to his chambers closed, the courtroom burst to life, and the media came at Tracy. Just as swiftly, she moved for the exit before it could become completely blocked and saw Finlay Armstrong clearing a path to facilitate her escape. "I need some fresh air," she said.

"I know a place."

Together they descended a back staircase and stepped out a side door onto a concrete deck on the south side of the building.

Tracy vaguely recalled standing on the deck during Edmund House's trial.

"I just need a minute alone," Tracy said.

"You'll be okay?" Finlay asked. "You want me to guard the door?"

"I'll be fine."

"I'll let you know when the judge returns."

It was numbingly cold, but Tracy was perspiring and her breathing labored. The finality and the magnitude of the proceeding stunned even her. She needed a moment to take it all in.

Scott's testimony that the hair samples found in the red Chevy belonged to both Tracy and to Sarah raised serious doubts about the integrity of that evidence. Then there was the added fact that the earrings presented at House's trial had not been worn by Sarah the day she was abducted, as well as the presence of plastic and carpet fibers calling into serious question Calloway's testimony that House had confessed to killing and burying Sarah quickly. Not to mention the job Dan had done discrediting Hagen. It seemed a foregone conclusion that Meyers would grant Edmund House a new trial. Now Tracy needed to think ahead. She needed to get the investigation into her sister's death reopened and she needed to get people talking. In her experience, nothing was more likely to cause conspirators to begin cannibalizing one another than the very real threat of criminal prosecution and going to prison.

The frigid cold, initially invigorating, began to burn her cheeks. The tips of her fingers had become numb. She started for the door and found Maria Vanpelt watching her.

"Will you be making a statement, Detective Crosswhite?"

Tracy didn't answer.

"I understand now what you meant about this being personal. I'm sorry about your sister. I overstepped."

Tracy mustered a nod.

"Do you have any idea who's responsible?"

"Not with any certainty."

Vanpelt stepped toward her. "It's television, Detective. It's about ratings. It was never personal."

But Tracy knew it was personal, for her and for Vanpelt. A homicide detective getting a murderer a new trial *was* good television. When the victim was the detective's sister, it was great television. And that meant not just better ratings for the station, but exposure for Vanpelt, and exposure was everything to someone like her.

"For you it's about ratings," Tracy said. "Not for me or my family. Not for this community. The impact of a murder is very real. This is my life. It was my sister's life and my parents' life. It was Cedar Grove's life. What played out here twenty years ago impacted us all. It still does."

"Perhaps an exclusive to tell your side of the story."

"My side of the story?"

"A twenty-year quest that looks as though it's coming to an end."

Tracy considered the first snowflakes falling from an ever more angry-looking sky, a sky that gave every indication that the weathermen had gotten it correct this time. She thought of Kins's and Dan's questions about what she would do when the hearing had ended.

"That's what you don't understand, what you'll never understand. When the hearing ends, you'll move on to the next story. But I don't have that luxury. It will never be over, not for me and not for this community. We've all just learned how to live with the pain," she said.

Tracy stepped past Vanpelt and pulled open the door, heading inside, eager to hear what Meyers had to say.

—

Tracy sensed a change in Judge Meyers's demeanor as he retook the bench, shuffled pages, and moved a stack of documents. He picked up a yellow pad, holding it at an angle and looking out at the half-empty gallery over the rim of reading glasses perched on the tip of his nose. Many had decided to leave and get home before the storm hit.

"I took the opportunity to check the weather report as well as to review the law to confirm the extent of my authority over these proceedings," Meyers said. "First things first. I've confirmed that a severe winter storm is scheduled to hit this evening. Knowing that, I cannot in good conscience delay these proceedings a single day further. I am, therefore, prepared to issue my preliminary findings of fact and conclusions of law."

Tracy looked to Dan. So did Edmund House. Both Dan and Vance Clark had cleared their tables during the break. Like those who'd left the gallery, they'd anticipated the proceedings had ended for the day, except for Meyers perhaps providing them with an estimated timeline for rendering his decision. Now they scrambled to get out notepads and pens. Meyers only briefly accommodated them.

"In my more than thirty years on the bench, I have never been witness to such a seeming miscarriage of justice. I do not know for certain what transpired some twenty years ago—that will be a matter, I presume, for the Justice Department to decide, along with the fate of those responsible. I do know the defense has proven in *this proceeding* that there are substantial questions as to the validity of the evidence put forward to convict the defendant, Edmund House, in 1993. While my written findings will detail those seeming improprieties in detail, I take this opportunity now because I cannot in good conscience send this defendant back to prison for even one more day."

House again turned to Dan, confused and disbelieving. A low murmur swept over what remained of the crowd. Meyers silenced it with a single rap of the gavel.

"Our judicial system is premised upon the truth. It is premised upon the participants in that system respecting and providing the truth, the whole truth, and nothing but the truth . . . so help them God. It is the only way our system of justice can properly function. It is the only way we can ensure a fair proceeding for the accused. It is not a perfect system. We cannot control those witnesses who have no regard for the truth, but we can control those who partici-pate in the judicial process—law enforcement officers and the men and women who have taken oaths to practice before this bench." In one sentence, Meyers had condemned Calloway, Clark, and DeAngelo Finn. "It is not a system without faults, but as my fellow jurist William Blackstone stated, 'It is better that ten guilty men go free than one innocent man be wrongfully convicted.'

"Mr. House, I do not know whether you are guilty or inno-cent of the crime of which you were accused, tried, and found guilty. That is not for me to determine. It is my opinion and con-clusion, however, based on the evidence presented before me, that serious questions exist as to whether you received a fair trial as is mandated by the Constitution and our forefathers who drafted it. Therefore, it will be my recommendation to the Court of Appeals that they remand this matter to the trial court and that you receive a new trial."

House had his palms pressed flat on the table. He dropped his chin to his chest and his huge shoulders rose and fell with an enor-mous sigh.

"I am not naïve," Meyers was saying. "I recognize that, during the past twenty years, evidence has gone stale and witness recol-lections will have likely eroded. The State's burden will be even greater than it was twenty years ago, but if that be a prejudice, it is a prejudice self-inflicted. That is not my concern.

"It will take some time to prepare my written findings of fact and conclusions of law, and I presume it will take time for the Court of Appeals to review them. I also assume it likely that the State will appeal my decision. There will also be the inevitable delay before the matter can be remanded to this Superior Court for the purpose of conducting a new trial, if that is to occur at all. Mr. House, those are not delays with which you need concern yourself."

Tracy realized where Meyers was headed. So too did those in the gallery, who continued to whisper and shift in their seats.

"I am, therefore, ordering your release, subject to your being processed at the Cascade County Jail and the imposition of certain conditions upon your freedom. I will not impose bail. Twenty years was more than a sufficient price. I am ordering, however, that you remain within the state, that you check in daily with your probation officer, that you abstain from alcohol and drugs, and that you obey the laws of this state and this nation. Do you understand these terms?"

Edmund House, mute for three days, stood and spoke. "I do, Judge."

CHAPTER 49

As Judge Meyers rapped his gavel a final time, reporters rushed to the railing, shouting questions at Dan and Edmund House. Dan pacified them as the correctional officers reapplied House's handcuffs and shackles to escort him out the back door to the Cascade County Jail for processing.

"We'll be holding a press conference at the jail just as soon as my client is processed," Dan said.

Finlay Armstrong stepped to Tracy's side to escort her out of the courtroom. In the midst of the commotion, she looked back over her shoulder, and for a brief moment she flashed back to that moment she had looked through Ben's truck-cab window and seen Sarah for the last time, standing alone in the rain.

Dan looked up and met her gaze, giving her a small, contented smile.

Finlay ushered Tracy out the courtroom door and down the marble staircase leading to the rotunda. Some of the reporters, perhaps sensing they would not get anything from Dan or House, hurried after her, cameramen rushing ahead to film and take photographs of Tracy descending the interior courthouse steps.

"Do you feel vindicated?"

"This wasn't about vindication for me," she said.

"What was it about?"

"It's always been about Sarah, about finding out what happened to my sister."

"Will you continue your investigation?"

"I will ask that the investigation into my sister's murder be reopened."

"Do you have any idea who killed your sister?"

"If I did, I would bring that to the attention of those who will be investigating."

"Do you know how your hair got in Edmund House's truck?"

"Someone put it there," she said.

"Do you know who?"

She shook her head. "No."

"Do you believe it was Sheriff Calloway?"

"I wouldn't know for certain."

"What about the jewelry?" another reporter asked. "Do you know who planted it?"

"I won't speculate," she said.

"If Edmund House did not kill your sister, who did?"

"I said I won't speculate."

In the marbled rotunda, more cameras and microphones assaulted her. Realizing it was futile to avoid them, she stopped.

"Do you think your sister's killer will ever be brought to justice?" a reporter asked.

"Today was about taking the first step to getting Sarah's case reopened. I plan on taking the rest of this one step at a time."

"What will you do now?"

"My immediate plans are to return to Seattle," she said. "But that will have to wait until the storm blows through. I'd suggest we all get to where we need to be."

She pushed through the crowd, Finlay assisting. Outside, several of the more persistent reporters continued to follow, but they quickly gave up, perhaps cognizant of the worsening weather. The snowflakes fell thick as a lace curtain, swirling in a persistent and occasionally gusting wind. Tracy pulled on a hat and slipped on gloves. "I can take it from here," she said to Finlay.

"You sure?"

"You married, Finlay?"

"Very. I got three kids under the age of nine."

"Then get on home to them."

"I wish. Nights like these are usually bad for us."

"I remember when I worked patrol."

"For what it's worth . . ."

"I understand," she said. "Thank you."

Tracy descended the courthouse steps. She'd not had a chance to change from her heels into her snow boots—the steps were slick and her footing treacherous. She had to take caution with each step. Moisture seeped through the leather of her pumps and she felt the cold invade her toes. She was going to ruin a perfectly good pair of shoes.

She raised her eyes to consider the traffic exiting the parking lot and beginning to back up on the road in front of the courthouse— cars and trucks, some with tire chains making a clinking noise that reminded her of Edmund House shuffling into the courtroom at the start of each morning and leaving each afternoon. A flatbed truck with large snow tires slowed as it approached the intersection. The right rear brake light illuminated. The left did not.

Tracy felt a rush of adrenaline. After a moment of hesitation, she picked up her pace, hurrying as quickly as the footing allowed. As she stepped from the bottom step, her foot came out from under her and she slipped, but managed to maintain her grip on the handrail in order to keep from completely sprawling onto the snow-covered pavement. By the time she'd pulled herself back to her feet, the flatbed had reached the intersection. She hustled across the street to the adjacent parking lot, straining to see, but it was too far a distance and the snowfall too thick for her to make out the letters and numbers on the license plate. A metal cage across the back window also blocked her view inside the cab. The truck made a right turn at the intersection, continuing on the road on the northern side of the courthouse.

Tracy slid between rows of the remaining parked cars. Exhaust belched from the tailpipes as drivers stood outside furiously scraping snow and ice from the front and back windows. Some backed from their stalls without clearing the snow. Others pulled forward to exit the lot, adding to the congestion. Tracy kept her eyes on the flatbed and didn't see the car backing from a parking space until the bumper nicked her leg. Snow covered its back window. She slapped the trunk to get the driver's attention and pivoted to avoid getting hit, but felt her shoe slip, and this time her knee smacked a patch of asphalt where the car had been parked, preventing the accumulation of snow. The driver got out, apologizing, but Tracy was already getting up, searching for the flatbed. It had stopped three cars from the next intersection for the main road. She cut between another row of parked cars, her lungs burning, calves aching from the strain of trying to maintain her balance. The truck reached the intersection and turned left into the blinding snow, away from her and in the direction of Cedar Grove.

Tracy stopped her pursuit and bent, hands on knees, keeping her head raised and watching until she could no longer see the vehicle. Her labored breathing marked the air in white bursts and the cold gripped her chest and lungs, stinging her exposed cheeks and ears. She realized that in her fall she'd torn her nylons and banged her knee, which ached. Her toes were numb.

She fumbled in her briefcase for a pen, bit off the cap, and wrote the letters and numbers of the license plate that she thought she'd been able to make out on her moistened palm.

Back at her car, she started the engine and turned the defroster on high. The wiper blades made a horrific noise as they scraped across the ice-encrusted windshield. Her fingers still numb, Tracy had trouble keying in the numbers for the call. She made a fist, blew into it, and flexed her fingers before trying again.

Kins answered on the first ring. "Hey."

"It's over."

"What?"

"Meyers ruled from the bench. House is getting another trial."

"What happened?"

"I'll fill you in later on the details. Right now I need a favor. I need you to run a license plate for me. I only got a partial so I'm going to need you to try some different combinations, whatever you can."

"Hang on. Let me get something to write with."

"It's a Washington plate." She provided him what she thought had been the letters and numbers on it. "Could be a *W* instead of a *V* and the three might have been an eight."

"You realize this could pull up a lot of possibilities."

Tracy transferred the phone and blew into her other fist. "I understand. It's a flatbed truck so it could be a commercial plate. I just couldn't get a good-enough look." She switched the phone again, flexed her fingers, and blew into her other fist.

"When will you be back?"

"I don't know. Storm is supposed to hit hard here. I'm hoping Monday at the latest."

"We're already getting hit here. I can hear the trucks out sanding the roads. I hate it when they do that. After a while it's like driving through a cat-litter box. Let me call this in so I can start for home. I'll let you know when I hear something."

No sooner had she hung up when her phone rang.

"I'm heading over to the jail," Dan said. "We're going to hold a press conference when House is released."

"Where's he going to go?"

"I haven't talked to him about that. Kind of ironic, though."

"What's that?"

"His first day of freedom and the weather has made prisoners of us all."

CHAPTER 50

Roy Calloway did not go home after the hearing. He went where he always went, where he'd gone nearly every day of his life for the last thirty-five years—rain or shine, weekday or weekend. He went where he felt most comfortable, more comfortable than his own living room, and why not? He spent far more time in his office than he did at home. He sat behind his desk, the desk with the nicks and scrapes on the corner where he had a habit of resting his boots. The desk at which he told people they'd find his dead body, because he wasn't leaving until then, or until someone got a crane to haul his ass out from behind it, kicking and screaming.

"Hold all my calls," he said to the desk sergeant. Then he sat back at his desk, propped his feet on the corner, and rocked in his chair while considering his mounted prize trout. Maybe it was time he acceded to his wife's wishes and retired. Maybe it was time to catch some more fish and lower his golf score. Maybe it was time to step aside and let Finlay take over, let a younger man have his turn. Maybe it was time for Calloway to go and spoil his grandkids.

It sounded good. It sounded right.

It sounded like a cop-out.

And Roy Calloway had never copped out. He'd never run from anything in his life. And he wasn't about to start now. He also wasn't about to make it easy on them. Call him stubborn, obstinate, proud. Pick one. He didn't give a shit. They could call in the feds, the Justice Department, the Marines, whoever the hell they wanted. He wasn't ceding his desk or his office to anyone, not without a fight. They could speculate. They could opine about the evidence being questionable. They could intimate wrongdoing. What they couldn't do was prove it.

Not one damn thing.

So let them come with their accusations and their pointed fingers. Let them come with their high-and-mighty attitudes. Let them come with their speeches on the integrity of the judicial system. They didn't know. They had no idea. Calloway had had twenty years to think it all through. Twenty years to ask whether he'd done the right thing. Twenty years to confirm what he'd known the moment they'd all made the decision. And he wouldn't change a thing, not one damn thing.

He reached for the bottle of Johnnie Walker in his lower desk drawer, poured himself two fingers, and took a sip, feeling the burn. Let them come. He'd be right here, waiting.

—

Calloway had no idea how much time had passed when his cell phone rang, bringing him back from his reminiscing to the present. Few people had his cell phone number. Caller ID said "HOME."

"Are you on your way?" his wife asked.

"Soon," he said. "Just finishing up."

"I saw on the news. I'm sorry."

"Yeah," he said.

"The snow's really starting to come down heavy. Best you get on home before you can't. I made stew out of the leftovers."

"That sounds appropriate on a night like this. I won't be long."

Calloway disconnected the call and slipped the phone in his shirt pocket. He slid the empty glass and the bottle from his desk back into the lower drawer, about to slide it closed when the distinctive shadow passed along the smoked-glass windows. Vance Clark didn't knock when he reached the door. He stepped in looking like he'd gone three rounds blocking punches from a heavyweight—shirt collar unbuttoned, the knot of his tie pulled low and askew. He dropped his briefcase and overcoat into one of the chairs as if his arms were too weary to hold them any longer and slumped in the other chair, the worry lines across his forehead prominent. As the County's Prosecuting Attorney, Clark was obligated to appear before the cameras and speak to the media following a big trial. The county had mandated it, though it had only happened a handful of times that Calloway could remember. Twenty years earlier, after Edmund House's conviction, Calloway had joined Clark at the podium. Tracy had also been there. So had James and Abby Crosswhite.

"That bad?" Calloway asked.

Clark shrugged, which appeared to be all the energy he could muster. His arms hung from the chair like limp noodles. "About what you'd expect."

Calloway retook his seat and retrieved the bottle. This time he set two glasses on the desk, poured two fingers in one, and slid the full glass to the corner where Clark sat. Then he poured himself another drink.

"You remember?" he asked. They'd drunk a toast in his office twenty years earlier, after Edmund House's conviction. James Crosswhite had been there too.

"I remember." Clark picked up his glass and tipped it toward Calloway before throwing back the alcohol and grimacing. Calloway lifted the bottle, but Clark waved off a refill.

Calloway spun a bent paper clip like a helicopter blade between his thumb and index finger, listening to the clock on the wall tick and to the low-pitched hum of the fluorescent lights, one still flickering and ticking.

"You'll file an appeal?"

"It's a formality," Clark said.

"How long before the Court of Appeals denies it and grants a new trial?"

"Not sure it will be up to me to decide. New prosecuting attorney might want to cut his losses," Clark said, apparently already resigned to losing his job. "He'll have a built-in excuse, blame it on the old guy, say I screwed it up so bad he can't win a retrial. Why waste the taxpayers' money? Why blemish his own record for someone else's shit pile?"

"Speculation and innuendo is all it is, Vance."

"The media is already running with their stories on corruption and conspiracies in Cedar Grove. God knows what else they'll come up with."

"People in this county know who you are and what you stand for."

Clark smiled, but it had a sad quality to it and quickly dimmed. "I just wish I did." He set the glass on the desk. "You think they'll come after us, criminal charges?"

Now it was Calloway's turn to shrug. "Could."

"I suppose I'll be disbarred."

"I suppose I'll be impeached."

"You don't seem concerned."

"What's to be, will be, Vance. I'm not about to start second-guessing myself now."

"You've never thought about it?"

"Whether it was the right thing to do? Not once." Calloway finished his drink and thought of his wife's admonition about the storm. "I suggest you get on home while you still can. Go kiss that wife of yours."

"Yeah," Clark said. "There's always that, right?"

Calloway looked again to the trout. "That's the only thing."

"What about House? Any idea where he'll go?"

"Don't know, but he won't get far or anywhere fast in this weather. You still got that .38?"

Clark nodded.

"Might want to keep it close by."

"I already thought of that. What about DeAngelo?"

Calloway shook his head. "I'll keep an eye on him, but I don't think House is that smart. If he was, he'd have filed an appeal based on inadequacy of legal counsel. He never did."

CHAPTER 51

Tracy backed up her Subaru, put it in drive, and gunned the engine a third time. This attempt, the tires bounced over the lip of snow and ice at the edge of Dan's driveway, followed by an ugly scraping sound beneath her car. She plowed far enough forward to leave room for Dan to park his Tahoe behind her. The noise awakened the alarm system, a chorus of yelps and barks erupting inside the house, though she could not see the dogs because of the plywood still covering the shattered plate-glass window.

When Tracy stepped from the car, her boots sank to midcalf in the snow that had buried the stone walkway. The partially buried lawn lights created pools of liquid gold. She found the spare key that Dan kept above the garage door and called out to Sherlock and Rex as she undid the deadbolt to the front door. Their barking had reached a fevered pitch. When she opened the door, she expected them to burst out and stepped to the side to avoid the impact, but neither dog came at her. Rex showed no interest, and Sherlock only stuck his head out the door, apparently to see if Dan was trailing her. When he realized Dan was not coming, Sherlock retreated.

"I don't blame you," she said, stepping in and shutting the door. "A hot bath sounds a lot better." The adrenaline that had fueled her for the week had dissipated, leaving emotional fatigue and stress, though her mind continued to struggle with the letters and numbers of the license plate of the flatbed truck.

Tracy locked the deadbolt and left her boots, gloves, and coat on the rug by the door. She found the remote control on the sofa and turned on the television, surfing channels for news of the hearing and Judge Meyers's unexpected decision as she made her way into the kitchen. She settled on Channel 8, which had been running Manpelt's reports as the lead story every evening, and grabbed a bottle of beer from the refrigerator, popping the cap. Returning to the family room, Tracy slumped into the cushions on the couch and felt her muscles immediately relax into the material. The beer tasted better than she could have imagined, cold and refreshing. She put her stocking-clad feet up on the coffee table and examined the scrape on her knee, which was just superficial. She should probably clean it, but Tracy didn't feel like getting up and going to the trouble. Dan might have to carry her upstairs to bed.

Her mind again drifted to the license plate. The *V* that could have been a *W* and the three that could have been an eight. Had it been a commercial plate? She couldn't be certain.

Tracy sipped her beer and tried to quell her thoughts. Everything had come to such a sudden and dramatic conclusion that she hadn't had time to absorb the implications of what had happened. Like everyone else, she'd thought that Judge Meyers would end the proceedings and issue a written ruling at a later date. She'd never imagined that Edmund House would leave the hearing a free man. She'd envisioned him being sent back to jail to await the Court of Appeals' decision on granting him a retrial. Her mind flashed again to that day at the Walla Walla prison when she had seen House's shit-eating grin. *I can already see it*, he'd said. *The*

*looks on the faces of all those people when they see me walking the
streets of Cedar Grove again.*

Now he'd get that chance, though not immediately. Nobody
would be walking the streets of Cedar Grove right now—not
tonight, maybe not for a few days. As Dan had said, the storm had
made prisoners of them all.

But House was no longer her priority. She didn't care what
might happen at House's new trial, or if there even was one.
Tracy would turn her attention to getting Sarah's case reopened,
which had always been her goal. She doubted that decision
would be up to Vance Clark. After Meyers's reprimand from the
bench, Clark would likely resign his post as county prosecutor.
Tracy took no pleasure in Clark's demise. She'd known the man
and she'd known his wife. Clark's daughters had attended Cedar
Grove High. Retirement also seemed Roy Calloway's best option,
though Tracy knew the man to be just stubborn enough to refuse.
It wouldn't matter whether or not Tracy was successful in lobbying
the Department of Justice to devote its resources to investigating
whether or not Clark and Calloway had participated in a conspiracy to convict Edmund House. She wasn't sure that such an investigation would include DeAngelo Finn, who was too old and too
frail, though he might prove to be a valuable witness.

She sipped her beer and found herself thinking again of her
conversation with Finn, as she had stood on the back steps to his
home.

Be careful. Sometimes our questions are better left unanswered.

There's no one left to hurt, DeAngelo.

But there is.

Roy Calloway had been equally pensive the evening he'd driven
to the veterinary clinic. *Your father . . .* , he'd started to say, before
something had made him stop.

She had wondered if, perhaps, George Bovine's horrific
recounting of his daughter's suffering had somehow convinced

her father and the others that, if they could not find Sarah's killer, the next-best alternative was to put an animal like Edmund House behind prison walls for the rest of his life. For years, she'd considered this the most plausible theory. Her father had always been a man of such high integrity and morals that it was hard to fathom him doing such a thing, but that man had not existed in the weeks following Sarah's abduction. The man she'd worked alongside in his office in their frantic search to find Sarah had seemingly been possessed of a different spirit. That man had been angry, bitter, consumed by Sarah's death. And, Tracy supposed, his own guilt that he had not been in Cedar Grove, had not gone with them to the shooting tournament, had not been there to protect them as he'd always been—as was a father's duty.

The local news began. Not surprisingly, Judge Meyers's decision to free Edmund House was the lead story, as the hearing had been the preceding three nights. "Shocking developments today in the post-conviction relief hearing of Edmund House in Cascade County," the news anchor said. "After twenty years, convicted rapist and murderer Edmund House is a free man. For more on the story we go live to Maria Vanpelt, who is braving a snowstorm and standing outside the Cascade County Jail where Edmund House and his attorney held a news conference earlier this afternoon."

Vanpelt stood beneath an umbrella in the glow of a spotlight. All around her, the snow swirled, nearly obscuring the Cascade County Jail, her chosen backdrop. Gusts of wind tugged at her umbrella, threatening to turn it inside out, and the fur lining of her hooded parka shimmered like a lion shaking its mane. "Shocking is exactly the word to describe today's events," Vanpelt said. She recounted Tracy's testimony, as well as the testimony of Harrison Scott that had led to Judge Meyers's decision to release Edmund House. "Calling the trial 'a travesty of justice,' Judge Meyers implicated everyone involved, including Cedar Grove's sheriff, Roy Calloway, and the county prosecutor, Vance Clark," Vanpelt continued. "Earlier this afternoon, I attended a news conference inside the building behind me. That was just before Edmund House walked out a free man—at least for the time being."

The camera switched to the earlier news conference. Dan sat beside House, a bouquet of microphones on the table between them. Their disparate sizes had been evident at counsel table but the difference seemed even more pronounced now with House dressed in a denim shirt and winter jacket.

Tracy's cell phone rang. She retrieved it from the couch and hit the "Pause" button on the television.

"I'm just watching you on the television," she said. "Where are you?"

"I had a few other interviews with the national media," Dan said. "I'm on my way, but I thought I better let you know the freeway's already a mess. There are spinouts everywhere. It's going to take me some time to get home. There are reports of power outages and downed trees."

"Everything's fine here," she said.

"I have a generator in the garage if you need it. All you need to do is plug it into the socket beside the fuse boxes."

"Not sure I have the energy."

"The boys are all right?"

"Lying here on the rug. You might have to carry them outside to go to the bathroom, however."

"And what about you?"

"I can make it to the bathroom myself, thank you very much," she said.

"I see someone's sense of humor has returned."

"I think I'm punchy. What I see is a hot bath in my future."

"I like the sound of that."

"Let me call you back. I want to watch the news conference."

"How do I look?"

"Still fishing for compliments?"

"You know it. All right, call me back."

She disconnected and hit "Play." Dan said, "We'll cross that bridge when we come to it. I suspect the Court of Appeals will act swiftly given the miscarriage of justice. After it does, we'll have to wait and see what the prosecutor decides."

"How does it feel to be a free man?" Vanpelt asked House.

House flipped his ponytail off his shoulder. "Well, it's like my attorney said, I'm not free just yet, but . . ." He smiled. "It feels good."

"What's the first thing you'll do now that you are free?"

"The same as all of you; step outside and let the snow and wind hit me in the face."

"Are you angry about what transpired?"

House's smile waned. "I wouldn't use the word 'angry.'"

"So you've forgiven those responsible for putting you in jail?" Vanpelt asked.

"I wouldn't say that either. All I can do is correct my past mistakes and try not to repeat them. That's what I intend to do."

An off-camera reporter asked, "Do you have any idea what motivated whoever was responsible for fabricating evidence to convict you?"

Dan leaned to the microphones. "We're not going to comment on the evidence—"

"Ignorance," House said, talking over him. "Ignorance and arrogance. They thought they could get away with it."

Vanpelt drew Dan's attention with another question. "Mr. O'Leary, will you seek the involvement of the Department of Justice to investigate, as Judge Meyers intimated?"

"I'll confer with my client and make that decision."

But House again leaned forward. "I'm not looking to the Department of Justice to punish anyone."

"Is there anything you'd like to say to Detective Crosswhite?" Vanpelt asked.

House gave her a tight-lipped grin. "I don't think words can express how I feel at the moment," he said. "But I hope to thank her in person someday."

Tracy felt another chill pass through her, as if a spider had crawled along her spine.

"What would you like now?" a reporter asked.

House's grin widened. "A cheeseburger."

The television cut back to Vanpelt outside the jail. She was straining to keep a grip on her umbrella, the wind also causing a rustling sound as it blew across the microphone. "As I said, that news conference was recorded earlier this afternoon, after which Edmund House left this jail behind me a free man."

The news anchor said, "Maria, it seems remarkable that a man who has spent twenty years behind bars for a crime that it now appears he did not commit could forgive so readily. What happens now to those who were potentially involved?"

Vanpelt had a finger pressed to the earpiece. She shouted to be heard over the wind. "Mark, I spoke with a law professor at the University of Washington this afternoon who told me that, regardless of whether or not Edmund House ever pursues civil charges for the violation of his civil rights, the Department of Justice could decide to step in and pursue criminal charges against those involved. It could also take over the investigation as to what happened to Sarah Crosswhite. So it appears that this story is far from over. This hearing may have raised far more questions than it answered. But tonight, Edmund House is a free man and, as you heard him say, in search of a good cheeseburger."

The anchor said, "Maria, we're going to let you go find shelter before the wind blows you away, but has there been any word from Detective Crosswhite?"

Vanpelt braced as another gust of wind swept over her. After it had passed, she said, "I spoke to Detective Crosswhite during a recess in today's proceedings and asked if she felt vindicated by the Court's ruling. She said the hearing wasn't about vindication. It was about finding out what happened to her sister. At the moment, that appears to be a lingering question that unfortunately may never be answered."

Tracy's cell rang. She checked caller ID. Kins.

"I just e-mailed the list to you," Kins said. "It's long but it's manageable. Is this the truck with the rear light out?"

"It's *a* truck with a rear light out. Could very well be more than one around here."

"We're getting news reports they freed House."

"Shocked the hell out of everyone, Kins. We all figured Judge Meyers would take the matter under advisement and issue written findings. But if he didn't rule today, it might not have been until after the weekend. He wasn't about to let Edmund House stay in jail."

"Sounds like the evidence was pretty overwhelming."

"Dan did a great job."

"So why do you sound so subdued?"

"Just tired, and thinking about everything. My sister and my mom and dad. It's a lot to digest this quickly."

"Think about how House must feel."

"What do you mean?"

"Twenty years in Walla Walla's a long time for him to find himself suddenly walking the streets a free man. I read an article once about Vietnam veterans being sent home from the war without any time to decompress. One day they're in the jungle watching people die, the next they're back home, walking the streets of Anywhere, USA. Many of them couldn't handle it."

"I don't think anybody will be out walking the streets tonight. They're predicting a blizzard."

"Here too, and you know these people can't drive these hills in the snow. Stay warm. I'm heading home before the crazies totally clog the roads."

"Thanks for this, Kins. I owe you."

"And you'll pay."

Tracy hung up and switched applications on her phone so she could open Kins's e-mail. Her initial pass through the materials he'd sent indicated that the list of potential license plate combinations was not insignificant. She scrolled through a second time, quickly scanning the names and cities of the registered owners, looking for anything familiar. She didn't see a name she recognized, but she did see the word "Cascadia," and stopped scrolling. The vehicle was registered to a "Cascadia Furniture." She took her phone to the nook where Dan kept his home computer, shook the mouse, and keyed the name into a search engine. "Wow," she said, surprised when the search resulted in close to a quarter of a million hits.

She added the words "Cedar Grove." It reduced the hits significantly, but there were still too many to efficiently go through. "What else?" she said out loud. After three days, her brain was fried. She couldn't think of any additional tag words to reduce the number of hits.

Tracy slid back her chair, about to grab another beer, when she recalled where she'd heard the name before. She looked about the kitchen. The boxes containing the files she'd accumulated during her investigation of Sarah's disappearance were stacked in a corner. There'd been no need for Dan to bring them all to court each day. She set the top box on the kitchen table and riffled through the files until she found what she was looking for. Sitting, she flipped the pages of the transcript containing Detective Margaret Giesa's trial testimony. She knew the trial testimony well, having studied it, and quickly found the portion of Giesa's testimony she was looking for.

BY MR. CLARK:

Q. Did your team locate anything else of interest in the truck cab?

A. *Trace amounts of blood.*

Q. *Detective Giesa, I am placing on the easel what has been marked as the State's Exhibit 112. It is a blown-up aerial photograph of Parker House's property. Can you tell the jury, using this photograph, where your search next proceeded?*

A. *Yes, we went down this path to search this first building here.*

Q. *Let's mark that building you're pointing to with the number one, then. Did you note anything of interest in that building?*

A. *We found woodworking tools and several pieces of furniture in various stages of completion.*

Tracy shifted her focus back to Kins's e-mail. "Cascadia Furniture," she said.

An explosion rattled the windows and shook the house, causing Rex and Sherlock to bolt upright and race to the plywood-covered window barking, just before the house plunged into darkness.

CHAPTER 52

Vance Clark was gathering his briefcase and coat from the chair and standing to leave Roy Calloway's office when the radio on Calloway's desk crackled. Finlay Armstrong spoke, though his voice was barely audible through heavy static.

Calloway adjusted the dial.

"Roy, you there?" Finlay sounded like he was talking in his car with the window down.

"I'm here," he said, then heard what sounded like distant thunder but quickly recognized to have been a single explosion. The fluorescent bulbs flickered and dulled and cut out completely. A transformer had blown. Calloway swore and heard the emergency generator kick in, like an airplane engine gearing up for takeoff. The lights came back on.

"Chief?"

"We just lost power for a second. Hang on, the generator is still kicking in. You're breaking up. It's hard to hear you."

"What's that?"

"You're breaking up." The lights dimmed, then brightened.

"Storm's picking up." Armstrong was shouting. "Wind gusts . . . You need to get out here, Roy. Something . . . You need to . . . here."

"Hang on, Finlay. Say again. Repeat. Say again."

"You need to get here," Armstrong said.

"Where?" The radio crackled. The static increased. "Where?" Calloway asked again.

"DeAngelo Finn's house."

—

The high winds had toppled trees and knocked out all power. Downtown Cedar Grove looked like a ghost town, with the wind whipping snow into drifts piled high on the deserted sidewalks, the streetlights and store windows blackened. Farther out of town the windows in the houses were similarly dark, indicating the power outage to be at least citywide.

Snowflakes slid over the windshield and swirled in the cones of light from the Tahoe's headlamps. They struggled to illuminate the branches that the wind had ripped from trees and left littering the road, which caused Dan to drive slowly and swerve frequently. As he approached the turn to Elmwood, he noticed a fire burning atop a telephone pole like a distant torch—a transformer. That explained the darkness. The entire electrical grid for all of Cedar Grove was down. The city had no emergency backup power, which was a costly upgrade that the city council declined to invest in several years back, reasoning that most residents had their own generators. Of course, backup generators didn't solve the problem of spotty cell phone reception in a mountain town, especially during a major blizzard.

Dan pulled into his driveway and saw tracks in the snow from a car's tires, but did not see Tracy's Subaru. It immediately worried him. He checked his cell. No bars. When he tried calling her, he got a persistent beep.

Where the hell could she have gone? he wondered.

He popped open the glove box and switched on a flashlight. Rex and Sherlock, who'd begun barking when he'd pulled up the driveway, became more animated as he approached the house. "Hang on," he called out, opening the door and bracing himself against 286 pounds jockeying for his attention. "Okay, okay," he said, petting them as he shone the flashlight about the room. He found Tracy's briefcase hanging from the back of one of the kitchen counter's elevated chairs. "Tracy?"

No response.

"Where is she, boys?"

He'd talked to her just thirty minutes earlier. She'd said all was fine.

"Tracy?" He walked through the house calling her name. "Tracy?"

His cell phone still showed no bars. He dialed again anyway. The call did not go through.

"Stay," he said to Sherlock and Rex as he pulled open the front door, though neither appeared too interested in following him into the garage, where he plugged in the portable generator he'd wired to the main electrical panel.

Back inside, the television was now on, though the sound was muted. He picked up a half-finished beer from the coffee table. The bottle remained cool to the touch. He hit the "Mute" button on the remote control. The local weatherman was using diagrams to explain the size of the storm and its path, talking about high- and low-pressure systems and predicting up to an additional eighteen inches of fresh snow by morning.

"The problem now isn't the snow, it's that the winds are increasing in ferocity," the weatherman said.

"No shit, Sherlock," Dan said. Sherlock whined at the sound of his name.

"Due to the recent warming and freezing pattern, ice is forming on the power lines and weakening tree limbs. Some of you may have seen the debris in the roads or heard those limbs snapping outside. We have at least one report that a transformer fire has knocked out electrical power to nearly all of Cedar Grove."

"Tell me something I don't know," Dan said.

The camera switched back to a news anchor sitting behind the studio desk.

"We'll continue to check back with Tim to bring you up-to-the-minute coverage on what is shaping up to be a major winter storm." Dan put down the remote and walked into the kitchen. "At the moment, we're getting reports of a fire on Pine Crest Road in Cedar Grove."

Dan's interest was piqued. He knew the road, of course, from growing up in Cedar Grove, but there was something more familiar about the name than a childhood memory, something more recent that jogged his memory.

"We're told the Sheriff and fire department personnel responded quickly and were able to contain the blaze, but not before the house sustained significant damage. A Sheriff's Office spokesman indicates at least one elderly resident lives at that address."

The memory clicked. Dan had used the address on the subpoena that had never been served, one to compel DeAngelo Finn to appear at the post-conviction relief hearing. He felt a chill. His stomach fluttered. He looked again to Tracy's briefcase. Then he picked up his car keys and headed for the door.

That's when he saw her note taped just above the deadbolt.

—

The lights atop Finlay Armstrong's patrol car and the two fire engines swirled and pulsed in bursts of red, blue, and white light as Roy Calloway drove down the block toward DeAngelo Finn's one-story rambler. The Suburban's headlights illuminated charred rafters poking through what remained of the roof, like the exposed rib cage of a dead animal picked clean.

Calloway parked behind the larger of the two fire trucks and stepped out. He trudged past firemen struggling to flatten and rewind hoses. Finlay Armstrong, standing on the front stoop, caught sight of Calloway and lowered his head into the wind and swirling snow, heading over. They met at the picket fence, a portion of which had been knocked down to run the hoses from the fire hydrant close to the house. Armstrong had the collar of his patrolman's jacket turned up and the earflaps of his cap pulled down and snapped beneath his chin.

"Do they know what started the fire?" Calloway shouted over a gust of wind.

"Captain says it smells like some sort of an accelerant. Likely gas."

"Where?"

Armstrong squinted. Snow and ice clung to the fur framing his face. "What?"

"Do they know where the fire started?"

"The garage. They think maybe a generator."

"Have they found DeAngelo?" Armstrong turned his head and pulled an earflap up. Calloway leaned closer. "Have they found DeAngelo?"

Armstrong shook his head. "They just got the fire out. They're trying to figure out if the house is safe to enter."

Calloway stepped through the gate. Armstrong followed him to the front porch, where two firemen stood discussing the situation. Calloway greeted Phil Ronkowski by his first name.

"Hey, Roy," Ronkowski said, shaking gloved hands. "A fire in a snowstorm. I've seen everything now."

Calloway raised his voice. "Have you found DeAngelo?"

Ronkowski shook his head. Then he stepped back and pointed up at the charred roof. "The fire spread fast across the roof and inundated just about every room. It had to be an accelerant of some kind. Gas probably. Neighbors said the smoke was thick and black."

"Could he have gotten out?"

Ronkowski grimaced. "Pray that he did, but we didn't see anybody when we got here. Maybe with the weather he went to a neighbor's, but nobody has approached us."

They heard a large crack and instinctively flinched. A tree limb crashed into the yard, scattering the firemen, taking out a portion of the fence, and just missing the back end of one of the trucks.

"I need to get in there, Phil," Calloway said.

Ronkowski shook his head. "Structure hasn't been determined safe yet, Roy. Not with this wind."

"I'll take that chance."

"Damn it, Roy. I'm supposed to be in charge here."

"Just make a note. This is my decision." Calloway took the flashlight from Finlay. "Wait here."

The front door's frame had been damaged from the forced entry. Black burn marks and blistered paint revealed where the fire had licked the sash in search of oxygen. Stepping in, Calloway heard wind whistling through the house and the plink-plink of dripping water. The beam of his flashlight danced off scarred walls and the charred remains of furniture. Framed photographs and knickknacks accumulated over a lifetime lay strewn across the carpet. He directed the light at a waterlogged piece of Sheetrock hanging from the ceiling like a wet bedsheet from a clothesline. Snow fell through a gaping hole in the roof. Calloway covered his nose and mouth with a handkerchief because the air inside still remained thick with smoke and smelled of burnt wood and insulation. His boots created puddles in the carpet as he stepped across the room.

He leaned through the doorway on his left and swept the light over the kitchen. DeAngelo was not there. He made his way across the living room debris and down a narrow hallway leading to the back of the house, calling out DeAngelo's name but getting no answer. He used a shoulder to force open the first of two doors, revealing a guest bedroom. The fire had done minimal damage, probably because the room was farthest from where Ronkowski believed the fire to have started. The fact that the door had been closed also would have reduced the flow of oxygen to fuel the flames. Calloway directed the light over a queen-sized bed, pulled open a closet door, and shone the flashlight over a bar and handful of wire hangers.

Retreating from the room, Calloway pushed open the second door, which also stuck in the sash. The master bedroom. Black smoke streaked the walls and the ceiling, but again, the damage was limited compared to the rest of the house. Calloway danced the light over a dresser partially buried beneath a piece of fallen Sheetrock, bent to a knee to lift a dust ruffle, and shone the light beneath the bed. Nothing.

He called out from his knees. "DeAngelo?"

Where the hell is he? he thought. The bad feeling that had started when he heard the report that Finn's home had been burned grew stronger.

Finlay entered the room. "They're coming in now. You find him?"

Calloway stood up. "He's not here."

"He got out?"

"Then where is he?" Calloway asked, unable to shake the bad feeling that had first come over him when he had heard Armstrong mention Finn's name over the radio. It was like a bad chill, a cold-to-the-bone feeling. Calloway walked to the closet and pulled on the knob, but the door was wedged tight in the jamb. "Check with the neighbors," he said to Armstrong. "Maybe he's disoriented."

Armstrong nodded. "Will do."

Calloway braced a hand on the jamb, about to apply more force, when he noticed two darkened points protruding through the door, roughly three feet apart. In the light from his flashlight they looked like two nails shot from a nail gun that had missed the studs and penetrated through the wall. Only these nails were significantly bigger, more like spikes.

"What the hell?" Calloway said. He yanked on the door. It didn't move, so he put a foot on the wall and yanked again. This time the door swung open faster than Calloway had anticipated, the weight and force nearly pulling the knob from his hand.

"Jesus!" Armstrong yelled, stumbling backward into the dresser.

CHAPTER 53

Tracy felt the Subaru's engine struggling as the car's tires fought to churn through the deepening snow. She couldn't see the center line or the edge of the county road. It was all a long white blanket. With the four-wheel drive engaged and the car in low gear, it plowed forward, but it remained slow going. The windshield wipers slapped a steady beat but couldn't keep the glass clear of the swirling snow, and visibility had been reduced to a few feet in front of her bumper. Tracy had to resist the urge to hit the brakes when gusts of wind caused the snow to fall in clumps from overburdened tree limbs, creating momentary whiteouts. If she stopped, she might not get the car moving again.

As she rounded another curve, a burst of light momentarily blinded her, causing her to steer closer to the rock face. A rush of wind from an eighteen-wheel truck plowing past in the opposite direction shook her car and spit snow from its tire chains. Maybe she was a fool to be out in weather like this, but she wasn't about to sit at Dan's and wait out the storm. It suddenly made sense, so much so that she was dismayed and angry that she had not considered the possibility before. Who else had access to the red Chevy truck? Who had the opportunity to plant the jewelry and the hairs?

It had to be someone whose presence on the property would not be conspicuous. It had to be someone who lived there on a daily basis, someone who Edmund House trusted.

Parker.

In their rush to convict Edmund, no one had checked Parker's alibi. Parker had said he'd worked a late shift at the mill, but no one had bothered to confirm it. There'd been no reason to, not with a convicted rapist to blame. It was just as likely that Parker, known to be a heavy drinker, had been out knocking back a few in one of the local bars, decided to drive home on the county road to avoid the highway patrol, and stumbled upon Sarah stranded and soaking wet. Parker would have been a familiar face. Sarah wouldn't have hesitated to get in the cab with him. What had happened from there? Had Parker made a pass and gotten angry when Sarah had rejected him? Had there been a struggle where Sarah had hit her head? Had Parker panicked and hidden her body in a garbage bag until he could safely bury it? Parker would have known about the dam going online. He lived not far from the area that was to be flooded. He also knew the trails in the foothills, and he'd been part of the search team, so he would have known when and where to bury Sarah's body. And maybe, most importantly, Parker had had a ready scapegoat to give up when Calloway came calling: his rape-convicted nephew.

The lumber mill in Pine Flat where Parker had worked at the time of Sarah's disappearance had since closed. How had Parker continued to make a living? How did he pay the bills? He'd made furniture as a hobby when Tracy had lived in Cedar Grove, selling a few of the pieces at Kaufman's Mercantile Store on consignment. Apparently he'd gone into business for himself—as Cascadia Furniture—and had bought a flatbed truck to deliver what he sold.

Tracy thought again of her question to Dan. Where would Edmund House go now that he was free? But House had already answered that question when she and Dan had first met him in Walla Walla.

I can already see it. The looks on the faces of all those people when they see me walking the streets of Cedar Grove again.

Where else could he go? Where else but to his uncle's home in the foothills? Edmund House had insisted that Calloway and Clark had conspired to convict him, and that had certainly seemed to be the case, but it didn't explain who had hidden the jewelry in the coffee can in the furniture shop and who had planted the blonde strands of hair. Neither Calloway nor Clark could have done it, not with Edmund at home and on high alert, not with an entire CSI team scouring over the site. Had Edmund also figured out that his uncle had been part of the conspiracy, and had willingly joined Calloway and Clark in order to cover his own crime?

Tracy briefly took her eyes off the road to check her cell phone. No bars. She wondered if Dan had made it home and found her note. She wondered if he had gone to get Roy Calloway. She spotted a pile of snow that looked to have been plowed from a side street and left along the side of the road, and slowed to have a closer look, trying to remember if that was the turn that led up the mountain to Parker's property. If she guessed wrong, she'd likely get stuck, with no way to turn around.

She made the turn and punched the accelerator to keep her speed up the grade. The tires of her Subaru fell into fresh ruts that had been made by a vehicle with larger tires and a wider wheel base—a flatbed truck. Her car shuddered back and forth as if on a track at a carnival ride, and the headlights bounced and shimmered off the trunks and limbs of trees swaying violently in the wind. Tracy leaned forward, peering through an ever-shrinking window of visibility as ice and snow gathered on the windshield, seemingly immune to the wipers and the defroster hissing hot air.

Tracy slowed into a corner, about to accelerate out of the turn when she saw a branch sticking up out of the snow. She braked hard and jerked to a stop. The headlights extended just far enough to illuminate two other trees that had fallen across the path. She'd get no farther in the car. Tracy looked about, uncertain how much farther it was to Parker House's property, or if she was even on the correct road. She again checked her cell phone. No reception.

Were Dan and Calloway on their way? She had no way to know. Instinct told her she didn't have time to wait.

She checked the magazine of her Glock, slapped it back into place, and chambered a round. After slipping two additional magazines into the pocket of her jacket, she pulled on her hat and ski gloves and grabbed the flashlight she'd found in a drawer in Dan's kitchen. Tracy shoved open the door, using her forearm to brace it against the howling wind and keep it from slamming shut. She steeled herself for the weather and what was to come.

CHAPTER 54

DeAngelo Finn hung crucified inside the closet door. His arms were raised shoulder height, metal spikes driven through the palms, blood dripping down the wood from each one. The weight of his body was held up by a rope tied around his waist and hung on a hook. Finn's head listed to the side, eyes closed and face ashen in the intense beam from Calloway's flashlight.

Roy Calloway put his ear to Finn's chest and heard a faint beat. Finn moaned.

"He's alive," Armstrong said, disbelieving.

"Get me a hammer, something!"

Armstrong stumbled out of the room, spilling whatever remained atop the dresser to the ground.

Calloway's instinct was to remove the belt, but if he did, Finn's weight would be transferred to the spikes through his hands. "Hang on DeAngelo. We got help on the way. Can you hear me? DeAngelo? Hang on. We're going to get you down."

Ronkowski and two of his firemen trailed Armstrong into the room. One carried a powerful lantern.

"Jesus," Ronkowski said.

"I need something to pull them out."

"You pry those nails out and the pain will kill him," Ronkowski said.

"What if we drive the points out from the back?" one of the firemen said.

"Same problem."

"We could cut around the spikes," Calloway said.

Ronkowski wiped a hand across his face. "All right. Let's do that. We can lift him to take the weight off his hands. Dirk, get the saw."

"Forget that," Armstrong said, stopping the fireman. "Just pull out the hinge pins and take down the whole damn door. We can use it like a stretcher."

"He's right," Ronkowski said. "That's better. Dirk, get a hammer and screwdriver." Ronkowski stepped closer to DeAngelo. "He's having trouble breathing. Lift him up to take the weight off his rib cage."

Calloway lifted Finn by the waist. The old man moaned. Armstrong returned with a chair from the kitchen and slid it under Finn's legs, but Finn was too weak to push himself up. Calloway continued to support his weight as Dirk returned with the hammer and chisel and started on the top hinge pin.

"No," Armstrong said, "take out the bottom bolt first. We'll brace the top."

The fireman knocked the bottom pin out of the hinge, then the bolt from the middle hinge. Armstrong and Calloway steadied the door.

"You got him?" the fireman asked.

"Do it," Armstrong said.

The fireman knocked out the top pin. Calloway braced against the weight of Finn and the door as he and Armstrong managed to turn the door and slowly lower it onto the bed.

"Get the tie downs," Ronkowski said. "We need to strap his body to the door if we're going to carry him out of here."

Ronkowski fitted an oxygen mask over Finn's face and checked his vitals. When a fireman returned with the straps, they removed the belt from around Finn's waist and maneuvered the straps under the door and cinched Finn about the ankles, waist, and chest.

"All right. Let's see if we can get him out of here," Ronkowski said.

Calloway took the end of the door by Finn's head. Armstrong grabbed the end near his feet.

"On three," Ronkowski said.

They lifted in unison, trying to avoid any sudden movements. Finn groaned again.

As they maneuvered the door through the jamb, Armstrong said, "Who would do it, Roy? Jesus, who would do something like this to an old man?"

CHAPTER 55

The cold bit at her, finding every seam in her clothes and pricking at her skin like dozens of needles. Tracy lowered her head into the wind, stepped over a fallen tree, and followed the tire tracks up the slope. She stayed in the ruts left by the tires, but her boots still sank up to her calves, making every step a struggle. She became quickly winded but trudged on, afraid to stop, pushing aside any thoughts of going back, telling herself it was futile since she could never reverse her car down the hill and turning it around was not an option. Besides, she'd put these events in motion. She needed to stop them.

Two hundred yards up the slope she came to the edge of a clearing. In the near distance, through the swirling snow, she could just make out the faint glow of a light and the shadows of buildings and snow-covered humps. She recalled the aerial photographs at Edmund House's trial, which had depicted multiple metal-roofed buildings, as well as cars and farm equipment in varying stages of restoration littering Parker House's yard. She didn't imagine it would change much. This was the right place. She turned off the flashlight and crept toward the light at the back of the property, stopping behind the bumper of the one vehicle not buried beneath snow—the flatbed she'd seen at the courthouse. She scraped the snow and ice off the license plate and confirmed it to be the same as the plate number that Kins had provided. Satisfied it was the same truck, she studied the ramshackle wood-plank structure. Two feet of snow had piled atop the roof. Foot-long icicles hung like jagged teeth from its eaves. No smoke came from the flue.

The wind found a space between the collar of her jacket and hat and sent a chill down her spine. Her fingers had gone numb inside her gloves. She feared losing more dexterity if she waited much longer.

She shuffled from the flatbed to the wooden steps, which had been recently shoveled. The wood sagged beneath her weight. On the tiny porch, she pressed her back against the siding and waited a beat before leaning to look through a window's glass panes, which were icing over on the outside and fogged on the inside.

Using her teeth, Tracy pulled off her gloves and unzipped her jacket. She reached for the Glock and felt the cold numbing her fingers. She alternately blew into each of her fists and reached for the doorknob. It turned. She gently pushed. The door stuck, and for a brief moment she thought it was bolted. Then it popped free of the jamb. The windowpanes rattled and she again waited a beat, the wind shoving hard at her back, nearly pulling the knob from her hand. Then she slid inside and, quickly and quietly, closed the door. She was free of the wind, which whistled through the house, but not the cold. The room was freezing and held the pungent smell of fermenting garbage.

She flexed her fingers, trying to improve circulation while quickly orienting herself. A table and chair sat beneath a small four-paned window. An L-shaped counter with a metal sink led to an opening to another room, in which was the source of the light she'd seen through the cabin's window. Though she stepped cautiously, the wood planks creaked beneath her feet, the sound only partially dampened by the muffled whirr of a generator—the likely source of power for the light. Tracy slid along the counter to the doorjamb between the rooms. Gun in hand, she leaned around the corner.

The light was especially bright because it was coming from a bare bulb. The lamp shade had been removed and it rested on the floor beside a rust-colored armchair that was facing away from her. An orange extension cord snaked along the floor and down a darkened hallway. Tracy stepped in. She stopped when she saw a crown of gray hair protruding just above the back of the armchair—someone was slumped in the seat. She detected no reaction to her presence. Tracy stepped in farther, angling around the side of the chair, the floor continuing to betray her presence. She stepped past the side table, the face of the chair's occupant coming into view from behind the wing of the chair.

"Jesus," she said, as the chin lifted, the eyes opened, and he turned his head to look at her.

It was Parker House.

CHAPTER 56

Parker House gave Tracy a startled, wide-eyed stare. It was not a look of surprise. It was the unmistakable lingering look of fear that Tracy had seen too often in her job, one that came from victims of violent crime. Blood saturated the arms of the chair where the metal spikes had been driven through the back of each of Parker's hands. Two more spikes pierced the top of each of his boots, driven through Parker's feet into the floor boards. A pool of blood flowed from beneath each sole.

Tracy pried her eyes from Parker's ashen face and quickly looked about the room. She noted the darkened hall just to the right of a wood-burning stove and switched on the flashlight. Heart racing and her head spinning, she fell back on her training as she crept down the hall, gun extended, flashlight sweeping left to right. She braced her back against one side of the hall, swung around a door frame, and danced the light over a rumpled bed and cheap dresser. Tracy swung back out and repeated the maneuver into the second room, finding it to also be empty, but for a single bed, dresser, and nightstand. She returned to the living room, trying to make sense of it.

Parker had closed his eyes. She knelt, touching him gently on the shoulder. "Parker. Parker."

This time, when his eyes opened, they remained hooded, half-closed, and he grimaced as if the small act brought him pain. His lips moved but emitted no words. He took in short rasps of air and swallowed with seemingly great effort. The words finally came in ghostly gasps. "I tried . . ."

Tracy leaned closer.

"I tried . . . to warn . . ."

His eyes shifted from her face to something above her, but she realized too late her mistake. The light had been a ploy to draw her in, a moth to the flame, the hum of the generator meant to deaden sound.

Tracy sprang to her feet but was unable to turn before she felt the dull impact against the back of her head. Her legs buckled and the gun slipped from her hand. She felt arms around her waist, catching her, keeping her upright. Breath blew warmly against her ear.

"You smell just like her."

———

Roy Calloway and Finlay Armstrong carried Finn and the closet door through the house and out the front entryway. With the storm gusting, they had to be careful it didn't catch on the door and pull it from their grasp like a kite.

"Take it slow," Calloway said. He could feel his boots slipping on the ice-covered front walk and shortened his steps, shuffling his feet until they'd managed to maneuver the door into the ambulance.

"Let's move," Ronkowski said.

Before stepping from the ambulance, Calloway leaned down and whispered in Finn's ear. "I'm going to finish this," he said. "I'm going to finish what I should have finished twenty years ago."

"We got to go, Roy," Ronkowski said. "His vitals are nose-diving."

Calloway stepped away. Ronkowski slammed the ambulance doors shut, and the vehicle lurched forward, fought for traction, and finally got moving. It plowed through the snow, lights rotating. Calloway watched it go with the remaining firemen. They stood beside Finlay as if frozen. Snow covered their gear and ice crystals clung to their facial hair.

"Is anybody's cell working?" Calloway asked.

Nobody's was.

He stepped to Armstrong. "I want you to take your car and get on over to Vance Clark's house. Tell him I said he and his wife are to go with you. Tell him I said to bring his gun with him and keep it close by."

"What's going on, Roy?"

Calloway grabbed his deputy by the shoulder but kept his voice even. "Did you hear what I said?"

"Yeah. Yeah, I heard."

"Then I want you to go to my house and get my wife. You bring all three of them back to the police station with you and you wait by the radio."

"What should I tell them?"

"Just tell them that I insisted. My wife can be stubborn as a mule. You tell her I said it is not open to discussion. You understand?"

Armstrong nodded.

"Go on now. Go on and do as I say."

Armstrong's boots sank into the snow as he struggled to reach his patrol car. When he'd driven off into the swirling snow, Calloway slid into his Suburban, pulled the Remington 870 shotgun from its clip, opened the breach, and loaded five shells. He shoved a handful more into his pocket. If these were to be his last remaining days in office, he was going to go out doing his job.

He started the car, about to pull away from the curb when headlights approached, aimed directly at his front bumper. A Tahoe plowed to a stop, sliding sideways the final few feet. Dan O'Leary jumped from the driver's side in a heavy jacket and hat. He left the door open, the lights on, and the engine running.

Calloway lowered his window. "Move the Goddamn car, Dan."

Dan handed Calloway a piece of paper. Calloway took a moment to read it, then crumpled it into a ball and banged his fist against the steering wheel. "Pull your car to the side and get in."

CHAPTER 57

Dan gripped the handle above the door and braced his other hand against the dash. He had his feet planted on the floorboard mat, but it only partially stabilized him as the Suburban bounced onto the county road, back tires fishtailing. Calloway corrected and punched the accelerator. The tires spun before gripping, and the big car lunged forward. Snowflakes assaulted the windshield and limited the reach of the headlights to dim cones that the darkness swallowed just a few feet from the hood. Dan repositioned himself on the bench seat as Calloway swerved to avoid a fallen branch.

"James was distraught," Calloway said. "We knew House had done it. We weren't buying his bullshit about a board splintering and cutting his face and arms but we couldn't prove it. I told James we'd never convict House without somehow tying him to Sarah. I told him that, without a body, without any forensic evidence, House would walk. No one had ever been convicted of first-degree murder without a body. The forensics weren't good enough back then."

"And he agreed to provide you with the jewelry and hair?"

"Not initially. Initially he wouldn't hear of it."

"What changed his mind?"

Calloway glanced over at him. "George Bovine."

"Branch!" Dan shoved his feet into the floorboards as Calloway swerved, just missing a large limb. After a moment to catch his breath, Dan said, "You put Bovine up to it, just like you put him up to coming to talk with me."

"The hell I did. Bovine came to speak to James when the news broke about Sarah's disappearance. I knew nothing about it. James called and asked me to come to the house. Bovine was already there. Tracy and Abby weren't home. James shut the doors to his den and Bovine told us what I'm sure he told you. A week later, James called me back to the house and handed me the earrings and the hair in plastic bags. I never considered the possibility that some of the strands might belong to Tracy. As I said, those kinds of things weren't on our radar as much back then. I put the jewelry and the hair in my desk drawer and thought it through for days before I brought in Vance Clark to discuss it. We both decided the evidence was of no use unless we could somehow get a warrant to search Parker's property, and the only way to do that was to get a witness to implicate House and put his alibi in question."

"How'd you convince Hagen to testify? The reward?"

The back end of the SUV slid as Calloway navigated a turn. When he corrected, the car shuddered and the engine revved until the tires regained traction. "Ryan's father and I went to the academy together. I'd known him since the day he was born. When his father was killed during a routine traffic stop, I started a fund for the family. Ryan would come in and talk to me whenever he drove through Cedar Grove."

"So he knew about Sarah."

"Everyone in the state knew about Sarah. During one of our conversations, I told him I needed someone who could say they frequently traveled that road at odd hours of the day and night. He checked his calendar and said he'd made a business trip that day. All I needed him to say was he took the county road and saw House's truck. I thought that when CSI found the evidence, House would realize he was screwed, tell us where he buried Sarah's body, and that would be the end of it. He'd take a plea, life without parole, and we'd be done with him. I never envisioned a trial."

Calloway slowed the car and whipped the steering wheel to the right. The Suburban bounced and bucked as it left the county road and started to ascend the mountain.

"Fresh tire tracks," Dan said.

"I see 'em."

"You brought the jewelry and hairs with you when you executed the search warrant?"

Calloway squinted and waited for a gust of wind to pass. "Couldn't do it with the CSI team present, and I couldn't make an extra trip out to the property without House getting squirrelly on me. Parker did it."

"Parker? Why would he set up his own nephew?"

Calloway shook his head. "You still don't get it, do you, Dan?"

CHAPTER 58

Sarah sang along to one of Tracy's Bruce Springsteen CDs, drumming her fingers on the steering wheel to the beat of the E Street Band. Tracy was the bigger fan; Sarah didn't even know all the words. She just liked the way the Boss's butt looked in jeans.

She sang the lyrics to "Born to Run," trying to take her mind off of the thought that Tracy was leaving. Not leaving physically, but getting married, that things would change.

The drive from Olympia had been long and melancholy. Sarah was happy for Tracy, but she also knew things wouldn't be the same now that Tracy had Ben. Tracy had always been Sarah's best friend and, in some ways, like a second mother to her. What Sarah was going to miss most were the late nights they stayed awake talking about anything and everything, from shooting to school and boys. She used to ask Tracy if they could still live together after Tracy got married. She smiled at the recollection of climbing in bed beside Tracy, her sister's comforting warmth helping Sarah to go to sleep. She thought of their prayer. She'd never forget their prayer. Many nights it was the only way Sarah could fall asleep.

She heard Tracy's voice in her head.

I am not . . .

"I am not . . . ," she said aloud.

I am not afraid . . .

"I am not afraid . . ."

I am not afraid of the dark.

"I am not afraid of the dark."

But she was, still, even at eighteen.

Sarah would miss sharing clothes and waking up with Tracy on Christmas morning. She'd miss sliding down the banister and waiting around a corner to scare Tracy and her friends. She'd miss their home and their weeping willow, the way she used to swing from its braids and dangle over the lawn engrossed in some fantasy in which the lawn was an Amazon River filled with alligators. She'd miss it all.

She wiped a tear from her cheek. She thought she'd prepared herself for this day, but now that it had arrived, she knew she hadn't. Nor could she have.

You're leaving next year for the U-Dub, she told herself. *At least now Tracy will have Ben.*

Sarah smiled, recalling how mad Tracy had been when they had handed her the silver belt buckle. She'd looked like a bee had stung her in the ass. She didn't have a clue why Sarah had let her win. She was too mad to even notice that Ben was wearing a new shirt and slacks. Sarah had helped him pick out both. God knew he couldn't do it on his own. Ben had called two weeks before the tournament and told Sarah that he wanted to propose at their favorite restaurant in Seattle, but he could only get a seven thirty reservation, which meant they'd be cutting it close unless they left straight from the competition. That meant Sarah driving home alone, and they both knew Tracy would get all "big sister" on her. Sarah had needed something to make Tracy not want to drive home with her, and she didn't have to think about it for long. Tracy hated to lose, but what she really hated was if Sarah *let* her win, at anything.

The rain fell in large drops, splattering the windshield, though they were still not the deluge Tracy had worried about. Like it never rained here? Please.

She belted out another line from the song, singing along with the Boss.

The truck lurched.

Sarah sat up. She checked her rearview and side mirrors, thinking she'd hit something in the road, but it was too dark to see behind her.

The truck lurched again. This time she knew she hadn't hit anything, but the truck began to buck and sputter, losing speed. The tachometer needle fell quickly to the left, and the gas light illuminated on the dash.

"Are you freaking kidding me?"

The red bar had dropped to "E."

Sarah flicked the plastic with her finger, but the needle didn't move. This was not happening. "Tell me this is not happening," she said.

It wasn't possible. They'd filled the truck on Friday. Tracy hadn't wanted to have to do it in the morning, worried they could be late. Sarah had bought a Diet Coke and bag of Cheetos in the convenience store for the ride.

You're going to eat that crap for breakfast? Tracy had chastised.

The engine quit. The steering wheel became difficult to turn. Sarah muscled the truck around the next curve. A slight downward slope allowed her to coast a little, but it certainly was not enough to travel the remaining distance to Cedar Grove, however far that was. As the truck slowed, she steered to the dirt shoulder, tires crunching on gravel, and slowed to a stop. She turned the key. The engine whimpered as if laughing at her. Then it just clicked. She sat back, suppressing a scream. Springsteen continued to moan and wail. She shut off the radio.

After a moment of anxiety, she said, "Okay, time to regroup." Their father always said to be adaptable and have a plan. "Okay, what's my plan?" First things first. "Where the hell am I?"

Sarah checked the rearview mirror. She did not see headlights behind her. She did not see anything behind her. She looked all about her surroundings. Sarah had once known the road well, but now she didn't take it as often with the interstate, and she'd not been paying attention. She could not get her bearings. She checked her watch and tried to calculate how much time had passed since she'd left Olympia, hoping she could calculate how much farther she had to Cedar Grove, but she couldn't be certain what time she'd actually left the parking lot. She knew that, once she exited for the county road, the Cedar Grove turnoff was twenty minutes. She estimated she'd been on the road for ten minutes. If that was the case, then her best guess was that it was another four to six miles to the turn. It wasn't a stroll in the park, especially not in the rain, but it also wasn't a marathon. Maybe she'd get lucky and a car would come along, though there wasn't much traffic on the county road anymore. Most people took the interstate now.

Promise me you'll stay on the interstate.

Why hadn't she listened? Tracy was going to kill her.

Sarah groaned, allowing a moment in which to feel sorry for herself. Then she got back to devising a plan. She contemplated sleeping in the truck bed, but thought of the panic it would cause when Tracy called the house in the morning—and Tracy *would* call to tell Sarah the news—and Sarah didn't answer the phone. Tracy would have their parents flying home from Hawaii and the FBI and everyone in Cedar Grove out looking for her.

"Well," Sarah said, thinking it through another moment. "You're definitely not getting anywhere sitting here. Time to start walking."

She slipped on her jacket and grabbed Tracy's black Stetson from the seat. The silver belt buckle lay beneath it. She slid the buckle into a pocket of her jacket, wanting to hand it back to Tracy in the morning to remind her of what a pill she'd been. They'd get a good laugh out of it, and the buckle would forever remind them of the night Tracy got engaged. Maybe Sarah could mount it on a plaque or something.

She was stalling. She was really not looking forward to a long walk in the rain.

She put on the Stetson as she stepped down from the cab, locking the door. As if to spite her, the rain increased in intensity, a rush of water that came with a roar. She walked along the edge of the pavement, hoping to find some shelter beneath the canopy of trees. Within minutes, water began to trickle down her back. "This is really going to suck, big time."

She pressed on, singing to pass the time, the lyrics of "Born to Run" stuck in her head.

"Everybody's out on the road tonight, but there's nothing . . . I don't know all the words."

Sarah trudged on. After another few minutes, she stopped and listened, thinking that she had heard the sound of a car engine, though now she couldn't be certain over the sound of rain beating on the canopy and trickling to the pavement. Sarah stepped farther onto the shoulder and looked back up the road, straining to hear. There. Headlights marked the pavement a second or two before the car came around the bend in the road. Sarah stepped to the shoulder, one foot on the pavement, leaning out and waving one hand overhead while using the other to cut the glare from the headlamps. The vehicle slowed and came to a stop in the road. Not a car.

A red Chevy truck.

CHAPTER 59

Tracy opened her eyes but she remained in complete darkness. Disoriented, her head in a fog of confusion and pain, she fought to shake away the cobwebs and remember what happened. She lifted her head, which caused a sharp pain to radiate across the top of her skull. She winced. When the pain lessened, Tracy pushed herself to a seated position, bracing on her arm for support. Her head pounded. Her limbs felt leaden. She took several deep breaths, continuing to gather her thoughts and trying to orient herself. The images came back in pulses.

The ramshackle house as she had approached.

The flatbed truck partially covered in snow.

The door leading to the kitchen.

Stepping into the main room.

The crown of hair just above the back of the seat.

Parker House turning his head and opening his eyes.

You smell just like her.

Someone had hit her from behind. When Tracy raised her arm to touch the back of her head, her wrist felt weighted. She shook her arms and heard the rattle of chains. Her heart raced. She struggled to stand, but a wave of nausea overcame her and she fell back down, on one knee. She inhaled deep breaths until the wave of nausea passed and tried again, slowly rising to her feet, stumbling but managing to regain her balance.

Tracy felt the manacles clasped to each wrist and ran her hand along what she estimated to be a foot-long chain between them. From the feel of it, a second, thicker chain extended from the chain between her wrists. She followed the links hand over hand to what felt like a rectangular plate. Her fingertips traced the contours of the heads of two hexagonal bolts. She braced a foot against the wall, wrapped the chain around her hand and tugged on the plate, sensing a slight give, but another wave of nausea and throbbing pain overcame her.

She heard a noise behind her. A wedge of dull light pierced the darkness, slowly widening—a door was opening. Someone stepped into the light, a shadow, and the door closed, plunging her back into darkness. She braced her back against the wall, raised her arms, and prepared to strike or kick.

She tried to follow the sound of footsteps shuffling about the room, but in the darkness, they seemed to come from all over. She heard an odd whirring noise. A sudden, sharp flicker of light followed, momentarily blinding her. Tracy dropped her gaze, waiting for the black–and-white spots to clear. Then she raised a hand to reduce the glare and saw that the source of the light was a single bare bulb dangling from a wire hung over a wooden beam, one of two beams running horizontally across a dirt ceiling scarred where a shovel had scraped.

Beneath the bulb, a figure knelt with his back to her, cranking a handle that protruded from the side of a wooden box. With each rotation of the handle, there was a sound like the beating wings of a swarm of unseen insects, and the filament inside the bulb pulsed. Its color changed from orange to red and, finally, to a bright white that pushed aside the darkness, revealing her surroundings and her circumstances.

Tracy estimated the room she was in to be perhaps twenty feet long, twelve feet across, and eight feet high. Four weathered beams served as vertical posts bracing the two ceiling beams. As she had discerned, rusted metal manacles cuffed each wrist with a foot-long piece of chain between them. The second chain, perhaps five feet in length, was welded to the rectangular plate she'd felt with her hands. The plate was bolted to a concrete wall. Scraps of mismatched carpet covered portions of the floor. In a corner of the room was a wrought-iron bed with a tattered mattress and, beside it, an equally worn sitting chair. Crude shelves lined one wall—canned goods on one, paperback books on another. Beside the books was a black Stetson that Tracy hadn't seen in twenty years.

Edmund House straightened and turned. "Welcome home, Tracy."

CHAPTER 60

A snow-laden tree limb slapped the windshield, exploding in a burst of white powder. Calloway didn't slow. He followed the tracks around another bend, about to hit the gas, then quickly hit the brakes hard, bringing the Suburban to a sudden stop inches from the back of Tracy's Subaru.

Snow covered the back window and the roof of the car, but it was only an inch or two thick. Dan looked ahead and saw branches sticking up from the snow, which had otherwise buried a tree that had fallen across the road.

Calloway swore under his breath and removed the radio microphone from its clip, playing with the radio's controls, using his call sign and asking if anyone could hear him. He got no response. He tried a second time, but again, the response was silence. "Finlay, you there? Finlay?"

He replaced the microphone in its clip and shut off the engine.

"Get what?" Dan asked.

Calloway eyed him. "What?"

"You said I don't get it. Don't get what?"

Calloway unlocked the shotgun, pulled it from its rack, and handed it to Dan. "We didn't frame an innocent man, Dan. We framed a guilty man."

He slid out the door into the storm.

Dan sat stunned. What the hell had he done?

He picked up Tracy's note from where Calloway had crumpled and tossed it onto a seat and unfolded it.

Truck that shot out window registered
to Parker House.
No one checked alibi.
Going to get answers.
Bring Calloway.

She thought it was Parker. She thought Parker had killed Sarah.

Dan pulled on his hat and gloves, stepped out into knee-deep snow, and immediately felt the biting-cold wind. He plowed his way to the back of the Suburban. Calloway was sliding the strap of a hunting rifle onto his shoulder and shoving bullets into his jacket pocket.

"How do you know?" Dan had to shout above a gust of howling wind.

Calloway pulled two flashlights from a rear-wheel well, testing one and handing it to Dan. He handed him two extra batteries.

"Roy, how the hell do you know it was Edmund and not Parker?"

"How? I told you how. I told everyone how. House told me he did it."

Calloway slammed the tailgate shut and stepped to the trail of footprints, which were already filling with fresh snow.

Dan pursued. "Why would he admit he did it?"

Calloway stopped to shout over the howling wind. "Why? Because he's a fucking psychopath, that's why."

He moved to the tree across the road and walked to where its stump was buried in snow. He dropped to a knee, and cleared the snow. Dan could see from the straight cut that someone had felled the tree with a chainsaw.

Calloway stood, squinting into the blinding snow as he looked up the hill. "He knows we're coming."

He started along the trail of boot prints, Dan behind him, carrying the shotgun. After a short distance, he was struggling to catch his breath. After a hundred yards, they both had to stop, breathing heavily.

"If he buried her body, why didn't you find it?" Dan said, struggling to get out the words.

A road map of red-and-purple veins traversed Calloway's exposed cheeks and nose. "Because that was a lie. House didn't kill her right away. He was playing us, playing me. And now he's played you."

"But you said you searched the property. If Sarah wasn't there and House didn't bury her, where was she?"

Calloway nodded in the direction of the mountains. "Up there. She was right up there the whole time."

CHAPTER 61

Sarah used her hand to block the glare of the headlights but could not see the face of the driver who had opened the truck's cab door and leaned out.

A man spoke over the rush of the rain. "That your truck back there along the side of the road?"

"Yeah," Sarah said.

"You need a ride?"

"I'm all right," she said. "I actually don't have far to go."

The man stepped down from the cab and hurried around the hood to where Sarah could see him. She assessed him in one word. Gorgeous. In fact, he looked like the Boss in a white T-shirt, blue jeans, and worn work boots. His biceps stretched the fabric of his shirt, which was getting wet and sticking to his chest. "What happened?"

"I think I ran out of gas," she said.

"I'll bet that made your night, huh?" He pulled his hair back off his face and folded it behind his ears. His smile made his eyes light up. "Don't beat yourself up over it. I've done the same thing. I try to see how far I can stretch a tank, you know." He pointed a thumb at his truck. "I got a gas can in the back. Unfortunately, it's empty. But I think there's a gas station in Cedar Grove."

Sarah said, "Not sure if Harley is still open. He usually closes around nine on Saturday."

"You live there?" he said.

That had been the point of using Harley's name. She was a local. She knew people. And people knew her. "Just outside town a bit."

He started for the cab. "Come on, I'll give you a lift."

But she didn't move. "Where are you coming from?"

He turned back, speaking across the hood. "I was in Seattle visiting my folks. Nice night to be driving, huh? Should have stayed, but I needed to get back. I live over in Silver Spurs. If the gas station's not open, I don't mind dropping you at your home."

"It's not far," she said, trying to sound casual. "I can walk."

"Come on, that's got to be, what, another five miles?"

"It's not that far."

"Yeah, but tonight you might drown." He smiled. "I'll tell you what. I'll drive ahead and see if the station's open. If it is, I'll get the gas and come back and we can fill up your tank. If it's not, I'll drive to your house and let someone know you're stuck."

Sarah knew Harley was closed and no one was home. Tracy was out with Ben and her parents were in Hawaii. She'd be sending him on a wild goose chase. "You don't need to do all that."

"No trouble." He approached and held out his hand. "I'm Edmund."

"Sarah," she said. "Sarah Crosswhite."

"Crosswhite? We got a Ms. Crosswhite over at the high school in Cedar Grove. Teaches science, I think."

"You work at the high school?"

"I'm one of the night janitors."

"I've never seen you."

"That's because I work at night. Only vampires see me. Nah, I just got the job."

She smiled. Gorgeous and funny.

"She's blonde, isn't she? Looks a lot like you."

"We get that a lot."

He nodded. "She's your sister. I can see it in the face."

"She's four years older. She teaches chemistry."

"I'll bet that's an easy A, huh?"

"Oh, no. I graduated. I'm going to the U-Dub in the fall."

"So you're one of those brainiac types?"

"Hardly." She felt herself blushing. "Tracy's the brains in the family."

"Yeah, I got a brother like that, a real junior Einstein."

The rain fell harder, another gush of water. His hair hung nearly to his shoulders. His T-shirt, now saturated, showed every ripple of his chest and stomach. He rubbed his arms.

"Well," he said, "why don't you wait under the trees by that mile marker over there, so I know where to find you, and I'll go see about getting you some gas." He started for the cab.

"It's okay."

He turned. "What's that?"

"I'll just go with you."

"You sure?"

"Yeah. It's fine. I don't want to make you drive all the way there and back."

"All right then." He hurried around the hood, climbed into the cab, and reached across, pushing open the passenger-side door and smiling down at her. "Let me help you with that."

Sarah handed him her backpack and used the door to swing up into the cab. She took off the Stetson and shook out her hair, craving the heat blasting from the vents. "I guess I'm lucky you came along."

"Instead of some freak job," he said, putting the car in gear. "Guy like that picks you up out here and you could disappear forever."

CHAPTER 62

D an knew Calloway was pointing in the direction of the peaks of the hills above Cedar Grove, but he couldn't see beyond twenty feet with the darkness and swirling snow.

"He kept her alive in a room in the Cedar Grove mine. He waited until the dam was about to go online and buried her where he knew it was going to flood."

"How do you know that?"

"Logical, given where we found Sarah's remains."

"No, how do you know he kept her in the mine?"

"We got to keep moving." Calloway trudged on, Dan at his side and straining to hear. "Parker found it," Calloway said. "Edmund used to leave the house on the ATV and go off into the mountains. After he was convicted, Parker thought of the mine and wondered about whether maybe Edmund had been going there on the ATV. He came and told me about it and we went up with bolt cutters and cut the lock from the gate at the entrance. At first we didn't find anything, but then I noticed the wall in the office seemed crudely built for a large mining company. When I looked closer I found a seam for a door. House had built a false wall and kept Sarah chained in a room behind it. We found a gray frock on the floor, manacles and chains bolted to the wall." Calloway shook his head. "Made me sick to my stomach thinking of Sarah in a place like that, what he must have done to her. We left everything as is, locked the entrance, and never went back."

Dan grabbed Calloway's shoulder, abruptly stopping him. "Then why the hell didn't you tell anyone, Roy?"

Calloway knocked Dan's hand away. "Tell them what, Dan? Tell them we all lied, that we manufactured evidence, but now we were sorry and want to do it right? House would have walked free and killed someone else's daughter. What was done was done. There was no going back. House had a life sentence and Sarah was dead."

"Then why didn't you tell Tracy?"

"I couldn't."

"Why the hell not, Roy? Jesus, why the hell wouldn't you?"

"Because I swore I wouldn't."

"You let her suffer for twenty years not knowing?"

The fur lining of Calloway's hat had completely iced over and ice crystals clung to his eyebrows. "It wasn't my decision, Dan. It was James's."

Dan squinted in disbelief. "Dear God, why would he do that to his own daughter?"

"Because he loved her, that's why."

"How can you say that?"

"James didn't want Tracy living the rest of her life with the guilt. He knew it would have killed her to know."

"She's lived with the guilt the last twenty years."

"No," Calloway said. "Not this kind of guilt."

———

Edmund House sat on the generator box. The light over his head crackled and emitted a low hum. "It's sort of ironic, isn't it?"

"What?" Tracy asked.

"All this time has passed and here we are, finally."

"What are you talking about?"

"I'm talking about you and me, here." He spread his arms, grinning. "I built this for you."

She hesitated, looking about the room. "What?"

"Well, the Cedar Grove Mining Company did most of the work, but I put in the little home touches like the carpet and the bed and the bookshelves. I knew you liked to read. I know it doesn't look like much now, but things go to hell when you don't keep up with the spring cleaning for twenty years." He smiled. "Honestly, I'm surprised it's still here, just as I left it. They never found it."

"I didn't even know you, House."

"But I knew you. I'd been studying everything about you from the moment I arrived in Cedar Grove and saw you at the high school. I used to go and watch the kiddies get out of school, and then one day out you walked surrounded by all these students. At first I thought you were one of them but then I could tell by the way you carried yourself that you were more mature.

"I knew from that moment that you were the one. I'd never had a teacher before, though I'd fantasized about a few. And I'd never had a blonde. After I saw you, I made a point of driving by in the afternoon when school got out. I needed to find out what kind of car you drove. But you can't park around a school too often without some nosy neighbor cluing in. Once I figured out you drove the Ford truck, I'd just look for it in the faculty parking lot, and if it wasn't there I'd drive into town. You used to go into that coffee shop and correct tests. I was there once, drinking a cup of coffee. If you weren't at the coffee shop I'd drive out of town past your house and see if the truck was parked in the driveway.

"I found a spot up the road where I had a better view of your bedroom window. Some nights I'd watch for hours. I liked the way you used to get out of the shower and look out your bedroom window with your hair wrapped in a towel like a turban. I knew what we had was special, even though you started dating that guy. Never did see what you saw in him, or why you'd move from that big old mansion to that shitty house. He complicated things, always being around. I couldn't just walk up to your front door or wait inside the house for you. I realized I was going to have to create my own opportunity. That's when I got the idea of messing with your truck so it'd break down."

The thought that House had been watching her made Tracy's skin crawl, but House's mention of the truck raised another, more sickening possibility. Sarah had been driving Tracy's truck that night. She looked to the black Stetson on the shelf.

"Threw me for a loop first time I saw your sister," House said. "She came into the coffee shop one time while you were working, snuck up behind you, and covered your eyes. I thought I was seeing double."

"You thought she was me that night."

House stood, pacing. "How could I not? Shit, it was like that Doublemint gum commercial with the twins. You guys even dressed alike. "

Though the cave was bone cold, Tracy had broken out in a sweat.

"When I saw the truck on the side of the road and then saw her walking in the rain, alone, wearing that black hat, I thought for sure it was you. Imagine my surprise when I got out of the truck and realized it wasn't. I was disappointed at first. I even contemplated just driving her home. But then I thought, hell, I'd gone to all that effort. And who was to say I couldn't have you both."

Tracy slumped against the wall, her legs weak.

"And now I have."

"You didn't bury her. That's why we couldn't find her."

"Not right away. That would have been a waste. But I couldn't have her escaping like Annabelle Bovine." House's jaw clenched and his face went dark. "That bitch cost me six years of my life." He pointed to his temple. "A smart man learns from his mistakes, and I had six years to contemplate how to do a better job the next time. We had some good times here, your sister and me."

Sarah disappeared August 21, 1993. The Cedar Falls Dam had gone online in mid-October. An acidic burn inched up the back of Tracy's throat. Her stomach lurched and cramped and she bent over, retching.

"But that asshole Calloway kept pressing me. When he told me about the witness, about Hagen, I knew it was just a matter of time. A man like that has no integrity. It's disappointing isn't it? I imagine you must have felt the same disappointment in your father."

She spit bile from her mouth and looked up at him. "Fuck you, House."

His smile broadened. "I'll bet your father never imagined that someday I'd use the jewelry and pieces of hair he used to frame me to get out of that hellhole, or that you'd be the one to help me do it."

"I didn't do it to help you."

"Don't be that way, Tracy. At least I never lied to you."

"What are you talking about? This whole thing was a lie."

"I told you they framed me. I told you they manufactured the evidence. I never once said I was innocent."

"You're fucking delusional. You murdered her."

"No." He shook his head. "No. I loved her. They murdered her—Calloway and your father, with all their lying. They didn't leave me a choice. With the dam going online, they forced me to do it. I didn't want to do it, but big-shot Calloway wouldn't let it go."

CHAPTER 63

Sarah lifted her head when she heard the squeak of the gate echo down the mine. He'd come back sooner than she'd expected. Usually the light died completely before he returned, but the bulb was still emitting a dull-yellow glow.

She hurried to finish what she was doing, picking up bits of the concrete and sweeping the dust into the hole she'd made. The light from the single bulb continued to grow weaker and she could not see well enough to be certain she'd found each piece, but she also didn't have time to keep looking. She put the stake in the hole and refilled it with dirt, tamping it flat.

The door in the wall pushed open as she shifted the carpet back in place, moved to sit with her back to the wall, and picked up the paperback he'd brought for her. Edmund House stepped in, set a plastic bag on a folding table, and cranked the generator handle. The filament brightened, making her squint.

House turned. He seemed to take longer than usual to consider her. His eyes shifted to the piece of carpet on the ground, and in the light she could see that she had not replaced it squarely in the same location it had been.

"What have you been doing?" he asked.

She shrugged and held up a paperback. "What can I do? I've read every book twice. Kind of spoils the story when you already know the ending anyway."

"You complaining?"

"No, just saying, you know. Maybe it would be nice to get a couple new ones."

By her calculations, it had been seven weeks since he'd brought her here. It was difficult to keep track of the days without any windows, but she used him as her clock. She put a scratch in the wall each time he came back, which she figured to be a new day. He'd taken her on Saturday, August 21. If she'd calculated correctly, it was now Monday, October 11.

A month into her captivity, she'd found a metal spike partially buried at the base of a vertical beam. She figured they used it to put in the tracks for the mining carts to haul the silver out of the mine. Ten inches long, it had a flat end that must have been used to hammer it into the ground. She'd been using it to chip at the concrete around the metal plate he'd bolted to the wall. The plate's bolts had some play in them that allowed her to dig behind the plate so he wouldn't notice. If she could loosen the plate enough, she might be able to yank it free of the wall.

"Did you get the supplies?" she asked.

He shook his head. He looked distracted, sad. Like a little boy.

"Why not?"

He leaned against the table, the muscles in his arms prominent. "Chief Calloway came back again."

She felt the flicker of hope but tamped it down. "What did that asshole want this time?"

"He says he has a witness."

"Really?"

"That's what he says. He says he has a witness who will say he saw you and me on the county road together. I don't remember anyone. Do you?"

She shook her head. "Not that I remember."

He pushed away from the table, approaching, his voice becoming angry. "He's lying. I know he's lying, but he says he has one and that his testimony is going to be enough to get a search warrant. What do you think he's going to find?"

She shrugged. "Nothing. You said you were careful."

He reached out and touched the side of her face with his fingertips. She fought the impulse to flinch and pull away. It only made him angry. "You know what I think?"

She shook her head.

"I think I'm being set up." He dropped his hand and walked away. "If they made up the witness, they'll likely make up some evidence to try me. Do you know what that means?"

"No."

"It means this could be the last time we see each other."

She felt a wave of anxiety. "They won't catch you. You're too smart. You outsmarted them."

"Not if they cheat." He sighed and shook his head. "I told Calloway he could go fuck himself. I told him that I'd already raped and killed you and buried you in the mountains."

"Why would you tell him that?"

"Fuck him," he said, now pacing, voice rising. "He can't prove it, so let him live with that on his conscience the rest of his life. I told him I'd never tell him where I buried your body." He started laughing. "You want to know the best part?"

"What?" she said, feeling more and more anxious.

"He wasn't recording the conversation. It was just the two of us. He has no proof that I said anything."

"We could leave," she said, trying to sound enthusiastic. "We could go someplace together, disappear."

"Yeah, I thought of that," he said. He pulled clothes from the plastic bag. She recognized her shirt and jeans. She thought he'd burned them.

"I washed them for you," he said.

"Why?"

"Don't I get a thank you?"

"Thank you," she said, though uncertain of his intent.

He tossed them at her feet. When she didn't move, he said, "Go ahead and put them on. You can't leave dressed like that."

"Are you letting me go?"

"I can't keep you here anymore. Not with Calloway on my ass."

She slid the frock he'd given her from her shoulders and stepped out of it, naked before him. He watched as she picked up her jeans and slid them on. They hung from her hips. "Guess I've lost some weight," she said, her rib cage and collarbones prominent.

"You had a few to spare," he said. "I like you skinny."

She held up her arms. "My wrists," she said.

He took the key from his pocket and unlocked the left manacle. She slid her arm through the sleeve of her Scully shirt and expected him to reattach the manacle. Instead, he unlocked her right wrist and let the manacles and chains fall at her feet. It was the first time in seven weeks that both her arms had been free. She slid the shirt on, snapping the buttons, fighting to remain calm.

"Where are we going to go?" she said. "We could go to California. It's big. It would be impossible to find us."

House walked to the shelving and shook her jade earrings and necklace from a can on the shelf. He picked up Tracy's black Stetson, seemed to consider it a moment, and then put it back on the shelf. He handed her the jewelry. "You might as well put these back on too. No reason for me to keep them."

She bit back tears. "You're letting me go?"

"I knew it would always come to this."

Tears flowed down her cheeks.

"Don't start crying about it."

But she couldn't stop. She was going home. "When are we leaving?" she asked.

"Right now," he said. "We can go now."

"I won't say anything," she said. "I promise."

"I know you won't." He nodded to the door. When she hesitated, he said, "Well, go ahead."

It was all she could do to keep from running, anxious to get away, to breathe fresh air again, to see the sky, hear birds, and smell the scent of the evergreens. She took a tentative step toward the door, and looked back at him. His face was a blank mask.

Sarah took another step and thought of seeing Tracy again, and her mother and father, of waking up in her own bed, in her home. She'd tell herself that it had all been just a nightmare, a horrible nightmare. But she wouldn't dwell on what Edmund House had done to her. She was going to get on with her life. She was going to go to school and graduate and then she'd come back to live again in Cedar Grove, just as she and Tracy had always planned. In her excitement, she did not hear him pick up the chain from the floor.

She'd reached the door when the chain wrapped tightly around her throat, strangling her. She tried to dig her fingers beneath the links, then tried to scratch his arms, but he yanked her backward with the chain, flinging her with such force he lifted her off her feet. The light through the door grew distant, as if she were falling down a darkened well. She reached for it, arms straining, and thought she saw Tracy just before the back of her head hit hard against the concrete wall.

CHAPTER 64

"I hated to kill her." Edmund House had resumed his seat atop the generator box, forearms resting on his thighs as if he were tending to a campfire and telling a ghost story. "But I knew I wasn't going to get an opportunity to get rid of her body like that again. And I wasn't going back to prison."

He sat up straighter. Anger crept into his voice. "I should have been in the clear. I'd planned it perfectly, bringing her here. But then Calloway made up all that bullshit evidence and got everyone on board—Finn, Vance Clark, your father. Even my uncle turned against me. So I decided, if I was going to hell for the rest of my life, I was taking Calloway with me, and I told him exactly what I'd done to her."

House grinned. "One big problem. He wasn't recording it. Man, I knew that would piss him off, but never in my wildest dreams did I think it would be used to hoist him by his own petard. How's that for irony? When they closed the door to my cell at Walla Walla that first day, I thought that was where I'd spend the rest of my life."

He paused, taking her in with his eyes in the way that made her sick. "And then you came to talk to me." He started to laugh. "And the more we talked, the more I realized they'd never told you what they'd done. You told me about the jewelry, how you knew your sister hadn't been wearing it that day, how she couldn't wear it, but that no one would listen to you. I got to admit, you got my hopes up, but then I realized that, with her body at the bottom of a lake, I'd screwed myself. So I settled in to do my time. I guess fate took over."

Tracy slid down the concrete wall, her legs suddenly weak. She knew who'd made the decision not to tell her. It was what DeAngelo Finn wouldn't say, that day she had gone to visit him. It was what Roy Calloway had nearly said outside the veterinary clinic. It had been her father's decision, and he'd made them swear to never tell her. Tracy was the one Finn was referring to, the one still left, the one her father had loved so very much.

Her father and Calloway had figured out that it was Tracy that House had wanted, that it should have been Tracy shackled in this hellhole, abused by the psychopath standing before her. James Crosswhite had forbidden them to say a word, knowing that the guilt would have been too much for Tracy to bear, that it would have killed her.

"I'm afraid I have to leave now." House stood. "I have unfinished business."

"You're never going to get away with this, House. Calloway knows. He's going to come for you."

House smiled. "That's what I'm counting on."

CHAPTER 65

Calloway stopped at the edge of what Dan surmised to be Parker House's property, both men breathing hard, the wind howling. "Harley found the break in the gas line. House must have done it in Olympia while they were at the competition. Maybe it was supposed to be a trial run to see what would happen, how far the car would go."

"That didn't come out at his trial," Dan said, bracing against a gust of wind. His hands and feet had gone numb.

"It was Tracy's truck and Tracy had given Sarah her black Stetson. She wore it that night to protect her from the rain. They looked so much alike. In the dark, House couldn't tell the difference. When he told me what he did to Sarah, how he'd repeatedly raped her before he killed her, he laughed and said, 'and she wasn't even the one I wanted.' That also never came out at trial. James didn't want Tracy living with that."

"It would have killed her," Dan agreed. "But Roy, why not stop Tracy before we got to this point? Why not tell her before it came to this?"

"Because I never thought it would come to this," Calloway said. "I forgot about the Polaroid and that Sarah couldn't wear the pistol earrings. Tracy held all that back, convinced it was a conspiracy. I also didn't know the strands of hair had come from a brush they both used. Didn't think about it back then. Besides, anything I said to try and convince her, she would have thought a lie, and her father was dead and her mother never knew. There was no one to convince Tracy to let it go."

Calloway looked to a faint glow of light coming from a building at the back of the property. "I never thought I'd be here again." He locked eyes with Dan. "I'm not sure what we're about to find in there. If anything happens, you just shoot. Don't even aim. You just pull the trigger."

They moved forward from one snow mound to the next, until they'd reached the ramshackle house. When Calloway removed his gloves, Dan did the same, shoving the gloves in his pocket. The stock of the shotgun was freezing cold. It hurt when he flexed his fingers, balling them into fists. He tried blowing into them, but his mouth was bone-dry, and he felt like he couldn't catch his breath.

Calloway held the .357's barrel up and reached for the door. The knob turned. He gave Dan the same knowing look he'd given him when he uncovered the tree stump. *He knows we're coming.*

He stepped in. Dan caught the door to keep the wind from slamming it open, followed Calloway, and quietly closed the door behind them. Inside the house, he heard the hum of a generator. He followed Calloway into an adjoining room, Calloway moving deliberately, his gaze darting left and right. Halfway in, he stopped abruptly, then moved swiftly to an armchair.

Parker House sat in the chair, spikes driven through the back of each hand into the armrests, which were covered in blood. Two more were driven through his boots into the floor, where blood had pooled. "Oh, God," Dan said.

Calloway put a finger to his lips. He stepped down a hall and turned on his flashlight, directing it into two rooms, along with the barrel of his gun. Then he returned and put two fingers to Parker's throat. The man was ashen, his lips blue. "He's alive," Calloway whispered, though it didn't seem possible. Parker opened his eyes and the tiny movement was startling, like the dead coming back to life. His eyes were dull. He looked like he was half-asleep.

Calloway knelt. "Parker? Parker?"

His eyes fluttered open.

"Does he have her?"

House looked about to speak, then grimaced, struggling to swallow.

"Get him something to drink."

Dan hurried back to the kitchen, opening and closing cabinets before he found a glass and filled it at the tap. When he returned, Calloway was dragging blankets and bedding from the hall. Calloway wrapped the blankets around House, took the glass, and tilted it to the man's lips.

House took a small sip.

"Does he have Tracy?" Calloway asked.

"The mine," Parker croaked.

Calloway set the glass on the floor and straightened, talking to Dan. "I need you to go back and get on the radio."

"The radio isn't working, Roy."

"The radio *is* working. We just didn't reach anyone. Finlay should be at the station by now and I told him to sit by the radio. You don't have to do anything except hit the power button. Tell him you need an ambulance and every available officer in Cascade County. Tell them to bring chainsaws."

"That will take forever."

"Not if you hurry. You get there, you do as I say, and then you get back here and build a fire. If you can't find wood, burn the damn furniture. Try to keep him warm until they arrive. That's all we can do at this point. When Finlay gets here, tell him to follow my tracks. Tell him House has her in the old Cedar Grove mine."

"If you're going up there, I'm going with you."

"We need more men, Dan. One of us needs to go back and get more men."

"You don't even know if I can reach anyone, do you?"

"You're wasting time," Calloway said. "Right now, I need you to do what I tell you. Tracy's alive, but she might not be much longer."

"How do you know?"

"Because House isn't trying to hide this time. He could have killed DeAngelo and he could have killed Parker. This is like a trail of bread crumbs."

"For who?"

"For me. I'm the one he wants. I'm the one he hates."

"That's all the more reason to wait."

"If I wait, Tracy might die. I lost Sarah, and I lost one of my best friends. I've lived with that too, for twenty years. I'm not going to let that son of a bitch take Tracy."

"Roy—"

"We don't have time to debate this, Dan. One of us needs to go back and get on the radio and get more men. You don't know where the mine is. Now go get help or they're both going to die."

Dan swore under his breath and handed Calloway the shotgun. "Here. Take this." Calloway tried to hand Dan the rifle but Dan shook his head. "I can move faster without it."

Calloway stepped to the back door, pushing it open. Wind rushed into the room, bringing flakes of snow.

"Roy."

He turned back. The big man had always had a presence about him. He was the law in Cedar Grove, and everyone living there felt better knowing it. But now, Dan saw a man beyond his prime, setting out into a blizzard to find a psychopath.

Calloway nodded once, stepped out, and was swallowed by the storm.

CHAPTER 66

The generator continued to hum, but the available light was quickly fading. Tracy did not have enough slack in the chain to reach the box and crank the handle herself. The filament had dulled from white, to red, and now a pale orange. The daunting onset of darkness made her think of Sarah chained to the wall—her baby sister, so afraid of the dark. What had she done all those hours alone? Had she thought of Tracy? Had she blamed her? Tracy looked to the lone patch of carpet leaning against the concrete wall at the back of the room and wondered if that had been the place where Sarah had sat. She touched it, needing to feel a connection, and noticed faint but distinct scratch marks in the concrete. She pulled back the carpet and leaned closer, seeing grooves in the wall. She traced them with her fingertip and realized they were letters.

Tracy bent closer, blowing away the fine white dust. She traced the grooves with her fingers. The letters became more distinct.

I am

Her stomach tightened in a knot. She blew harder and wiped with a greater sense of urgency, tracing the indentations.

I am not

She scraped at a second line of letters just below the first row.

I am not afraid

A third line was scratched below the second, though the grooves were not as distinct.

I am not afraid

She ran her hand farther down the wall but did not feel any other grooves. She angled herself so her body did not cast a shadow on the wall, but she did not see the rest of their prayer. Sarah had apparently never finished it.

To the right of the prayer, Tracy felt more scratch marks but these were vertical grooves. Again she angled her body so as not to block the remaining light.

Tracy sat back, hand covering her mouth. Tears streaked her cheeks. "I'm sorry, Sarah," she said. "I'm so sorry I couldn't save you."

Another thought came to her. The reason for the calendar was obvious, Sarah was keeping track of the days of her captivity, but why their prayer? Of all the things Sarah could have written, why would she have written something only she and Tracy knew? She could have written her name. She could have written anything.

Tracy turned and looked to the door in the wall. Her gaze migrated to the black Stetson on the shelf and it brought a realization.

"He told you, didn't he? He told you I was the one he wanted," she whispered.

Sarah must have feared Tracy would someday be chained to the same wall, and she had left her a message—but it wasn't just the words that were meant for Tracy. There was more to it than just their prayer.

"What did you use?" She felt the scratch marks again. Sarah clearly hadn't made them with her fingernails.

She had to have used something sharp and rigid. Twenty years ago the concrete would not have been weakened by the years of moist soil above it and damp air.

"What did you use?" She looked about the floor. "What did you use? And where did you hide it from him?"

—

The mine shaft would be more than a mile and a half up the hill, if Calloway could even find it. When Parker House had led Calloway up the mountain twenty years earlier, nature had already reclaimed much of the mining road. In the intervening two decades, the lush vegetation had likely completed its reclamation—not to mention the fact that the road was now buried under several feet of snow.

Calloway directed the beam of his flashlight over the snow, searching for footprints. He instead found sled marks, the kind made by a snowmobile. The tracks led away from a shed behind the house and carved a path up the mountain. He stepped inside the shed and swept the light over an ATV and rusted and dilapidated equipment, but did not see a second snowmobile. His breath marked the air. Calloway directed the beam along the wall, stopping when it illuminated a pair of antique snowshoes made of wood and woven rope, hanging on a hook.

He pulled the shoes from the wall and removed his gloves to put them on. His fingers quickly became numb. The toeholds on the snowshoes weren't quite big enough for his boots, but he forced them on and adjusted the straps as best he could to secure them. He slid his hands back inside his gloves and stepped outside. The wind gusted as if to greet him, or to warn him. He lowered his head into it and followed the sled marks up the hill. The first few steps in the snowshoes were awkward, the wooden frames kept digging into the snow. He kept his weight distributed more on the balls of his feet and soon got the hang of it.

Within minutes, his thighs and calf muscles burned, and his lungs felt as though he had a weight compressing his chest and preventing him from getting enough oxygen to fill his lungs. He concentrated only on putting one foot in front of the next, using a mountain climber's rest step to conserve energy and catch his breath. But he kept his body in motion, fearful that if he remained idle, his body would shut down. He took another step, straightened his leg, rested a beat, and continued, step after step, fighting off exhaustion and the unrelenting voice that he stop and turn back. He couldn't turn back. He knew what this was about. House wanted his pound of flesh. He wasn't hiding Tracy the way he'd hid Sarah, and he wouldn't wait long for Calloway. He'd kill Tracy. The wind that battered him was also erasing the snowmobile tracks, making them more difficult to follow. Still he pressed on, up the mountain.

This time he intended to finish it.

He had no doubt that was also Edmund House's intent.

CHAPTER 67

Dan collapsed against the Suburban's snow-covered hood, panting and wheezing. He couldn't catch his breath. His chest ached and his lungs felt like they were about to explode, like he was suffocating. His face, hands, and feet burned from the cold. He could not feel his fingers or his toes. His legs and arms were leaden.

He had plowed back through the snow as fast as he could, using the trail he and Calloway had carved while getting to the property. He had not allowed himself to stop. He thought only of getting to the Suburban, radioing for help—if the radio even worked in the storm—and getting back to help find Tracy. A part of him still believed that Calloway had sent Dan away just to get rid of him, not wanting to put him even further in harm's way.

Stumbling along the side of the car, he nearly fell, but gripped a door handle to keep himself upright. When he tugged open the door, snow tumbled from the roof onto the floorboard and seat. He gripped the steering wheel and used it to pull himself up, laying his flashlight across the bench seat. Inside, he took only a moment to catch his breath, which marked the air inside the car with white bursts. Dan removed his gloves, blew into his fists, and tried to rub life back into his fingers, which felt swollen. He flipped the power switch on the radio. It lit up—the first good sign. He unclipped the microphone, took a deep breath, and spoke in gasps. "Hello? Hello, hello."

Static.

"This is Dan O'Leary. Is anyone there? Finlay?" He paused to catch his breath. "We are in need of any available backup at the Parker House property. Bring chainsaws. Trees across the road."

He threw his head back against the seat, waiting, hearing only static. Swearing at the lack of response, he turned the dials as he'd watched Calloway do before, and tried again. "Repeat. In immediate need of any available backup. Send ambulance. Chainsaws. Parker House property. Finlay, are you there. Finlay? Dammit!"

Again, the response was static. Dan repeated the message a third time, got no answer, and put the microphone back in place. He hoped someone had heard him, but he couldn't wait any longer. He could feel his body already wanting to shut down, his limbs becoming heavier. His mind and his instinct for self-preservation were fighting against his need to go back into the freezing wind and blinding snow.

He flexed his hands, blew on them a final time, and fit the gloves back on. Then he grabbed the flashlight from the seat and pushed open the door.

The radio crackled. "Chief?"

Tracy studied the white concrete dust and efflorescence leaching from the cracks. She brought her fingers to the tip of her tongue. The paste tasted bitter and acidic. She smelled it and detected the faint odor of sulfur.

She sat back and looked up at the scarred dirt ceiling. Above it grew a forest of ferns, shrubs, and moss—an entire ecosystem that had bloomed and died with the four seasons for millions of years. The decaying plants and decomposing animals had trickled back into the soil, where the persistent rain and melting snow forced the chemicals they created to seep through the rock and earth. Concrete was not meant for such damp conditions. The sulfates caused chemical changes in the cement, weakening the cement binder.

She got to her knees and picked at the concrete. It had become pitted and came away in small flakes. Tracy tugged on the chain and felt the plate attached to the wall give just a fraction. The bolts embedded in the concrete had likely rusted and expanded, causing the concrete behind the plate to crack further and allow for water intrusion. She pulled again. The plate pulled half an inch from the wall. Tracy felt behind it and her fingertips traced etchings where someone had chipped at it—Sarah. She'd been working the plate free of the wall, but twenty years ago, that would have been a more difficult task.

"How? How did you do it?"

Tracy stood and stepped as far away from the wall as the chain allowed, defining the area Sarah also could have reached. She walked in an arc. The light overhead continued to fade. Shadows crept down the concrete wall, shading Sarah's message.

I am not
I am not afraid
I am not afraid

Tracy considered the square patches of carpet and dropped to her knees, lifting them, feeling for imperfections in the ground. She began digging with her hands.

"Where is it? What did you use?"

The filament inside the bulb grew weaker, now a faint orange. As the circumference of light shrunk, the shadows crept farther down the wall.

I am not afraid

Tracy dug faster. Her fingertips touched something solid. She increased her pace and uncovered a small, round rock. She swore and looked to the door in the wall. She had no idea when House would return, but she could never dig up the entire area she could reach. It was simply too big, and Tracy had a sense that House did not intend to stay in the cave long, as he had with Sarah. She sensed he was on some kind of mission, settling scores. She continued to feel, now almost in blind darkness, and had the strange sensation that someone took her hand and guided it to just a few inches from the hole where she'd uncovered the rock. Tracy felt an imperfection in the ground, a mound of dirt. She ran her hand over it and felt a slight depression beside it. She dug. Just an inch below the surface she hit something solid. Tracy worked her fingers along the object's surface, scraping the soil away, no longer able to see. Whatever the object was, it was not round. It was straight, rectangular. She dug around the object, trying to find a defined edge. When she found it, she worked her fingers deeper and felt the bottom of it. Tracy secured a fingerhold and tugged at the end, feeling the earth reluctantly give it up. She worked another finger beneath it, then a third. She gripped it and, with a final effort, yanked it free.

A metal spike.

CHAPTER 68

Roy Calloway pushed himself beyond what he thought his body still capable of doing. Mercifully, the snow had temporarily let up, though the wind continued to pummel his unprotected face as he climbed higher. The muscles in his legs had begun to cramp in knots. His lungs felt as though they would burst from his chest. He could not feel his hands or his feet. The urge to stop and catch his breath, to rest, grew stronger. After a few more steps, the trail flattened, triggering a recollection of his hike with Parker House twenty years ago when they'd come to a crest in the hill. If he remembered correctly, the entrance to the mine would be on his left. But could he find it?

He recalled the entrance as having been rectangular, not much bigger than a single-wide garage door. The wood beams supporting it had already begun to list to the left as if about to collapse, and, as with the decades-old road, the mine entrance had also been partially obscured by foliage. It would likely now have been completely overgrown, but Calloway was counting on the fact that Edmund House would have needed to clear the entrance to take Tracy inside.

Calloway swept the beam of his flashlight over the snow. He no longer saw the snowmobile tracks, nor did he see the machine. House must have hidden it and carried Tracy the final distance. He looked more closely and picked up a single set of boot prints.

The mine could not be far.

He used the beam of light to follow the footprints. They led to what he first thought to be a rock, but was, in actuality, a black hole in the side of the hill. The snow had been recently shoveled out to expand the opening.

Calloway knelt and used the light to look about. He slid the shotgun from his shoulder and removed his gloves, flexing his fingers, trying to restore feeling. He unstrapped the snowshoes and staked them in the snow, listening, but hearing only the howling wind, his eyes scanning the darkness. He blew again into his fists, gripped the shotgun, picked up the flashlight, and got to his feet.

He shone the light on the ground and took a step. His boot sunk knee deep. Calloway yanked his leg free of the snow, took a second step, and again plunged to his knees. He moved to his left where the trail of footprints had tamped down the snow, and made better progress up the hill, though he was still plodding. Closer to the hole, he stepped with his right leg into the next depression, but this time his boot did not sink. It struck something solid.

The snow beneath his foot exploded like a geyser, spraying Calloway in the face. He heard a loud snap, a microsecond before metal teeth bit into the flesh of his leg, followed by a second, sickening snap.

Calloway screamed in agony and toppled face-first into the snow.

Something heavy landed hard on his back, driving the wind from his lungs, burying him further, suffocating him. He strained to lift his head, in search of air. Someone grabbed his arms, yanking them over his head. Cuffs pinched his wrists.

He lifted his head, still partially blinded by the snow and pain. A hooded figure walked backward, dragging Calloway by his arms up the slope toward the black hole, like prey being dragged into an underground den.

CHAPTER 69

Horrific screams reverberated down the mine shaft. It sounded like the baying of a wounded animal, but Tracy knew it to be human. House had returned, and he was not alone.

The filament in the bulb had nearly extinguished, and the room had returned to near darkness. Tracy hurried to make a final scratch in the wall, determined to finish what Sarah had started.

> *I am not*
> *I am not afraid*
> *I am not afraid*
> **of the dark**

The cries grew louder, echoing wails of agony and pain. Then, just as suddenly and horrifically, they stopped.

Tracy swept the remaining bits and pieces of concrete that she'd chipped from around the bolts holding the plate to the wall into the hole she'd created while unearthing Sarah's metal spike. She covered them with dirt and patted it flat. A clattering and banging arose from the other side of the wall as she aligned the piece of carpet with the others.

The door banged open.

House entered with his back to her, grunting as he struggled to drag something heavy into the room. He dropped his kill near one of the vertical wood beams in the gray light from the doorway. The shadows prevented Tracy from making out the body's face with any clarity. She assumed it to be Parker.

Next, House threw a length of chain over the nearest horizontal beam, gripped it, and stepped back. He pulled on the links of chain hand over hand, as if he was raising a boat's sail. The body rose, arms extended overhead. House continued to pull until it hung like a slab of meat in a butcher's window. He gave a final grunt and slid a link of the chain onto a hook protruding from the vertical beam, holding the body up. Finished, he fell back against one of the other posts, hands on his knees, bent over and breathing heavily. After a minute to catch his breath, he jabbed at the air with a fist, staggered forward, and fell to his knees. Tracy could hear his labored breathing as he cranked the generator handle. The filament pulsed and glowed, the drone becoming louder. The circumference of light took back the shadows, slowly revealing the body.

Roy Calloway hung by his wrists, slumped against the vertical beam, the horizontal beam not high enough for him to hang free. As the light fell across Calloway's face, Tracy thought he was dead. Snow and ice clung to his face and clothing. The light filtered down his body, and over the .357 still in its holster on Calloway's hip. Farther down, the light revealed his right leg sticking out at an odd and twisted angle just below the knee, where the metal teeth of the bear trap gripped his leg. His pants were torn and saturated in blood.

Tracy got to her knees and moved toward Calloway, but there was not enough slack in the chain to reach him.

House stopped cranking the handle of the generator and fell back against the table, chest still heaving. Sweat and melted snow matted his hair to his head and dripped down his face. He pulled off his gloves, unzipped his coat, and shook it free, throwing everything onto the bed. His long-sleeved shirt stuck to his chest. He stood staring at Roy Calloway as if to admire a prize elk. One he was about to gut.

Calloway moaned.

House reached out and grabbed his face. "That's right. Don't you dare die on me, you son of a bitch! That would be too good for you. Death is too good for any of you. You're all going to suffer in a way that will make twenty years feel like they were nothing." House turned Calloway's head to face Tracy. "Take a look, Sheriff. All your efforts and lies and you still failed."

"You're an idiot," Tracy said.

House released his grip. "What did you call me?"

Tracy shook her head derisively. "I said, you're an idiot."

He came toward her, though still out of her reach.

She said, "Have you really thought this through?"

Calloway shifted his legs, tried to stand, and screamed in pain, regaining House's attention. House leaned an arm against the beam, his and Calloway's noses nearly touching. "Do you know what solitary confinement is like, Roy? It's like someone stuck you in a hole and deprived you of all your senses. It's like you don't exist, like the world doesn't exist. That's what I'm going to do to you. I'm going to keep you in this hole and make you feel like you don't exist. I'm going to make you wish you were dead."

"You really are a first-class fuckup," Tracy said.

House pushed away from the beam. "You don't know shit. If you did, you wouldn't be here."

"I know you screwed up, twice. I know you got caught, twice. And I know you ended up in jail, twice. Did you ever stop to think maybe it's because you aren't as smart as you think you are?"

"Shut the fuck up. You don't know anything."

"A smart man learns from his mistakes," she said, mocking him. "Isn't that what you said? It doesn't look like you've learned shit to me."

"I said shut up."

"You brought the Sheriff of Cedar Grove here. How fucking stupid can you be? Parker is still alive, Edmund. Do you think Calloway came alone? They know where you are. You're going back to jail. Strike three. Three strikes and you're out, Edmund."

"I'm not going anywhere until him and me are finished. After that, I'm going to take care of you." House lifted the generator onto the table and turned it around. The back of the crate was open, revealing wires protruding from large battery cells just as Tracy had suspected.

He loosened the wing nuts and fastened stripped-copper wires around the bolts projecting out of the top of the battery. When he turned to speak to Tracy, the ends of the wires inadvertently touched, causing a spark. House grimaced and flinched at the shock. "Goddamn it."

"Jesus, you're stupid."

He took a step toward her, still holding the wires. "Do not call me stupid."

"How do you think he got here? Did you stop to think about that? They're coming for you, Edmund. You're going to lose again."

"Shut up."

"You haven't learned anything. You were in the clear. They weren't even going to retry you. You were going to walk away free, but you let your ego get in the way."

"I didn't want to get away. I wanted my revenge. And I'm getting it. I've had twenty years to think through what I would do to them and to you."

"Which is why you're a two-strike loser. Because you're an idiot."

"Stop calling me an idiot!"

"You had the chance every convict hopes for, dreams for, and you blew it because you're too stupid."

"Stop calling me—"

"You haven't won anything. You've lost, again. You're just too stupid to know it. You're an idiot."

He dropped the wires and rushed her, eyes wide, enraged. Tracy waited, letting him come, her hand on the flat end of the spike in her boot. When House was nearly upon her she rose up, pushing off her back leg with all her strength, her arm swinging up from the ground. She drove the sharpened tip of the metal stake just beneath House's rib cage, his momentum and all of her strength embedding it deep in his flesh.

House roared in pain and fell back.

Tracy spun, shoved a boot against the wall, wrapped the length of chain around her hands, and yanked hard on the metal plate. Bits and pieces of cement and plaster dust sprayed the room as the rusted bolts ripped free of the wall. Her wrists still manacled, the foot-long piece of chain between them, she lunged for the big revolver on Roy Calloway's hip. She was fumbling to free the snap on the holster when she was yanked violently backward. Edmund House had grabbed the chain and tugged on it like a leash. She fell onto her ass, got to her knees, stood, and reached again for the gun. House wrapped the chain around her neck. She lifted a boot against the beam and shoved off, propelling herself backward into him.

They crashed into and overturned the makeshift table, sending the generator to the floor. Tracy landed with her back atop House. He continued to choke her. She whipped her head backward, trying to butt him, and kicked and elbowed behind herself too. The chain tightened. Tracy fought to dig her fingers beneath the links, but House was too strong and her fingers wouldn't fit. She lowered a hand, searching, felt the head of the spike and applied pressure. House screamed and cursed but the chain remained tight.

She yanked up on the spike, hard. House screamed. The chain loosened. This time, when she whipped her head back, she struck something solid, and heard the bridge of his nose crack. The chain slackened more, enough for her to pull it over her head. She rolled off, fighting to catch her breath, her throat on fire. She crawled across the ground, hoping there was enough slack in the chain, which remained wrapped around House's hand. She reached Calloway and freed the snap on the holster. This time she'd gripped the handle of the revolver before the chain pulled taut, yanking the manacles around Tracy's wrists and violently jerking her arms. The gun flew from her hands, landing somewhere in the shadows across the room.

House had staggered to his feet, the chain wrapped around his massive forearm. Blood stained his shirt where the end of the spike protruded and dripped from his nose down his chin.

Tracy tried to stand but he yanked the chain again, causing her to sprawl onto the floor. He came toward her. The generator lay on the ground beside her. She grabbed the two copper wires and started to her feet. House tugged again. She did not resist.

She flew into him, knocking him backward. When they landed, she pressed the stripped copper wires to the iron spike, creating a spark. There was a loud snap, and the smell of flesh burning. House quivered and twitched and jerked as the electricity passed through his body. In her head, she heard her student Enrique at Cedar Grove High shouting *conductor*. She lost the connection, found it again. House's body jolted. Then he went limp.

Tracy rolled off. This time she pulled the chain from his arm as she scrambled across the room in search of the gun. House moaned behind her. She looked back over her shoulder and watched him somehow roll to his hands and knees, like a bear struggling to get up. She felt blindly along the ground where it met the wall.

House rose.

Tracy's hand swept the ground.

House stumbled forward.

She swept along the wall and felt the gun.

House quickly crossed the room, too quickly for almost anyone to get off a shot. Almost.

Tracy rolled onto her back, already pulling back the hammer. She fired, cocked the hammer, fired, cocked, and fired a third time.

CHAPTER 70

Tracy used her own body weight to counter Roy Calloway's dead weight on the other end of the chain. When she had enough slack to free the chain from the hook that had been holding him up, she slowly lowered him to the ground. Calloway muttered incoherently. His breathing came in short, raspy breaths. He seemed to be slipping in and out of consciousness. He was alive, but Tracy did not know for how long.

Across the room, House lay face down on the ground. The first bullet had pierced his sternum, stopping his forward progress. Before he'd hit the ground, Tracy's second shot had pierced him two inches to the left of the first bullet, exploding his heart. The third bullet had left a hole in his forehead and blown out the back of his skull.

She found the key to the manacles in House's pants pocket. After freeing herself, she cut House's discarded clothing into strips and tied a tourniquet around Calloway's leg. She did not attempt to remove the bear trap, fearing that she would further open the wound and Calloway would slip into shock, if he did not bleed to death. She cradled Calloway's head in her lap. "Roy? Roy?"

Calloway opened his eyes. Though the room remained bitterly cold, sweat beaded on his face, as if he were running a deadly fever. "House?" he whispered, voice weak.

"Dead."

Calloway gave her a thin-lipped smile. Then his eyes fluttered closed.

"Roy?" She slapped at his cheek. "Roy? Does anyone else know we're here?"

Calloway whispered, "Dan."

CHAPTER 71

Dan met Finlay Armstrong, a second deputy, and two Cedar Grove locals with chainsaws at Roy Calloway's Suburban. Leaving the locals to cut through the downed trees and clear a path to Parker House's property, Dan and the two deputies took off up the mountain toward the house and littered yard.

The snow had let up and the wind had lessened, making the trek not as difficult and bringing an eerie peace—as if they were in the eye of a tornado. When they reached the building, they found Parker alive, but he looked to be in even worse shape than when Dan had left him.

"You stay here," Armstrong said to Dan, "and wait for the ambulance to arrive."

"Not a fucking chance," Dan said. "I'm going with you to get her."

Armstrong looked about to debate, but Dan used the same line Calloway had used on him.

"We don't have time to debate this, Finlay. Every second we remain down here is another second for House to kill both of them." He started for the back door. "Let's go."

Armstrong and Dan climbed the mountain. Having grown up in Cedar Grove and hiked the hills their entire lives, they knew the way to what had been the Cedar Grove mine. The snow made everything look different, but their path was carved by footprints that must have been left by Calloway.

Twenty minutes into their hike, they found snowshoes staked in the ground about fifteen feet below what looked like the entrance to a cave. Someone had recently carved it larger. Deep boot prints had created a path to and from the opening, and there was a long imprint that looked as if someone had been dragged across the snow. That was disconcerting in itself. More disconcerting was the trail of blood that streaked the snow and led to the mouth of the mine.

They knelt outside the entrance, and Finlay shone his flashlight into the tunnel before he entered the mine first, his shotgun at the ready. Dan clutched the rifle. Their flashlights sent two cones of light down the shaft.

"Turn it off," Dan whispered, shutting off his own flashlight.

They were plunged into complete darkness. After a few seconds, however, Dan saw a faint orange glow emanating about twenty feet down the tunnel. They walked toward it and came to a doorway leading into a room. Finlay paused outside, then flipped on his flashlight and spun in, shotgun extended. Dan followed with his light and rifle. The cones of light swept over what had apparently been an office, with metal desks and chairs and army-green file cabinets.

The orange glow was coming through an opening in the paneled wall at the back of the room.

"Here," Tracy said. "I'm in here."

Dan started for the door but Finlay grabbed his arm. "Tracy?" Finlay called out. "You all right?"

"Yeah," she said. "House is dead."

Finlay stepped into the room, Dan behind him.

A bare bulb dangled from a wire. Beneath it, resting against a wooden beam, Tracy sat cradling Roy Calloway's head in her lap. In the far corner lay Edmund House, blood saturating the back of his head and his shirt.

Dan knelt and hugged her. "You all right?"

She nodded, then looked to Calloway. "He's not going to last long."

—

Morning dawned and with it, the storm passed. Tracy stood near the mine's entrance, which had been dug out by Finlay and the others who had responded to his call for help. She wrapped the thermal blanket around her shoulders as she considered the patches of blue sky and shafts of sunlight knifing through the cloud layer in hints of magenta, rose, and orange, a post-storm sky. In the distant valley, the rooftops of the houses in Cedar Grove looked like tiny pyramids. Smoke spiraled from chimneys and curled into wisps in the dead air. Tracy had had a similar view from the window of her bedroom, and the knowledge that she knew so many in those homes had always brought her a sense of peace and comfort.

A noise from farther down the mine shaft drew her attention, and she looked back and watched paramedics carry Roy Calloway, bundled in blankets, out of the mine on a sled. Calloway turned his head and made eye contact as they carried him past. Tracy followed them outside, watching as they lowered the sled to the snow and tethered it between two snowmobiles.

"He's still a tough son of a bitch, isn't he?" Dan said, walking up behind her.

"Like a two-dollar steak," she said.

Dan wrapped an arm around her shoulders and pulled her to him. "So are you, Tracy Crosswhite. And you can still shoot. No denying that."

"What about Parker?" she asked.

"He's critical. DeAngelo Finn is too."

"DeAngelo?"

"Yeah. Looks like House was settling up with everyone. Hopefully we reached them in time. Hopefully they'll all be okay."

"I'm not sure any of us is going to be okay," she said.

He adjusted the blanket around her shoulders. "How'd you do it? How'd you get free?"

Tracy watched a tendril of smoke that had spiraled up from one of the chimneys, which hung motionless, like the vapor trail left by a jet. "Sarah," she said.

Dan gave her a quizzical look.

"House wanted me all along," she continued.

"I know, Calloway told me. I'm sorry, Tracy."

"He must have told Sarah he intended to bring me here next. She carved me the message in the wall. Even if he'd seen it, House wouldn't have known what it meant. Only I knew. It was the prayer we used to say together at night. It was a message to me. Sarah wanted to let me know she'd found something to dig at the wall, to loosen the bolts. She must have just run out of time, and the concrete would have been stronger twenty years ago than it is now."

"What do you mean?"

"It's chemistry." She sighed. "That wall was poured some eighty years ago, maybe longer. Over time, the chemicals from the decaying plants wicked down through the soil and interacted with the concrete. When concrete deteriorates, it cracks, and we know that water will always find its way through cracks. When water reached the bolts, it caused them to rust. When the bolts rusted, they expanded, cracking the concrete even more. Sarah scratched the message in the wall, but what she was really doing was using the spike to chip away at the concrete behind the plate and around the bolts."

"Mrs. Allen would be proud," he said.

Tracy rested her head on his shoulder. "We used to say that prayer together when Sarah was young. She was afraid of the dark. She'd sneak into my room and crawl in bed next to me, and I'd tell her to shut her eyes and we'd say it together. Then I'd turn out the lights and she'd fall asleep." She started to cry, not bothering to wipe away the tears. "It was our prayer. She didn't want anyone to know she was afraid. I miss her, Dan. I miss her so much."

He squeezed her tight. "Sounds like she isn't gone. Sounds like she's still with you."

She quickly raised her head and pulled back to consider him.

"What?" he asked.

"That's the strange thing about it. I felt her, Dan. I felt her presence here with me. I felt her leading me to that spike. There's no other way to explain why I dug in that exact spot."

"I think you just did explain it."

CHAPTER 72

The snowstorm had stranded the media, which had come from all over the country to attend the post-conviction relief hearing, in Cedar Grove and the nearby towns. When news broke about DeAngelo Finn and Parker House, and about what had happened in the Cedar Grove mine, reporters and their cameramen rushed from their hotels to their vans. Maria Vanpelt was in her glory, broadcasting from all over town and telling anyone who would listen that she had been first to break the story on *KRIX Undercover.*

Tracy had watched the media frenzy unfold on the television from the comfort of Dan's couch, Rex and Sherlock on the floor beside her as if to protect her from the horde of reporters who had camped outside Dan's home. Knowing the media would not leave them alone until she had addressed them, Tracy sent word she would hold a press conference at the First Presbyterian Church, the only building in Cedar Grove big enough to accommodate the anticipated crowd. The church where they'd held her father's funeral.

"I'm doing it to appease the brass," she told Kins over the phone.

"Bullshit," he said. "I'm not buying that for a second. If you're doing it, you have an ulterior motive."

———

Tracy and Dan stood in an alcove at the front of the church, hidden from the crowd that filled the pews and stood along the aisles.

"You did it again," Dan said. "You've managed to make Cedar Grove relevant. I hear the mayor is telling anyone who'll listen that Cedar Grove is a quaint little town full of opportunity and ripe for development. He's even talking about reviving the long-abandoned plans for Cascadia."

Tracy smiled. The old town deserved a second chance. They all did.

She peered out at the sea of faces, her gaze flowing over the standing-room-only crowd. The media throng sat up front with notepads and tape recorders. Cameramen had established positions in the aisles from which to film. The locals and the curious had also come, many of the same faces that had come to Sarah's service and sat through the hearing. George Bovine sat in a pew near the front, his daughter Annabelle seated between him and a woman who was presumably his wife. He had told Dan over the phone that he thought the finality of the event, that knowing that Edmund House was indeed dead, might help his daughter finally find closure and begin to slowly move on with her life.

Sunnie Witherspoon and Darren Thorenson had also come, and toward the rear, Tracy saw Vic Fazzio's unmistakable mug a foot above the crowd, along with Billy Williams and Kins.

"Wish me luck." She stepped from the alcove into the clicking of dozens of cameras and whirl of flashing lights. The bouquet of microphones taped to the podium was even more substantial than the one that had greeted Edmund House at his post-hearing press conference at the jail.

"I'd like to keep this short," Tracy said. She unfolded a sheet of paper containing her prepared notes. "Many of you are wondering what transpired following the hearing that culminated in the release of Edmund House. As it turns out, I was correct. Edmund House was wrongfully convicted. I was wrong, however, in thinking him innocent. Edmund House raped and murdered my sister, Sarah, just as he confessed to Sheriff Roy Calloway twenty years ago. But he did not kill or bury her right away. He kept Sarah captive for seven weeks in an abandoned mine in the mountains. Shortly before the Cascadia Falls Dam went online, he killed her and buried her body. The area flooded, seemingly covering his crime forever."

She took a breath and gathered herself. "Many of you are wondering who was responsible for convicting Edmund House. I've wondered the same thing for twenty years. I now know that the person responsible was my father, James Crosswhite. For those of you who knew my father, I understand that this is probably hard to accept, but I ask you not to condemn him. My father loved Sarah and me with all his heart. When she disappeared, it broke him. He was never the same man." Tracy looked to George Bovine. "What he did, he did out of love for her, and for every father who loves his daughter; he was determined to ensure that no father would ever suffer the grief that he and George Bovine had suffered because of Edmund House."

She took another moment to gather her emotions. "The only logical and reasonable conclusion is that after Edmund House confessed to Chief Calloway, taunting him that they would never convict him without my sister's body, my father gathered the strands of hair from the hairbrush in the bathroom that my sister and I shared in our childhood home, and placed that evidence in the Chevy stepside. And it was my father who hid Sarah's earrings in a sock in a can in the toolshed on Parker House's property. As a country doctor, my father made frequent house calls, including calls on Parker. It was my father who reviewed every tip received about Sarah and who called Ryan Hagen and convinced Mr. Hagen that he'd seen the red Chevy that night he had driven through town. My father acted alone in doing these things. I want to emphasize that neither Roy Calloway, Vance Clark, nor anyone else, to my knowledge, played a part in my father's wrongdoing. My father's actions were born from grief, despair, and desperation. We can all question his actions, but hopefully you won't question his motives.

"For those of you who knew my father, I ask that you remember that man—a faithful husband, a loving father, a loyal friend." She folded her notes and looked up. "I will be happy to answer your questions."

And the questions came in a flurry. Tracy bobbed and weaved around them, answering what she could, deflecting others, and pleading ignorance when necessary. After ten minutes, Finlay Armstrong, the Acting Sheriff of Cedar Grove, stepped forward and ended the conference. Then he provided Tracy and Dan a police escort out of the church and back to Dan's home, where they again went into seclusion, protected by the best security system in town.

—

The following day, Tracy walked into Roy Calloway's room in the Cascade County Hospital. She found Calloway sitting up, though leaning back at a forty-five-degree incline with his leg suspended in a sling above the bed. "Hey, Chief."

He shook his head. "Not anymore. I'm retired."

"Did hell freeze over?"

"For three days," he said.

She smiled. "You got that right. How's the leg?"

"Doctor says I get to keep it after a few more surgeries. I'll walk with a limp and need a cane, but he said it won't keep me out of the streams."

She took his hand. "I'm sorry I put you through this, Roy. I know my dad told you not to say anything, and when I kept pushing for answers, I put you in a situation where you felt the need to protect Vance and DeAngelo and try to convince me to let it go and just leave."

"Don't go making me out to be some hero," he said. "I was covering my ass too. You know, I thought about telling you."

"I wouldn't have believed you," she said.

"That's what I figured. That's why I didn't try. You'd made up your mind, and I knew you were as stubborn as your old man."

She smiled. "More."

"He didn't want you suffering any more than you already were, Tracy. He'd lost Sarah. He didn't want to lose you too. He was afraid that the guilt would be too much for you to live with. He didn't want that, Tracy. He didn't want you thinking Sarah died because of you. She didn't, you know. House was a psychopath. He killed her because he got the chance. But I guess I don't need to tell you that. I imagine you get a fair share more of those types of killers than we get here in Cedar Grove."

"What do you think happened to him, Roy?"

"Who? Your father?"

"You knew him as well as anyone. What do you think happened?"

Calloway seemed to give his answer some thought. "I think he just couldn't get past the loss. He couldn't get over the grief. He loved you both so much. He felt so much guilt because he wasn't here. You know how he was. He thought if he had just been here, he could have stopped it somehow. It hurt their marriage, you know?"

"I figured it did."

"He blamed her for him not being here, for them being in Hawaii. He didn't, but . . . he did. And then when he thought that we weren't going to be able to get justice for Sarah, I think it just kind of put him over the edge and it snowballed on him. He was a man of such high character. I'm sure that planting the evidence just weighed on him even more. Don't judge him, Tracy. Your father was a great man. He didn't kill himself. The grief did that."

"I know."

Calloway took a deep breath and let out a sigh. "Thanks for what you did at the news conference."

"I just told the truth," she said, unable to suppress a grin.

Calloway chuckled. "I'm not sure it will satisfy the Department of Justice."

"They've got bigger fish to fry," she said. Besides, Tracy thought there was merit to what DeAngelo Finn had said to her, about people not always being entitled to the answers, not when those answers could do more harm than good. She felt no guilt blaming her father. "My father would have wanted it this way," she said.

"He had broad shoulders." Calloway reached for a glass on a table next to his bed, took a sip of juice through a straw, and set the glass back down. "So, will you be leaving?"

"Still anxious to get rid of me, aren't you?"

"Actually, no. It's been too long."

"I'll be back to visit."

"It won't be easy."

"You can't bury the ghosts if you don't confront them," she said. "And now I know I don't have to let Sarah go, or my dad, or Cedar Grove. They'll always be a part of me."

"Dan's a good man," Calloway said.

She smiled. "Like I said. I'll take it slow."

"So, you're going to be okay with it, knowing?" he asked. "If you ever have a need to talk, you call me."

"It's going to take time," she said.

"For all of us," he said.

DeAngelo Finn was just as philosophical when she visited his room.

"I would have been with my Millie," he said. "And that's not such a bad thing, you know."

"Where will you go?" she asked.

"I have a nephew near Portland who says he has a vegetable garden in need of weeding."

—

Last on her rounds was Parker House. As she entered his hospital room, she remembered her father telling her at the trial that Parker was suffering too. She could only imagine what he was feeling now.

House had bandages on both his hands and presumably his feet, though he lay beneath a thin hospital sheet. He looked pale and gaunt, more than normal, and Tracy wondered if, in addition to the shock from his wounds, Parker was also experiencing the shock of not having a drink for several days.

"I'm sorry, Tracy," Parker said. "I was drunk and I was scared. He wasn't right. Edmund wasn't right from the moment he first came to live with me, but he was my brother's boy, and I felt responsible for him."

"I know," she said.

"I didn't mean to hurt you or Dan or his dogs. I was just hoping to scare you from going forward with it. I guess I just never thought there would come a day when he might get out, and it scared me to think of what he was capable of doing. I just panicked, I guess. It was a dumb thing to do, shooting out that window."

"I want you to know that my father never held you even the slightest bit responsible for what happened, Parker. I don't either. Not then and not now."

Parker nodded, his lips pressed tight. "You were a good family, Tracy. I'm sorry about what all came about, everything that happened because of him. Sometimes I think about what might have happened if he'd never come around, what Cedar Grove might have been like. You ever think about that?"

Tracy smiled. "Sometimes," she said. "But then I try not to."

CHAPTER 73

She stayed in Cedar Grove as long as she could, but by Sunday afternoon, Tracy could not put off the inevitable any longer. She needed to get back to Seattle. Back to her job. She and Dan stood on his porch, Dan's arms wrapped around her. His kiss lingered. When their lips parted, Dan said, "I don't know who's going to miss you more, me or them." Rex and Sherlock sat beside them, looking forlorn.

Tracy punched him lightly in the chest. "It better be you."

He released her and she rubbed the bony knob atop Rex's head, now free of the plastic cone. The vet said he'd be as good as new. Not to be forgotten, Sherlock nuzzled her hand for attention. "Don't worry, I'm not going to forget either of you," she said. "I'll be coming back to visit, and you can come see me in Seattle, although you're going to have to wait until I get a house with a yard. And Roger's not going to be too happy about the two of you." She could only imagine her cat's reaction when more than two hundred eighty-five pounds of dog invaded his sanctuary.

During the days she had spent convalescing in Dan's home, Dan had never asked what their future held, whether she might consider staying. But as she'd told Parker House in the hospital, sometimes she couldn't help but imagine the Cedar Grove she'd known, even when she tried not to. It was a part of her. Still, she and Dan both knew that they had separate lives and that neither could be immediately disrupted. Tracy had a job to do, and Dan had made a life again in Cedar Grove. He had Sherlock and Rex to care for. His criminal defense practice also looked like it was about to explode due to the notoriety brought by his defense of Edmund House, as well as the aftermath.

Dan and the two dogs walked Tracy to her car. "Call me when you get home," he said, and it felt good to have someone care enough to worry about her.

She put her hands on his chest. "Thanks for understanding, Dan."

"Take your time. We'll be here when you're ready, me and the boys. Just keep swinging that sledgehammer."

She waved as she backed down the driveway into the street, then again as she drove away, wiping a tear from her cheek. When Tracy reached the freeway entrance, she passed it, no longer anxious to leave, and instead turned right and drove into Cedar Grove. The downtown area looked better in the sunshine. Everything always did. It seemed more vibrant, the buildings not as dilapidated. People walked the streets and cars were parked in front of the storefronts. Maybe the mayor would succeed. Maybe he'd revitalize the old town. Maybe he'd even get a developer to finish Cascadia and make Cedar Grove a vacation destination. It had once been a place of great joy and comfort for a young girl and her sister. Maybe it could be again.

Tracy passed the single-story homes with kids in snow clothes playing in the yards, the remnants of their snowmen almost completely melted. Farther out of town, she came to the larger homes on the bigger plots of land, the ones with rooflines protruding above manicured hedges. She slowed as she approached the largest hedge, hesitating only briefly before she drove between a gap in the hedge framed by two stone pillars and up the driveway.

She parked in front of the carriage house and walked to where the weeping willow had once stood like a majestic guardian of the property. Sarah used to climb the braids and pretend the grass was an alligator-infested swamp. She'd dangle above the lawn, crying out to Tracy to rescue her from their snatching jaws and razor-sharp teeth.

Help! Help me, Tracy. The alligators are going to eat me.

Tracy would step carefully along the path to the stone closest to the tree, lean out over the lawn, and stretch out her hand.

I can't reach, Sarah would say, fully enveloped in her fantasy.

Swing, Tracy would reply. *Swing to me.*

And Sarah would start to move her legs and body to get the braids to swing. Their fingers would brush. On the next pass, they would touch. Finally, she'd be close enough for Tracy to grasp her hand, and their fingers would intertwine. *Now let go,* Tracy would say.

I'm scared.

Don't be afraid, Tracy would say. *I'm not going to let anything happen to you.* And Sarah would let go, allowing Tracy to pull her baby sister to safety.

The front door of the house pulled open behind her. Tracy turned. A woman and two young girls stood on the porch. Tracy guessed the girls' ages to be twelve and eight. "I thought it was you," the woman said. "I recognized you from your picture in the newspaper and on the news."

"I'm sorry to intrude."

"That's okay. I heard you used to live here."

Tracy looked to the two girls. "Yes, with my sister."

"It sounded so horrible," the woman said. "What happened. I'm so sorry."

Tracy looked to the older sister. "Do you slide down the staircase banister?"

The girl grinned and raised her eyes up at her mother. Her sister laughed.

"Would you like to come in?" the woman said. "Take a look around? The house must hold a lot of memories for you."

Tracy considered what had been her home. That was exactly the reason she'd driven out to the property, to begin the process of reminiscing about the good times her family had shared there, instead of the bad. She smiled again at the two sisters. They were now whispering mischievously. "I think I'm okay," she said. "I think I'm going to be okay."

EPILOGUE

Tracy adjusted the knot of her red bandanna just off center, dug at the ground with the toe of her boot, parted her legs, and squared her shoulders. Then she mentally went through the progression of shots.

"You ready, Kid?" the range master asked. "I can go over the sequence again if you need. I know it can get confusing keeping it all in your head. We like to give everyone a fair shake, especially the beginners."

On this early Saturday morning, a month after Tracy had returned to Seattle, the sun filtered through the canopy of trees. The sunlight added intrigue to the façades of makeshift storefronts built to replicate an Old West town, and cast shadows across the dozen other competitors. Dressed in old-fashioned cowboy attire, they chatted amicably or readied for their turns to shoot.

Tracy looked again at the targets through her yellow-tinted shooter's glasses. "Sure," she said, sensing he wanted to run through it again. Besides, her father had always taught her to take any competitive advantage she could get.

"Two shots each," he said. "Then you move to the second table and use the shotgun to take down the tombstones. When you're finished, you run to that storefront and shoot out the window at the five orange targets. One shot each."

"Thank you," she said. "I think I got it."

"Okay, then." He stepped back and called out. "Shooter ready?"

"Ready," she said.

"Spotters ready?"

Three men raised their heads and stepped forward. "Ready."

"On the beep," the range master said. "You got a line you like to use?"

"A line?" she asked.

"It's something to let me know when you're ready. Some people say things like, 'I hate snakes.' I say, 'We deal in lead, friend.' It's from *The Magnificent Seven*."

She considered what she'd always said in competition, what Rooster Cogburn had said in *True Grit* right before he'd ridden across the open field, guns blazing. *Fill your hands, you son of a bitch.* "Yeah, I have one."

"Well then, let's hear it when you're ready."

She took a deep breath and exhaled. Then she shouted, "I am not afraid of the dark!"

The timing mechanism beeped. She grabbed the rifle from the table, shot, and levered the second bullet as the first shot hit metal with a ping. She hit the target a second time, levered, shot again, and continued until she'd hit the four remaining targets twice in rapid succession. Already on the move, she picked up the shotgun from the second table and hit the first tombstone. Before it had hit the ground, she'd already pumped and fired at the second target, taking them left to right, the big gun barking. She placed the shotgun down and hurried to the makeshift storefront, stepped inside, squared her shoulders to the window and drew the pistol from across her body. She shot out the window and hit each target in sequence, multiple pings ringing out.

When she finished, she spun the pistol and fit it back in its holster.

"Time!" the range master yelled.

No one spoke, not a word, though every competitor now stood watching.

Wisps of smoke filtered in the morning air and brought that familiar, sweet smell of gunpowder. The three spotters each held up a fist, looking to one another as if uncertain.

Tracy had no doubt. She knew she hadn't missed a target.

The range master considered the timer, looked to another competitor as if disbelieving, and considered the timer again.

"What is it, Rattler?" The question came from an older competitor seated on a barrel. He had his legs apart, his hands resting on his thighs. His cowboy handle was "The Banker" because he wore a bowler hat and a red-paisley vest with a gold pocket watch and chain. "Did it malfunction?" he asked, though his handlebar mustache twitched as he said it, and his mouth broke into a shit-eating grin.

"Twenty-eight point six," Rattler said.

The other competitors looked at Tracy, then at one another. "Are you sure?" one of them said.

"That can't be right," another said. "Can it?"

Tracy's time was six seconds faster than that of the fastest shooter, three seconds slower than her best time when she'd seriously competed.

"What did you say your name was?" the range master asked.

Tracy stepped from the storefront and reholstered her Colt. "The Kid," she said. "Just the Kid."

—

As the light of day faded, Tracy pulled her rugged cart across the dirt and gravel in the direction of the parking lot. It was the same cart her father had handcrafted for her. She'd retrieved it from storage, along with her guns, when she had gone to get some of her parents' furniture. She'd moved into a two-bedroom home in West Seattle and needed to fill the rooms. It had a big yard for when Rex and Sherlock came to visit.

The Banker, who had kept a keen watch on Tracy throughout the rest of the competition, came up beside her. "You leaving?"

"I am," she said.

"But they haven't announced the winner yet."

She smiled.

"What should we do with the belt buckle?"

"Is that your granddaughter I saw shooting today?"

"Yeah, she's mine."

"How old is she?"

"Just turned thirteen, but she's been shooting damn near since she could walk."

"Give it to her," Tracy said. "Tell her to never stop."

"Appreciate that," he said. "Twenty years ago, I saw a shooter, went by the name Kid Crossdraw, I believe, though everyone just called her 'The Kid.'"

Tracy stopped.

The Banker smiled and continued. "I saw her in Olympia. Best shooter I ever saw, until today. Never saw her again after that, though. She had a father and a sister that were pretty good too. You wouldn't happen to have heard of her, would you?"

"I have," Tracy said. "But you're mistaken."

"What about?"

"She's still the best shooter."

The Banker played with an end of his mustache. "I'd love to see it. Do you know where she might be competing next?"

"I do," Tracy said. "But you're going to have to wait a bit. She's shooting at higher targets now."

ACKNOWLEDGMENTS

As always, there are many to thank. First and foremost, before anyone e-mails to tell me I don't know my geography, Cedar Grove is a fictional town I created in the North Cascades. Yes, there is a Cedar Grove, Washington, but I've never been there. I created the town name because I liked the ring of it, and when I later learned of the actual town's existence, I didn't want to change it. So there!

I've received so much help from so many sources that it is hard to know where to begin. This book was a long time in the making, so some of the interviews and research go back several years. As always, the people acknowledged are experts in their fields. I am not. Any mistakes or errors are mine and mine alone.

Thank you to Kathy Taylor, forensic anthropologist with the King County Medical Examiner's Office, for all of her insight on the excavation of a decades-old grave site in a wooded, hilly terrain. Thank you also to Kristopher Kern, forensic scientist and member of the Crime Scene Response Team with the Washington State Patrol, for his similar but distinct expertise.

Thank you to Jennifer Gregory, PhD, LICSW, Western Regional Medical Command Care Provider Support Program Supervisor of Joint Base Lewis-McChord, and to David Embry, PhD, PT Research Program Coordinator, Children's Therapy Unit of the Good Samaritan Movement Laboratory. David approached me at the Pacific Northwest Writers Conference when I shared with an audience a general idea for my next novel, and he put me in touch with Jennifer Gregory. They provided fascinating insights into the minds of sociopaths and psychopaths, which are truly frightening. Their assistance helped me to write this novel and the next.

I've also been fortunate to meet many wonderful people in the police community who are always generous with their time and their knowledge. I could not have written this book without the assistance of Jennifer Southworth, Detective, Violent Crimes Section, Homicide Unit, Seattle Police Department. Jennifer first helped me when she was working for the CSI unit. She has since been promoted to Homicide and became an inspiration for this novel. My thanks also to Detective Scott Thompson, King County Sheriff's Office, Major Crimes Unit/Cold Case Homicides. Scott's willingness to always help me with his knowledge, or to put me in touch with others who can provide needed information, has been invaluable. One of those individuals was Tom Jensen, King County Sheriff's Office, Major Crimes Unit. Some say he was the last man standing on the Green River Killer Task Force which, after twenty years of dedication, finally obtained the evidence to convict Gary Ridgway.

Thanks also to Kelly Rosa, Senior Paralegal at the King County Prosecuting Attorney's Office and lifelong friend. Kelly has helped me on just about every novel I've written and promotes them like crazy. I thought it time she took the next step and became a character, and decided that a forensic anthropologist would be just perfect. Thanks, Kelly—you continue to be the best!

A shout-out also to Brad Porter, Sergeant with the Kirkland Police Department. I met Brad during a horrific trial in King County related to a case where he was the lead detective. Brad has remained a friend and sounding board. He's also the physical inspiration for the character Kinsington Rowe, the Sparrow, though Kins's personal life is fictional.

Thank you also to Sue Rahr, former King County Sheriff and now Executive Director of the Washington State Criminal Justice Training Commission, the Police Academy. I didn't know it when I wrote the novel, but Tracy also has bits of Sue in her: toughness, determination, and a sense of humor. Thanks for taking the time to give insight into your career in what remains a largely male-dominated profession. I want to thank Detective Dana Duffy, Violent Crimes Section, Seattle Police Department, for the same reason. Detective Duffy was Seattle's first female homicide detective; she too took the time to speak with me candidly not only to describe her career and her job but also to provide necessary perspective.

My thanks to Attorney Kim Hunter of Covington, Washington, for her expertise on the post-conviction relief process and criminal law. I was stuck when I met Kim, and she helped get me unstuck!

The best part about my job is all the cool things I get to do, like attend a Cowboy Action Shooting competition on a foggy winter morning at the Renton Fish & Game Club. That was a hoot, like stepping back into the Old West. The participants are in full costume and take their responsibilities, including gun safety, very seriously. Their skills are likewise serious. These men and women can flat-out shoot. They welcomed me and provided me with insight and information that I could have never found in a book. So, thank you to Diamond Slinger, Jess Ducky, Driften Rattler, Dakota, and Kid Thunder, among others, who all took time to answer my questions.

Another fun part of my job is giving away characters in books for charity—in this instance, to raise money for my son's high school, Seattle Prep. Thank you to Erik and Margaret Giesa for their generous contribution in exchange for allowing me to use their names as characters in this book. I wish I had space to print Erik's e-mail describing his wife. Every wife should be so lucky to have a husband describe her as "incredibly beautiful, with great curves and incredible calves and a smile that reflects in her heart." Happy twenty-fifth wedding anniversary.

I do a lot of reading to research my novels and usually don't acknowledge those printed sources, but I want to take the time to identify just a few of the books, manuals, and articles that I found helpful:

Godwin, Maurice and Fred Rosen, *Tracker: Hunting Down Serial Killers*

Reichert, David, *Chasing the Devil: My Twenty-Year Quest to Capture the Green River Killer*

Yancey, Diane, *Tracking Serial Killers*

Keppel, Robert D. and William J. Birnes, *The Psychology of Serial Killer Investigations: The Grisly Business Unit*

Morton, Robert J., *Serial Murder: Multi-Disciplinary Perspectives for Investigators*, Behavioral Analysis Unit, National Center for the Analysis of Violent Crime

Brooks, Pierce, "Multi-Agency Investigative Team Manual," United States Department of Justice, National Institute of Justice

Thank you to super-agent Meg Ruley and her team at the Jane Rotrosen Agency. Meg just keeps working wonders for me. I'm grateful to have been one of her writers for nearly a decade. She has an infectious personality that always sees the glass as half-full. I am indebted to her and her team, who read my drafts and offer suggestions. I do appreciate all of your support. I couldn't do it without you.

Thanks to Thomas & Mercer for believing in *My Sister's Grave* and in me. Special thanks to Alan Turkus, senior editor; Charlotte Herscher, editor; Kjersti Egerdahl; Jacque Ben-Zekry; Tiffany

Pokorny; and Paul Morrissey. If I missed anyone, you know you have my thanks.

Thanks to Tami Taylor, who runs my website and does a fantastic job. Thanks to the cold readers who labor through my early drafts and help make my manuscripts better. Thanks to Pam Binder and the Pacific Northwest Writers Association for their tremendous support of my work.

Thank you also to the loyal readers who e-mail me to tell me how much they enjoy my books and await the next. You are the reason I keep looking for the next great story.

I've dedicated this book to my brother-in-law, Robert A. Kapela. Robert was a good man with a big heart and bigger smile. Over the last few years, he lost his joie de vivre while suffering from the lingering effects of a severe medical issue and in the midst of a contentious divorce. Robert's life ended March 20, 2014. My family was blessed to have Robert come and live with us the final week of his life. My kids loved their "Uncle Bert," and my wife loved her brother. He was the "fun" uncle who made summers especially memorable on his boat.

I realize the tremendous hole that is left when a loved one dies. I felt it when my father died six years ago and think of him every day. The hole will never fill completely. Robert's death has touched us all deeply. The morning after he died, I sat on the porch to watch the sunrise. My wife joined me. It was a brilliant magenta sky, and as we sat watching I suddenly remembered that the day before I got married, the priest had asked me what I wanted, and I had said, "I want to watch the sunrise with Cristina for the rest of my life." I am certain the sunrise that morning was Robert's gift to us, reminding us to see God's beauty in every day, to feel his love, and to always stay in the light. My prayers and thoughts remain with Robert and his three sons.

To Cristina, the love of my life and my soul mate, who has stood beside me with each step of this life journey. You get more beautiful with every day. Remember the sunrises we've promised each other, and always see the beauty, love, and light in every day. To my son, Joe, now a man, I wish for you everything in life that you need to make you happy—love. To my daughter, Catherine, you light up every room you enter. Never lose that glow or joie de vivre.

ABOUT THE AUTHOR

ROBERT DUGONI is the critically acclaimed and *New York Times* bestselling author of the David Sloane series, which consists of *The Jury Master, Wrongful Death, Bodily Harm, Murder One,* and *The Conviction.* He is also the author of the best-selling stand-alone novel *Damage Control,* and the coauthor, with Joseph Hilldorfer, of the nonfiction expose *The Cyanide Canary.* Dugoni's books have been likened to Scott Turow's and Nelson DeMille's, and he has been hailed as "the undisputed king of the legal thriller" by the *Providence Journal* and called the "heir to Grisham's literary throne." *Bodily Harm* and *Murder One* were each chosen as one of the Top Five Thrillers of 2010 and 2011 respectively. *Murder One* was also a finalist for the 2012 Harper Lee Prize for Legal Fiction.

C. DUGONI

Visit his website at www.robertdugoni.com, and follow him on Twitter at @robertdugoni and Facebook at www.facebook.com/AuthorRobertDugoni.